ALSO BY VANESSA VESELKA

Zazen

The Great Offshore Grounds

THE
GREAT
OFFSHORE
GROUNDS

Vanessa Veselka

 ALFRED A. KNOPF   NEW YORK   2020

THIS IS A BORZOI BOOK
PUBLISHED BY ALFRED A. KNOPF

Copyright © 2020 by Vanessa Veselka

All rights reserved. Published in the United States
by Alfred A. Knopf, a division of Penguin Random
House LLC, New York, and distributed in Canada
by Penguin Random House Canada Limited, Toronto.

www.aaknopf.com

Knopf, Borzoi Books, and the colophon are registered
trademarks of Penguin Random House LLC.

Library of Congress Cataloging-in-Publication Data
Names: Veselka, Vanessa, author.
Title: The great offshore grounds : a novel / Vanessa Veselka.
Description: First edition. | New York : Alfred A. Knopf, 2020.
Identifiers: LCCN 2019057825 | ISBN 9780525658078 (hardcover) |
    ISBN 9780525658085 (ebook)
Subjects: LCSH: Domestic fiction. | GSAFD: Mystery fiction.
Classification: LCC PS3622.E85 G74 2020 | DDC 813/.6—dc23
LC record available at https://lccn.loc.gov/2019057825

Jacket image based on: *A Breaking Wave* by David James (detail).
    Photo © Christie's Images / Bridgeman Images
Jacket design by Kelly Blair

Manufactured in the United States of America
First Edition

This novel is for Violet Luna, my girl.

BOOK I—HENRY HUDSON

Health to buzzards

Cash to the drivers

Euler for the lords

An' Greasy luck to the lifers!

1 The Wedding

FIFTEEN MILES south of Seattle and halfway across Puget Sound to the west is Maury Island. Shaped like an arrowhead aimed at the mainland, green as the inner fold of a grass blade, it can be seen from the air cradled in the crook of an elbow of water. Tourists ride over on ferries to watch for whales and UFOs. Jets turn around overhead on their final approach to the airport. Even on days when there is no rain, mist filters through the evergreens until it pulls apart like threadbare cloth and burns off.

The wedding was to be held in the afternoon at Point Robinson, the site of an old fog-signal station that once housed a steam whistle fed by coal fire and water to warn away ships. In 1897, at the dawn of massive capital expansion and speculation, the whistle sounded for five hundred and twenty-eight hours, nearly killing the man who had to shovel the thirty-five tons of coal. The cargo had to be kept from the rocks, but who can halt the lumbering desires of the world?

In 1915, the lighthouse with its state-of-the-art, fifth-order Fresnel lens was built. Powered initially by oil vapor lamps, its beacon could be seen for twelve miles. The lens was the perfect manifestation of Victorian technology, replacing simple flat lenses with faceted, crystal domes, prisms cut into tiers that made it both astonishingly beautiful and a breakthrough in optics. The Fresnel lens had a theoretically infinite capacity to capture diffuse light and, by way of internal reflection, cast it like a spear through darkness. It lit stages and celluloid, Polaroid shots and retinas for ID scans, and on Point Robinson, it lit Puget Sound.

These days, every modern ship has a GPS and the little lighthouse is just a decoration on a brochure, a destination for a grade-school field trip. The mechanisms that rotated the original lantern remain on the first floor, which is now a tiny museum of technology with gauges and wheels and iron bolted into the base with lines that lead nowhere and do nothing.

Back across the sound in Seattle, Livy looked out the window of her basement apartment. Her father was getting married that afternoon, and though it was already late April, a cold, wet breeze still whistled through the gaps in the caulking turning her skin to gooseflesh. A few feet away stood her sister, Cheyenne, poorly slept but already dressed.

"I'm freezing," said Cheyenne. "I'm turning on the space heater."

"Turn on the oven. They charge us for electricity," Livy said.

Cheyenne rolled her eyes but went over to the little white gas stove. Cranking the temperature to broil, she leaned back against the oven door so she could feel the heat on her hamstrings while the oven warmed.

Yesterday they'd spent the whole day picking rocks out of Livy's landlord's garden in trade for a patch of soil near the sunny side of the fence so that Livy could grow food. It wasn't political. Livy didn't care about pesticides or permaculture. She was just the cheapest person Cheyenne had ever known. She lived off past-date groceries. She washed her clothes once a month with a teaspoon of dish soap in a tub. She made her own bras. Cheyenne was pretty sure she would have rinsed and reused dental dams if she thought it would work. Recently, Livy had become convinced she could feed herself off three square yards of land. It was ridiculous, but since Cheyenne had appeared out of nowhere and moved in on her without warning or rent, she didn't have much of a say.

Taller and unfreckled, Cheyenne had chosen a rose-colored capped-sleeve shirt with eyelets and a pair of black pinstriped suit pants. She could pass in the crowd they'd be in today. Her second-hand clothes came off as vintage, while her misadventures in body art made her seem a fine vase, badly cracked and chipping but a gritty accent to any room.

"Cyril didn't come to my wedding," Cheyenne said. "Why should I go to his?"

"Did you invite him?"

"Hell no. He would have arrived like a lord and expected to walk me down the aisle. Here. Let me give you away. Oh hey Dad, I'm pretty sure you did that."

"You're right. He would have," said Livy.

"So why are we even going?"

"I have a day off work and it's cheaper than a movie. I'm tired of ramen and hot dogs and there'll be rich-people food so I'm taking Tupperware."

"Please don't make it obvious," said Cheyenne. "We're already going to look so out of place."

"Because you have jailhouse tats of hearts and clubs on your knuckles? Or because I don't shave and look like a landscaper?"

Cheyenne spread the fingers of her left hand. "Not just clubs and hearts. The one on my thumb is a diamond and the pinkie is a spade. You just can't tell anymore."

Livy crossed to where she'd laid out her newly washed blue painter's pants and pulled them on over her long johns. "I'm going to the wedding because it's a show of support that costs me nothing. I have never thought of him as a dad so I don't care. At his worst he's just a big blank. A disappointment. He gets a clean slate. That's my wedding present. A pass. It's the only decent move."

"I shot my better angels," said Cheyenne.

"They're angels. You can't kill them."

"If they were real you could."

Livy could feel Cheyenne's eyes burning holes in her ribs. She zipped her fly and flattened her pockets.

"I have clothes if you want to borrow something," said Cheyenne.

Livy froze for a second then bent down to roll the cuffs, making sure they were perfectly even on both sides and all the way around. "I have a white shirt. It has buttons. I can tuck it in," she said.

"What do you think his bride will be like?" asked Cheyenne.

"A full-blown voodoo narcissist like him."

"He couldn't take the competition. I predict Anglo geisha."

"I can see that," said Livy.

"We should at least get drunk before we go."

"I'd rather do it on his dime," said Livy.

"I bet inviting us isn't even his idea. I'll bet it's the bride's."

Livy smiled. "Maybe he has cancer and his doctor warned him that guilt suppresses the immune system."

Cheyenne propelled herself off the stove with her back foot.

"Yes!" she said. "No." She held up her hand. "Wait," she said, "I have it. He found God . . . and God said unto him," Cheyenne threw her arms wide and boomed, "Stop being such a dick! A dick, a dick, dick . . . echo, echo, echo . . ."

Neither sister had seen their father since they were fourteen. The wedding invitation had arrived only two weeks before the date of the ceremony, just on the heels of Cheyenne's reappearance, something their mother, Kirsten, considered prophetic. It was obvious from the short window that the decision to include them was, at best, the result of a long debate or, at worst, an afterthought. Their initial instinct had been to ignore it and the invitation was repurposed as a coaster for days before it was seriously considered. But in the end they could not ignore it. It tapped at a hidden door . . . *Shh . . . he is a king in a castle; he has only stashed us away in the village to keep us safe; someday he will call for us, claim us, and make everything right.*

"I kind of understand why we're going to the wedding," said Cheyenne, "but why is Mom going?"

"For her own reasons."

"Without a doubt."

Livy's eyes met Cheyenne's for a second then moved to the clock. "What time is Mom picking you up?" she asked.

A car honked outside.

"Now," said Cheyenne.

Kirsten's twenty-year-old Toyota was stopped in the middle of the street with the hazards on blocking half the road. She was wearing a black velvet camisole with a long black skirt and black cardigan. There was a ring on every finger and totemic silver jewelry hung around her neck. Tiny zircon studs pierced the indigo blue sun and the crescent moon tattooed on her earlobes. Cheyenne took one look at her and knew that her mother was totally prepared to make an awkward situation more awkward.

"Get in or we'll miss the ferry," said Kirsten.

The dashboard of Kirsten's car rattled with the engine.

"Keep the window rolled down," she said. "The defroster doesn't work."

Kirsten and Cheyenne hadn't spent any time alone since Cheyenne returned so Cheyenne had agreed they would go out to the wedding together, while Livy rode in with their brother, Essex. The minute Cheyenne got into the car, though, she regretted it. Kirsten had questions. About Cheyenne's failed marriage. About its aftermath. About Cheyenne's spiritual analysis of this moment in her life. Cheyenne tried to change the subject to one of Kirsten's many interests—domestic violence legislation, her coven, what books she was reading—but it always turned back to Cheyenne's psyche and the archetypal trauma that must be feeding her cycles of disintegration. Cheyenne told her mother she was tired and pretended to sleep but Kirsten talked anyway.

"You're a mystic by nature," Kirsten said as they drove onto the ferry. "You're drawn to shadowlands."

Cheyenne rolled over and fell into a deep fake nap.

When they arrived, Kirsten went to find out where they were supposed to park. She saw Cyril, dressed in white, in the distance by the edge of the water. Walking over, Kirsten noted that his black hair was still long in front and combed behind his ears as it had been when she'd first met him, a rail-thin twenty-four-year-old holding forth about social norms and Hesse, quoting the Dalai Lama. It had all turned out to be plumage.

She'd never held him to any kind of child support outside the occasional hospital bill, but recently her attitude about that shifted. She didn't expect anything out of him, but maybe the girls should. She wasn't sure. Cyril was one of those rich people who viewed his wealth as the natural fruit of his spiritual voyage.

The rain had stopped but the air was chilled and her shoes were wet by the time she reached him.

Cyril kissed her on both cheeks.

"Thanks for coming early," he said.

"You said you had something for the girls."

"Yes, but not now. I've set aside time before things get too hectic," he said.

Kirsten watched a large foamy wave burst into a white star on the rocks behind him.

"I'm not young anymore," she said. "I could have cancer or drop dead of some zoonotic disease and you'd be their only blood relative."

He smiled. "I have faith in your immune system."

"Won't save me from getting hit by a bus or shot by some teenager with an AR-15."

"That's a little dramatic," he said.

She eyed him without expression, then laughed.

"I just hope it's good," she said. "Whatever you're giving them. Like a house. Or an education."

He turned to the water. Facing the sound, the breeze caught his hair.

He raised his hand to point at something and Kirsten walked off. Such a fucking Leo. Returning to the car, she knocked on the window to rouse Cheyenne.

———

Guests began to arrive in taxis. They clustered by the lighthouse, wandered as far as the radio tower, then came back to the catering tents where the bartender was stocking the open bar.

Around one, Livy arrived with Essex. They drove up in a beater AMC Eagle that Essex had borrowed from his landlord. Essex had brought a date, a honey-haired stripper who happened to be his cash fare one night. Livy brought an empty cooler. Kirsten met them at the car window and told them where to park, then directed Essex to take all their things to a small house on the edge of the sound. By now the caterers had set up the tables and were unloading white folding chairs onto the grass, which was freshly cut and verdant, save for a few raised knuckles of brown earth where it had been mown to the mud. Cheyenne stood on one of those like a pitcher on a mound. Livy saw her and walked over.

"What's the lowdown?" asked Livy.

Cheyenne pointed at Cyril, who was chatting with friends near the lighthouse.

"Have you talked to him?" Livy asked.

Cheyenne shook her head. "I still think this whole thing is a bad idea."

"Any sign of the bride?"

"No, they keep her stashed away until he signs the paperwork and gets to keep her."

Livy smiled, but it was show. Cheyenne's eyes darted everywhere except in the direction of Cyril. The back of Livy's hands itched. At the last minute she had gotten nervous about how she was dressed and made Essex stop by Kirsten's so she could change. But borrowing clothes from Kirsten's closet had been a terrible mistake. Standing now, planted on the grass in a sleeveless floral print dress that exposed both the worker's tan she had from the elbows down and the eggshell white of her muscled upper arms, she was miserable. She hadn't worn socks and her mother's black cotton Chinese slippers were soaked from the dew. Although she'd done her hair as usual, two braids pinned across her head like a wreath, she'd braided it too tight and it was giving her a headache. She narrowed her eyes at Cheyenne, who was now fidgeting with the leather bracelet on her wrist, with her head hung crown-down, hair shaggy in her face.

"Let's get this done," said Livy. "Then we can fade into the background."

As they approached him, Cyril stepped away from his friends and opened his arms.

"Cheyenne, Livy. I'm so glad you could come."

He kissed them each on the cheek and rested his hand on Livy's shoulder until his friends excused themselves.

His cell phone rang and he answered it.

"I don't go to weddings," whispered Livy. "What happens now?"

"People come. Someone reads something by Hafiz or Rumi. There is an original vow contest, then everyone gets drunk."

Cyril hung up and turned to them.

"I was hoping we could spend a few minutes together before the ceremony. I'm really excited for you to meet May. She's heard all about you."

Livy coughed. Cheyenne started to say something but Cyril turned to the panorama behind him. He'd chosen the spot for its view of the mountains across the sound. The lighthouse was an accent. A Dutch windmill in the tulips. A Scottish manor in the background. Something to decorate the moment but not a part of it.

"Stunning, isn't it? The Indians believed these mountains were made to divide those who were greedy from those who weren't because the people had forgotten to be grateful. The gods locked the ungrateful ones on the dry side of the mountains where nothing grows. A lesson." He turned back to them. "We're all so lucky. You two most of all. So few concerns."

Behind him, a wind-shaped, hundred-year-old apple tree flowered at the brink of land, each petal that fell from it a skiff sailing uncaptained to the underworld.

"Cheyenne." He smiled at her. "Kirsten said you were divorced?

I'm sorry it didn't work out. I hope it didn't go too badly." He squeezed Livy's shoulder. "Any young man of yours I need to meet?"

"She doesn't like men," said Cheyenne.

Cyril dropped his hand.

"I'm sorry. I shouldn't have assumed. Forgive me. Well," he scanned the sweeping coastal range with the pride of ownership, "we all have our own road. Pardon me. I have to go take care of a few things. I'll come find you in a bit and we can visit a little more."

Kissing each of them again he walked back toward the small parking lot.

"How can he not know you're gay?" said Cheyenne. "Half of our first-grade class knew you were gay."

Essex emerged from one of the houses and shaded his eyes. Livy smiled and waved him over.

"You know he's been waiting," Livy said. "You can't dodge him anymore."

"I'm not dodging him. Some people you have to be in the mood for," said Cheyenne.

"I'm pretty sure you're one of those people," said Livy.

Cheyenne smiled a little but kept her eyes on Essex. Abandoning his date, he came toward them. She hadn't seen him for two years and only sporadically for several years before that. She was struck by how much bigger he was in person than in her memory. This dissonance between the Essex in her mind and the real Essex was familiar but still jarring. Always in his presence she saw a large and broad-shouldered, if clumsy, man, but as soon as he was out of sight, he became the eleven-year-old boy she'd found on the street and dragged home when she was a teenager. She saw him beaming as he got closer and winced. You don't get out of saving someone from themselves.

Reaching her, Essex wrapped her up in his arms, lifting her slightly in a hug. She kissed him and stepped back. He'd dyed his hair but the roots had since grown out so that from his scalp to the top of his ears it was light brown and from there to his chin, black. It reminded Cheyenne of a two-tone leather van seat.

"Where's your date?" asked Livy.

Essex pointed to a drink table.

"Livy said you broke up with her," said Cheyenne.

"Different girl," said Essex.

He glanced at the ground, then squinted at Cheyenne, tilting his head, causing a short curtain of hair to fall across half his face.

"Do you think being here is a good idea? He's never done a thing for you guys," he said.

"At least he's related to us," said Cheyenne. "You have no excuse."

"I'm here to tell him what an asshole he is," said Essex.

"Bet you don't," said Livy.

"Watch me."

Cheyenne peered into his blue eyes. He flinched. She shook her head. "You won't. None of us will. We should and we won't," she said.

Livy folded her arms tight against her body. "He's not worth it," she said.

Essex saw Cyril heading toward the lighthouse and he turned and walked toward him. The sisters looked on. From their spot across the lawn they could see Essex's mouth begin to move until Cyril put his hand on his shoulder and smiled. Essex smiled back.

"Coward," said Cheyenne under her breath.

2 The Keeper's House

UNDER A WHITE CANOPY with garlands wrapped around the metal tent poles, guests, about fifty of them, stood scattered on the grass near an arbor with a trestle, wineglasses in hand. No one was wearing anything particularly fancy, but money was everywhere, hidden in the make of a hiking boot and in the confidence with which people asked for things.

Hors d'oeuvres were coming out and Livy, seeing an opportunity, went into the kitchen tent and embedded herself within the Filipino catering staff, who were sick of being mistaken for Mexicans. She sympathized and ate off the trays as they were plated while they bitched in Tagalog. Outside on the lawn were the Tibetan workers from one of Cyril's warehouses, invited more as accessories of enlightenment than for their intimacy with Cyril and the bride.

Inside the kitchen tent, two pots of jambalaya were being kept warm. One pot was marked "Beef" and the other "Shrimp." On the beef pot was a piece of masking tape with the words "Save for Tibetans" on it. Livy sidled over and started spooning some into a Tupperware bowl she'd stashed in her bag. The cook caught her and put the lid back on the pot.

"That's for later," said the cook, "and not for you."

"Why can't we have the beef?"

"It's for the Tibetans. The shrimp jambalaya costs too many lives."

Livy frowned slightly then grinned in a rare, wide smile. "Because it's only one cow," she said.

"One cow," said the cook.

It was such a dazzling moral parry. A harm-reduction approach to reincarnation Livy could get behind.

Essex tried to make himself useful. He carried chairs and kegs and drove tent poles deeper into the ground, so he wouldn't have to look anyone in the eye. Years of promising himself he would tell Cyril off if he ever had the chance, and he'd blown it right away. *Say it! You are an awful father (and I should know because I had an awful father)*, but when the time had come to say it, his courage had abandoned him.

When there was nothing left to lift or carry, he joined Livy and Cheyenne under the canopy. Trays of cheese and fruit appeared.

"I like how they do this," said Essex. "At most weddings they starve you and keep you sober until after the vows."

Cheyenne cut a half-moon slice off a wheel of Manchego. Livy filled two plates and went with Essex's date to stake out a table in the corner of the tent.

"I watched your showdown with Cyril," said Cheyenne. "He'll never recover."

"What do you want me to do? It's his wedding." Essex put a cluster of grapes on his plate, picked the last of the cheese off one platter and moved to the next.

Cheyenne's back muscles tightened. She could never figure out why feeling sorry for Essex turned into feeling sorry for herself.

Essex took a slab of feta to go with his other goat cheeses. Cheyenne palmed a heel of Bavarian farmer's bread. Having filled their plates with as much food as they could, they made for the corner where Livy was. They spread out, taking up the whole table, lounging like lions. Servers brought carafes of water and bused empty plates. Essex and his date fell into a side conversation about someone they knew.

"What's her name?" whispered Cheyenne.

"Jennie," said Livy. "Or Jessica?"

Livy looked at her watch. A passing server refilled their wineglasses.

"So Essex said he isn't your real brother. How did you all meet?" asked Jennie.

"I was hanging out on the Ave," Essex said.

"When Cheyenne was seventeen she dragged him home off the street," said Livy. "He was the most pathetic kid you ever saw. I'd have left him."

"She would have," said Essex. "She's not joking."

"I just thought we were going to give him a shower and bus money," said Cheyenne.

"Kirsten let me stay," said Essex.

"I heard someone say the bride is super young," said Cheyenne.

"Did they say it like a compliment or a slam?" Livy asked.

"Look at these people," said Cheyenne. "Compliment."

Cheyenne ate a cracker while staring down the horizon line. Livy stole the last piece of Gouda off Essex's plate as his date watched with the soft eyes of a seal pup. Servers cleared the bread and lit cans of Sterno beneath the chaffing dishes.

Cheyenne looked at her sister. "Do you think it's too late for us?"

"Too late for what?" Livy said.

"To be something. Not in some stupid get-married-or-look-at-me-I'm-a-lawyer way but in a real way. Look at us. We're thirty-three."

"Thirty-three and a half," said Livy.

Cheyenne tore off a piece of black bread and popped it in her mouth.

"What do you do, Cheyenne?" asked Jennie.

Livy laughed.

"I'm in a transitional time," said Cheyenne.

"Permanently," said Livy.

"That's not fair. She just got back," said Essex. "She'll figure it out."

"No I won't," said Cheyenne, and Livy laughed louder.

It wasn't a bad moment. Cheyenne tore off another piece of bread.

"I always try to think about where I want to be at the same time next year," said Jennie.

Livy put both hands on the table. "I want to be up north fishing and the rest of you can go to hell."

Jennie looked to Cheyenne.

"I'm playing it by ear," Cheyenne said. "I'll probably stay here for a while."

Livy's stomach went a little sour. In the two weeks Cheyenne had been at Livy's, she hadn't once talked about paying any rent. Cheyenne was a barnacle. Livy was going to have to scrape her off the hull at some point and it wouldn't be pretty.

Livy turned to Jennie. "Essex says you're in nursing school. When do you graduate?"

"It was supposed to be next year but I'm taking time off to go to Africa."

"Why Africa?" asked Cheyenne.

"I want to see the world before it's gone."

Jennie laid a slice of baked brie on a hummus crostini. A man in white began to weave through the guests. Livy noticed him before the others.

"When's the last time you saw your dad?" Jennie asked.

Livy looked at Cheyenne. "Eighth grade? But we only saw him once or twice a year before that."

"He used to take us to work for show-and-tell," said Cheyenne. "Two kids from his polyamorous youth to vet him as an unconventional thinker."

"They had free Coke machines and candy," said Livy. She gazed solemnly at her sister and lowered her voice by an octave. "You know, Cheyenne, the Indians say—"

Cheyenne slapped the table. "Which Indians? Which Indians, Cyril?"

"They say bad Indians get left with dry land. So be a good

Indian. Don't be greedy. Honor the earth and it will provide." Livy patted Cheyenne on the head. "Hope that works out well for you people while I frack the hell out of what land we left you."

"God it kills me!" said Cheyenne. "Which Indians? Exactly. Which. Indians? Cyril."

"I think it's Cowlitz myth," said Livy.

"That can't be right," said Cheyenne. "Also I don't care. It's a lousy myth."

Essex pointed with his cheese knife to warn them that Cyril was within earshot.

The lighthouse keeper's house, and the assistant lighthouse keeper's house, opened onto the sea, not the land. It was a fundamental orientation when they were built, but now it was no longer important to the wedding guests who came in and out what was once the back door.

Cyril had rented both for the night. He and his bride would stay in one and Kirsten and the girls in the other. It was a gracious act of hospitality toward them that cost him nothing. They had not followed his career; when he lost interest in them, they lost interest in him. Still they knew the broad strokes. He had started in software development. Rich in stock, he had branched out into sidelines like the import-export business that employed the Tibetans. From there, it was less concrete. He had, it seemed, transcended goods and services almost entirely, diversifying into multiple shell companies, replicating and mirroring, acquiring and sloughing off; unmoored from states of reality—like warehouses and people—to become an algorithmic superstructure of predatory capital, ever moving, ever present, unfixable in space and time. And yet he had called them all here. What he had to give his daughters must be worth it. At least that was the hope.

After fetching them from their table, Cyril welcomed Livy and Cheyenne in through the back door of the keeper's house. Built in

1919, the house had undergone a restoration on the heels of a bad 1970s remodel, elevating something claustrophobic about the layout, a Victorian hangover, which exposed a dread of open, common space.

"May is upstairs," he said. "Let's go into the parlor to talk."

His voice was pregnant with so many possible futures that Cheyenne's heart began to race, but she couldn't tell if it was excitement or apprehension. He brought them into the parlor. She had expected a room with darkly stained walnut furniture, dollhouse chairs upholstered with hard, candy-striped cushions. The room was plain, though. A few heart-shaped chair backs, a standing cabinet. A large picture window from the bad remodel, which had been too expensive to remove, offered a clear view of dark waters. Cyril took a chair. The girls sat on the overstuffed couch, instinctively moving closer together until, inches apart, swapping electrons, they radiated and crackled. Upstairs they heard laughter and voices, giggling and a squeal. Cyril ticked his head toward the ceiling.

"May and her friends getting ready. I'm told I have to vacate the premises soon." He nodded to himself. "She's wonderful. An old soul."

Someone started playing Beyoncé above them and the floor began to sink and rise as people danced. Cyril ran his hand along the arm of the chair.

"The bardo," he said, "the land between."

Cheyenne looked sideways at Livy.

"A test," he said. "Do it right and you are reborn into a better world." He smiled at them. "The Tibetans have it right. We rarely know our journeys." He clapped. "The carnival of human experience is magnificent! Have you ever been overseas?"

Livy and Cheyenne both shook their heads.

"Neither of you? Well don't put it off. You'll live a smaller life. Travel made me a citizen of the world." His eyes wandered to the window and the sound beyond. "The bardo. You can get caught in illusions." He looked to them for recognition and saw none. "You can take on what isn't yours."

Outside, the DJ checked the sound system.

"May is pregnant," he said.

"Congratulations," said Cheyenne.

"Thank you."

Livy gave him a tight smile.

"We're going to Singapore. As things develop, we'll probably settle in China afterward. That's where things are really happening."

He leaned forward with his elbows on his knees, pressing his palms together, bringing his fingers to his lips, tapping them. Then he stopped.

"Everything," he whispered, looking from one sister to the other, "everything feels new. It feels like this is my real first child. Not technically, I know. But in all the real ways." He took a long breath. "And I need to allow myself this moment and fully experience it. I never had a say in being a parent. There were other choices. I'm not sorry—you both turned out well. But it's time for me to leave the bardo and move on."

He stood and crossed to a dresser where an envelope lay. "Tonight marks a beginning," he picked it up, "and an end."

He handed it to Livy. Things tilted slightly beneath her. The skin on her forearms got hot.

"I wanted to leave you something," he said. "The obvious thing would be money, but I truly believe money will ruin the two of you."

Cheyenne laughed sharply. "It already has."

Cyril's eyes sparkled at Cheyenne, as if the joke were his.

"I feel pretty comfortable letting the universe guide your fate," he said.

Cheyenne's stomach contracted. Livy opened the envelope. Her breath caught. Cyril pointed to it.

"I tried to anticipate any genetic questions you might have. That's a summary of family medical history, some cancer, some hypertension, a little asthma. Not too bad. Anyway, it's there for you."

Livy blinked. "Thanks, Cyril. I appreciate the medical info. If I ever have decent health insurance I'll make sure they get a copy."

"There's more," he said.

Livy looked in the envelope and saw a second sheet. She unfolded it. On it was the address of a monastery in Montana and a name: Ann Radar.

As girls they'd been fed a fairy tale: Two women loved the same man. One wanted a baby and the other wanted to chase the North Star. Each became pregnant, so they made a plan. The one who wanted the baby would take both children and the one who wanted the North Star would continue on. The first mother was happy and the second mother was happy.

But which daughter was which? It drove Livy and Cheyenne fucking bat-shit crazy.

Kirsten had never given them a name or a way to reach the other woman. She refused to say which girl belonged to which mother, and Livy and Cheyenne had never been able to figure it out. Each sister had Kirsten's black hair and mannerisms, her broad shoulders—but so did a lot of people. Mostly they looked like their father, Cyril, who also had black hair. Every now and then, though, one sister would see something in the other and think, that's totally her mouth, but they could never be certain. Paperwork didn't clarify anything either. Theirs was a home birth, and Kirsten was listed as the mother on both birth certificates.

When they finally got the real story, it didn't help because it wasn't much different from the fairy-tale version. Kirsten met Cyril when he was in grad school. They had an open relationship. Then Cyril fell in love with a girl who was new to town. The girl and Kirsten became friends. Not long afterward both women got pregnant. Since one was ready for a baby and one was not, they struck a deal over a bottle of wine and some tosses of the *I Ching*. One woman became a mother of two girls and the other became a Buddhist nun. Cyril, not as much of a polyamorous adventurer as he originally thought, didn't stick around, and Kirsten raised the girls alone.

———

"That is the other woman I was with at the time of your conception," Cyril said now. "I was never a part of the agreement your mothers made and don't consider myself bound by it. Do what you like with the information."

A chill ran through Cheyenne's arms. They had never had a name. They'd never even had a hint. All the fights the sisters had growing up. Guessing. Over whose mother was whose. Over who had the North Star in them and who didn't. In middle school they had both wanted to be Kirsten's daughter. In high school neither did. Ann. That was it? Ann. Such a ridiculously plain name. Cheyenne took the paper from Livy.

A girlish voice called down the stairs, "You all need to go now. You can't see the bride."

"Yes, get out," squealed a second voice, laughing.

Cyril made a face at his daughters. "I guess it's time," he said, standing, walking them to the kitchen door. "I'm proud of how you two turned out. You'll find your path." He opened the door, ushering them out. "The world won't know what hit it."

The door closed behind them.

They retreated to the other keeper's house. Once inside, Cheyenne coughed and teared up.

"That was hugely fucked. I'm so angry I can't see straight. He gets all this power. For nothing. We just give it to him." She laughed but tears rolled down her cheeks. "What bullshit."

She kicked the brocade corner of a sofa and paced the living room.

"I don't even know what a bardo is," said Livy.

"Ask Mom. She'll tell you all about it." Cheyenne stopped dead. "We should leave," she said.

"No, I'm getting food and alcohol out of this. If nothing else, we get that."

Cheyenne shivered. She was dressed for a fucking wedding and might as well stay.

Kirsten came in through the kitchen.

"I'm not ready to talk to her about this," said Cheyenne.

They slipped out the front, standing on a strip of grass between house and water, a welcome mat for sea gods and ghosts. Cyril's bride emerged from next door in a netting of white tulle. Hemmed in by a man-made bulkhead of rocks and driftwood, she knelt on the steps of the porch. Her thick black hair blew into her face as she tried to light a cigarette in the wind.

"Oh shit!" said Cheyenne. "She's actually Asian."

"We wouldn't have to make it up if he'd cared enough to introduce us," said Livy.

The bride, who was a few years younger than they were, lit her cigarette and sat down on the steps. The wind changed direction and a stray piece of her tulle caught fire. It flared like a wish lantern and she jumped up, clapping her hands over it until it was out, then sat back down and lit another cigarette.

Livy felt the change in barometric pressure and looked instinctively toward the west where clouds had formed several miles off.

"I'm cold. I'm going back in," she said.

When Kirsten found out about the address of the monastery, she hit the roof. She screamed at the absent Cyril until Cheyenne told her the whole stupid thing was her fault in the first place.

"It's a myth of belonging!" yelled Kirsten.

"To a goddamned star!" Cheyenne shouted.

"There are worse myths," said Kirsten, "believe me. You could be Daphne, running from a rapist and getting turned into a tree," which was the end of the conversation.

Ten minutes later Kirsten packed her bags and left.

Cheyenne looked at Livy. "I guess I'm riding back with you."

Unsure of where to be, Livy and Cheyenne walked back outside. The wind kicked up. A folding chair went over. The poles holding up the canopy where the tables of gifts and banquet tables were shivered as the canopy billowed like a sail for a second, then settled.

Essex found them twenty minutes later, sheltered under a tree. Something was different but he wasn't sure what.

"What did Cyril want?" he asked.

"To tell us he's moving to China and not to expect more excellent parenting," said Livy.

"Did he give you anything?" asked Essex. "Kirsten thought he might give you something."

"Advice on reincarnation," said Cheyenne.

Essex looked at her but saw no bitterness in her expression.

"Nothing feels worse than shame and hope," he said cheerfully, trying to help.

"Or the death of something you thought was dead that wasn't. That's good too," said Cheyenne, but now there was an edge to her voice.

"He gave us the address of the monastery where our other birth mother went," said Livy. "That's why Kirsten left."

"Kirsten left? Should we go?" he asked.

"No, she's fine. This is all actually her fault," said Cheyenne.

3 The Tower

THE CEREMONY was scheduled for 3:30 but nothing was happening. Chairs were on the lawn by the trellis and people congregated but the cues weren't coming. A man in a blue suit told everyone there would be a delay. By 3:15 it was clear something was wrong.

Cyril soon made the announcement that it was still going to be a little while but they would bring more wine. Not five minutes later somebody else made a new announcement that there was no preacher coming. The man had gone to the Point Wilson lighthouse on the Olympic Peninsula instead and there was no way to get him here in time. Cyril asked people to call friends who might know someone who could come on short notice. Cell phones lit in every hand, and cupping them like vigil candles against the wind, people were beetling around and bumping into each other trying to get reception. No one was coming up with anything until someone got the bright idea that the old Coast Guard captain who came with the lighthouse could perform the ceremony if they just got far enough off land. But then somebody looked up the actual laws regarding captains marrying people and found out that it was an urban myth, which the old sea captain could have told them if they'd asked. As it turned out, though, the old Coast Guard captain was also a justice of the peace.

Within an hour, everyone was gathered on the lawn by the trellis; the retired Coast Guard captain had run home to shave and returned wearing a blazer. Nearing eighty but sharp, not drunk but just a little high, he waited at the end of the chairs now lined up in rows.

It was dusk when the bride came out of the keeper's house with two friends following. Her white dress and torn tulle whipped around her in wind that was now strong and steady. Drops of light rain fell, guests tried not to flinch. Her bare shoulders were wet and everything was gray—the people, the clothes, the air. As she walked down the grassy aisle the sky darkened and the sun sank. A powerful gust sent empty chairs tumbling. The Coast Guard captain, who'd spent most of his career on icebreaker ships, was unfazed, but just as she arrived next to him, the bride was blown sideways into Cyril.

It started to pour and the captain began to incant, his voice cutting through the wind and rain. Cyril yelled for everyone to head for the catering tent, but no one heard him over the captain's voice and the captain wasn't stopping. Something about the waves, those that lift us, those that wipe us out. Finally, the bride turned and ran for cover and everyone followed. They reached the catering tent, a mob, clearing away folding tables to make room underneath it.

The captain, though, stared straight ahead, watching the mainland vanish into a descending fogbank. The tent canopy snapped in the high winds and finally tore in one long awful sound, ripping lengthwise while several people screamed, the poles collapsing sideways around them. The caterers immediately leapt to kill the propane tanks in the portable kitchen, the butane fire and Sterno under the jambalaya pots. The sky flashed with lightning.

"To the houses!" a man yelled, but he was overruled by the captain's voice rising over the blow like a deep and terrible singing bowl. "To the tower!" he intoned in the key of the storm itself.

Everyone ran for the tiny lighthouse, though it was far too small to hold them all. At the door, the captain went calmly through his keys as the crowd surrounded him and Cyril and the bride shivered by his side. He opened the lighthouse door and hit a switch. Compact fluorescents shone grimly down on a room that looked like the boiler of a deep-draft ship with its layers of glossy gray industrial paint, meters, and pipes. Cyril and his bride stepped inside. Livy, Essex and his date, Cheyenne—all of whom had been spotted as family—were pushed to the fore.

"Where is the ring bearer?" shouted the captain at the shadows on the lawn.

A drenched man in a beige windbreaker made his way forward. Once he was inside, the captain led the wedding party up the red spiral staircase. Livy wanted to see the view from the lighthouse, but Cheyenne resisted. Every time she tried to step back, though, someone pushed her ahead. Essex, too big to push or pass, kept his place near Cheyenne, dragging his date along. Behind them, people crowded into the first-floor museum room, and the stairwell, and the alcove on the second floor that held the old coal stove, and up the final steps to the tower. But only a quarter of the guests made it into the lighthouse itself. The rest were left in the yard where thunder rumbled and the sky blackened and it was no longer possible to tell storm from night.

In the gloomy stairwell, Essex felt breathless. He lost the hand of his date, found it, and lost it again. The wedding party climbed up and around the final turn and into a tiny circular room at the top of the tower with windows on all sides. The captain turned on the lantern and prismatic light compressed by the Fresnel lens shot out over the point, burning like a new star.

Six of them stood around the light. Livy and the captain, Cyril and his bride, the best man and Cheyenne. Essex remained with his date on the final step watching the scene over Cheyenne's shoulder. The rest of the guests wound down the stairs.

The captain tried to direct people. Livy looked at Cheyenne. Her sister was shading her eyes, staring into the light. Livy saw Essex whisper in Cheyenne's ear but couldn't read his lips.

"Is this hard for you?" Essex asked.

Cheyenne turned. "Do you mean do I look at fucking Cyril and his child bride and imagine it's the same as me and Jackson only with millions of dollars and bad weather?"

"Yeah," Essex said, raising his voice, "that's exactly what I mean."

"Quiet!" said the man on the step below Essex.

Essex leaned over her shoulder so his mouth was close to her ear. "Do you remember what you said to me the night we met?"

"No, and I don't care," she said.

"You said . . . 'Go away.'"

She laughed. The man behind them hissed.

"I meant it," she said.

"I treasure the moment," said Essex.

The wind dropped off momentarily, exposing the silence beneath it. Cyril's bride stared out the black windows.

Below, Cheyenne saw a few people on the ground who had been unable to fit in the tower migrating across the lawn in the downpour. Some to their cars, others to the half-collapsed catering tent. She would have traded places with any of them. Pinned into a room she had no interest in being in, her skin on fire. Everyone breathing on the stairwell behind her and in the floors below—all one animal. A few muffled coughs, a few comments meant to lighten. But after all, it only has to end in marriage to be a comedy. She could wait it out.

Two people in the stairwell left and the crowd turned clockwise as it adjusted. Now Cheyenne was directly across from the bride, who was pressed against the curved wall of windows. A blast of wind shook the tower and the panes rattled. The icebreaker captain, who, Cheyenne was starting to realize, was an utter diva, took a step forward and began the ceremony in earnest.

"We are here today," he bellowed, "to witness this couple's marriage in the sight of the greatest of all gods, weather."

Something smashed against the window near the bride's head and everyone jumped. The captain shrugged. "Birds. These sudden storms."

Someone in the stairwell laughed and everyone shifted a little, but not the bride. She stood perfectly straight, gazing blankly at her own reflection in the glass.

"And yet these powerful forces that drive us together," said the captain, raising his voice again, "can also drive us apart! We must always be vigilant. These are icebergs. These are U-boats. What we see is but a little of what's there. Never forget the great depths of this world!"

Livy glanced at Cheyenne, who would not look at her, afraid she'd laugh. Outside, a cloud turned white with hidden lightning and the rain fell sideways.

"As black as this storm is," said the icebreaker captain, "it will pass. Rings!"

"We actually have some vows we'd like to read," said Cyril.

"Oh yes. Vows!"

Cyril unfolded a piece of paper: "You are my fragrant morning, my spring, my light blossom, my May. Like a lotus—"

There was a huge crack as lightning struck something on another part of the island. People looked around, suddenly aware that there was a radio tower in the field a hundred yards away from them.

"—spinning in a stream, you teach me who I am. You help me, see me."

A flash lit the sky just as another bird hit the window near the bride.

"And I know now that the roads we have walked down separately have only prepared us for being together."

He folded his paper and waited for her. But the bride wasn't listening. She kept staring out the windows where her own face danced, contorted and wavering as people shifted in front of the Fresnel lens.

Cheyenne saw Cyril glance at May. What was in that look? Something so naked, so desperate. The simple desire to be comforted, to be assured of what no one can ever be assured of, that it will all turn out all right. That the things which come to pass, like ghost stories, like demon lovers, will all cut a path toward home. It reminded her of the other things too, things she couldn't put into words but which still hurt. Cyril put his hand to May's face and she jumped, startled, and reached for her own slip of paper.

"I am your lily. I am your love. I will be faithful to you and god." She folded the paper back up.

"Rings!" said the icebreaker captain.

The man in the beige windbreaker held out two rose-gold bands that glinted on his open palm. The rings went on and the couple kissed and the crowd in the stairwell cheered as one more deafening gust shook the tower windows.

"Yes!" boomed the captain. "We may well rejoice and celebrate. But may we never forget the terrible depths of this world!"

4 Irish Lord

FOR THE PAST SEVERAL SUMMERS Livy had worked long-lining for halibut in the Gulf of Alaska. The family that employed her ran a small outfit out of Ketchikan: their boat, a marginally buoyant piece of fiberglass; their skipper, a third-generation fisher-man utterly without instinct. As a student of what not to do, Livy studied the man as she would a rare and dying plant.

When he got excited, she too felt a thrill and paid particularly close attention.

"The fish are there!" he'd yell. "I feel it!"

He was always wrong. Pointing at a vague patch of glassy black sea and shouting, *Down there!* It was the moment he lived for; though it underscored their ever-bleakening prospects, it was his moment, his to take. *Down there!* Yes. Down there, with the starfish and the Irish lords, down with the albino space shrimp. The most unimaginable things came up on those lines, none of them halibut. Over time Livy learned where the fish were by where the captain didn't go.

After months of blisters and vomiting over the side of the rail, Livy was often glad when the season ended and she returned to Seattle and went back to driving a cab at night. Floating through the intersections at bar closing time, fishtailing on the barest shimmer of rain in a Crown Victoria, making money, her own captain at last. Yet no eternity exists more vividly than 5:00 a.m. in a Dairy Queen parking lot holding some jackass's empty wallet as collateral while he tries to borrow the fare from his dealer.

This was how it went for three years. Back and forth, migrational. But now Alaska had fallen through. After a winter of pull-tab binges in Juneau, the family she'd always worked for had sold their boat, converted to Mormonism, and moved south in the embrace of the church. Without another Alaska connection, Livy was out of luck. Driving a cab was changing too. Every jerk with a car was a cabdriver now and all the real money was gone out of the game.

So she got a job refurbishing vintage yachts at a marina on Lake Union. The position flew under the radar of state minimum-wage requirements by claiming to be training—*Here's a scraper, there's the paint, go forth*—so getting up to minimum wage took three months, but she worked without supervision and that was worth a lot.

Then in the early spring Livy found her basement studio; built without permits and well below code, it absorbed 80 percent of her income, but it was the first time in her life that she'd had real privacy. Until Cheyenne showed up and ruined it. Now her boxes of books and records filled the corners. Her chatter was constant. She boiled up all the macaroni and drank all the Folgers. With every economic microaggression she created a soft and persistent financial pressure, reminding Livy of how tentative existence was. A broken arm could shatter Livy's livelihood. Bronchitis could soak up an entire paycheck. One minor bike accident, that's it, watch below. Because that's all it would take to end up on her mother's couch. Livy began walking to and from work just to be alone, an hour each way. She walked along the ship canal, under the Aurora Bridge, along the edge of the lake, sometimes thinking of it as the edge of a vast and horizonless sea instead.

Coming home one evening, two weeks after the wedding, Livy found the studio empty. Cheyenne had run into an old acquaintance and was out for the night. Livy almost cried in gratitude. Getting out of her work clothes, she sat naked in the lamplight. She sang to herself and drew on her body with a ballpoint pen. She outlined her scars—the dot from a nail gun, the oval on her knee from where she had taken the stitches out too early with a safety pin and a toenail clipper. She stopped at the circular, nickel-sized scar on her upper arm.

She'd done it to herself with a car cigarette lighter the last time she and Cheyenne had lived together. It had been their senior year of high school, a period now referred to as the Year of the Great Crisis, the first of Livy's elliptical, low-grade depressions, which arrived like a comet and would return about every seven years. The tiniest thing had set it off. Livy had met two girls earlier that fall and the three of them started hanging out around the clock. One night, six months in, she found out that the two girls were dating and had been for months. The idea that you could feel so close to people and not know what was going on, that you could be so very mistaken, caused a foundational crack. She lost weight. Counselors called her into their offices to tell her it was okay to be gay, which she already knew. Kirsten was convinced she'd been in love with one of the girls and had her heart broken. Only Cheyenne got it right.

"She's fine," she said, "she just doesn't like being wrong."

One evening, just before summer break, Livy borrowed Kirsten's car and drove to the ship canal. Parking near the fish ladder, she left the motor running. Furious at herself, she started to cry. Enraged at her own weakness, she pushed in the cigarette lighter. When it popped out, she yanked her T-shirt sleeve up over her shoulder and pressed the orange coils into the meat of her upper arm. It hurt like hell and smelled god-awful. She counted to three as it burned then jumped out of the car, walked to the canal, and threw the lighter into the water.

Sitting naked on the rug in the lamplight, she felt the echo of that time. Cheyenne's presence exposed a fragility that was more than economic. Ever since her sister moved in, Livy had started to doubt herself in ways she hadn't since she was a teenager. Having the name of the other mother now, after all these years, only made things weirder. Ann Radar—and what is Radar anyway? Kirsten said a lot of people made up names back then. It might have been a band she was in or an idea. It was a lead, though, of some sort.

The sisters hadn't been able to reach an agreement on what to do with the information. Having the address and not using it made Livy feel more in control, whereas it made Cheyenne feel out of control. Cheyenne began to fixate on the idea that one of them might have come from people who had something. *Maybe they want a granddaughter? Maybe she wants to be a mother now?* Livy wondered if her sister wasn't right, and if maybe there wasn't an opportunity there.

In the morning Livy found a note slipped under her door. It was from her landlord. On a letterpress card with a daffodil in the bottom corner it said: If your sister's going to stay here then I'm raising your rent by half and doubling your utilities. I'll also need a larger deposit and $30 for a background check. Thanks!

Under different circumstances Livy would have marched upstairs and threatened to rat out her landlord to the building permits office. But this just might have solved Livy's problem. Cheyenne would never be able to come up with the rent money and Livy had none to front. Now she could herd Cheyenne along and they could both raise a glass and fairly say, *Damn the landlords of this world!*

But when Cheyenne came home and Livy handed her the note, Cheyenne had little reaction. We'll figure it out, she chirped, and then she ate more than her share of the eggs, didn't do the dishes, and rolled out a yoga mat in the center of the room.

Livy tried to find respite at work but couldn't. Everything irritated her. Marlinspike in hand, she looked around the repair bay and wondered which of the two rich hippie owners she needed to gut to get NPR turned off. Livy put her earplugs in and ran her hand across the side of a battered sloop.

The bubbling gray paint had blistered and cracked and the wood beneath was rotting. Jesus, what's wrong with people? The beautiful thing about a bowline knot is that it's simple. You can even make it one-handed if you're injured or maimed. The boat Livy was looking at had been rigged and sailed by an imbecile. The mast had snapped in a small storm and the boat had been abandoned, an ark in the weeds. This was her bosses' specialty, flipping old boats for outrageous prices on a clever paint job and polish—everything is reparable if you change your definition of fixed. Livy grabbed a paint scraper and began to work.

When lunchtime came, she got her food and went outside to eat in the sun. At the end of the dock she saw Kirsten coming toward her. She hadn't seen her mother since the wedding.

As Kirsten approached, Livy saw she had on her battle shirt. It had faded from purple to lavender and was thin from years of washing. There was a harmless blueberry muffin in the upper left and the words AIN'T NO LOVIN' LIKE SOMETHING FROM THE COVEN written across the top. Kirsten wore it when gearing up for a fight. Livy had seen her throw an entire tray of lasagna at a couch when she was wearing that shirt.

The shirt made Livy feel like a child.

"I only have a minute," Livy said when her mother was within earshot.

"We can take a quick walk," said Kirsten.

They had gone only a few feet when Kirsten started in.

"Cheyenne says you are thinking of going to find Ann."

"We might. I don't know," said Livy.

"This isn't something Ann did. She didn't give you the address. Cyril did. Following his whims instead of respecting Ann's decision is tantamount to firebombing all of second-wave feminism for a pat on the head from the Man."

"Firebombing?" Livy said.

Kirsten lowered her voice like the FBI was listening. "Would it make a difference if I told you this whole Ann Radar thing was more about Cheyenne than you? It's her path, not yours."

"Can we please not talk in terms of paths?" said Livy.

"It's her story."

"Are you saying that Ann is her mom?"

Something pulled at Livy. Unlike Cheyenne, she'd grown away from obsessing over whose mother was whose, but that didn't mean she liked the idea that other people knew something about her life that she didn't. On its surface, this talk with Kirsten was a typical lecture. *Don't look outside yourself for what you need. Nothing but you will make you whole.* Yet the subtext felt like a confession. Then again, Kirsten considered it her job to make every moment a potential initiatory experience. Which pointed toward this not being an admission of parentage so much as a test. An apple from the hag in the forest who is not really a hag.

5 1040-EZ

KIRSTEN, NOCTURNAL AS SHE WAS, rarely woke before 4:00 p.m. If she did, it was for administrative reasons: DMV lines, unpayable bills, courthouses, community college. She preferred these things to come at her half-asleep so she could protect the best of herself for later, because at night she had a shining-diamond mind.

She had come home from meeting with Livy and begun to work through her list of chores since she was already awake, but then stopped in the middle. She was anxious and hadn't known it. The day had a haze to it. It felt like a future memory, each moment framed like she wasn't there but looking back at it already. It was a natural step from that feeling to the realization that what was bothering her was Ann. Beneath her visible frustration at Cyril's violation and the way that it might throw her daughters off course was something moving that she could not name, an undertow.

Kirsten pulled a box out of the closet. Beneath ten years of 1040-EZs, she found her earliest journals and brought them to the kitchen table. On top was her first. It had a denim cover with a gnome at the bottom and she had carved the words FOOD IS EVIL. SLEEP IS FOR LOSERS into the cover. She'd written it back when she was still starving herself and living on Pop-Tarts cut into tiny squares. It was written in the summer she met Margaret, a public-health nurse and midwife from Boston.

———

Fifteen-year-old Kirsten had walked into Planned Parenthood looking for birth control. Too skinny, stripping her black hair to frost it blond, worried the pill would make her fat but frustrated by slipping diaphragms, creeped out by the sponge, sick of condoms—she demanded Margaret give her something better, as if it were the nurse's fault.

Margaret started listing all the options but Kirsten did not like what she was hearing.

"This sucks," she said, jumping off the examining table. "No wonder people pull out."

"What do you call people who use the withdrawal method?" asked Margaret.

Kirsten glowered. "Parents."

"Heterosexual," said Margaret.

Kirsten looked at her but Margaret remained straight-faced.

"Fuck, I wish I was gay," said Kirsten.

"Well if you're dead set against condoms you could try the cervical cap. No protection against STDs but it works pretty well if you do it right, and it's smaller than a diaphragm. Most women are just too chicken to touch themselves and would rather poison their bodies, but you're not chicken, are you?"

Kirsten tried to figure out if it was more pathetic to be proved a coward or to get goaded into something because someone calls you one. She pulled her pants off and lay back on the table while Margaret measured her cervix. Pulling a small latex cup out of a box, she showed Kirsten how to get it up inside her and get the suction right.

"We'll have to order the cap. It'll take a few weeks."

On the way out, Margaret grabbed some granola bars from a basket in a break room and shoved them into Kirsten's hands.

"The Man wants you too thin to act. Too thin to think."

It's hard to overestimate the impact of meeting someone who is truly free. Pre-Margaret, Kirsten felt flat. Everything washed in pastel, the hideous institutional color palette of the day: baby blue, peach, coral, salmon, pale aqua, taupe. After Margaret, everything began to change. Over their next few appointments she worked on Kirsten like a fucking glorious unicorn of feminism. She came at Kirsten with everything she had. In one summer, she freed Kirsten from nearly every cultural bind, a radical form of rare magic.

Turning the pages of the old journal, rage shot through Kirsten. It wasn't Cyril's choice. The agreement she and Ann had made had nothing to do with him. She turned to the back of the journal where she'd kept a list of Ann's addresses. The one Cyril gave the girls was years old. Ann had left the monastery in Montana when they were in middle school. She also didn't go by Ann anymore. But that didn't mean there weren't ways to find her.

It was best to warn Ann. Sitting down at the table, Kirsten got out pen and paper and wrote a short letter. Then she ripped out the page of addresses and took it to her altar on the bookshelf.

Once it had been a busy collection of small statuary, Hindu death goddesses, superheroes, laminated Klimt bookmarks. Now it was spare. She was long past thinking the images she'd clung to as a young woman still held power for her. Like an old erotic map, they were just too familiar to work. Now her altar was simple. A leaf. An abalone shell. A poem she'd screenshot and printed out at the library. She tore the addresses into strips and, burning them on the altar, applied the first lesson she'd ever learned from Margaret: *Never give the Man what he wants.*

6 Triumph

CHEYENNE SAT in the temp office watching the woman behind the desk peel the label gum off a bottle of hand sanitizer. The lobby was empty. The daily work assignments had been dispersed and all the other new applicants processed. Cheyenne was the last appointment of the day and had to make a big show and cry to get the slot. Now she sat in a burnt orange upholstered chair covered in brown stains watching a reality show about people getting mangled on crab boats.

It was interrupted every few minutes by teasers for the news—a record of halfhearted diplomatic gestures, the traditional mating dance of the war gods, some updates on general cruelty, and, inexplicably, a picture of a beach. Then it was back to the crab boat and someone in a yellow spacesuit getting swept off-deck into the arctic swell.

She looked down at her application and saw a job history comparable to any intellectually ambitious recovering meth head. Newspaper delivery, nonprofit program director, bookstore clerk, nonprofit program director again, university administrative assistant, Christmas retail, university administrative assistant's lackey, study-skills tutor, bad wife. Then a murky period of off-grid employment that wasn't worth explaining. She turned in the form and went back to her spot on the orange chair.

Ann Radar was at least a direction. Cheyenne was surprised that Livy agreed to go find her, but Livy set the bar for the trip at $1,000, an impossible amount. *Get your half of the money together and we'll go.* Complicating things further, Ann was no longer in Montana. They had spoken to the abbot there and the only lead they had was shaky, a woman who might have once been Ann who was now at a monastery in Boston. They called to see if she was there and were told that she was. And that was enough for them. Three weeks after the wedding, though, they were no closer to making the trip. It would be the same in a month or two or three. Unless Cheyenne started to make some money.

At five o'clock people started leaving the temp office. At a quarter after, the associate placement counselor called Cheyenne back into the administrative catacombs. The associate sat her down, reviewed her clipboard, and told Cheyenne she had a wonderful future in servitude. If she had the right outlook. Which she didn't. Cheyenne made it through with her eager face on, though barely. The counselor congratulated her on her wealth of hard-won but unrelated skills. *We'll call you for sure. Meanwhile get some slacks.*

The bus came and Cheyenne got on but couldn't face going back to the apartment. Instead she went to find Essex. There was no one better to complain to about work—the idea of it, the reality of it, the lack of it—because on all our tombstones it will say: RIP independent contractor. Most likely they'll write it on a billboard over a mass grave as deep as a valley. Essex would at least find that funny.

Cheyenne hadn't been to his place but knew of it: Neighborsbane, a legendary, run-down Victorian mansion that rented rooms to all the outcasts who found their way to the Pacific Northwest. Seattle's Ellis Island. Everyone knew someone who had lived there. The owner, Lester Minus, was equally famous. He occupied the top floor and rumor had it that climbing the stairs to his apartment you could feel the exact point where the floorboards stopped creaking and the walls were no longer white but the color of aged bone, and the floors became old-growth fir. All of it, famously—the period fixtures, the rehung windows, the leaded glass—was testament to Old World deal-making. Short on rent? Replumb my bathroom. No deposit? I'm sure there's something we can do.

Taking a turn onto the block, Cheyenne saw it in all its broken splendor. At the door, she was let in by a petite trans man with a Bible Belt accent. She wandered into an unfinished kitchen where people were listening to Norse synthpop and boiling beets. She asked them where Essex's room was. They shrugged and pointed at the ceiling.

Upstairs, Jared, Essex's oldest friend, sat cross-legged on a mattress on the floor with Scorpions records fanned out in front of him. A few feet away was Essex, his back against the purple wall, his legs stretched out and crossed at the ankles. Balanced on his thigh was a paper plate with a rectangle of Spam in the center surrounded by an aura of grease. Essex had been carving the Spam into a deer with a key. He'd gotten the triangular shape of the head right and was working to free the animal's spine from the gel and meat.

"I know you avoid me," said Jared. "I'm not an idiot."

"I don't avoid real you. I avoid stupid you. It's okay to avoid stupid you. What does your mom say?" asked Essex.

"She thinks it's great I'm enlisting."

"And she doesn't mind you getting killed or having PTSD the rest of your life."

"I can do both of those things here," said Jared.

Jared's hair was crimped on one side, a nod to metal, and shaved on the other, a nod to Southern California '90s punk. His Iron Maiden shirt, a breastplate; his skull tattoo, a seal, a coat of arms—because how else would we know each other? In this vacuum, in these empty halls. At least Jared saw himself somewhere. Essex couldn't find his place in any of it. He went back to sculpting the Spam deer, working on the haunch. Jared pulled a record out of its sleeve.

While Essex's respect for Jared had dissipated over the years, his loyalty to him had not. They had been kids on the street together, bound in permanent jail solidarity, so when Jared called to tell him he was joining the marines, Essex made a point of hanging out. Now, having seen each other almost every day for the past week, each joke had become a blade that both cut away the years but also laid bare their current emotional distance.

Jared put the record down.

"You should enlist," he said. "They'd love you. All big and strong. You'd be totally *Call of Duty* if you worked out at all."

Essex instinctively shrunk, caving his shoulders, a habit. Raised by women, he was sensitive to his size, and what had started as awareness had evolved into a bit of a nervous twitch. His attempts to manage his presence in a room made him clumsy, which resulted in everyone being reminded of exactly how big he was, when, inevitably, he tripped into someone or knocked something over.

Jared looked at Essex with envy and a little bitterness. "They would take you in a second," he said.

"I would never do anything that stupid without a good reason. Hanging out with you isn't one," said Essex.

Jared's eyes strayed to the pink block that held his friend's attention. Picking a pen up off the floor nearby, he reached over and sank it into the Spam deer's back, where it stuck up like a spear. He laughed. Essex remained still for a heartbeat then held the deer with the pen in its back up to Jared's face.

"Finish the job," he said.

"Fuck you."

"Finish the job."

"Leave me alone."

"Coward," said Essex and took the pen out.

Using the shaft of the pen, he cut the Spam deer in half. It bothered him, though it shouldn't have. It wasn't a real deer. But that's the problem with imagination. There was a knock and Cheyenne came in.

Essex jumped up. Brushing his hair back, he kicked some dirty clothes into a pile, but she didn't notice.

"I was just at a stupid temp agency for hours then had to wait in the rain forever for a bus and I'm going to kill Livy for being such a cunt about the money but I can't until I have another place." She took off her jacket and dropped it by the dresser. "The whole thing sucks."

"How much does she say you need?" asked Essex.

"Five hundred dollars for my share. The abbot we talked to in Montana thinks her real name might be JoAnn Colson, but he's not sure. He gave us the address of a place in Boston called the Fire Blossom Temple."

"Is she there?" asked Jared.

"Some lady named JoAnn Colson is, but that's all I know."

"Can't you borrow Kirsten's car?" asked Essex.

"She wants no part," said Cheyenne.

"You could still ask."

"No I couldn't."

"Five hundred dollars is a lot," said Jared.

"It's the minimum. Car rental. Gas and oil. Food. Lost wages." Cheyenne's eyes started to burn. "The most, the most I can make temping in a week is three hundred and twenty. And that's without disruptions, which never happens—*Oh, I'm sorry, I thought you knew QuickBooks. Oh, I'm sorry, you're actually supposed to be at our satellite location. It's just past fucking Pluto. Should I mark you for a half day?*"

Jared laughed. "I'd talk to this JoAnn woman before driving all the way across the country."

Cheyenne's eyes snapped to Jared. "Well it isn't your deal so it doesn't matter what you'd do. Besides, we're counting on the pathetic nature of our presence to work the magic."

"Can you sell anything?" asked Essex.

She smiled. "My ass. Down on the corner. That's the fucked thing. I'm a haggard thirty-three not twenty-two. It's not like I can just go make bank in some strip joint."

"Not haggard," said Essex, and smiled.

"You could sell plasma," said Jared.

Cheyenne laughed. "There's no way I'm going to spend all day waiting in line, then hooked up to a pump, so some leech-farming blood baron can give me twenty-five dollars and a cookie. Only ass-holes make that deal."

"What about selling some of your records or books?" asked Essex.

"I sold almost all of them today and got nothing. It'll cover food and bus passes until I get my first check, but that's it. And," she began to gesticulate, "that check won't come for three weeks. And it will only be for a couple of days because of where the stupid pay period falls. And it will have a onetime administrative fee deducted from it. And the fee for not doing direct deposit. And the fee to cash the check." Stopping abruptly, she let her hands drop. Her throat was dry. She swallowed but the tightness stayed.

"If you had the money, could Livy get the time off?" asked Essex.

"They said she could have next week off or wait to see if next month works." Cheyenne crossed to where Jared was and sat beside him on the mattress. "I don't want to talk about it anymore." She looked at Essex. "Are you going to drive a cab tonight?"

"I don't know. I didn't make any money last night and the night before I didn't cover my lease. Livy says I'm the worst cabdriver ever."

"She's probably right," said Cheyenne. "I can't imagine you doing it."

"Why doesn't Livy drive anymore?" asked Jared. "As a chick she'd make double in tips."

"She doesn't like drunks. She always used to make money, though," said Essex.

"So how come you can't?" Jared asked.

Essex shrugged. "People are always talking to you. I feel bad cutting them off and the time adds up."

"Livy would cut off your dying words if she saw a fare behind you," said Cheyenne.

"She's got the long view," said Essex.

Cheyenne turned to Jared. "Essex said you're enlisting. That's stupid. Why?"

"It's not like I have anything else going on," said Jared. "I don't think it'll make a man out of me, if that's what you mean."

Cheyenne leaned into his space. "You know what women do when they've got nothing going on? They get pregnant. Having one decision you could make that made the rest get made for you." She slapped his thigh. "Good luck with that, man."

Jared pulled another record out of its sleeve and spun it on his finger until it toppled, rolling onto the floor and into the wall.

"Which branch?" she asked.

"Marines," said Jared. "If they don't take me, then the army."

"It's fucked that you need a college degree to go into the Peace Corps," said Essex. "There should be some way to sign over your life without killing something. I wouldn't mind digging ditches for the next twenty years if there was a good reason."

"I'm sure someone wants you to dig a ditch. Go find them," said Cheyenne.

"I'm just saying there should be global use for a person with low standards and a shovel," Essex said.

Cheyenne rolled her eyes but giggled. She crawled off the mattress and stood. She felt better but didn't know why. The night seemed different.

"You know, if Livy kicks you out they have a room coming up here," said Essex, "one of the nicer ones. If I drive more I might be able to front the move-in costs for you." He paused. "You can also stay in here if you want."

Jared started to hum.

"God fuck no," she said.

Jared laughed.

"But thanks." She smiled at Essex.

Cheyenne picked her jacket up off the floor. Essex walked her out.

When Essex came back Jared was looking through liner notes. "My dad was in the military. I think that's why he killed himself," said Jared.

"I thought he got hit by a car," said Essex.

"Might have."

Essex laughed and gathered up the Scorpions records. "I always heard my dad was in the marines, but I've never seen proof."

"Bet he was a Coastie," said Jared.

"Bet your dad wasn't there at all."

Essex pulled open the top drawer of his dresser. "I should drive." He plowed through a jumble of black shirts.

"You'll just drive half the night and go home the second you make your lease."

"There's no reason I can't force myself to stay out. If I have a good night, I can help Cheyenne."

"*Oh Cheyenne, you can always stay in here with me . . .*"

"What?" said Essex.

"Your feelings aren't exactly brotherly."

Essex stopped going through shirts and turned. "So you're a pre-pubescent boy on the street—"

"Like we were," said Jared.

"Like we were," said Essex. "And a hot, seventeen-year-old girl who is smarter than anyone you ever met picks you up and takes you home to live with her family. For. Ever."

Jared clicked his tongue.

"Tell me," said Essex, "tell me it wouldn't make an impression."

Jared shook his head. "You have a crush on your sister, man. It's gross."

"Oh," said Essex, "it's way more than a crush."

7 Crown Victoria

ESSEX DIDN'T HAVE A STEADY LEASE. If he wanted to drive, he had to go down and ask for a cab, put his name on a list, hang out in the tunnel for hours, and wait for the dispatchers to call out a number for the cab he could take. There were rules, though. You couldn't leave and come back even if you were at the bottom of the roster because it wasn't a first come, first served kind of thing. The list was just so they didn't forget you existed. They went down it according to their own logic: *Let's me see . . . Yeah, he's good—give him 112 . . . He's got a sick kid—give him 38 . . . Oh no fucking way, he wrecked last week . . . No . . . Caught stacking . . . No . . . Oh, definitely man, she's cute—give her 26 . . . Oh her? She's totally cute—122 . . . And—god brother, are you kidding me? HOT 88.* Luck or lightning could strike. Sometimes you got a free lease because the dispatchers didn't like the owner of your cab and comped it on a technicality. Sometimes you got charged a fee that didn't exist or were made to wait hours on a cab that wasn't coming because they were curious how you'd react. Once Essex spent a whole week driving around with a roasted chicken under his seat because the dispatch guys had a bet to see how long it would take for a precooked bird to rot to the point where you could smell it.

Sometimes Essex would slip into the dispatcher's office and listen to them tell stories. It was his favorite part of driving, watching the steady drivers pass through, the smooth-shaven Eritreans in pressed shirts and lemon cologne, the Caribbeans with thin gold chains and silver teeth, the middle-aged Persians with low voices and rich accents. Far from being a sacred sphere of enlightened multiculturalism, though, the dispatcher's office was the epicenter of unchecked stereotyping.

"Don't you people pray, like, five times a day? Where's your rug?"

"Man, I don't know. I must have left it at the S-Y-N-A-G-O-G-U-E."

"Hey, amigo! *Como estas?*"

"I'm fucking Egyptian, you idiot."

It was the kind of gloves-off diversity found the world over in places where people of different backgrounds actually lived together. The parade went on with nicotine-stained Vietnam vets with felonies, men who used hair spray, Lebanese, Macedonians, African Americans eating lactose-free chocolate bars, and the tattooed white kids who knew every cool bartender in town and where the shows were happening—all people who would rather risk a gun to their head than have a boss. People who'd work a twelve-hour shift for nothing but a slice of pizza over their lease and return night after night looking for that mythical six-hundred-mile cash fare, that fat halibut, which meant a week off from work because these were the most motivated to be unmotivated citizens of the planet. Gamblers each, and everyone had a game. You played wide, ran the hinterlands, and went long on the chance at a twenty-mile airport run; you stuck inside, hitting short rides, darting from club to club all night where the fares were smaller but tips were bigger; you took anything you got and let fate play out, but what you didn't do was mix it up. You had to have a strategy, a philosophy, or you were nowhere. Essex was nowhere.

Most nights he drove he went home early. Once he covered his lease and gas all ambition bled right out of him. No matter how he tried, he couldn't make himself care. Every night he had an excuse for why it was better to leave and swore he'd make up for it the next night by working his full twelve but never did. Over his twenty-seven years Essex had failed at most everything conferring social value. School counselors, fry-cook managers, concerned citizens strained to make real to him the costs of his behavior. He wore his ability to suffer consequences like a merit badge. But he really did want to help Cheyenne. Which wasn't to say his feelings for her weren't a problem. They were. Just not one he expected to solve. Or as the Egyptian said to him one night, "No one drives for money." Essex wanted to thank Cheyenne in a way that would matter to her. So he went down, signed up, and waited in the tunnel.

He tried to become more visible to the dispatchers, waiting patiently while they played video games, while they each ate an entire pizza. It only half worked. *So Sanders says he should get a haircut and Gil turns bright pink and says, "Yeah? Yeah? Well you tell Sanders this," and he pulls out a knife with a ten-inch blade then I kid you fucking not, grabs his own ponytail and starts sawing it off, throws it on Sanders's desk and walks out. The next morning it's lying there like a dead fox when Sanders comes in— Essex, are you still here?*

On the weekend when there were more drivers than cabs, the lease drivers gathered in the break room for the lottery. Leaning against the walls in faded black Western shirts and baby-blue Cuban button-downs they talked shit under the florescent lights or sprawled on metal folding chairs with their eyes on the trashed gray carpet. Then one of the dispatchers would come in and make a speech about safety, share a few horror stories from the previous week, and end with "It's raining, go make money." He'd shake a coffee can of Scrabble tiles and everyone would line up to take a piece, one letter for each cab going out. Rarely were there Z numbers of cabs. In general, A through H would go out in the first hour. Then I through M might get a five-to-five short an hour or a six-to-six cab.

Any letters after that and you might not go out at all. That's where the gamble came. Sometimes it was better to throw the tile back in and go play video poker instead, try another night. If you'd had a bad run, someone might hand you a B and say you owe them.

On the weekend the cashier's office was closed. Which meant you didn't have to pay up front for your lease. You could actually drive Friday, Saturday, and Sunday, then drop the lease for all three nights early Monday morning. It allowed for a longer game. You could have a lousy night, totally blow it, then cover the lease out of the next night's take. If you drew a good Scrabble tile and got a cab.

On Friday Essex pulled a C from the coffee can and drove the full twelve. The first part didn't go so well. He got locked in rush-hour traffic coming back from a short fare and watched, helpless, as requests for rides stacked up. By the time he was free it was dusk and he was in the doldrums. Everyone had gotten home from work, but no one was going out yet. Then around 9:00 p.m. bartenders, strippers, dealers, and bouncers started coming in to work and that was a wave worth money because they tipped at 50 percent, so you give them your number and hope they call you for a ride home. But then you were into the night. It would move fast and you had to be sharp. Ultimately Essex did all right.

Saturday night he pulled an A, his first and only ever. He got some grocery runs right away, cranky old people who didn't tip and were half crazed from loneliness and social-services paperwork. Next he got a group of girls from the suburbs going into town to drink. Better to get them on the way in. On the way out they'd throw up in your cab. There was a fine for that but it wasn't easy to get money out of someone in a blackout who was about to throw up again.

Around 11:00 p.m. Essex hit that elusive stream of pure fortune. His cab was never empty, his fares were cash, his tips were generous, and no one was on meth or talking about their gun collection. His timing was symphonic and it became possible for a few hours to imagine handing Cheyenne the money and basking in her gratitude. But just before the bars closed the fuel pump went and his night ended. There was no extra cab for him to switch into. He'd lost the richest cut of the night and had to walk home.

Sunday had to be his day. The dispatchers gave him a five-to-five cab but it was available by 3:00 p.m. so he had fourteen hours to work with. The shift started smoothly. He got a couple of medical runs taking boxes of blood from one hospital to another. No tips but the mileage rate was higher, and on a slow afternoon it was okay as long as you didn't get lost in the basement maze of some hospital under construction trying to find someone to sign for a delivery. After that he swung south and worked the semirural areas before picking up a couple of pot dealers heading back into town. The night was taking on an even tempo, no big money, no long waits, just steady.

As it got dark, work began to taper off and the gaps between rides lengthened. Essex pulled over in a movie theater parking lot, booked into the zone, then turned off the car to save gas. When it was this slow, moving made no sense. Around 10:00 p.m. he walked to the corner to get a falafel from a stand. When he came back, he saw that he had missed two rides. An idea, which would take root later, planted itself in his mind. Around midnight he picked up some bartenders going home early. At 2:00 a.m. he made the mistake of counting his money. After gas and falafel, he'd made only $150 total over what he owed for the three nights' leases, just enough to keep the landlord off his back, nothing else.

Now it may be possible that Essex was the least effective cab-driver who ever worked, but that didn't mean he didn't love it. Every night he joined the antiauthoritarians of all nations in an anthem of freedom, a kind of American work song that marked where servitude ended and possibility began. Some of his best moments were spent chatting with the Russian drivers at the taxi stands, learning to cuss in Persian, gliding over the highways at dawn doing ninety miles an hour in an ex–cop car with 350,000 miles on it while the sunlight pierced the clouds and struck the city gold.

"It's the greatest job in the world," said one driver. "I quit every night and get hired again the next day."

Essex pulled into the garage just before 5:00 a.m. but didn't fill his gas tank like he should have. That was $40. He parked the car without cleaning it. That was another $5. He hung his keys on the hook. Day drivers were trying to switch out fast to catch the last of the early-morning airport runs as the sky turned into a softer blue.

"Look at them," said the Egyptian, gesturing at the lease drivers waiting in the tunnel, "with their Scrabble tiles and their silly plans to make money tonight. What a mess. Pathetic. But," he jabbed his finger at one driver after another, "look at them. Humans. Every one."

Essex thought of Cheyenne. She was the most human person he knew. The things she wanted changed so often that it seemed to others she wanted nothing at all. In this moment in time, though, her wants were simple: $500 to find Ann Radar.

That night, Essex turned in the car but did not fill the tank. He did not drop the three nights of lease money into the slot by the office either but walked out with $443 in his pocket.

He was going to miss driving cab.

8 The Great American Desert

CHEYENNE AND LIVY left in the evening, heading east through the pass. The late-spring rains had fallen as snow in the mountains, which, plowed to the shoulder, turned the road into a gray gully as they climbed. Slush froze, giving grip to the wheels. Slopes flashed white. Livy had flat-out refused to buy chains for a rental so the car skated on glassier sections of ice. She remained hyperalert. Because it only takes one trucker jacked up on crank. She reached for her thermos of coffee. It wasn't dread but another thing entirely that had her. This was what she wanted, this trip. A way to get Cheyenne moving and see if the momentum would inspire her to go somewhere else. Not a plan so much as an instinct about how her sister worked, but now that they were in motion, all she felt was the loss of control.

Dropping in elevation they drove through the lowland pines as the highway ran straight. It was so bright in the full moon they could have driven without headlights. Livy pulled over on the side of the road to pee; mud starred with ice crystals glinted in the moonlight beneath her, the sky was a giant bowl above. When she got back in the car, Cheyenne was eating a bag of corn nuts Livy'd stashed in the door well on her side. Livy gunned the engine as she pulled out, but it only buzzed. Watching the road over the dash, they came into high desert. Gold haze light, towns that turned out not to be towns but a gas station with an outbuilding or a closed rest area lit by state funding.

Soon the highway rose in a steady incline as they approached the Columbia, which cut down through basalt cliffs to a man-made lake above a dam, a new body of water born under the pressure of great plans, azure in daylight and easily seen from space, spanned by a bridge, the lake's surface rippling in wind that whistled through canyons etched with petroglyphs. Wordless in the moonlight, they crossed flooded lands, the sedge houses of the Wanapum under the current, a shelter for fish.

Cheyenne dozed. She tried to get one leg tucked under her but kept hitting the stick shift. At least they weren't fighting. She felt sixty. Maybe it was already too late for anything real to change.

Thinking that, Cheyenne felt her lower back ache. Too many aspirations. She was getting her period soon so she hoped it wasn't that. The added hormonal stress in a small car on a long drive could blow everything apart.

When Cheyenne got her period for the first time, Kirsten had called her into her bedroom, lit candles, handed her a cup of raspberry tea, and talked about the Goddess. Cheyenne barely listened. She wanted to look like Kirsten, who she found beautiful. Cheyenne had been watching her own body and bone structure to see if it was heading that way. Though she wasn't paying attention to Kirsten's speech, she did remember being super proud of herself for getting her period before Livy. Then Kirsten told her about the other mother and the North Star. When Cheyenne realized she wasn't joking, her eyes went from her mother's face to the wall. She felt the way she had when Kirsten gave her too much cough syrup because she had misread the dosage. Kirsten reached over to touch her hand but Cheyenne yanked it back.

"So you might not be my mom?"

"There's more than biology."

Cheyenne jumped off the bed. Confused, ashamed that she thought she might look like Kirsten when there might be nothing connecting them at all, she ran to tell Livy. And that's when she found out Livy had been having her period for months, knew all about the other mother and hadn't said a thing.

Cheyenne watched her sister in the driver's seat. She saw that Livy's braids had loosened, freeing the short fine black hairs around her face. She could see Livy's breath. Her eyes wandered to the shoulder of the road. She tried to daydream to pass time, but to orchestrate a triumph you need a certain kind of story. *I am an underdog. I am coming-of-age.* It wasn't the kind of story she could tell herself anymore.

Livy unscrewed the thermos cap and took a sip of lukewarm coffee. "You can't keep staying at my place. I can't take the rent increase and you can't cover it. You need to find a place of your own."

"Can you get me a job where you work?"

Livy laughed. "You'd be crying by lunch."

"Maybe not."

"Then you'd quit and I'd hear about it forever."

Livy screwed the cap back on and checked the mirror.

Something moved outside the car window and Cheyenne bolted upright.

"Deer!"

Livy saw it but they were going too fast. The deer leapt. Livy glanced in the rearview and saw it standing on the center line of the highway, its mirror eyes reflecting in the taillights. Adrenaline raced in their bodies. Cheyenne started laughing. It took several minutes for Livy to realize she was going more than ninety miles an hour and slow down.

"Do you want me to drive?" asked Cheyenne.

"I'm good."

"Mom would call that an omen."

"Mom calls everything an omen," said Livy. "Burnt toast. A utility bill."

Cheyenne turned in her seat and adopted her best imitation of Cyril. "You know, Livy, the Indians say—"

"Oh god stop it," said Livy. "You know, to be fair, Mom's not any better."

Cheyenne shifted her bearing to match Kirsten's, adopting the matter-of-fact tone she used for all mythological nagging. "Livy, the Indians say that the deer is a gentle guiding spirit and when it appears it's trying to tell you something. Can you hear what it's trying to tell you?" Cheyenne leaned into Livy's space. "Conform to female gender norms," she whispered. "Cover yourself in blood and strap-on antlers because you're going to face death."

Livy cracked up.

"You'll come to understand in the fullness of time," said Cheyenne.

"It's not like you aren't just as superstitious as she is," said Livy.

"I'm not superstitious at all."

Livy pulled out the ashtray. In it was a dull half-dollar coin. Cheyenne pushed the ashtray closed.

"You put that there. I didn't even have to look," said Livy.

Cheyenne didn't deny it. "You'll never go to jail when you're riding with a Kennedy," she said. Cheyenne's eye line shifted to the shoulder. "I think I'm getting my period," said Cheyenne. "Remember when I ran to tell you I got my period first and found out you'd been having yours for two months."

"You sucker-punched me when I was brushing my teeth," said Livy.

"I forgot about that."

Cheyenne flashed on the memory, the foam of bloody toothpaste sprayed on the shower curtain, the chocolate shag rug Livy tackled her on. The elbow that would have come down on her face if Kirsten hadn't pulled them apart.

"You deserved to get punched in the face," said Cheyenne.

"You always make such a big deal out of me not telling you something personal."

Livy rolled the window down to air out the car. The wind blew and they couldn't hear. Cheyenne's hair, which was unbraided and shorter than Livy's, became itching, stinging little snakes whipping her face.

They were below empty on gas when they hit Spokane so Livy pulled over at a truck stop. After seeing the prices, she refused to fill the tank but decided to hit the next station up the road to see if it was cheaper. Cheyenne groaned.

"Six cents a gallon—or whatever it is—is not going to make a difference."

"It does," said Livy, "it adds up."

"And when you're fifty you'll be able to take a vacation," said Cheyenne. "Come on. Tell me. What is it you want? I mean for real. Not what you used to want, but what you want now."

Livy pumped $5 of gas into the tank and said nothing. When she was done she put the nozzle back and got in the passenger seat. Cheyenne gave up and came around to get behind the wheel.

"Drive," said Livy.

Cheyenne put the car in gear and accelerated. Lurching slightly, she turned onto the frontage road and was soon doing eighty.

"I want a fishing boat," said Livy.

Cheyenne laughed. "That's it? That's what you want out of your whole life?"

"Pretty much," said Livy.

"Well that's fucking attainable. Take out a loan."

"Hi. I make one dollar over minimum wage. It took five years to get these skills. Invest in my future."

"Get someone to lie for you," said Cheyenne.

"I don't want anybody to lie for me. I don't want to owe anybody anything. It took me three years to pay off the loan I took out to get to Alaska that first time. This is the first debt-free year I've had since. Do you even know how much you owe me? Almost a month of rent, nearly every meal you've eaten, pocket change, and bus fare—you're going to need two jobs to pay me back."

"There's no way I'm working two jobs," said Cheyenne.

Livy's skin tingled. "You're the reason you're in this stupid situation," she said.

"We're all in stupid situations," said Cheyenne.

They came up on the exit where there was supposed to be another gas station but there wasn't so Cheyenne continued on. Ten miles later, she saw a turnoff with a sign for Chevron and took it. She drove three miles but still no station. The car began to slow as it ran out of gas. Cheyenne coasted onto the shoulder, too tired to be enraged. There wasn't an electric light to be seen for miles.

"We're going to have to hitch to the next gas station," she said.

"I'm not leaving the rental with our stuff in it."

"I'm not hitchhiking back to the interstate alone in the dark."

Cheyenne crawled between the seats into the back and positioned herself so the moon wasn't on her face. "It's freezing," she said.

"Our body heat will warm it up."

"I have to go to the bathroom."

"I'll kill you if you get out," said Livy.

Livy took the rubber bands off her braids, letting the bands roll onto her wrists. Shaking her hair out, she finger-combed it and twisted it out of the way. She was asleep in minutes.

Cheyenne could see her sister's breath. She couldn't sleep. A strong wind rattled the car. She twisted and stared at the unlit dome light. Minutes passed. If a thirty-three-year-old learns to play the violin in the forest, does it make a sound? How late is too late to throw everything at the wall? Does a desperate attempt at greatness crack open some kind of universal magic? Maybe this is what it looks like to flunk adulthood. Maybe there are no points for boldness. Maybe at this age you only get points for grace.

She rolled onto her side and pulled her shirt up over her nose so her breath would warm her face, but it just made her skin damp so that when wind came through the invisible spaces in the car door her cheeks stung with cold. The seat belt dug into her temple. She sat up.

She saw Livy's eyelids flutter and knew her sister was awake. The moon was down lower and the starlight that turned the highway from jet to indigo did not penetrate the car. She and her sister were in a cave of their own. Like they were as children, sharing a bed under electric blankets. Cheyenne tugged the drawstrings of her hoodie tight, leaving only an oval around her eyes.

"I slept with Jackson's students," said Cheyenne. "Like, a lot of them."

Livy opened her eyes. "You're kidding," she said.

"Nope."

"Oh fuck, that's bad, Cheyenne. What is wrong with you?"

"I honestly don't know. It was like I had this golden ticket out of here and into the banquet and I just tore it up."

"I thought you were in love with him."

"I was. Totally," said Cheyenne. "That's what made it so golden."

Livy sat up. "You know, I always thought you would go back to school."

Cheyenne scoffed. "I love how people tell you to go to college when they don't know what else to tell you." She looked lost for a second then grinned. "Son, I can see in your eyes you have the makings of a phlebotomist or a drug and alcohol counselor." Her voice frayed along the midrange edge. She blew a cloud of hot breath into her hands. "The place where Jackson taught was incredible. All carved stone and spires. The library had books from the eighteenth century. The seasons were like the seasons in movies. And the weirdest part was that everyone was physically stunning too," she said. "East Coast royalty."

"What do they do with the fat and ugly people?" asked Livy.

"I don't think they let them in. Maybe that's the real point of the admissions interview. Sir, I can see from your application that you have terrible acne scars."

"Why didn't you enroll?"

Cheyenne laughed. "Do you know who goes to schools like that? Future prime ministers. Senators."

"So what? You're smart. You have your associate degree."

"An associate only makes it worse. Those places want to think they've discovered people like us."

"That makes no sense," said Livy. "The whole thing sounds gross."

Cheyenne shook her head. "It wasn't. It was beautiful. I just fucked it up."

Livy squinted at the clock over the steering wheel. It was 4:30 a.m.

Cheyenne leaned between the seats. "You know, I was thinking," she said, "as long as we're driving this far we should take a more scenic route, slow down a little."

"It's going to take me months of overtime to recoup these five days."

Cheyenne pulled two crumpled twenties out of her back pocket. "This is all I have left after what I gave you for the trip. Take it." She slapped it onto the dash. "I don't say I'm broke. Last week I had nothing and I still took you to dinner."

"On the fifty dollars you borrowed from me."

"That makes me twice as generous."

Livy became a dot in a sea of rage. Then an idea came. "If we take an extra day," she said slowly, "you find another place to live as soon as we're back. No excuses. And you pay me back from your first check."

"Deal," said Cheyenne.

Noticing a faint line of rose blue on the horizon, Livy pointed. Within seconds, the line turned into a pale orange plane of light that radiated over the low tawny scrub brush now gilt with frost and dew.

"You'll be able to hitchhike in a few minutes," said Livy.

Cheyenne grabbed Livy's fisherman's cap and pulled it down over her ears, waiting.

"Should I feel bad that Essex can't drive a cab anymore?" she asked.

"No, he was a terrible cabbie."

Cheyenne took the twenties off the dashboard and got out. Two hours later she returned with a trucker and a five-gallon plastic can of gas. By midmorning they were well into Montana.

A few hours past Missoula the land changed again, flattening and turning brown, scoured by wind. They crossed the Yellowstone River, then followed it as it ran, north by northeast, fed by the Yellowstone Lake. It had poured over the falls and through the Black Canyon before they ever knew it. Past Billings the Yellowstone joined the Bighorn, which carried with it the Little Bighorn and the Tongue. As they drove they saw signs for reenactments. Custer. Stand with or against! Your choice. And they heard talk in the rest area of a magnificent new state-of-the-art jail created from nothing but investor money and high-interest loans.

Then they came to the great Powder River, which was fed by the Little Powder, as well as oil from pipeline breaks, Red Cloud's War, and benzene as it joined the Yellowstone. The Yellowstone, which already had inherited so much, the Bighorn and the Wind and the Tongue, as it flowed toward the Missouri River, which had no choice but to inherit the watershed as it drained toward the Mississippi, that unstoppable force. And maybe there just is no way out of history. No matter how much you want to come from a different story, you can't.

They traveled from high elevations and scrubland to prairie to chain stores, and settled into the doldrums of flat grass, sunburnt and feral, another unwelcome thing upon the land. After Miles City, they dropped south through the hunting grounds of the Crow people. In the periphery, Livy saw a new future, free again. Cheyenne saw a woman with a changing face. Now this. Now that. The mother narcotic. Maybe a different past would mean a different future. Maybe there was another history to claim. Passing through the Black Hills, north of Mount Rushmore and Pine Ridge, south of the Bakken Formation and Standing Rock, they drove the Badlands.

East of the coal beds, west of the Black Hills, they passed a rash of square and Sputnik-era buildings, each half as tall as the flagpoles in front of them. An elementary school, a middle school, a high school. Decorated with signs leading to bomb shelters, furnished with government-issue desks made of moon shots, school bells cocked like a gun for lunch periods and air raids, they passed white chalky pits of bentonite clay terraformed by bulldozers missing only the great hand of a giant three-year-old descending from the heavens. There were ripples in the land; the sun was a patina on the highway. Tangled spaghetti creeks glinted and irrigated farms lined one beside another like jade mah-jongg tiles. Livy looked through the windshield as she drove at the grassland steppe on either side of the road.

They could hear the subsonic songs of red rock and scrub bush. In an unsparing white flash of midday light, they drove through miles of the cash crop ethanol, a pentimento of buffalo skins behind it, untanned and rotting in piles on the prairie; they, too, were shadows. Drive to the sea here; drive to the sea there. Raise a great army. Nantucket to the Arctic to Panama—growing in all directions like a deep breath.

They drove across the Great American Desert. An empty and lifeless wasteland, it stretched from the Midwest to the Rockies and served as an initiation for pioneers and speculators seeking the spoils of the west. Only the desert was not lifeless and not empty. It was not the Kalahari or the Gobi but a prairie overrun with life, a prairie covering a great aquifer, from which grain, future dust bowls, and the Monroe Doctrine would be drawn. Wagons brought whale oil to new towns. Oil for light and lubrication. Bones for corsets and collar stays. Ivory for the keys of Midwest parlor pianos. Girls stretched their hands wide over the white keys. Dreaming of marriage, future typists, future salaried masses, secretaries. Tapping out notes, imagining, still, a world made of whale teeth and ribcages, brown fat and ambergris.

Was this where it had all gone wrong? Livy saw a man alone in the arid expanse. Flickering in and out of existence, preening in an Elizabethan ruff with a fistful of charters, bent down to check the soil for tobacco. Finding it too dry to plant, he strode forth, oscillating over the steppe, to the gold and salt and light rumored to be in the hills to the west. She watched him vanish into a pinprick in the rearview mirror, a small white star degenerating toward collapse.

9 Draft Horse

ESSEX MET JARED FOR LUNCH. Thirty minutes at the diner and their table was a carnage of torn sugar packets and empty cream decanters. The waitress had stopped refilling their coffees. Jared pulled apart the second half of his grilled cheese sandwich and dipped it in ketchup. He began to eat, his bony face exposing his state-funded teeth chinked with mercury amalgam.

"Is an army of cabbies after you now?" Jared asked, swabbing the last of his crust.

"No, I just can't ever drive again."

"What are you going to do?"

"Probably landscape. Stand by the freeway and get day-labor gigs."

"You ever done that?" asked Jared.

"Yeah, it sucks. Either you get picked up because you're white so they can bro down with you on guns and immigrants or you don't get picked up because you're white and they're afraid you won't work hard enough for shitty pay."

"You should make a sign that says 'It's okay to fuck me over.'"

Essex laughed. "I thought that's what the look on my face said."

Jared squinted. "No, it says 'I'm starring in day-labor porn.'"

Essex tossed an orange skin onto Jared's plate.

"Enlist," said Jared. "You have no money. Soon you'll have nowhere to live and you're obviously out of ideas."

"Cheyenne will pay me back," said Essex.

"Cheyenne never pays anyone back. Especially not you."

"She would if I needed it." He smiled. "Maybe."

Jared laughed. Essex leaned back in his chair.

"There really should be day-labor porn," said Essex. *"Truck boy! By the yard-waste bags, yes, you! Find me my fluffer!"*

Jared stared at his cleaned plate. "Come with me to the recruiter," he said. "You don't have shit going on. Tell me you don't want something to change. Tell me you don't want to be different."

Over Jared's shoulder by the entrance was a glass box with the silver claw. A seven-year-old was trying to navigate the metal arm over the stuffed animals and getting frustrated. Even from where he sat, Essex could see stains on the napless fabric of the animal the boy wanted. The boy lowered the claw and snagged a small tiger by the neck, which dangled and dropped. Essex felt an overwhelming urge to go over, break the glass box, and get the tiger. Strike a blow against the machine. Everybody gets a stuffed animal. The boy gets two for his anguish. Physical strength should be good for something. But then what would happen? He would be in jail or entangled in the mental health system bound to some poor caseworker who didn't need him any more than Essex needed a caseworker. That's the problem with critical thinking. It always ends in a big nowhere.

"So you sign up and you're gone," said Essex. "When? The next day? A week?"

"I wish it was like that. There's a bunch of stuff they make you do first."

Essex picked up a fork then set it down. "I'll go," he said.

Jared laughed. "You're kidding."

"What?"

"I don't know. I just didn't think you'd say yes."

"I'd join about anything right now."

The waitress dropped the ticket. She'd kissed the back, leaving a lipstick print, and drawn a little heart next to the total. Essex flipped the ticket between his fingers with a snap so Jared could see the lip print.

"Here's somebody who should enlist," he said.

They started to get up and realized they were blocked in by an old woman struggling with her walker. The woman inched forward in such incremental motions it seemed for a second Essex was observing a problem of scale and not speed. She'd been to the beauty parlor but slept since and the back of her hair was pressed flat, curls awry on one side of her head, her white powdered skin with its lacelike neural net of fine lines, intersections, all down along her arms, age spots, hematomas, suns and galaxies. Essex realized she was nearly blind. When she was a few feet away she halted, slowly turning her head. Her filmy cataract eyes, glazed and blue, fixed on Essex.

"Honey, I thought you were dead," she said. "I'm so glad you're not."

She came toward him, a tanker drifting into port, but then saw that he was someone else and began to shake. Because she was not a tanker. She was a dry leaf weathering a gentle breeze as if it were a harsh wind, holding with everything fast to the tree.

10 Wolf Spider

THE MORNING after the girls left for Boston, Kirsten stalked the living room in her cornflower slip, her hair pinned into a knot by a chopstick. Finally she sat back down at the kitchen table.

Kirsten looked at the envelope addressed to Ann on the counter. The second letter. The demonic chrysalis. The wolf spider. It wasn't worth writing again. She had expected Ann to be angry at Cyril for violating their agreement, but she wasn't. Instead her responses were flippant. *The girls' karma is their own. If they're meant to find me they will.* That was it. If they're meant to find me they will? For the first time ever Kirsten had come down hard against karma. Fuck karma, Ann. We had a deal. She'd heard nothing more.

What did she know about Ann anyway? Even if she'd wanted to tell them. She knew Ann was still a Buddhist but not what kind. She knew Ann traveled extensively but not how. Perhaps she had married well or come into money. It was also possible that cut away from children and the need to shell out money for a two-bedroom apartment for twenty years, Ann had floated upward into the realm of homeownership and 401(k)s, health care and cars with airbags.

Kirsten looked back at her laptop where several windows were open. All health-care plans, none of them worth a shit, but she was tired of getting bounced on and off of Medicaid every time assholes in the legislature decided to redefine poor. Normally she could weather the tides of eligibility, but not this time. Something was wrong and she didn't know what. Her stomach hurt. Her appetite flagged. She'd gone for her annual at the women's clinic and everything seemed fine. But she knew her body well enough to feel a change. She went to the tarot cards and did a few readings. She got the Lovers and the Star and the Universe—who doesn't want that in their life? She clicked through the benefits on each plan. *Any preexisting conditions?* Oh I don't know, how about capitalism?

So here she was. Wide awake in the blazing daytime, having scrolled through online postings, and now sitting with *Nickel* ads flayed to the classifieds, looking for a job.

You can't just call anymore. That's a flag. You can't ask a reasonable question like what shift or how much an hour. That's a flag. You can't even walk in and fill out an application. Everyone wants a résumé. Whore out your personal charm just to wash dishes.

"A flexible team player with experience and a positive attitude wanting to move ahead."

She annotated in her mind.

~~Flexible.~~ No boundaries, no kids.

~~Experienced.~~ Needs no training.

~~Positive attitude.~~ Obsequious yet entertaining.

~~Wants to move ahead.~~ In responsibility but not pay.

For years Kirsten had made her own deal with the government. I fill out paperwork, you give me money to live on. It was an honest paycheck in her opinion, a reallocation of federal funds to support the work they should be doing and weren't. How many nights had she spent on the suicide hotline talking someone off the ledge? The number of times she'd opened for the early shift at the domestic violence center. Every night she showed up reliably alive. Not dulled by meaningless jobs, she met the messed-up world intact and offered it an all-hours humanity. The government had gotten more than its money's worth. They're fucking lucky I only charge them food stamps and $850 a month.

But none of it looked real on paper. She closed the *Nickel* ads. If you were over twenty-five and looking for a job, everyone expected a pageant of humiliation and a good story. Are you a recovering addict? Are you married to a bride hoarder? Are you a homemaker new to the market with an autistic son or a husband with cancer? Tell me. *No, tell me. What exactly is your excuse for being fifty-two and broke?*

It's not like she didn't know how to weather the opinions of others. A mom of two toddlers at twenty, living off food stamps, she was used to the scouring glance. In the DSHS office while the girls crawled on the floor then ran wild over the seats, then squirmed, and fought, and yanked hanks of hair out of each other's heads. If she ignored it, she got told off for not disciplining them. If she yelled at them, she got told she was abusive. And both girls were hard in their own way. Cheyenne was a danger to herself in public. Livy was a danger to herself in private. She was unreadable when you most needed to read her, whereas Cheyenne would tell you point-blank every shitty thought she had about you. But Cheyenne had a deep sense of wonder. She could see herself in the stories Kirsten told. She was mythic by nature. Or had been. Kirsten couldn't seem to get anything out of her that way anymore. And there weren't any federal aid programs for that. Hello, ma'am, yes. Can you tell me which form I should fill out for a failure of faith in the universe? It would be pages for sure. *How long has it been since you last had faith in the Universe? Have you tried in the past week?*

The parking garage that hired Kirsten charged her $35 for the shirt they gave her and told her they'd dock her if she didn't wear it. It would come out of her first paycheck, which would come after her third week of work. But none of the uniform shirts they had fit Kirsten—men in Indonesia not having breasts—so she had to settle for one that came down to her thighs. They suggested she buy two.

On her first day she put it on in the bathroom. It was plastic and creased like a Halloween costume. When she came back to the office, her supervisor showed her how to fill out the time card and gave her a no-solicitation policy to sign. He rented her a flashlight and handed her a patch.

"Make sure you sew it on right here," he said, patting the meat of his upper arm. "Otherwise it looks fake."

Fake like we're not really cops? Fake like your grievance process? She flipped through the employee manual. It would take three months to clear the probationary period and get health-care coverage. Then most of her check would go to covering the premium, but it was better than bouncing on and off of Medicaid every time the qualifications changed. And down the line—her new employer assured her—it was a career. She wondered if they believed that.

Leaving the office, Kirsten thought of her daughters.

You don't like your myth? Well I don't like the one I'm in either.

Her stomach started to hurt. The bowl of oatmeal she'd made for breakfast was still full. She scraped it into the trash. It would take three months to get on the company's health plan, but once she was on, she would get all the tests. Between now and then, it was best not to have a record of stomach complaints. Not until she was off probation.

11 The Locust

THE STORM came up from Nebraska. When the high winds began, they had to stop to wait it out. Tornados touched down and lifted. Mad ballerinas, storm goddesses, they danced across flatlands and floodplains. When the winds died, they drove again, racing power outages and wild skies. They turned north and talked less. Neither sister had seen the rust belt but it was apparent that a giant metal locust had crawled across this part of the country, leaving behind its discarded shells in the form of smelters, bridges, ironworks. They drove along the Great Lakes where tall ships were reenacting a famous battle, their sails flying, circled by helicopters from cable channels. They, too, were after a different history.

"I want something hot to eat," said Cheyenne. "There's got to be some restaurant bar around here with cheap food."

Cheyenne saw a motel with a medieval turret and a sign that read HAPPY HOUR.

"There," she said, "turn there."

The bar was red leather and the faces were pink. A TV was on and video poker games were talking to themselves. Bread bowls of clam chowder were the special of the day. Livy ordered one to split. To go.

"They have jojos," said Cheyenne. "Give me money for jojos."

Livy handed her $5. "I'm going to hold you to our deal."

But Cheyenne had lost interest and was watching the TV behind the bar.

"I hate it when you do that," said Livy.

"I think I'm getting my period," Cheyenne said. "Do you have tampons?"

"Roll your own," said Livy.

"I plan to but I just think it would be good to have some in case we're somewhere without toilet paper."

The bartender came with the bread bowl.

"Do you sell tampons? Like in a vending machine or something?" Cheyenne asked.

"Only condoms," he said and put her jojos in a white paper bag.

Back in the car Cheyenne put her feet on the dashboard and reclined the seat. She undid the top buttons of her pants and drummed her fingers on her belly so it quivered like Jell-O. "I'm glad we're doing this together."

Livy ate her share of the clam chowder, carefully cutting away the top inch of the bread bowl with her Leatherman until it was a detachable bread rind. She handed the rest to Cheyenne. Cheyenne drained her chowder in a few sips then bit into the bread bowl as if it were an apple.

"You know Jackson's school isn't far off our route," she said, chewing.

Livy gaped. Cheyenne swallowed and laughed.

"Don't look at me like that. I just wish you could see it, that's all."

"Then maybe you shouldn't have slept with all his students." Livy reclined her seat. "Wake me when it's my turn to drive."

Cheyenne finished the jojos and the bread bowl. Turning on the radio as she drove, she began to sing along to the pop songs she could recognize. Three hours later when Livy opened her eyes they were on a rural highway.

"Where are we?" asked Livy.

"New York State. Don't worry, all the people I slept with have graduated by now."

12 Ribcage

THE COLLEGE where Jackson taught was on the perimeter of a town with brick houses that had been built on foundations that sloped following the drop of a creek. Snowy hillsides in winter, canopies of green, the foliage of fall, it cut down through mineral-rich black earth and struck the bone undercarriage of an enormous bleached ribcage. That's where the whale was. You could track the spine straight back up the hill to where the town fathers had planned their homes; they were well safe from floods but not from erosion, as far above the creek sings to the slope its cradlesong. *If you cannot reach the hill, the hill must come to you . . .* And now there are no right angles to the town's rooftops, only tendencies toward them; there are no surrounding mountains, only the roots of mountains worn away. Carved in salt and light, a white schematic on a white page, invisible as Wonder Woman's plane, the town was reminiscent of its source though it no longer reflected it.

For Cheyenne it was the site of a personal explosion of assumptions and aesthetics. It had gone off inside her like a nail bomb. Constructed of James Taylor, maple syrup, Celestial Seasonings tea boxes, *Little House in the Big Woods,* and Cat Stevens before he was an asshole, it was a supernova of subterranean longings. It had blown with incredible force. Enough for the blast to send her backward through a wall into a room with a wood floor and a woodstove surrounded by ceramic cookware and trays of whole wheat spinach lasagna. At first it had sated a deep hunger for something she was convinced was unnameable, but in the end, it did have a name. The students she met called it whiteness. According to them, it was everywhere on her and in her. A new unspeakable shame to lay over the other shames she knew. But it was her reaction that did the damage. Moving from one body to another, one dorm room to another—she already felt so out of place—and when the dust from that nail bomb settled, the town was still serene, the college was still sacrosanct, Jackson was still willing, but she had stepped into a wasteland.

She hadn't been back since.

"I can't tell if it's creepier to be here and not tell Jackson or to tell him and not see him," said Livy when they got out of the car.

Cheyenne stopped in front of a shopwindow filled with colonial antiques.

"Jackson's parents' house is full of this stuff."

Next door was a sandwich shop where they got morning glory sunflower seed muffins and ate under a mural of Frodo smoking a pipe.

"I can't imagine you living here," said Livy.

Cheyenne waved at the room. "These people run the world."

"Not my world," said Livy.

"Don't kid yourself."

There was a crack of thunder and a heavy East Coast rain began. By the time they got to the car they were soaked. But the rain wasn't cold, and the wet earth smelled like life.

"You drive," said Cheyenne. "I want to be able to hide if I need to."

Cheyenne directed Livy up the hill toward the college. As they got closer, Cheyenne sank lower until her knees were on the car floor and her back arched up over the seat.

"Stop at the convenience store and get beer," said Cheyenne. "It'll be on the left. They'll have something cheap."

"You're a sinkhole of cash," said Livy, but she stopped.

Livy ran in and came back with a six-pack. She pulled a beer from the plastic noose and handed it to Cheyenne, who was still on the floor but had repositioned herself so that her stomach and elbows were on the seat.

"It's out of your share," Livy said.

"Fine. Go to the top of the hill, make a left, and it's about a mile down."

The rain, which had paused for a few seconds, came down harder, beating the windows and hood. Livy slowed to ten miles per hour.

"Do you see a spire?" asked Cheyenne.

"I don't see anything."

Cheyenne opened a beer and held it out to Livy.

"I don't want open beers if we get pulled over."

"Down it. I downed mine."

"What's in your hand?"

"Your beer," said Cheyenne.

"In the other hand."

"My second beer. These things are mostly water."

Now slowing to a stop in the downpour, Livy took the beer and chugged it without taking her eyes off the windshield. She handed the can back to Cheyenne who crushed it into a disk and stashed it under the seat.

"I see the spire," said Livy.

Cheyenne opened a third beer. "It's made of elephant tusk and England."

"Would you stop with the beer?" said Livy. "It's your turn to drive."

Coming over the rise Livy saw the cathedral library and its surrounding orchards blown pink with cherry blossoms.

"Wow," she said, "it's like pictures of places like this."

"That's deep."

Students ran between buildings in the rain. Women played lacrosse in a spray of mud on a field by a glade. Pulling back out onto the road, Livy drove a mile, then rolled onto the shoulder, took a beer, and drank it.

"Your turn." She got out and Cheyenne came around.

"Man. I think I'm drunk on two beers. I feel like such a light-weight," said Livy.

Cheyenne put both hands on the steering wheel but didn't move. "I'm drunk too."

"You said you were fine!"

"It hadn't hit me," said Cheyenne.

"I would never have had another beer if you weren't going to be able to drive."

"It's your fault for starving us."

Cheyenne watched the rain splatter. She put the car in drive and lurched onto the road.

"I have to go apologize," she said.

"Oh god fuck no. Please just leave it."

"He deserves an honest apology," said Cheyenne, making a hard right at the next corner.

Jackson's house was back up in the woods. Cheyenne turned by a mailbox and drove a quarter mile up a driveway, then stopped within sight of the house and turned off the car.

"I'm sure he heard us," said Livy.

"No he didn't. I can't even tell when this car is on."

Cheyenne looked at the porch through the woods.

A light in the house came on. Cheyenne froze. Jackson stepped onto the porch. In the shade of the forest, she could see him. Light pierced the clouds, painting him white and black, sharp and beautiful like an old woodcut. Cheyenne put her hand over Livy's mouth. Jackson looked around then went back inside.

"This is stupid," said Livy. "I'm driving."

Cheyenne crawled over the gear shift into the warm wet seat where her sister had been. Livy backed down the driveway, pulled out, and drove toward town.

"Future Chinese minister of agriculture," said Cheyenne. "Saudi overlord."

"How do we get back to the highway?"

"Turn left. Shark tank, think tank, President Whatever. Lobsters. Alan Watts."

"Are you all right?" asked Livy.

"I hate this part of the country."

Livy, though, had never been to New England. She'd never been east of Idaho. When the rain cleared she rolled down her window and let in the honeysuckled breeze. Green hillocks and ponds cut out against a robin's-egg blue sky, a color so saturated and unnervingly homogenous and vivid that the whole landscape seemed shot on a green screen, an absolute chromatic shunting parallel. They drove through mill towns named after sunken frigates. Lowell, Massachusetts, the City of Spindles where women wove slave-picked cotton to scratchy cloth, struck for wages, were crushed, and went back to weaving again.

> *Oh! isn't it a pity, such a pretty girl as I—*
> *Should be sent to the factory to pine away and die?*
>
> *Oh! I cannot be a slave,*
> *I will not be a slave . . .*
> *For I'm so fond of liberty*
> *That I cannot be a slave . . .*

Coming into the capital, Livy and Cheyenne hit rush hour. The effects of alcohol wore off and they arrived at the temple itchy and dirty.

They got out of the car.

They stood before the door.

Burnished streets of Boston, flooded with gold-orange late-afternoon light. Moving through honey, every hesitation crystallizing them, they stepped into the entranceway.

13 The Essex

ESSEX WENT WITH JARED to meet the recruiter. He was half hoping something would stop him from doing what he was about to do. Nothing did. With only a few words, he had propelled himself forward; with no one in his way, no circumstances to consider, inertia had taken over. Frictionless, he passed through Kirsten's neighborhood and then Livy's on the bus. He didn't regret giving Cheyenne the money.

The recruiter showed him a video and gave him coffee, doughnuts, and brochures. He was somewhat cheered by the pay and benefits. The idea that he could get financially stable stirred something in him he hadn't known was there. He owed them, all of them. He knew that he could never pay them back, but also that it would be a freedom to be out of their debt.

The first time Essex saw Cheyenne she was in line at the takeout window of an all-night falafel place on University Way. He was eleven. He was in a recess by the post office where he and his friends went to avoid cops. It was raining and he was alone, trying to stay awake.

He noticed her for two reasons. First, because she was an older teenage girl and he'd been noticing them a lot in the past month. Second, she was telling a dramatic story. He could tell because her gestures were big and people were smiling. They gave her space, stepping back into the rain themselves. He tried to hear but couldn't, only the single words, which sailed like shots over the street noise— Why? Stupid. Saltpeter. Curry of course. Witch! Dumb ass—then she stamped her foot and, looking skyward, yelled, "I mean who would ever do that?" Everyone laughed. The falafel man handed her a falafel. Someone paid for her. Cheyenne made the appropriate expressions of shock and gratitude, but Essex doubted she was surprised.

Taking a bite, she stepped into the street looking both ways for traffic and walked toward him as if he were a mailbox or a bus stop bench. As she got closer he felt the urge to step out of her way, but two feet away she thrust her falafel in his face.

"It's gross. Take it."

He did and she walked off. After he ate, he fell asleep and slept the sleep of the dead. Someone kicked his leg. She was standing over him.

"What is wrong with you?" she asked. "Go away. How old are you?"

"Fifteen."

She laughed.

"Twelve. Mostly."

Her shoulders sagged.

"Oh fuck you," she said, yanking him up. "Come on. It's a long walk."

He didn't know where she was taking him but he went. She walked fast and seemed to have nothing to say to him. Crossing the bridge over the interstate he asked her name but couldn't hear what she said and was too embarrassed to ask again.

It was 3:00 a.m. when he met Kirsten. She opened the door fully dressed, as if it were the afternoon.

"He needs somewhere to go," said Cheyenne, and ushered him in.

"What's your name?" Kirsten asked.

"Christian."

Cheyenne pointed to the couch. "Sit." She said it like she'd just about had it up to here with him, which made no sense.

Kirsten brought him a plate of spaghetti.

Cheyenne left without a glance in his direction.

He pointed at the door. "Does she live here?"

"Sometimes," said the woman. "Do I need to call anyone for you?"

"Not really," he said.

He met Livy the next morning. She definitely did live there because she told him if he touched her shit she'd kill him. According to her, there were already two people too many living in the house. He wasn't sure which two she meant but knew he was one of them. Periodically over the next few months, Cheyenne would swing by but she ignored him. Livy usually did too, but one afternoon, after a particularly bad set of decisions on his part, Livy ordered him into her room. She waved a paperback with a painting of a ship on the cover.

"I've been reading a book about people like you. They're called whalers. They sign on for anything. Assholes on a ship called the *Essex*. Every disaster they should have seen coming, they ignored. You're like that right now."

"But I didn't do anything," he said.

"The hell you didn't. Look around yourself. You're fucked. You're three thousand miles out to sea with no way to get back and it's all your fault. Now you have to get on a raft and eat your friends. It's the only way out of the problems you've created."

Every time after that when she passed him in the hall, she whispered, "Essex."

Then Cheyenne started calling him Essex and he decided he didn't really mind. He was the *Essex*. To survive he was going to have to cut loose almost everyone he ever knew up until then and head for land. All these years later, it wasn't very different. The raft, the sea. He was twenty-seven with nothing. Lost.

The recruiter handed him information on where to go for medical screenings. The process was going to be much slower than he had hoped but was at least a direction and a destination. Some ships navigate by charts and landmarks, piloting through understanding the larger picture and their place within it. Other vessels have to rely on dead reckoning. They know only where they came from and how long it took to arrive at this moment in time. From this they can try to make the thousands of minute calculations and course corrections necessary to reach the shore.

14 The Fire Blossom Temple

THE FOYER of the Fire Blossom Temple had a rack for shoes and a table with cups and an electric teapot. Against one wall was a long church pew, its bench no longer level, worn by generations; it saved seats for families long gone. The walls behind it were ablaze with light from a window in an adjacent room. Cheyenne and Livy took off their shoes and sat on the hard wood bench across from a giant ensō that hung from the ceiling, weighted by bamboo rods. Brushed into a banner of silk, a black circle not quite closed, a shackle, a handcuff on a field of white.

The roshi, once JoAnn, and possibly Ann, was expecting them. The abbot had called ahead. Cheyenne's feet itched. Her socks were still damp from the rain. Livy's braids had become unpinned and she chewed on the paintbrush tip of one, something Cheyenne hadn't seen her do since childhood.

A woman appeared. A black shadow with the sun behind her from a west-facing window. They stood. Ann Radar had been a foil or a myth, something to which one sister would be intimately connected and the other, not. All the conversations they'd had, about what she might look like or if she'd have an East Coast accent—*Do you think she wants to see us? I'm sick of caring what she wants*—yet all of a sudden, they did. The idea that they might be, for the first time since birth, in the presence of their real mother, broke each sister open in private ways. *Are there still cracked bits of shell in my hair? Can you see the new skin? Will you shade me with your body?* A searing and unbearable sensitivity spoken in a language of pinpricks and nerve signals marking a soft spot that had never quite closed.

"Let's talk in my room," the roshi said.

They followed her past the zendo and a kitchen into a small apartment that looked out on an alley. There was a window, open a few inches. The roshi shut it.

The room was spare and dustless. There was a single bed, its top sheet folded in hospital corners, a tatami mat, a meditation bench, a small desk and two chairs; she asked them to sit. They took the chairs and she sat on the floor. Cheyenne got up but the roshi waved her back down.

"I prefer it," she said.

The roshi stretched out her legs. Fat and flexible, her head covered in a short gray stubble and scars, she reminded Cheyenne of a brawling stray dog.

On the desk Livy saw a framed photo of a young woman. She had on thick black eyeliner and was wearing a *Star Wars* T-shirt and leather jacket, and she pointed above her to a marquee that read TONIGHT! THE CURE. Livy trained her ears on the sounds of rush-hour traffic, which came through the walls and window—honking geese and birds of prey—interspersed with sounds from the kitchen.

The roshi's blue eyes moved from one sister to the other. Livy's skin got hot at the throat and behind her ears. She wanted to scream and that anger made her tear up. But the idea that the older woman might think she was crying was too much, so she began to glare back.

"I am not your mother," said the roshi. "If you had called ahead, I would have told you."

The roshi let the words fall, ax-like. Cheyenne's breath caught. Livy looked away.

"There is a chance that I knew her, though," said the roshi, crossing her legs. "The abbot told me some of the story you told him. I'd like to hear it from you."

"We were born on the same day," said Livy.

"Same father, different moms," said Cheyenne.

The roshi nodded. "That's quite a hat trick."

"Our moms threw the *I Ching* and the midwife lied on the birth certificates," said Cheyenne. "There was all this myth around it."

"We were told she was the North Star," said Livy.

"People tell kids all sorts of things," said the roshi. "A lot of people are adopted."

"It felt different from other adoption stories," said Cheyenne.

The roshi smiled. "Everyone's personal story feels different than other people's stories."

The older woman glanced at the sunlight now disappearing from the alley. As she turned her head, her eyes flashed, reflecting. There was a bell in the corridor and the sisters turned toward the sound.

"It's for the dinner crew," said the roshi.

A minute later, the sun was entirely gone from the alley and the roshi's room had gone from tawny to dark rose and was now almost too dark for the three women to read one another's expressions.

"There was one woman," she said. "She came to the monastery around the right time. The right age too. Her name was Justine but later someone told me her real name was Ann. We weren't close."

15 The Universe

AT AGE NINETEEN, Kirsten had quit eating meat and started living solely on cheese fries. Two months later she showed up at the clinic where Margaret worked, anemic. Kirsten's visits had become rare. In the earlier years of their relationship she'd seen Margaret every few months. Now she only grabbed condoms occasionally and waved. The nurse-midwife, while still elevated in Kirsten's summation of the world, was no longer new to it. She might be outgrowing Margaret; she wasn't sure, but since she was overdue for a Pap smear and felt like shit she made an appointment.

Margaret put Kirsten in a gown and drew her blood. She made her pee in a cup and have a breast exam, then told her to get dressed. While waiting for the test results, Kirsten told Margaret about all the wild things that had been happening. Kirsten had been hanging out in metaphysical bookstores; she'd been throwing staves and tying colored yarn on candles.

"It's like I'm talking to the Universe and she's talking back," she told Margaret. "It's like there's a conversation between everything that's going on all the time and I finally understand what's being said."

Margaret didn't seem interested. It turned out the Unicorn of Radical Feminism was a materialist. Kirsten refused to let that stand.

"But in history they used to worship goddesses and everyone was peaceful, not asshole warmongers, and that's how we have agriculture and writing. They believed in the great mother so they didn't kill things all the time. That would be better than this, right? If we had goddesses, it would be totally different."

"Yes," said Margaret, "except the only country on earth that actually worships goddesses engages in wife burning and promotes fetal scans to determine the baby's sex so they can abort it if it's a girl."

Seeing Margaret was fucking depressing.

The medical assistant knocked and handed Margaret a slip of paper.

"I think I'm psychic," said Kirsten.

"You're pregnant," said Margaret.

After leaving Margaret, Kirsten had walked to the arboretum, where the trees flushed green and knotted buds were just starting to crack in the soft spring heat. She could feel her new body. Pregnant. All in. Kirsten pushed open the door to Cyril's studio apartment. Neither Ann nor Cyril was home. The Murphy bed was down and unmade. The tile counter of the kitchenette was stacked with several days' worth of dishes and the black-and-white-checked floor, splattered with spaghetti sauce. Something had been shifting in the apartment between the three of them. She could feel it even when the others were gone. They were all sliding toward something they couldn't see.

When Ann returned, Kirsten barely waited for her to get through the door.

"I'm pregnant," she said.

Ann shrugged. "So am I."

Kirsten stared.

"It's not a miracle," said Ann. "We've both been here a couple of months. Our cycles lined up. Are you going to use pennyroyal?"

"I'm not sure," said Kirsten.

"Pennyroyal's way better than a D&C," she said. "It just takes a few days."

"What if it doesn't work?" asked Kirsten.

"You take more."

Maybe it was her vegetarian's sense of ambivalence about causing any form of death or perhaps only teenage sentimentality, but
she couldn't imagine aborting. The Universe is either talking to you
or it isn't.

"I'm going to keep it," said Kirsten.

Ann gave a whip-crack laugh. "Then maybe I will too," she said.

When they told Cyril, he paid up for two months of rent and left.
Good riddance.

As the months passed, their hair thickened and twice as much blood
filled their bodies. They got health care, and free cheese and peanut butter. Something began to bother Kirsten, though. Ann was
thrilled to be pregnant. She was fascinated by the drama in her
body. Yet there was something forensic in her interest. She had no
reaction to strangers touching her belly, whereas Kirsten wanted to
knife anyone who tried.

"Do you believe in destiny?" Kirsten asked Ann one night.

"Of course."

"Do you think everyone has one?"

Ann laughed. "Some people are doomed to be boring stupid
peasants."

"Do you think it's possible for someone to miss their destiny?"

"How can you miss it? That's the point."

"Maybe it's like talent," said Kirsten. "Maybe you can have it
but let it go to waste."

Ann was a devout believer in her own brilliant future, and Kirsten
could see the idea bothered her. Kirsten pulled a book she'd gotten
from the library out of her backpack.

"Have you ever heard of the *I Ching*? You throw coins and look
up the hexagrams and it tells you about your superior path so you
don't miss it," she said. "You'll like it. It's kind of like Chinese dice."

Ann loved games of chance. She considered any loss she suffered
an anomaly. She was fascinated with her own destiny.

"We should play for something real," said Kirsten, and got three pennies.

It would be a home birth. Totally underground. No drugs. No permission.

Kirsten got a bottle of wine out of the fridge and a fifth of vodka out of the freezer. She put them both on the table next to a loaf of day-old challah and a tub of roasted garlic hummus. It was her night to host the coven. After thirty-one years of meeting they had become less of a magic circle than a place for microloans, chiropractic recommendations, and unwanted advice.

She got out the glasses and cut the challah on the breadboard. She hadn't heard from Livy or Cheyenne since they left. Maybe now they knew that the woman they were going to see wasn't Ann. Or maybe they were just about to find that out. She didn't care. *Hate me for it! Go ahead. I owe you nothing.*

Having an organizing myth is good. This had been her thinking. Myths give heroic shape to adolescence in a time devoid of initiation. The story was supposed to free them from the mundane. It was a condom to lower the risk of spiritually transmitted diseases like monogamy and patriarchy. But to have power, myths need drama. They need transcendent beauty. And in the ugly blocks of subsidized housing, surrounded by fast-food chains, penned in by arterial roads without sidewalks, over that year when they had moved from one dismal apartment without natural light to the next, always with black mold blooming on walls punched with jacks for cable you can't afford to use, how was she supposed to give them that? And in order for them to work, myths require initiation and initiation requires profound emotional confusion. You need to lose something you hold dear. Something you thought made you what you were.

That's the price of entry.

16 Polaroid

"JUSTINE?" ASKED LIVY.

The roshi nodded. "She got mail addressed to Ann sometimes. Like I said, we weren't close."

It was night now. The roshi raised herself on one knee and turned on an electric light that flared their faces white.

Justine, Justine, Justine . . . Cheyenne said the name under her breath. A chill went through her, a current she transferred to Livy.

"Do you know where she is?" asked Cheyenne.

"I have no idea how to reach her. It's been years. I heard a rumor she went to Bolivia but that may not be true. Why do you have a right to know?"

Cheyenne and Livy looked at each other. It wasn't a question they'd expected.

"You know, the older I get," said the roshi, "the more I wonder if there is something colonial about curiosity. If I want, I should have. If I'm curious, I should know." She straightened. "Who exactly do you think comes to places like this? I mean comes and stays. Massage therapists and tour guides? Who turns over the keys to their life and says shave my head and tell me what to do? People who can no longer trust themselves. The suicidal and mentally ill. Those with violent intentions. The past is different for men than for women. Even here, though we like to pretend it isn't. When men become monks they can talk about almost anything they did. They can say they murdered someone and people don't make much of it.

It's almost romantic. But women don't talk about leaving a child behind. Not if they were adults when they did it. Justine could have had that story. Every woman I've ever known could have had that story, and I would never have known."

Livy flinched. It was all too easy to imagine. The roshi smiled softly.

"What was she like?" asked Cheyenne.

"I didn't know her well. She had a kind of ambition I found unsettling. I'm sure she was just a messed-up kid like the rest of us." The roshi paused. "I might have a picture of her."

The roshi went to the bookshelf and pulled out a beat-up copy of the *Tassajara Cookbook*. Inside the pages were Polaroids. She sorted through, then picked one out.

"This was taken at Great Prairie in Montana the first year I was there."

She handed the photo to Cheyenne. A group of young women stared into the lens. Their eyes burned, newly arrived, magnetic. One had a freshly shaved head, the others didn't. The roshi touched the face of the woman with the shaved head. "That's Justine."

The woman with the shaved head was freckled with full lips. Her expression reminded Livy of Cheyenne, but only a little. Cheyenne thought maybe she saw a shade of the young Livy. Mostly what they saw was someone who was very young.

"You can have it," said the roshi.

Livy took the Polaroid from Cheyenne, holding it carefully by its edges. Something untranslatable stirred, a vertigo she could not push away. She handed it back to Cheyenne, who put it in her jacket pocket.

Watching the reaction of the sisters to seeing the young woman, the roshi added, "I have to tell you, it's hard for me to imagine the Justine I knew carrying an unwanted pregnancy to term. She was not sentimental."

17 The Wharf

OUTSIDE THE MONASTERY, a Friday night in Boston swallowed them whole. Noise from the bars and the streets, the early drunks, the taxis, and the tourists everywhere around them.

"It can't be over," said Cheyenne.

Livy rolled her shoulders and squeezed her eyes shut. "Fuck, I can't believe I let you talk me into missing this much work. Drive us out and I'll take a shift once we're on the turnpike."

Exhaling, she trotted goat-like down the steps.

"I need to walk first," said Cheyenne. "I'm too wound up to get in a car."

"We need to go now."

Cheyenne glared at her sister. "You're really making this worse. It's bad enough as it is."

Livy saw that Cheyenne was on the verge of crying, which might come out in several ways. "Chill out," she said. "We can walk a bit."

"Thank you," said Cheyenne, but didn't move.

On the corner, a group of young men spilled out of a bar.

"Lawyers," Cheyenne said.

"How do you know?"

"Jackson and I used to come here for conferences."

"I can't imagine you at a conference."

"I didn't go. I wandered around and showed up when they were done."

Two tears welled, balanced on the bottom of Cheyenne's eyelids, then broke and ran down her cheeks.

"Oh hold it together," said Livy. "She might have been my mom."

Cheyenne laughed loud enough to scare a pigeon off the rim of a trash can but seconds later had new tears in her eyes.

"Will you stop blubbering if I let you stay at my place another month?" said Livy.

Cheyenne wiped her cheeks. "Yes, I promise."

But Livy knew it was a mistake—felt sick thinking about it.

Cheyenne started walking. One of the guys on the corner yelled a girl's name into the traffic. Cheyenne crossed the street away from them.

They reached the Common. From where they stood, the fountain ahead was black and they couldn't tell if it had water in it.

"Congratulations," said Cheyenne, "you're on the Freedom Trail." She pointed to the green. "They do reenactments here sometimes."

"Of what?"

"Revolutionary War things. The whole reenactment thing is so fucked up. All those Civil War guys?"

"A Japanese guy I fished with said it's the same with samurais."

Cheyenne laughed. "Can you imagine if they reenacted women's history? Hundreds of teenagers in bonnets dying in childbirth? It would be fucking perfect. Heroic midwives race between bedsides covered in blood. I hate this part of the country."

Reaching the wharf they stopped. Schooners were docked with sails furled. A re-creation of an eighteenth-century tall ship rocked gently in the quiet water. Livy watched someone near the bowsprit light a cigarette then cup it, take two drags, and throw it into the water.

"Well this is the end of the tour unless we jump in," said Cheyenne.

Livy shook herself alert then pulled out her phone to check the time. There was a voice mail from an unknown number. She listened and handed the phone to Cheyenne. It was a job assignment from the temp agency she'd signed up for. Cheyenne played the message back and called the number. Listening, she punched in a few numbers and hung up.

"It's automated. You can accept or deny jobs." She gave Livy the phone.

"When do you need to be back?" asked Livy.

Cheyenne put her hands in her pockets and twisted one way, then the other.

"I've been thinking about what you said about how you thought I would go back to school and I think I will. If I go back I won't have to dodge the student loans from last time anymore so I'll have credit and," Livy began to speak but Cheyenne put her hand up, "I'll qualify for grants and loans so I can pay any back rent I owe in one lump sum with interest."

Livy felt queasy again.

They reached the car and Cheyenne got in the driver's seat.

"God I feel so much better," she said. She pulled into the street. "History or art therapy," she said. "One of those, at least to start."

As she drove, Cheyenne chattered about being a teacher or a counselor or a spiritual adviser—but the kind that doesn't really believe in anything but still wants to help—until they were back on the turnpike. Finally Livy cut her off.

"Did they say how long this temp job would be?"

"I don't know. I declined it."

Livy burned but said nothing. Half an hour later they stopped at a travel plaza to switch off driving. Cheyenne popped the trunk and got her bag out of the back.

"I want to change clothes," she said, and handed Livy the keys.

Livy handed her the credit card. "Go put thirty dollars on pump number two and get a quart of oil. I'll fuel up."

After she filled up and parked, Livy went to the bathroom and washed her face. Cheyenne came in without oil. She went into the stall to change, pulling out a blue cotton shirt stained with ketchup and a pair of black pinstripe pants still damp from where she'd tried to scrub off dried peanut butter the night before. She put them on and stepped out of the stall.

"That peanut butter stain looks like cat vomit," said Livy.

Cheyenne put her leg up on the counter and turned on the other sink. She poured a few palmfuls of water over the peanut butter until the whole leg was soaked. She went for paper towels but there weren't any so she wrung out the cuff and gave up.

Livy washed her jeans and the green shirt in the sink and rolled them tight.

"Here's your card," said Cheyenne, handing it over.

Livy put it in her wallet and took out a twenty. "Go get the oil with this so we can have change for tolls," she said.

Cheyenne rolled her eyes and took the bill.

"Take my bag," Cheyenne told Livy.

Sitting in the car waiting, Livy realized the trip was a financial disaster but also a lesson. Her sister was her sister.

Cheyenne came out of the restaurant side of the building and crossed the parking lot. Her dark, shaggy hair had an orange luster from the neon of the illuminated food court. Her blue shirt looked gray. The ketchup looked like blood. The wet leg of her black pants clung to her calf, wrapping at the hem, exposing her sockless ankle. In one hand, a gallon of water, in the other, a Hershey bar the size of her head. Still with no oil.

Livy started the car. Her sister was the most resourceful person she'd ever known. She had charm. And she must have at least one friend in the area somewhere, Jackson if no one else.

Cheyenne stopped to roll up the wet pant leg.

Livy freed the emergency break and put the car in drive. Cheyenne froze and they met eye to eye for a full second. Then Livy took her foot off the brake and floored it.

Cheyenne had twenty dollars and the world's largest chocolate bar. She'd be fine.

BOOK 2—THE LAY

All the money gone I could not find it (find it)

Booze was left I poured into a glass (glass! glass! glass!)

The bitch I saw in flip-flops must a took it (took it)

And paid her passage with her . . . high-interest credit card!

—Melody repurposed for autoharp
  by smokers on the porch at Neighborsbane

18 New Archangel

SITKA HARBOR faces the Gulf of Alaska with the Tongass at its back, a forest thick as whale fat and dense as sea otter fur. You want to get to another place? Go around, says the Tongass. Swim. Build a boat. I don't care.

During the reign of Tsar Paul, tall ships came to Alaska, under the guise of Russia's first joint-stock venture, the Russian-American Company. Hunting their way up the Aleutian Islands, they left behind a trail of small wooden churches on bony subarctic hillsides. Martyrs in egg tempura and gold leaf brushed onto wood panels. Archangels, like Michael. Saints, like Nicholas, the intercessor of sailors. But in this new place, new saints were also born as heaven made room. Saint Herman, who held back a Kodiak tidal wave. Saint Jacob, who established the parish in Atka to watch over two thousand miles of grassland and minister to the souls of killer whales.

Carving the waters along the coast, the Russian-American Company sailed into what would someday be Sitka, which was under the watch of a large Tlingit fort. High on an outcrop, cliffs on three sides, the fort presided over the salt water below as it had for a thousand years. Fearing the Tlingit, the company staked the ground a few miles down the coast with colonial confidence. After all, Lewis and Clark had reached the confluence of the Columbia.

Aleksandr Baranov, a former glass merchant from the backwoods of Siberia who wore chain mail to work, even on the advent of gaslight, now a corporate executive charged by the company with the care and feeding of the Russian aristocracy's venture capital, chased the glossy pelts of otter into the Tongass. Baranov, a product of rampant speculation and the hiding-behind-the-drapes-soon-to-be-assassinated, middle-aged Tsar Paul, valiantly slaughtered forth.

He christened their outpost Redoubt St. Archangel Michael. In the shade of the vast cedar and hemlock forest, on land sculpted by glaciers and pockmarked, they were unafraid.

Yet the Tlingit kicked the Russians out. *Gunalchéesh!* because the Tlingit were children of Raven and Eagle. But Baranov returned with more ships. Moving back across the gulf, he passed the Kenai and Chugach mountains and the breathtaking Yaas'éit'aa Shaa, which the Russians called Mount Saint Elias—Elias, also known as Elijah: Elijah, whose speech is a burning lamp, Elijah, who was secretly fed by ravens. By hugging the coast and sailing through Tlingit land, Baranov was confident his brigs and schooners, cannon, and foreign faces would terrify. With every nautical mile he displayed his gunship plumage and gasconade of company vessels, adorned with Aleuts. But perhaps he was mistaken. Perhaps he was not the center of the story so much as a subplot. And perhaps his fleet was not terrifying so much as fascinating, rare. Rare like pods of killer whales in an urban harbor, or alien and beautiful like clear footage of dry rivers on Mars. Something new in the world.

The Tlingit now held the Russian redoubt. With young saplings they had fortified it against cannon from the sea. Baranov fired over and over on the fort, but the iron balls bounced off the angled green wood and rolled into dugouts where they were captured and reclaimed by the Tlingit at night.

The Battle of Sitka lasted six days. In the end, Baranov strode ashore. Wounded, he waited for a surrender that never came. The Tlingit had disappeared into the woods, victorious. The Tlingit win was not without cost, though. The Kiks.Ádi houses taking part in the battle were the Steel House, the Clay House, the House on the Point, the Strong House, the Herring House, the House Inside the

Fort, and some of these houses have doors that have not opened for a long time. Because while the birth of Raven and Eagle is beyond memory, clans and houses are more fragile. They are born of the experience of the People and when a maternal line breaks, like ghosts, their stories walk into the woods. This is also true.

Coming ashore, looking at the ruins of his settlement, it was clear to Baranov that the Archangel Michael had abandoned them. To whom should they look for shelter then? Already they imagined a time of starting over. Lie to me about where I come from. Count from now. Wash me clean of history.

Livy was done with caring about where she might have come from. A sea and a sky, a ship and a real star to steer by—she needed nothing else.

She had arrived in Sitka in late July with $82 in her pocket and a job. She'd gotten it through a deckhand she'd fished with two years earlier, a Tlingit from Sitka named Michael. Michael's uncle had suddenly come into a boat, the *Jani Lane,* and they needed someone to help fish. All you have to do is get here, he said.

After her debacle with Cheyenne, Livy had returned a day late and her boss had fired her. He hoped she understood. A window was probably opening for her right now, he said. Her landlord had given her notice and she had two weeks to pay rent or entangle herself in an eviction and lose a reference. She called the credit card company to see if she could do a balance transfer, but since she had recently run up a bigger bill, they'd cut her credit line to half of what she currently owed and raised her interest to 29.9 percent. They also hoped she understood.

With no other options, she sold what she could of Cheyenne's things and moved onto Kirsten's couch. She hadn't lived with her mother since she had gotten her first full-time job at seventeen. The sense of failure was excruciating. Then Michael's offer came, but she needed $1,000 for gear and a plane ticket. Kirsten didn't have any money. Neither did Essex, not until he started boot camp. The idea that she had work but couldn't get to it was worse than anything.

"Maybe call Cheyenne?" said Essex.

Her sister, as predicted, had ended up on Jackson's couch while he was away for the summer. Livy didn't want to know how that conversation went. She and Cheyenne had still not spoken.

Livy would have totally spiraled if Kirsten had not gone to the coven for help. Like most feminist collectives, the coven was entirely made up of poor people but they usually had their methods. With everyone running so lean, Kirsten doubted they could help but had to try. Living with Livy was unbearable.

"Please, give me money," Kirsten begged the other women. "It's like having some angry laid-off steelworker on the couch yelling at the radio and whining about honest work. I can't take it."

Her desperation set gears in motion. As long as Kirsten could get the money back to them by winter solstice, nothing bad would happen.

In the airport, a one-way ticket to Alaska in hand, Livy was again herself. She hit the Starbucks and poured their entire decanter of half-and-half and all their sugar into her canteen. Because fuck me if I'm going to pay for a teabag I can get free on the plane. The young woman behind the counter saw but didn't care. Why should she? Slave, servant, associate, technician, team member. Do you want to try our Iced Whipped Strawberry Bouffant Bliss Blowjob today?

Livy preferred an elemental boss. Her first captain had screamed in her ear, "The sea doesn't care about you!" Which was great and fair because it meant the sea didn't care about him either.

Once in the air she drank three cups of free orange juice, and ate two packages of free pretzels and pocketed two more.

They were almost overheaded due to low fog coming into Juneau and forced to fly to Anchorage. Ten minutes after they landed, the fog rolled in lower and thicker and it was clear no plane was getting out. Livy was cutting it close already. She needed to get to the docks. She spent the last of her money on a ferry leaving that night.

A baggage handler offered her a ride to the ferry terminal in a rust-eaten station wagon that smelled like wet dog and Febreze. Livy was in no position to turn it down.

"Watch the floor," she said as Livy got in, "you can put your foot through."

Cigarette smoke filled the car. Streaming by outside in the dark were decrepit ranch houses and somewhere, deeper back through the trees, a still and glacial lake. The road would end and there would be nothing but the Tongass. Black wolves denned in roots that wound around granite boulders studded with garnets calling to their gumboot and herring roe cousins. Fog rose into the forest canopy, warp the branches, weft the cloud. Hemlock, spruce. Cedar grown taller than two hundred and fifty feet. In her half-awake moments, she saw the trees as they were, Chilkat dancers caught mid-spin, umber spines, slope-shouldered, they gathered like chiefs along the shore. In headdress crowns of reed shivs, piercing the day into the starlight, they danced at a potlatch that began long ago.

They came to the terminal. The woman cranked the emergency brake and idled.

"There's a box of Cheese Nips in the back I keep for my grand-baby. You can take those."

As Livy picked the half-empty box off the floor, the woman pulled a worn plastic baggie out of her purse.

"Here's some weed if you get stoned. It's mostly shake but you might be able to sell it." The woman held the bag to the light and wrinkled her nose. "Maybe. It'd be a hard sell. It's pretty much only seeds. I'd try a teenager."

She laughed like she'd been punched in the gut and dropped the bag into Livy's lap. Her laugh turned into a coughing fit. Once she caught her breath and wiped the tears out of her eyes she patted Livy's leg.

"That's bad, isn't it? Sometimes it's just that way. Easy to forget how low things can go. Always good to have something to sell. Especially something that's not attached." She cracked up again. "Am I right? I'm right. You know what I mean, I know you do."

On the solarium deck of the ferry, Livy went to the rails as they pulled out into the channel. The soft burnt yellow light of the heat lamps behind blacked out her night vision and she saw only shapes. Soon they would be coming down the back of the Great Island Home of Bears. On the other side, the city, an amalgamation of pull tabs, salmon bakes, folk rock, and totem poles. Down past that was Sheep Creek. And past that, the old Juneau mine where runnels of rainwater carved deltas no bigger than handprints beneath the moss-covered piles of broken tailings and drained onto the beach. Livy knew that beach. She had crawled around its derelict boats. They were all over Alaska. Abandoned where storms had left them or shipwrecked elsewhere and brought up by the tide. Dead seiners and skiffs, trollers, their power blocks and pots scavenged, spools and splintered pallets, lines unlaid and spliced with seaweed. Even processors with food still on their galley shelves, Miracle Whip labels not peeling but blanched, a white dust over everything. Long-liners. Gillnetters. Capsized or sunk to the portholes with holds full of barnacles and engine rooms full of sand, keel sides cracked in two and driven down into spit or bar, now a shelter for tide pools and kelp. Sometimes strange jellyfish washed across in a rare tide and illuminated the sand like gumdrop deck prisms. Orange, purple, red, they pulsed and beat and dried in the air amid rotting nets and bleached orange buoys tangled and strewn among the rocks.

Once, a Japanese tanker cut from its moorings by a great tsunami had appeared on the horizon, its engines quiet. No sailors, no captain, a ghost in the shipping lanes without running lights, it vanished in the dark. Livy never saw it herself, but she'd heard fishermen argue over it. Tow the damn thing in! There's got to be a killing to be made in copper and salvage oil. Oh just leave it alone and forget about it. How many dead satellites are floating around in space anyway? The Coast Guard blasted it with a heavy barrage of 25 millimeter shells but it didn't go down. Rasputin, Franco-Methuselah, it came on with flames licking from every socket, great fountains of black smoke billowing from its decks, listing now and riddled by cannon fire. They shelled it again with heavier shot. This time it did sink. It fell more than a thousand feet. *Step handsomely around the snow crab. Run your hands over the rusted rails. Hold your breath and count starfish. Anyone who can't face this should stay home.* But what had the ship done? It was only courseless. Drifting. Mindless of its effect, it was nothing but a lost child returning to the arms of its true mother, the graveyard coast.

19 The Miracle of Aunt Jennie

IT WAS EARLY in the afternoon when Livy got to Sitka Harbor. The sun was burning through the fog and steam rose off the docks and lines. Crabbers and trollers, purse seiners and vintage skiffs, liveaboards with polished wood trim and tarps battened with pristine twine all bobbed in their slips.

She found the *Jani Lane* out on the tidal grid awaiting repair, half out of the water and listing. She stood before it like she'd come upon a corpse. A thirty-six-foot wooden gillnetter with old lines, the *Jani Lane*'s nets were tangled and her hull was stained with algae. The wood that should have made her collectible was rotting and the deck was covered in trash bags.

"Livy!"

She saw Michael jogging up with his arms full of duct tape and pancake mix.

"I thought I wasn't going to make it," she said.

"If you got here this afternoon you'd have missed us. Here."

He handed her a family-size box of Bisquick.

"What's the deal with this boat?" she asked.

"My uncle got her in the settlement. Isn't she awesome?"

Livy looked at the duct tape weatherizing the windows of the gillnetter.

"We didn't want to put money into her until we had the permits," said Michael.

"I thought we were seining."

"Well there was a seiner but it turned out to be in pretty bad shape," said Michael. "Besides," he clapped his hands, "who wants to be some mindless jerk seining for pinks and dogs when we can go totally old school in a boat like this. Get some reds, some coho. That's the best part. We're going to Bristol Bay."

"The season there is half over."

Michael shrugged.

Livy looked at him. She examined the small freckles dotting his broad cheekbones. She looked at the creaseless skin between his eyebrows. He was like Essex and about his age. She knew if she stared at him long enough he would smile. If she stared longer, he would stop. She shook her head and looked away.

"You got to trust me," he said, "this whole trip was meant to be. Written in the record books before we were born."

"I don't want to hear about how something is meant to be just because it's happening."

But she couldn't complain because the haphazard work ethic that led to the *Jani Lane* leaving this late in the season had also led to her having a job.

A man appeared on the deck of the boat. Shirtless and pasty white with a brilliant aura of red shoulder hair, he took a quick look around, reached back and yanked the rubber band from his frizzy pigtail and threw it in the water.

"Boat's fucked. Another day," he said.

He spat over the side and went back below. Michael set the box of duct tape down.

"Is that your uncle?" asked Livy.

"Maybe we should get out of here for a bit."

They went to a liquor store that served food. A gray rectangle with photos of bearded men next to full holds or halibut the size of teenagers. Michael paid for the beer.

"Does your uncle know anything about fishing?" she asked.

"It's been a while, that's why I'm here. Want to see my new tattoo?"

He pulled his shirt up and twisted. On his ribs was the jackal-headed god Anubis.

"What's wrong with you? Don't you know how many hippies in the Lower Forty-Eight would kill to be native? Cover yourself with killer whales and eagles. Lord it over them. They deserve it."

Michael pulled his shirt down. "I like the idea you can weigh a heart." He fiddled with a pull tab. "Last year was the worst since my mom died. Getting tattooed was the highlight. I was so low. But the darkness was just part of the magic."

"I don't want to hear about magic," she said.

Michael leaned forward. "I'm telling you, Livy. We could go out there with nothing and still come back with fish. This trip is blessed. I've seen it in dreams." Michael grabbed her forearm. "You were there. That's why I asked you to come. We were on the deck of the *Jani Lane* sailing over a copper bay and our whole boat was flashing silver with salmon. Destiny."

Livy heard Cheyenne's voice. *Wait. What's the difference between fate and destiny? Give up? A six-pack of beer!* It was her sister's favorite joke in high school. It's stupid, Livy told her. It doesn't mean anything. It's not funny. Except that it was.

They got back to the boat around midnight. Michael's uncle was nowhere so Livy felt weird about going below. Instead they stretched their bedrolls out between the trash bags and lay down under the lilac sky. A month from now she would be out of debt to the coven. In two months, she'd be back to where she was before Cheyenne had shown up.

She closed her eyes and listened to the small tides. She felt something hard in her pocket. It was the little black tourmaline marble Michael had given her on their way back to the boat. To help with her negativity.

"They met in rehab," said Michael.

"Who?"

"Aunt Jennie and Uncle Jeremy." Michael scooted closer and propped himself up on his side. "In Juneau when they were teenagers. Uncle Jeremy was a speed freak then. They got kicked out of rehab for messing around but it was extended care and she was already six weeks pregnant so they got married to keep things cool but she miscarried and they broke up anyway. She was going to file for divorce but the day she went to do it the woman at the clerk's office had to leave early because she had a restraining order on her own ex and had seen him across the street so she didn't want to leave at the regular time so she told Jennie to come back the next day but Jennie couldn't because she was leaving for Angoon the next morning. Turned out it was better for taxes to be married so they just left it. Aunt Jennie hated paperwork. She walked into the woods in June. When we cleaned out her place it was full of unopened letters and bills. Years of it. The night she died she appeared to Jeremy in a dream. She told him to go to Fish and Game first thing in the morning and file a claim for the fishing permits she inherited from her dad. She told him to make sure he applied for an emergency transfer through widows and orphans, or sole survivors, or whatever they call it now. Then he called me because she told him to take me fishing. Take care of my nephew, she said." Michael's voice broke like a wave over a rock on the word *care*. "And when I got the call? I was lower than I'd ever been. I'd spent my dividend on my girlfriend right before she left me. Then I found out all the appliances were rented. They took the fridge. Wheeled it out in front of me. Threw all my frozen food on the lawn like I could just go buy more. I had nothing, Livy, nothing, and that very night, Aunt Jennie comes to Jeremy in a dream and tells him to take care of me. That very night. I hadn't even heard about her dying but I swear I felt something. I don't care what you call it—Jesus, Eagle, Odin, Anubis—I have absolutely no fear left, and that's all I had before. It was magic. Fucking total magic. I mean, even you have to see a hand of greater purpose shaping everything. This thing goes so far back. She took care of me. I have no more fear and Livy, that was all I had before. It was everywhere, and now it's gone."

Livy rolled away but Michael kept talking. She held the little black marble up to the sky between her fingers and moved it slowly over the moon. Even you, Livy, even you, he said, even you have to know this is bigger than us. Even you have to see that none of this should be happening. But it is.

20 Athens and Sparta

LIVY WOKE when Uncle Jeremy stepped across her body to piss over the side of the boat. She was sitting up when he turned around.

"Pump's dead. Head's fucked." He yawned and stuck out his hand.

She shook it.

"Livy, right? Let's get this fucking trash off the boat."

Grabbing a yard bag full of debris he lobbed it onto the dock.

Jeremy wasn't terrible, just surly, a trait Livy generally trusted in a skipper. But everything on the *Jani Lane* needed work. They had fooled themselves if they thought they were going to sea, or that they could have possibly sailed yesterday. The engine had problems, the electrical was a mess, and there was rot beneath the waterline. As the tide went out farther, it exposed a sizable hole in the fiberglass hull. Binge-watching YouTube for guidance, Jeremy had tried twice to patch it and failed. Over the next few days, as word got around about the size of the hole, the *Jani Lane* became a punch line in the bars. The jokes fell on Livy and were all about letting women drive. *Hey, what was the last thing they said on the shuttle* Columbia*? Oh, I don't know. Look at the stars?*

She counted down the hours until they could leave.

The only encouraging thing was that Bristol Bay, where they were now headed, was having a record-breaking salmon run. Everyone down to the green deckhands were making bank. The idea that in just a few weeks she would be able to pay the coven back and still have money to get her through winter, and maybe beyond, buoyed her and made whatever stupid things people said meaningless. But first they had to get there.

The daylight was never quite gone. Working within the limit of the tides they moved to a twenty-four-hour clock. Up at 3:00 a.m. to take apart the bilge or change oil, down for an hour, up for an hour, sleep for two. In some sense, they were already at sea.

Livy's phone buzzed all the time with texts from Cheyenne, who apparently had her own phone now. At first the texts were angry rants. Then they turned into statements of fact and metaphysics. *Being here is perfect! I should really thank you for dumping me on the Massachusetts Turnpike. You're an instrument of the Universe.* Livy never responded, but it didn't matter. Cheyenne's messages continued, morphing into delicate haikus of manipulation. *I don't think pennies have real copper in them . . . There's a plywood coffee table on the corner and people are just passing it by . . . Did you know they don't call it food stamps anymore? How the hell did I miss that? . . .* After one particularly bad day the phone buzzed and Livy threw it as hard as she could on the concrete. But the phone was too cheap to break. *Hey Livy, I made this one for you. What's the difference between an Athenian and a Spartan?* I don't know. A six-pack? *Years of counseling! . . . I wrote the roshi a thank-you letter and signed it from both of us.* Livy texted back. *You do not speak for me.* Hitting Send, she realized what she'd done. The phone was buzzing in seconds. Livy walked into the nearest bar and sold it.

The day they were to leave she was walking toward the *Jani Lane* when she heard the sound of a chainsaw's high whine, downshifting when buried in wood. She saw Michael.

"What the hell is going on?"

"I guess there's a length limit in Bristol. No boats over thirty-two feet," he said.

She looked at the thirty-six-foot *Jani Lane* and realized Jeremy was sawing the extra four feet off the front of the boat.

He was already three feet into the bow. The weather rail kept him from getting into a good position so he couldn't get the angle of the cut. Livy jumped forward but not fast enough. The chainsaw kicked back.

"My fucking face!" screamed Jeremy and dropped the twitching chainsaw.

He buckled over with his head in his hands. Blood ran between his fingers.

Michael dropped the line and was on deck behind Livy.

Jeremy was rocking back and forth.

"You're going to have to let us see it," said Livy.

Michael grabbed a T-shirt he'd been using to clean the engine. "Get some pressure on it."

They waited for a few minutes until the blood flow slowed enough for them to get a look. He'd missed the eye. The main cut was short and deep and came from some kind of shrapnel, not the blade.

Jeremy kicked a nearby bag of supplies. "I'm not going to pay any damn ER when I've got a drawer full of Neosporin and superglue."

They worked the rest of the afternoon and evening unbowing the boat. When they were done they faced a new problem because there was two tons of scrap.

Jeremy came above.

"Leave it!" he yelled. "I don't care if we get banned from this port forever."

At that moment, neither did Michael or Livy.

By 11:30 they were aboard and ready. Despite the fact that crossing the gulf in a boat like the *Jani Lane* was a terrible idea, Livy could not fend off joy. They were leaving. The moon, that great and reliable force, brought the bigger tides and raised the boat. She bobbed under a rose sky, streaked with lavender and pale blue lines. Jeremy with his superglued face backed them off the grid and out into the harbor.

Livy stood beside him in the wheelhouse. He was flushed and chatty in a way she hadn't seen before. Jeremy rolled a cigarette. Something else she'd never seen him do. She wondered if he might even be a little drunk. But his speech was clear and fast, his attention to detail, sharp. He couldn't stop cleaning and saw dirt on the dashboard where there was none. Livy's job was to fish. The rest she didn't want to know about. She took a spot on the sawn-off bow by the half-cut weather rail. The deck was covered in sawdust, broken chainsaw teeth, and twisted drill bits. She swept them over the side with her feet as they motored out into the channel past the rubble-mound breakwater and out into the open ocean.

21 The Unicorn of Feminism

SITTING ON THE EDGE of her bed, Kirsten faced the bookshelf. It was a particleboard piece of junk she had painted gold when the girls were toddlers. The shelves sagged, the back was missing, the gold had all but chipped off, but Kirsten couldn't let it go. It was the first piece of furniture she had owned that wasn't donated. On it, she kept the books that made her who she was— *Spiritual Midwifery, Gyn/ecology: The Metaethics of Radical Feminism, The Good Vibrations Guide to Sex, The Power of Myth.* She'd carried them from apartment to apartment. Looking at them now, she saw nothing worth crating around.

The world she'd tried to make for the girls had blown up. Cheyenne was gone again and Livy was somewhere in the Bering Sea. Cheyenne's absence wasn't new, nor Livy's fishing trips, but this was different. It was a fundamental rejection of everything she'd built. Neither of them cared fuck all for metaphor; they had no interest in growing, only in surviving. And they were barely doing that. The very thing she'd created, the myth of the North Star, had not led to a transformative understanding of what matters but had made everything more petty and desperate instead. Even Essex would be gone soon, also dragged down by the search for Ann.

Kirsten pulled a shoe box off the bookshelf. They were the only photos she had and she wanted to see her younger face. Sorting through the pictures she found only one of herself. It had been taken right around the time she'd first told the girls about Ann. She'd been thirty-one. Her hair was long and her skin was duskier. She still had fat in her cheeks. That was it. One photo. She wasn't camera shy; there had just been nobody else around to take pictures.

She'd never expected Cyril to stay. She'd outgrown him even before she found out she was pregnant. Ann, she expected to stay. Not literally but emotionally. Kirsten sighed and tears of rage came to her eyes. She was mad at no one but herself. She couldn't fully blame Ann for cutting ties. Hadn't she also cut ties? At the time they knew each other, Kirsten had truly believed she was creating something new in the world. *I feel like we're explorers,* she'd told Ann. *No one has been here before. We get to make it all again.*

Disgusted, she tossed the photo of herself onto the floor and went back to the bookshelf. Pulling each book off the shelf, boxing them up, she went outside in the blaring noon. Someone probably needed this shit, but it wasn't her.

She saw a dented blue Chevy by the chain-locked trash containers. The car belonged to a teenager she often saw crying and chain-smoking in the stairwell after fights with her parents. She went down to the Chevy and tried the handle. The door was open like most cars in the lot—better to lose a cheap stereo than face a deductible you can't afford and have to drive around like a jerk with duct tape and cardboard over your window for a year. The backseat was full of laundry and water-logged textbooks. A fast-food uniform was carefully laid over the headrest. Kirsten put the books on the floor by the gas pedal. Her shift at the parking garage would start in a couple of hours. She wondered if Ann worked, and if so, how many hours and for how much.

Two hours later in her own uniform, she patrolled a row of identical hybrids. She had to ask what the hell she was doing. How had she ended up here? It's not like if she came upon someone trying to break into a car she was going to do anything about it. She kicked the nearest tire. What allegiance do I have to you? She closed her eyes and listened to the echo of sounds off concrete and voices outside on the street. Her stomach hurt. She was sick of everything.

———

The clinic Margaret had started in a run-down neighborhood thirty years ago, once the site of transgressive midwifery, was now as sterile as a coffee shop, all butter-colored walls and black-and-white portraits of pregnant mothers and babies nursing happily. Kirsten looked at a photo of a young bearded man cradling a newborn with downy thatches of hair and unfocused eyes. She imagined the effect real photos of birth on the walls would have. Women covered in blood and feces. Faces swollen in pain. Eyes wide with fear as an Apgar score turned out poorly.

Kirsten let the receptionist know she was there. She hadn't seen Margaret in several years and wasn't entirely sure why she was there now. Going to the midwife when something was wrong was an old instinct more than a considered decision. And Margaret was also partly to blame for all this because she was a part of who Kirsten was. She glanced at the photos and shook her head. She suspected she and Margaret still shared things in common. Like an awareness that the new world they thought they were creating had never been born. Kirsten took a seat. So what if the pathologizing of birth was replaced by the demand that it be pretty. Who cares what other people do? She flipped through a magazine and put it down.

Margaret appeared in the hallway. She looked the same as she had the last time Kirsten had seen her. Her curly Sephardic hair was no more silver than it had been then. She had the same color to her face and way of standing that made her seem taller. She still wore black cotton pants and button-down shirts. And she still made Kirsten feel like a teenager.

Margaret led Kirsten back to her office and turned on a white noise machine. Kirsten sat in a wide cushiony chair.

"Your practice is crazy busy. Is that weird?" she asked.

"I'm used to it. I don't get to attend births much but I don't miss being up for days."

"There are stupider reasons not to sleep."

"Undoubtedly," said Margaret. "How are the girls?"

"Livy's in Alaska and Cheyenne is back East with Jackson. They're not together. I don't know what she's doing. We don't really talk. Cyril gave them Ann's address so they were running around trying to find her for a while."

Margaret drew her chin back. "How did that go?"

"They didn't find her," said Kirsten.

She looked out the window, avoiding Margaret's eye.

"You didn't give them an address?" said Margaret.

"Don't lecture me," said Kirsten.

Margaret clicked her tongue. Kirsten let her gaze wander. She noticed Margaret's hair was still thick whereas hers was dull and thinning. Margaret's voice was shakier than it had been. Something rich was missing from the timbre, though you could barely hear it. Kirsten wondered if her voice had changed too.

"Kirsten, why are you here?" asked Margaret.

Kirsten tried to say it but couldn't. My stomach hurts. It can't be ulcers. I'm not a receiver, I'm a giver. I think the psychic sponge in my gut that soaks up all the bad in the world is finally saturated. I don't know.

She took a breath and looked Margaret in the eye. "I still believe the Universe is talking to me but I no longer like what it's saying."

22 The Storm

THE STORM that hit the *Jani Lane* two days later nearly sank her. Gusts of wet wind blasted the wheelhouse, whistling in the duct-taped seals, and water ran down the walls in the steering room and pooled in the corners. Ocean came through the hatches and tin seams of the sutured hull.

They were farther out from shore than they should have been. The coastline was gone. Livy thought of the cracked preservers, the ancient GPS, and their single survival suit. The radio had already shorted but that wouldn't matter much if she went over. She had gone over once in a drill in Puget Sound. It was a sunny day with waves under a foot tall yet she could not see the boat. The green deckhand who pulled her aboard was more shaken than she was. We could barely see you, he kept saying, you were nowhere. It was so clear. You were nowhere. She quickly learned what no sailor or fisherman wants to know, that if you go over there's usually jack-all chance.

Skipper Jeremy was trying to drive the boat back into the waves but it was getting harder. A large swell two points off the starboard bow crashed over them and knocked Jeremy sideways. *One hand for yourself, one hand for the ship!* Drilled into her brain, and thank god because she was almost thrown down the ladder to the cabin.

"Where's the fucking key!" Jeremy yelled. "Look for the fucking key!"

The ignition switch was stripped and the key had fallen out. With his left hand on the wheel, he dropped to his knees and felt the floor for the key ring. Another wave hit and he lost the wheel.

"Drive the fucking boat!" Livy shouted. "You drive the fucking boat!"

She saw the key in the corner, snatched it up, and thrust it at Jeremy. He was sliding it into the ignition when a huge wave broke over the wheelhouse and he fell with his hand still on the key ring, accidentally turning off the engine.

The harmonic convergence of the resonating ocean rang the little gillnetter like a tuning fork. Livy got down on the floor and yanked aside the hatch cover behind Jeremy's feet to get at the engine. The starter was shot. It had died the week before and they'd been starting the engine by striking it with a wrench but she didn't see the wrench anywhere. Jeremy put the key back in.

"The wrench! Where did you put the—"

A giant wave smashed straight down onto them, blowing out the wheelhouse windows and hurling them against the portside wall. Water rushed into the tiny steering room. Livy and Jeremy scrambled on their bellies through freezing seawater and tempered glass to get the hatch cover back over the engine.

"Get to the cabin!" Jeremy yelled.

The next rush of water swept them backward toward the open hatch, which was working now like a basin drain. Feet through the hole she swung down, hands on the overhead rail, but slipped on the ladder and fell to the cabin floor. She felt Michael's hand on her arm and grabbed him as he pulled her in. Jeremy, just behind, managed to get the hatch cover on, killing the last shaft of light as a new wave scoured the wheelhouse.

They were adrift without power or light, GPS or radio. The one survival suit was stowed in the abandoned wheelhouse, which was probably now an aquarium. The sea anchor and whatever ballast it offered had long gone, the bilge pump was still and the hull was filling with water. Even if they could get down there and bail they would only be moving the ocean from one part of the room to another. They braced as a wave hit. Livy had to jam her back and shoulders into the curved wall behind her and press her heels hard against the lip of the bunk to keep from getting thrown into the galley cabinets.

The subsonic hum of the ocean vibrated their bodies. The terrible sea breath syncing now with the circulation of blood through their hearts; the crashing, the howling, they were one thing. Over the next two hours the hull filled with water. They got thrown hard larboard as the *Jani Lane* slid sideways into fifteen-foot troughs, and slammed starboard as she was dragged up the other side. Eventually the storm began to die. By the time they could go above, the cabin was more than a foot deep in water and the sea was coming up from everywhere. She found the wrench and mercifully was able to start the engine. The pump began to work and they began to bail. With all clocks stopped and everything shorted out or soaked they had no idea what time it was. In the weirdness of the Alaskan summer light and with the storm still muting the sky it could be 4:00 a.m. or noon. A light wind out of the southwest began to blow.

The mooring lines were ripped off, nets torn right on the reel. The sea anchor and three wheelhouse windows were gone. The phones, the batteries, the computer keyboard were all soaked in seawater, but the three of them were better off than they had been two hours earlier.

Jeremy emerged from the wheelhouse braiding his frizzy pigtail. His shoulder hair a copper haze in the sun, he crossed to where Livy squatted, jamming electronics into grocery bags filled with instant rice.

"That was a bitch," he said.

He swatted her on the shoulder, a mano a mano gesture meant to turn all events into an adventure—*Here's to brotherhood!* (or ineptitude) *Raise a glass!* (hopefully not of your own urine). Behavior like this deserves a three-thousand-mile skiff ride in open sea.

"I don't want to talk to you," she said.

He pointed to the rice where his cell phone was half buried. "Will it work?"

She emptied the last box of Uncle Ben's over his phone and tossed the box aside.

"I'm glad you're here. You're solid and I appreciate it," he said.

She looked at Jeremy. He was in the same white sleeveless shirt he'd worn since Sitka. Stained with coffee and engine grease and with a yellow patch along one side the size and shape of a liver, which Livy guessed was powdered lemonade. His face had not fully healed from the chainsaw accident but the superglue was holding the skin together. Despite her rage and the fact that she didn't respect him at all, at his words a rush of pride ran through her. That betrayer, that craving for the compliments of men.

"It'll be better when we're in Bristol," he said. "We'll be drowning in fish and none of this will matter."

Reaching the Homer Spit they came along a yellow bull rail. Michael made fast to a deadman and Jeremy jumped off.

"I'm for the harbormaster."

Half an hour later Michael returned but Jeremy was gone for hours. They looked for him around the dock and on the barstools of the Salty Dog but could not find him. That evening he came back carrying a shitty computer and singing a song he made up.

"Down the chain! Down the chain!" He handed the computer to Livy. "We go tonight. Straight south!" he said, for some reason pointing at the sky.

"Are you crazy?" said Livy. "We're going to miss even more of the season."

Michael came up from below. "What's going on?"

"Your uncle wants us to sail this piece of junk six hundred miles down the Aleutian fucking Island chain and all the way back up instead of dragging it sixteen miles across those mountains." She jerked her head toward Cook Inlet. "Right there."

Michael took the computer from her. "I thought we were going to portage," he said.

"Fuck portage," said Jeremy. "Too expensive. We go around."

"We'll make the portage fees back in one day of fish," said Livy.

Jeremy stretched his hand out gravely like an opera singer. Taking a deep breath, he tucked his chin and puffed out his chest. "Down the chain! Down the chain!" he sang in his best basso profundo.

"We have enough money to do it," Livy said.

"Had," said Jeremy. "Had."

He clapped and made a clownish face. Livy shook her head. Michael walked away with the computer.

All night, Jeremy was in an exceptionally good mood, wide awake and sweating in his tank top; tiny rivulets cut pink paths through the dirt on his face. He talked twice as fast as he normally did and chain-smoked, even though Michael said he had quit years ago. Watching him grind his teeth and sing Pure Prairie League songs, Livy got an idea about what had happened but there was nothing she could do.

Driving the boat away from the dock, the mild breeze and the twilight made the water and coastline beautiful. As they passed dead boats, derelict and weathering on the spit, Jeremy rolled one cigarette after another, smoking them down to his fingers then tossing the butts out one of the broken windows. Chatty again, buoyant, he spoke of various skippers he'd fished with when he was a teenager.

"Jennie told me a story once," he said, "about a fisherman she met years ago. A Tlingit from Kake. He'd grown up near her and was a few years older. She said he had this boat, the prettiest little seiner she'd ever seen. Cherrywood, sunny yellow trim, a little brass bell, and he named the boat after his girlfriend. One day he goes out into the channel and doesn't come back. The other fishermen go look for him. Coast Guard. A helicopter. Nothing. But his girlfriend won't believe it because there's a Tlingit story about a man who went out like that and it turned out he was down south stranded on an island full of oranges and finally made it back—you know how people grasp at hope, anyway. One night this girl and Jennie and some other folks are doing acid on the beach near the old dryfish camp. Halfway through the night the girl starts freaking out saying she'd made the whole thing happen and that his death is all her fault. Nobody knows why but she's crying and starts taking off her clothes and wading into the sound, which is fucking freezing. Jennie tries to get her to come back but she won't, so Jennie wades out. She said the girl's feet are all cut up and kelp is tangled all around her ankles. They get her ashore and the girl sits down on the wet ground and refuses to move, so Jennie gives up. Then the girl begins to sing in Tlingit. An old song about a lost canoe full of young men. As she's singing, her boyfriend's fishing boat starts to come back. First the nets wash up. Then the wheel. A few pieces of painted trim float on the tide wrapped in seaweed. The girl starts to walk up and down the beach singing and the broken little boat keeps washing up. She fishes each piece out and drags it up above the waterline so she can put it all back together. Apparently it went that way all night."

"That's a really fucked-up story, Jeremy," said Livy. "Now I'm going to go down and eat a box of powdered mashed potatoes and forget I ever heard it."

Michael laughed. "Ha! You're superstitious."

"I am not but the people around me are so I have to deal with it."

Jeremy talked through the night then crashed for two days straight. They motored south and west, passing between the abandoned World War II military installations on Kodiak Island and Katmai, land of eruptions. On the other side was Bristol Bay, but between the *Jani Lane* and fish were moonscapes of pumice with ash flows the color of clotted cream or tan in places like the torched top of a meringue. Livy could not see the flows from her vantage on the deck but knew they were there, otherworldly. She was also aware that with every nautical mile traveled they were actually moving farther away from where they needed to be, not closer.

Hugging the coastline of the Aleutian arc, the land changed. She saw cliffs like a cut cake, rich brown under the green carpet of summer grasses, cotton grass, eelgrass, crowberries and blueberries, volcanoes shrouded in fog. Eventually they came to Unimak Island, the point where they could cut through the chain. They turned into the shallow waters of False Pass, where baleen gray whales escaped the toothed whales, orcas that hunted them in roving packs. It was night when they came through but not dark. On the southern tip of Unimak, where a lighthouse with a Fresnel lens once stood, an automated beacon signaled land to passing ships.

It was two weeks later when they finally arrived at where they were to fish. Looking across the bay, Livy was stunned by the number of vessels. Crowded against the imaginary line in the water demarking the boundary between where they were allowed to take fish and where they weren't, the boats were so close that from where she was it looked like they were all bobbing into each other, driving across each other's nets and cutting away the fish. They moved frenetically. A hive. Each attending the queen salmon, her spine whipping S-like beneath them. Set all the nets you want! Pull the purse strings, drop your pots. I owe you nothing, said the sea.

Over the marine radio, announcements came every three hours calling the openings and closings—fish, don't fish, fish—as officials tracked the shoals beneath the boats. And when a close was called, skippers on the flying bridge yelled for hands to get the nets in, pick the fish faster. Deck load! Drop the fish anywhere. Throw them in the fo'c'sle, stuff them in your pockets. All futures narrowed and grand plans became less grand, as the great mother salmon sounded by the line.

23 The Bed

CHEYENNE STOOD on Jackson's porch with a plastic sack of lunch meat in her hand and a backpack stuffed so tight it was almost round. She'd fucked up. Again. She'd slept with Jackson the day he came back from vacation. The next morning, after the euphoria of a possible reconciliation wore off, she had to tell him she was leaving. Again. Go back and try that other way. Walk through the doors of an empty house to see if it's still empty. Close the box that is already closed. Lose a day, lose two—this whole place is a faerie mound. With no better ideas, she called Essex and begged him to come get her. He said he'd be there in three days.

Essex arrived in a '70s Ford Supervan. Spray-painted white, the red cross from the ambulance company that had originally owned it showed through.

"Wasn't that in the blackberry bushes at Neighborsbane?"

"Lester rented it to me," said Essex.

"Will it make it home?"

"Hope so. I have to be back in three days."

His skin was tan on one side from driving, his brown hair grown to his shoulders, and what remained of the black dye was blue-gray in the overcast day.

"Is Jackson around?" he asked.

Cheyenne laughed, wrecked. "Are you crazy?"

In the month and a half that had passed she'd put on weight, rounding her cheekbones, filling her bra. Anyone who knew her would have known it wasn't weight from enjoying life. Her skin was newsprint white except for the circles under her eyes.

"I promised to be gone by tonight," she said. "The bed's in the basement. Heavy as fuck. Solid brass. Watch your head on the basement stairs."

Once down, Cheyenne flipped a light switch. Boxes of wine were stacked next to a wicker chair. Triangles of firewood lined a wall. Cheyenne gave the root-cellar door a yank and the smell of wet earth and clay dust filled the air. A single window spared the cellar from total darkness. The brass headboard leaned against the stone cottage wall. Undertones of marigold and sea green flickered in the spindles and castings as the tree branches near the window shivered. Even pulled apart, rails stacked, the bed took up half the room.

"It's been in his family five generations." Cheyenne held up her hand, fingers spread apart. "Five. We got it as a wedding gift. Heirloom. Heir. Loom. Did you ever think about that?"

She wrapped her hand around a bed knob, a starfish on a rock.

"Are you sure we should take this?" said Essex.

"His exact words were, 'Sell it. It's got to be worth something to someone.'"

"Well that's pretty clear."

They started with the rails, which banged to the concrete floor like seesaws and struck the rafters, nearly shattering a light fixture and narrowly missing Cheyenne's cheek. Then the hardware. All out onto the grass by the van next to the sack of lunch meat. The footboard. Navigating the doorways, they had to take breaks.

"This thing must have been huge," said Essex. "Did you actually sleep in it?"

"We had to rearrange the whole house around it, but it worked. I didn't even know it was in the root cellar until three days ago, which is some pretty Blackbeard shit." They stopped to angle the footboard to make the corner. "I just assumed it was in storage somewhere, waiting for a better wife."

It took twenty minutes to navigate the headboard up the stairs and get it out into the yard. It wasn't until they leaned it against the Supervan that they realized it would never fit.

Cheyenne tossed the slats she was carrying onto the grass. Stomping back inside she realized she'd locked the door and left the keys on the table. Reaching down she tore a handful of grass out of the yard and threw it as hard as she could.

Tiny green blades fell lightly to the earth.

"We'll just have to tie it to the roof. It's that or leave it," said Essex.

"Fuck no. Leaving this bed on the lawn is the only thing worse than taking it."

They found a pair of gardening shears and a thick coil of manila rope.

"Will Jackson mind if we take these?" he asked.

"Not if I go with them."

They hoisted the massive brass headboard onto the roof of the Supervan, laying the footboard in the opposite direction on top. Looping rope around the belly of the van they cinched it tight, but the bed still stuck out an arm's length on either side. Cheyenne got in and jammed her backpack between the seats and held the lunch meat on her lap. Essex started the van and it rattled to life.

"Fuck, hang on, I'm going to throw up."

She jumped out and ran to the woods but didn't make it. After she vomited she tore a few more handfuls of grass out to cover the spot so it wasn't obvious, then stalked back to the van.

"Are you pregnant?" he asked.

"No, I just can't be here anymore."

Essex did a three-point turn on the yard.

"You know we're going to have to stay with the van now or someone will just cut the ropes and take the bed," said Cheyenne.

"Or take the van."

As they turned onto the road, Cheyenne kept watch, making sure nothing came undone. Essex saw Cheyenne's face in the side mirror as she monitored the ropes. Her outgrown bangs whipped across her cheeks in the hot wind. When she was not looking at him, she looked as he had first known her, soft-eyed, unpredictable; she wasn't particularly affable but he'd rarely met anyone as kind. Most people were kind for show; Cheyenne was kind because she had no choice. The result of a deal struck between her nature and the universe, which she couldn't escape. Twice they had to pull over and resecure everything. Once, turning off for gas, the bed slipped and she had to lean out of the window to grab the rope to take up the slack until they could stop.

"Do you think it's better to be left for someone? Or for no one at all?" she asked. "If you had to choose." She looked over at him. "Oh lord. You're laughing. Why are you laughing?"

He coughed. "Ask Jackson." Looking at her face he instantly regretted saying it.

By afternoon she was dizzy from staring backward—forced to keep your eyes fixed on the past to get free of it? That's funny. Funny like the Greeks. She wished she could wipe the last week away.

They spent the night in a rest area on the Ohio border. Lying on the corrugated metal floor of the van with their clothes for pillows, Essex asked Cheyenne if she was okay. She didn't move and he thought she might be asleep, but a minute later in a precise voice she said, "I hate the *Moosewood Cookbook.* I hate educated white people. I hate Emily Dickinson. I hate snow and transcendentalism, and soup."

Then she rolled over and went to sleep with her face on an iron bed slat.

She woke in the early morning to a scratching sound, like rat claws on metal. She waited to see if it would stop. When it didn't, she got up and slipped quietly into the passenger seat. The sound was gone. Then it started again. Outside it was getting light. She peered around the parking lot then saw a face. A skinny white man with fuzzy blond hair and big freckles, bug-eyed and hollow-cheeked, was sawing at the ropes with what looked like a car key. She slipped into the back where Essex was, picked up one of the detached rollers from the bed, then slammed it against the inside of the van where the man was sawing. Essex bolted upright, terrified.

Cheyenne checked the damage outside. One rope was sawed halfway through.

"Jesus. We're going to have to tie it up all over again."

Essex looked at the greenway of bushes and thin trees behind the rest-area bathrooms.

"What was his plan?" he asked. "Drag it into the woods?"

"He was trying to cut five strands of one-inch rope with a key. He didn't have a plan."

But that wasn't true because she could see the plan too—a gleaming cage with a slatless frame. A sodden mattress on the forest floor, grass blades growing through the rails. King of the Brass Bed, he stands. In his hand, a goblet of acetone, his keys, a scourge, his scepter, a road flare, a ring of rock salt and Sudafed encircling the marriage bed over which he lords.

"We're a magnet for bad ideas," she said.

They relashed the ropes and the day heated as they drove the upper Midwest. They stopped for frozen burritos at a gas station and took turns watching the van. Cheyenne bought blue Gatorade but was too freaked by the color to drink it and poured it out.

Moving west, their meth-head problems got worse. In a gas station on the outskirts of Chicago they made the mistake of running to use the restroom at the same time and came out and found screws all over the ground from where someone had tried to detach a rail and slide it down under the ropes.

They crossed the Mississippi around dinner and pulled into a family restaurant. They parked the van right in front and asked to be seated by a window. They never took their eyes off it for more than a second, but when they went to check the ropes they found saw marks on one of the legs.

The next day, sun-dried and crack-lipped, they drove until noon without saying or hearing a word of human speech. The first person to talk to them was a short dirty man with metal teeth who offered them $100 for the bed while they were putting gas in the tank. They didn't say anything to the man and just got back out onto the interstate.

"Those were homemade teeth," said Cheyenne after a few minutes.

"They don't usually come in that shape."

Cheyenne dug out her phone to check for messages.

"Have you talked to Livy? Does she know I'm coming home?"

"She's in Alaska. Fishing. I'm not supposed to get into details."

"What do you mean?"

"Try her yourself."

"I have." Cheyenne shifted onto her other hip.

"Are you still mad?" he asked.

"No, I deserved it. But I do consider all debts resolved."

"What are you going to do when you get back?"

"I'm going to spend a week in bed and touch everything that's mine and doesn't belong to some guy and figure it out after."

Essex drummed on the steering wheel with his thumb. "Livy sold your bed," he said.

Cheyenne shrugged. "It was just a futon. I got it from the Buy Nothing people."

Essex looked pained. "She sold the rest of your records and books too. I tried to keep a few of your favorites, but she found them. Everything's gone."

She stared at him like he was a talking lobster.

They hit the channeled scablands. Their final night they took turns staying on watch. The rest area was filled with eighteen-wheelers, running motors and torn mud flaps, amber running lights. Both Cheyenne and Essex were restless in the cold desert wind that whistled through the van. In the morning when she was checking the ropes, Cheyenne saw that the two big brass bed knobs on the headboard were gone. They had been unscrewed in the night.

She kicked the side of the van. Essex came out to see what was happening.

"No one is ever going to want this bed. It's massively damaged and missing things and will never be what it was."

"Hold on, it's not that bad."

"It's not worth anything to those fucking people if it's not perfect. I know them. They're like that. You have to be perfect. God. We're doing this for nothing. Jackson gave me his family's bed and I can't even keep it in one piece." She slammed her forearm onto the side of the van. "Fuck!" she screamed.

"Stop doing that, it's stupid."

"There's not going to be a fresh start, not even a small one."

He reached for a lock of her hair. She grabbed his wrist to push it away but he shook her off.

"You have cheese in your hair and I'm trying to get it out."

She dropped her hands.

"I think it may be gum. But you don't chew gum, do you?"

He got the cheese out of her hair, which turned out to be peanut butter.

"I need to tell you something," he said.

Her bones turned to lead. "Please don't tell me anything," she said. "There's nothing I need to know that I don't know already."

"We've always been close. You know me like no one else."

"Don't. Just leave it."

She slipped sideways, buying space between them.

"You know how you love people," he said, "and feel responsible for them but how loyalty isn't always good? Like how I'm loyal to you and it isn't always good. But it's because we understand each other. We're special."

She closed her eyes to brace for what she knew was coming.

"I joined the marines," he said.

She let out a breath and laughed. "You're too old. There's no way they would take you."

"I leave for boot camp in two days."

Her eyes locked on him but her expression was predatory.

"The good news is I can help you out once I start getting paid," he said.

She started to shake. "What have you done?" Her voice scraped the words, the iron in her blood shivered, she laughed again. "Nothing? You have nothing to say."

She began to circle him. His shoulder blades knit together.

"What the hell do you think you're joining? You won't get a bank account because you think the interest goes to the NSA." Her voice rose. "You don't even think we should have agriculture! I've been in more fights than you have. If someone shot at you, you'd apologize to them."

He showed his palms and stepped back. "Isn't it better to have someone like me there than some psycho?" he said.

"You think this is a joke. That's what you think? A joke."

"That's not what I was saying."

"The president's own. Do you know what that means? They kill you first. Call them," she said.

"What am I supposed to say?"

"Say you made a mistake and you can't come. Tell them you're useless because it's true. Tell them you took a sheet of acid and thought you were in a movie where you actually gave a fuck about international politics!" Her voice was turning into something he'd never heard come out of a human; it soared, half growl, half whistle; she shouted, "You can't even bring yourself to hunt!"

She stopped and looked around. Seeing a trash can a few feet away she walked over and knocked off the metal lid. She saw a nest of beer bottles at the bottom. She grabbed one and walked over to Essex and smashed it at his feet.

"What are you doing?" he said.

She went back to the can and grabbed a second bottle. Essex, who had come out without his shoes on, pressed himself against the van. She threw the bottle at his feet. A trucker rolled down his window and threatened to call the cops.

"You're going to get us arrested," said Essex.

She found and smashed a third bottle.

"Why are you doing this?" she hissed. She stepped in at arm's length to him. "What the fuck are you thinking?"

"I don't know." He couldn't look at her. "I've got nothing going on. I want to know what I've got in myself. I can't tell. I could be anybody."

"And you can't think of any other way to figure that out? You can't think of anything? Like martial arts. Like hiking the Appalachian Trail. Spend a year alone in a cabin without water. Track a fucking bear!"

He raised his head and dropped his shoulders. His resistance gone, he looked at her.

"All those things are great, Cheyenne. But this only takes a signature."

She stepped in until she was six inches from his face. Her skin was the color of roses and her eyes were bronze. Every bottle she broke was a universe ending.

24 One Good Reason

KIRSTEN HEARD THAT CHEYENNE was back in Seattle from Essex, not from Cheyenne. She texted to say Cheyenne should come over for dinner once she got settled. Cheyenne's reply was polite and noncommittal. Kirsten sent back a large red heart, but only because there wasn't an emoji for mythic ambivalence.

Before Essex had left to get Cheyenne, Kirsten made him promise to stop by before boot camp even though she'd already said goodbye to him three times. She was hoping for a stroke of genius, some indestructible argument to keep him from going, but every reason she offered was met with a shrug. It was like he was twelve again. Saying nothing, changing nothing, shuffling around. The image of him at that time was still vivid; Essex, already big, sitting on the couch, shoulders caved, feet on the ground, eyes on the coffee table, knees up to his face—when had he turned into such a fucking follower?

"What happens if you change your mind?" she'd asked him. "Things don't always feel how you think they're going to feel."

"I don't think the marines care much about how I feel," he'd answered and then given her a little smile. "I also don't care much about how I feel right now. I'm going in circles." And she could see that he was.

She was too. At night, she was sure something was very wrong with her and she would start to sweat lightly as a kind of panic set in. The feeling was more akin to guilt than fear, as if she had done something very wrong and everyone was about to find out. In the daytime, it was gone. If something were truly wrong with her, she'd know it. It wouldn't be a mystery and she didn't need the medical-industrial complex to prove it.

She opened the door after Essex had left to let the breeze in. It was hot for summer in the Pacific Northwest and the blackberries on the bush by the parking lot were fully ripe. Livy said the berries in Alaska were sweeter and bigger. She couldn't imagine that being true. She wondered if Livy had talked to Cheyenne.

A week from now her health-care coverage would kick in and she would have her first doctor's appointment. She had promised Margaret that she would get all the tests her high premiums, slim paycheck, and $10,000 deductible would allow. By then Essex would be covered in mud and getting screamed at; Cheyenne would be wandering around avoiding her; Livy would be out in the Bering Sea chasing security, surrounded by salmon, covered in salt.

25 Egypt, Again

CHEYENNE STOOD in the front yard of Neighborsbane, waiting. Jackson's bed was fully assembled on the lawn. She'd advertised as an estate sale to draw more buyers. The scrap-metal guys were already circling. One, a man with white Brillo hair in thrashed overalls, pulled over in a tiny red truck piled high with refrigerators and offered her fifty bucks. The guy across the street had a brother looking for a bed who would probably give her $300 he said, but she was holding out for the antiques freaks.

The first wave came. Their alabaster skin in black Victorian clothing, they stretched forth hands with Georgian rings to touch the bedposts and frame. *Where are the bed knobs? Are those . . . saw marks?* They clicked painted fingernails on the headboard and offered her $1,000 but she couldn't stomach the thought of giving them her marriage bed. The price is fixed at $2,000, she said, and they floated away like driftwood.

She almost sold the bed twice but each time she could not imagine letting the buyer have it. By lunch the estate-sale folks were gone and the scrap-metal guys were back. Would she take $100? Cash right now.

Then a man in a brown vintage suit came up the street looking for the sale. Behind him several trucks laden with future scrap metal converged.

The man in the brown suit crossed the yard. "How much for the bed?" he asked.

The scrap-metal guy parked in the middle of the street and jumped out.

"Two thousand," said Cheyenne. "It's an heirloom. Totally irreplaceable."

The man examined the frame. "Okay, I'll go two thousand."

"I'll give you one-fifty cash," yelled the guy with Brillo hair, huffing across the grass.

The man in the brown suit took out his checkbook. He was offering her a kind of freedom. Starter money, an edge on the coming hustle. A little bit of grace and dignity. But her mind strayed to magic. The magic of being all in. The magic of being unafraid. Looking at the check she counted up all the different freedoms he was making possible: the freedom to leave or stay, the freedom of food preferences—but Cheyenne didn't care about freedom. What she wanted was liberation. She'd fucked up. She'd let everyone go in her life again. The man held out the check. Cheyenne reached past him and plucked three fifty-dollar bills from Brillo guy's hand.

"Take it," she said. "Melt it down."

Cheyenne went back inside and up to Essex's old room. It came with a stained mattress, purple and red walls with silver trim, a window that looked out on sewer work, and no sign that he had ever lived there.

There may have been a better way to persuade Essex to stay out of the marines than throwing bottles at him. There may have been a better way to apologize to Jackson for dragging him through her indecision than by having lots of sex then leaving again. There might have been a better way to reconnect with Livy than destabilizing her life by making her go on a road trip she couldn't afford.

All that remained of Cheyenne's personal things, which Essex had attempted to rescue, was a paperback edition of *The Guinness*

Book of World Records. Livy had apparently used it as a doorstop to carry out the rest.

DOG WITH THE LONGEST TONGUE, LARGEST GATHERING OF NATURAL REDHEADS, MOST BEER MATS FLIPPED AND CAUGHT, MOST MOUSETRAPS RELEASED ON TONGUE, MOST ENTRIES IN A 2-PERSON PANTOMIME ANIMAL RACE

—though 37 seemed low . . .

GREATEST DISTANCE FLOWN IN A WING SUIT. FASTEST TIME FOR DUCT-TAPING A PERSON TO A WALL. LARGEST STRUCTURE BUILT BY A TERRESTRIAL MAMMAL

—setting aside the Boeing factory, the Target warehouse, and the Berlin hangar for giant airships because one thing is obvious; the world is full of people with ambition.

BEST EMPIRE

—Egypt, again.

She looked at a picture of the beautiful black drag queen sporting the World's Longest Fingernails. Below was a footnote about the former champion who had held the record for decades but lost her nails in a tragic automobile accident. She had never been outgrown, but had reigned since the book's inception, each curling nail fascinatingly grotesque. The editors' reluctance to let her go touched Cheyenne. As if they could not bear to print an edition without her. She was no longer titled, but it was not her fault—and anyway if you blame yourself for every wreck that happens, even those you know you caused, you'll go crazy.

Selling the bed for $150 was not a triumph. It was not a chariot. It was not Roman, like victory. It was Greek. Like fate. The Universe had not broken open and rewarded her for boldness over grace. From the second the scrap-metal man banged the brass bed apart to strap it onto his truck, Cheyenne knew she had made a mistake. Jackson had cut off her phone plan and she had no credit for another. She'd sold the phone but that just bought a bag of groceries and a bus pass. The temp agencies she had signed up with the first time she'd come back had marked her as unreliable, and all she'd been able to find was a part-time minimum-wage job as a hostess in a chain restaurant where everyone, including the manager, was younger than she was.

She renegotiated terms with her landlord-roommate, Lester Minus. She would pay him $2 for every hour she worked. She would supply the pay stubs as proof. In return he would let her stay, under certain conditions. He could rent her room out on a nightly basis to travelers while she slept on the couch. She would receive a 20% cut of the profits. However, since she was also, in effect, renting the couch, 5% would go toward that, which left her with 15% on the room.

All boats rise.

26 Physics

ESSEX HAD THIRTY-SIX HOURS. He wanted to see the Section 8 housing projects where he had grown up. Passing through the parts of town with playgrounds and grocery stores, it started to rain. He walked on the thin dirt footpath along an arterial road, between bushes and intermittent guardrails, every passing car spraying him with water. It went on like this for a mile. Not all miles are the same. The mile between you and digging a ditch is shorter than the one between you and the body of someone you love—and that mile is different from the one between you and the person who needs money as much as you do, that you can't pay back. The mile he was walking felt like a combination of all three.

Arriving at a plywood outbuilding that had been turned into an AA clubhouse, Essex could already taste the weak coffee and fake creamer. It had been years since he'd been there, but it was the same. Brown carpet and baseboard heating, the same fold-out tables with Styrofoam cups and cubes of sugar on top, the same dry-erase boards with anniversaries and announcements.

The 5:00 p.m. meeting was going. The chair was a kempt and beefy man in a white dress shirt that was rolled neatly up his fore-arms, exposing an old India ink tattoo under a carpet of blond hair. Essex could smell his aftershave from the door. The guy was just the type he'd hated as a teenager. He didn't feel that way now. People should have a home. There should be someplace for everyone to go.

In the back of the room behind a small bar with a couple of stools, an old man was washing coffeepots in the sink. On the counter sat a half-eaten birthday cake.

"I'm looking for Sandy K," said Essex. "Is she still around?"

"Sandy K? Oh sure."

"Do you know where she lives?"

"Are you a bill collector?"

"I'm her son."

"I hate bill collectors. Talked to one last week. He's like, 'Aren't you folks supposed to make amends and pay everyone back?' So I told him Steps are in an order for a reason, fucker. First I got to get over my resentment and you ain't helping." He clapped Essex on the shoulder. "Wreckage of the present. Those assholes never have any sense of humor. Set yourself on fire in a motel and marry the same woman three times, then you'll have a sense of humor. People ask me how I can laugh at things like that. I tell them, I don't laugh because it's funny. I laugh because it's true."

Essex liked the old man immediately.

"Cake?" said the old man. "We're just going to throw it out."

Essex said no but the man cut him a slice and stuck a plastic spork in it.

"I know Sandy lives close by. Linda will know where. She's chairing the next meeting if you can hang out."

While Essex waited he ate the whole cake.

Sandy's new apartment was in a concrete honeycomb complex, plastic tricycles on the landings, a banner of a pot leaf or an eagle carrying a flag here and there, built on a slope with gray boat paint covering rotting stairs ready to slide into the nearest gulley with enough rain or a minor earthquake—like every place they'd ever lived.

He knocked on Sandy's door and she opened it.

"It's Christian," he said to save them both.

"Oh! My big baby." She opened the door and tapped her cheek. "Give me some. Come inside. Tell me everything."

He remembered her hair as dark, but it was light brown now. The muscle tone in her freckled shoulders was still there but her waist was wider and her legs skinnier. He recognized the chairs around the kitchen table. The walls were hung with platitudes, crosses, and dream catchers in no particular hierarchy. A sliding glass door opened onto a concrete balcony that overlooked a tennis court with a dipping net and piles of wet leaves.

She offered him a seat on the couch next to a bookshelf of ceramic dolphins.

"I collect them. My sponsees give them to me."

Reaching over, she pulled a pillow out from under him that had the Serenity Prayer in needlepoint on it. "One of my girls made it. She just did her fifth Step. Poor thing was trembling like a leaf. No need to be nervous, I told her. It's not like I'm going to hear anything new."

That, he could believe. By the time he was nine he'd heard all about abortions and car crashes and what dead people looked like. He could also make daiquiris and pronounce the word *cunnilingus.*

"I joined the marines," he said.

"At your age?"

"They took me."

"Are you thirsty?" she asked. "I have pop."

"I leave tomorrow. I thought you should know."

"You have your own higher power watching over you, baby." She walked to the fridge.

He felt sick but thought it might be all the frosting he'd eaten.

She came back with two sodas and handed him one.

There was a knock at the door and two girls came in. One was college age. The other had skin weathered from exposure or over-tanning and he had no idea how old she was.

"Hey Mom," she said.

Sandy tapped her cheek and she kissed it.

"Give me some sugar," Sandy said to the younger girl. "These are my newest babies. This is my son, Christian. He's going to be a marine."

Essex stood up to make room on the couch, but when he started to sit Sandy motioned for him not to. "Honey, it's almost seven and I lead a women's Step study on Wednesday nights so I'm going to have to ask you to leave."

His face got hot as he took it in. His feet were heavy and his head got light. It was the same feeling he used to have as a boy when he thought something would turn out one way and it turned out another.

She showed him out and kissed him noisily on the cheek.

"You'll let me know where they send you, won't you, baby? Another chick out of the nest," she said, not to him but to the women in the room, and closed the door.

He slept at Jared's. They played video games and ate half a pan of leftover lasagna Jared's mom had made. The next morning, they reported to the recruiting station where they were taken for a final round of medical evaluations and then from there to a hotel for the night. Neither he nor Jared had ever stayed in a hotel before, which wasn't something they realized until they were handed a room key. In the elevator up to their floor, Essex kept reminding himself he'd made a momentous decision, but also kept forgetting.

At dawn the new recruits were put on a bus to the airport. There were five of them, all under twenty, Essex guessed. He probably had five years on the sergeant. One of the recruits realized he'd set his camera on the ground when he threw his bag beneath the bus and left it. He turned to go back down the aisle but the sergeant blocked him.

"First lesson. Keep your shit together."

The recruit thought he was joking but the sergeant didn't move and eventually the recruit went back to his seat and the bus got back on the road.

"How bad do you think boot camp is going to be?" Jared asked.

"Probably awful."

He looked around at the other recruits. Even here, he was bigger than everyone else.

"I think I'm going to be carrying things," he said.

"Maybe we'll be snipers."

"I fucking hope not. The only person I'd feel okay about shooting is you."

Essex had never been on a plane before. He slowed everyone down in the security line because he wasn't sure for a minute if the TSA agent was joking when he asked him to take his shoes off.

They found their row. Jared had the window seat but Essex made him trade since Jared had flown before. Jammed in against the molded plastic, Essex tried to stretch his legs but it turned out flying wasn't made for people who were tall and square.

Across the aisle were two more recruits, Aggies from Texas, brothers, from their conversation. He pieced together that they had gotten drunk on a road trip, ditched their car, and signed up. One of the Aggies, the older one, finally went to sleep and conversation stopped. After a while the younger brother also dozed off, sleeping with his head on the other brother's chest. In their minds, outside the Brazos flooded like the Nile leaving jewels in the soil. Crystals that turned into mesquite trees buzzing with life, into locusts and copperheads and lightning.

As the plane began to taxi, then took off, Essex watched the runway drop away beneath him. Soon he could see the irrigated grasslands of central Oregon. Through the clouds he saw verdant fields dotted with what looked like giant marshmallows.

"What are those?" he asked.

"I think they're hay," said Jared. "Hey, how did you find Sandy?"

"Throw a rock in a clubhouse, hit a sponsee."

"Sandy K. More will be revealed . . ." said Jared.

"More always is."

The coastal range was closer now and the hills began to roll again. The white-dot hay bales disappeared. Rivers cut through fields and mountains to the ocean.

Thinking about Cheyenne, he felt more gone than ever. Someone told him if you rub a crystal hard enough it can change electrons on the other side of the universe. Electrons can't share an energy state. If one electron moves in, the other has to move out. On the other hand, if time happens all at once and nothing beats the speed of light, Cheyenne was here now and he just couldn't see her because he wasn't far enough away. Clearly this was bullshit. He probably shouldn't have learned his physics from hippies. But he liked the idea that wherever he was, whatever he did affected her. Because whatever she did certainly affected him.

Essex turned to Jared, who had fallen asleep. He wished he felt close to him or to any man. It has to happen when you're really young, though, or it never does. Even as a kid, each new neighborhood, each new school it was always the same closed ranks. Sorry boy. Should have been here in kindergarten. The only other path to brotherhood was to get nearly killed with someone else, which he and Jared had almost managed, but cars and drugs don't really count.

In San Diego the recruits were transferred onto a bus to the marine depot. As soon as they were driving, the lights went out and someone yelled, *Get your head down! Get your fucking head down!* Essex tried to see what was happening and a sergeant shouted full force into his face, *Head down! Head down now!* Then there was a loud bang and he ducked. Another bang. *Between your knees!* shouted the same sergeant. Fuck man, said Jared, what is this? I don't know, man, I don't know. There was a series of shot-like sounds from another part of the bus and a different sergeant barreled down the aisle. Essex lifted his head and caught a glimpse of the neighborhood going past. It looked normal. Then the sergeant was over him. *Keep your fucking head down. Between your knees! Between your knees! Now! Now! Now!* Essex tried to put his head back down between his knees but the bus lurched and his head hit the plastic back of the seat in front of him, jamming up his neck, and more loud noises he couldn't identify came from several directions. Both sergeants were shouting now and it wasn't stopping; the noise, the shouting, the lurching, the banging, it went on and on. Just when silence fell and he thought it would stop, it started again and after a while the periods of silence were worse than the noise. He lost his sense of time. He knew they were doing it. They were trying to scare them. Jared kept whispering, his words a single stream of sound—*I wish they'd fucking stop it's not funny Jesus what's happening is something happening I wish they'd fucking stop fuck can you see outside can you see where we are I can't see anything can you see?* And Essex could see because he had been raised by Kirsten and knew exactly what was going on. It was a play—the kidnapping, the darkness, the noise and fear—classic stage-one initiation. He could see the mechanics, but it's kind of like porn. Even if you know how it works, it works. If you're the type. Essex could see what the sergeants were doing yet he was consumed by fear. He was the type.

Get off the bus you fucking pussy! they yelled at the depot. Pussy? Essex laughed. What's bad about a pussy? Oh shit, apparently a lot. The guy shouted into Essex's ear with so much force the tiny hairs on his skin tickled. *Tubs!* yelled the man. *Tubs!* Essex looked around. Recruits were throwing everything they had into red plastic tubs. *Tubs! Are you deaf? Tubs!* Guys were tossing in billfolds and phones, taking off rings and crosses, pulling out photos of children. Essex didn't have anything but his driver's license and ten bucks. Jared slid two copper bracelets off his wrists and threw them in the tubs like they were snakes.

Essex had never seen so many men together. There must be women too but he didn't see any. If he had he would have walked over and stood next to them, which would be as nonsensical as anything else going on. After all, it wasn't like he could carve ten thousand years of history out of his belly. He'd know how to be, though; don't be a dick; don't touch anything; take it and don't say a word—his entire concept of masculinity came down to a list of what not to do. The line moved, pushed by a noise wall of strategic emasculation. His mood sank. It wasn't working anymore. It had on the bus, now it wasn't. He wanted to go back and put his head down between his knees in the darkness so it would work again.

27 Graveyard Point

LIVY HAD BEEN FISHING in Bristol Bay for weeks and the *Jani Lane* wasn't even close to breaking even. Every day boats headed south, shares split and done. Sometimes Livy heard them celebrating on shore. From the beginning, it had been a slew of failures. The sawn-off gillnetter was a floating textbook of structural weakness problems. Cracked fiberglass, swollen wood, leaking hull; every time she saw the welding on the reel's wheel mounts, she had visions of Jeremy on his knees with a cigarette lighter and a can of hair spray.

Most nights, Jeremy let the boat go dry in the shallows. *Fuck me if I pay to dock!*

Take a deck shower. Here's a bucket. Livy was pretty sure it was his own behavior ashore that he feared.

Life with Michael unfurled like a bad play.

LIVY: Hey Michael. When are you going to cash that check you found and pay me back for the beers you drank?

MICHAEL: If I pay you back now I'll just have to lend it to you again whereas if you give me the last of what you're holding it'll all work out because you won't have to borrow any money because I'll have it.

LIVY: Cash the check.

MICHAEL: I'm pretty sure it's worth more uncashed.

As the season ticked down, the situation became more grim. The only bright spot was the day Jeremy let Livy board the salmon tender *Dinah* to do the fish tickets.

"Maybe you can find out if that deckhand you like is also a pussy muncher," he said.

Okay weird Santa, fuck you, thought Livy.

LIVY: Hey Michael, what are you going to do with all your take?

MICHAEL: I'm going to build a spaceship palace out of T1-11.

LIVY: I'm going to buy a hundred pounds of gold and mint some coins with my face on both sides.

When the *Jani Lane* finally did break even the season had less than forty-eight hours to go. Whatever they caught in that window would be all they got. Every hour they could fish, they did. When they offloaded, the numbers would be sad but all profit.

On the final day a huge shoal of fish passed beneath them. A gift from the Great Mother Salmon, the promise of Michael's aunt Jennie. They filled their nets. Then the radio blared. Closing time. Jeremy yelled to reel faster and shouted, *Deckload! Deckload! They've called it. It's done. Get those fuckers on board.* And Livy saw the undulating silvery waves come to the surface. She'd never seen so many fish in a single haul.

Jeremy jumped down to help. I can't fucking believe it, tears flooding his eyes and running over his cheekbones into his beard. Then Livy heard a terrible creak and lost her balance. Grabbing the rail she looked toward the sound and saw the reel, straining against the nets full of fish, begin to shiver.

"Stop!" she yelled.

"Reel faster!" shouted Jeremy.

"The wheel mounts!"

"Fuck the wheel mounts!" He motioned for Michael to continue.

Livy waved her hands but it was too late. The mounts gave and the whole reel snapped off, plowing like a freight train down the center deck, just missing Livy and Jeremy before it took out the back of the boat and sank, dragging their nets and all the fish to the seafloor. Livy stared helpless as she watched her money slip away.

They had nothing. There was nothing.

Free of the weight of the reel, the *Jani Lane* bobbed happily in the water, oblivious. Jeremy turned to her. She saw madness in his eyes. A second later he bolted for the wheelhouse. The engine screamed as he turned the boat. She grabbed the rail again as she lost her footing.

He was accelerating, driving full throttle toward the shore of Graveyard Point. The closer they got to the beach, the faster Jeremy went. Soon she could see the faces of the subsistence fishers along the beach coming into view, their expressions frozen in a moment of disbelief as the *Jani Lane* approached. Surely the shallows would stop him. But the *Jani Lane* gained momentum the closer to shore it got. Jeremy was not going to stop. Livy and Michael looked at each other and jumped into the hold.

"Grab something!" yelled Livy.

Michael braced himself back against the box, wrapping his arms around a tangle of torn net that had snagged when the reel went over. The *Jani Lane* hit ground. The impact threw Livy forward then back, knocking the wind out of her, and she saw things fly over the hold and heard them crash onto the deck. The *Jani Lane* plowed forward, driving well up onto the beach where it finally stopped, half buried in wet sand. Jeremy hopped over the side of the boat and walked off, trailed by angry Alutiiq set-netters.

Livy and Michael hid in the hold until it was silent. Climbing out, they looked around. The deck was destroyed, there was nothing to save. They grabbed their seabags and went over the rail of the shipwrecked *Jani Lane*. Michael stared shell-shocked at the bay.

"I was here in my dreams. We both were. The water was copper-colored and we were riding a river of silver fish. I don't understand."

"There's no way in hell I'm going home without money," said Livy.

28 Mantra

ON HER NINETY-FIRST DAY as a security guard Kirsten had gone to the doctor and sat in the clinic answering questions about her appetite and sleep. *Were there any new stressful situations in her life?* Other than, say, all of them? Draped in a cotton square with flowers on it, sitting on an examining table covered with paper that crinkled each time she moved, she had tried to be thorough.

Technically, her doctor wasn't a doctor but a physician's assistant, and technically not that, since she was still in training, but no one else was taking new patients. The woman had been thoughtful, though, and demonstrated the ability to listen, which was better than most Kirsten had seen.

"We'll run tests," the woman said once Kirsten had laid out her symptoms.

The woman seemed nervous. Kirsten had wondered if it was her first time with something like this.

"A full blood panel and screening," the PA had said.

"How much will it be?" Kirsten had asked.

"That depends on your deductible."

The first round of tests led to an endoscopy, which led to a biopsy. Several days later Kirsten had to call in sick again and wait in a daisy-flower robe for them to tell her what she suspected by this point, that she had stomach cancer. Now they wanted to know the stage. Taking her back, they made her drink a silvery white metal. It's for the imaging, the CT tech explained. That's a shame, said

Kirsten, I was hoping it would turn me into a superhero. The CT tech laughed but Kirsten got the sense that the laughter was rote.

Kirsten had to call in sick to work again for the molecular tests. It's the flu, she'd said. It's going around, they'd said. You'll have to make up the hours, they'd said. Then a week later the doctors needed her to come in and talk about the results so she had to call in sick again, using the last of her accrued sick time. Her boss had informed her she would need to bring a doctor's note if she wanted to keep her job. She could bring the note but that wasn't going to save her job. She knew the drill. From now on she was going to have to be the perfect worker. Show up early and go home late. Leave those extra hours off her time card. Ingratiate herself to some schlub in human resources.

A month after her first appointment, the doctors were finally able to fully describe in detail the kind of cancer she had, its profile and prognosis. They were a little less clear on what she was supposed to do with that information.

"The oncologists say you need to get started on treatment," said the nurse navigator.

"I can't drop below benefited hours."

"They can't fire you for having cancer."

"They can fire you for every other made-up reason," said Kirsten.

The woman scraped at a piece of paint on her desk. "I wish we'd caught this earlier."

"I can't run to a doctor every time I have a stomachache."

"I understand." She closed her laptop. "We deal with what we've got, though, don't we?"

"No shit." Kirsten laughed.

"Do you have support at home?"

"My son will be back from boot camp at some point but I don't think they'll let him stay."

"Do you have other family?"

"Two daughters."

"Do they live here?"

"I'm not sure."

"You need to find out."

Fuck. It rang in Kirsten's head. Fuck like a mantra. Fuck like a song.

29 Eagle Ring

ESSEX HAD BEEN ALLOWED one call when he arrived at
the marine depot. He was not to converse but to read the paragraph
they handed him and nothing else.

I HAVE ARRIVED SAFELY AT MCRD SAN DIEGO.
PLEASE DO NOT SEND ANY FOOD OR BULKY ITEMS. I WILL
CONTACT YOU IN 3 TO 5 DAYS VIA POSTCARD WITH MY
NEW MAILING ADDRESS. THANK YOU FOR YOUR SUPPORT.
GOODBYE FOR NOW.

After that, all non-written communication had been cut off. He
wanted to tell Kirsten about the whole initiation thing and how the
marines were really good at it, mostly because he thought she'd
appreciate that (she certainly didn't appreciate anything else about
the marines), but despite his good intentions, when he sat down
with pen and paper his stamina for the story flagged. He had never
written a long letter.

After his thirteen weeks of boot camp he was to be sent to Camp
Pendleton for the next phase of training. Essex asked his drill sergeant if it was true. *You don't need to know fuck all, recruit! Because
it is no longer your job to ask why things happen to you. Things will just
happen to you.* Then the man pointed to the ground and told him to
do push-ups. Essex did as the man asked. A great calm flooded him.
There was no decision for him to make. His preferences, his expec-

tations and opinions, they no longer mattered. Kirsten had trained him to be the center of his own story, but he'd never really believed it. Now he was the center of nothing, and it was okay.

In the barbershop on base there was a sepia photo on the wall of a man long dead with thick lips and big ears in a wool-and-leather hat. With his hide strap across his chest, trim as a mailman, the man in the picture stared past Essex in the barber's chair. At his neck, a kind of priest's collar with an eagle, globe, and anchor on either side. A patch with a star holding an Indian inside. Stars on his shoulders too, each button an eagle, globe, and anchor stacking like sefirot down the front of his chest.

"Who is he?" Essex asked the barber.

"That's John A. Lejeune. The ultimate marine's marine," said the barber.

Essex wanted to be a marine's marine. It wasn't likely.

John A. Lejeune entered and left his mind at various points during the day. Sometimes he watched Essex in silent approval. Essex imagined his praise, spoken in code, nothing said, all understood.

It was week ten, just before the Crucible, his final test before becoming a marine, that the ghost of Lejeune visited Essex. Covered in Indians and eagles, anchors and stars, he waited for Essex to do something, but Essex didn't know what the man wanted him to do. He asked him, but John A. Lejeune looked through him like he didn't see him at all. A wicker man of leather, each eye a solar eclipse.

30 The Mother Narcotic

LATE IN THE SUMMER, after months of paying Lester a cut of her wages and sleeping on the couch when he Airbnb'd her room, which was rare, Cheyenne was actually deeper in the hole to him than when she started. What she had told herself when she first moved in, that a new direction would present itself, that she would hear something about Justine, that she was in the part of the story just before redemption, all that had faded. She was whatever she was going to become and not at the beginning, middle, or end but past it, living out the part not worth telling because nothing was going to happen.

Now at her lowest, she took a bus to the meth edge of the city where the plasma donation centers were. Hours later she was in a cubicle lying about lifestyle questions. The woman behind the desk tagged her fingernail with a glow-in-the-dark marker.

"Don't worry, it'll wash off in about a week. It's so we can tell if someone has donated elsewhere in the past five days. It's for your safety."

Cheyenne wondered if the woman believed that.

In the waiting room, a man in his forties sat down next to her. He had a black leather jacket, an India ink tear tattoo on his cheekbone, and a bandanna tied around his wrist.

"New client?" he asked. "That's an extra fifteen dollars."

It was crowded and the chairs were full. A security guard stood by the door with his arms folded, watching the room like any one of them might hatch into a lizard.

"Don't you hate that we're called clients?" she said.

"Better than 'population,'" he said.

The man laughed like Santa and unwound his bandanna.

"It's good to be new," he said. "I'm about to be new again myself."

Taking out a small nail clipper, he extended the tiny file. Glancing at the guard he began to file the nail with the glow-in-the-dark tag off his index finger. He did it quickly with his hands between his legs so that from a few feet away it just looked like he was twitching.

It took Cheyenne a second to get what was going on. Looking down at his other hand, she saw that his middle finger was also missing a nail. She was in awe of the sheer will it took to do that. He had made a decision. He had applied his determination to an idea and done it 100 percent. Livy, Kirsten, Essex—whatever their flaws, they could all do that, whereas Cheyenne could not.

Soon she was abed with a needle in her arm watching a cop-show marathon. A fat, hairy man in Snoopy scrubs came to check on her progress. The man without fingernails had filled his decanter and was rewarded with a fraternal smile. He would be released. He had done well. The phlebotomist looked at her decanter, sniffed, and turned up the draw.

"Some people are just slow," he said.

When she returned to Neighborsbane, she handed the money she'd earned from the plasma center over to Lester and he gave her the mail he'd been holding hostage. Among the junk circulars marked "Resident" was a letter. She thought it might be from Livy but it was postmarked North Carolina. The return address said Justine. She snatched it out of his hands and went to her room.

Sitting on her mattress with her back against the wall and knees tucked to her chest, she turned over the envelope. It was thin: It wasn't a long letter. She couldn't quite bring herself to open it. She dug her journal out of her backpack and got out the Polaroid they'd gotten from the roshi.

She traced Justine's face with her finger. She thought she saw sadness; she hoped that maybe she and Livy had something to do with that sadness, but the longer she looked, the more the woman's expression shifted until Justine's face went blank.

Cheyenne weighed the letter on the flat of her palm. She let her imagination run scripts of what might be in it: declarations, revelations, a check for a million dollars with a note that said, "Sorry." She wondered if the letter was better unopened. She scooted forward on the bed until her knees were in the square patch of natural light from the window. A jackhammer started outside. The crew on the sewer work yelled over the noise. The jackhammer stopped then started again.

Cheyenne ran her finger under the seal. Because inside it was change, and any change was good.

Dear Cheyenne,

Kirsten said you were looking for me. I believe you and Livy are 33 now? Is that right? I leave for a three-year retreat in Southeast Asia this fall. If you can get yourself here before that, we can talk.

Justine (formerly Ann)
Wat Dhamma
Bolivia, North Carolina

Cheyenne began to shake. Not because she had finally heard from Justine but because Kirsten had known where she was all along. She'd let Livy and Cheyenne traipse around the country, blowing up their relationship and going broke; she'd seen Cheyenne twice since she'd been back and never said a thing.

Cheyenne threw her journal at the opposite wall. After the high of righteous anger passed, hopelessness set in. This was worse than not knowing where Justine was because now Cheyenne knew but could do nothing about it. She had no car or credit. She was falling behind every day.

———

A week later, looking down the row of beds at the plasma donation center, Cheyenne wondered what had gone wrong. She was paralyzed. She couldn't even go yell at Kirsten. She was stuck. The people in the beds next to her were stuck. The whole place should be a roiling cauldron of revolutionary sentiment but wasn't. And what if some jail-tatted Norma Rae stood up on a roll-a-bed and held aloft a full decanter of plasma and yelled, *You get $25 and they sell it for $2,500!* Would they all swarm the receptionists and strike the donation centers nationwide? Would the men in the beds around her write talking points on lottery tickets? But instead of ripping out tubes and emptying their plasma onto the floor, they all lay there. Bickering over the TV channels.

Nothing was going to deliver any of them. Her plasma wasn't. Her minimum-wage job wasn't. Her desire to get to North Carolina wasn't. She thought about everyone she ever knew. How many worlds can you move through? Make a list of those you love. Do you love them now? The alcoholic and emotionally feeble, the old friends who had vanished into salaried jobs and attachment parenting groups, the academics, the sex workers, the twenty-year-old dishwasher at work and the twenty-five-year-old manager. A curving universe of interactions driving ever toward limits moving closer at higher speeds. The asymptote. The surface tension pulling everything upward. She could see why Justine had bailed. The mother narcotic appeared, still young. With supple movements and a blank expression, she leaned over and checked the plasma decanter and shook her head. Some people are just slow.

31 Raleigh

THE BERING SEA had unearthly beauty. The lead-colored water, the glacier-blue sky, the wild grass blown sideways; Livy was in the home of the jackass sublime. She and Michael had hitched a ride to Dutch Harbor on the salmon tender *Dinah*—Dutch Harbor, a shanghai of boats, a rhetoric crab. Perched at the outer edge of North America, it surpassed all other US ports in fish catch.

New Bedford. Former whaling capital of the world. Still recognized as the premier US port. In the dawn of the American self-concept, New Bedford had made its name hunting right and sperm whales. Drawn by bodies so full of oil and lamplight, sailors rounded the Horn for a lay ever longer, sailing into the vast Pacific. But as the whale populations dwindled and fossil fuels were discovered, the market collapsed. Who can compete with an endless supply of fuel? New Bedford was forced to turn its attention to other fish, but the port continued to decline as those populations also plummeted. Then borrowing on the genius of incentivizing depletion while stoking desire, a different economic driver could be engaged: rarity. It was the scarcity of sea scallops that helped revive the port—because who does not want what is about to be gone for good? As the price of sea scallops went up, so did the number of fishermen. It was a perfect solution. Profits soared. New Bedford could now rest secure in the knowledge that her last scallop would be worth more than all other scallops put together.

But how do you measure the wealth of a port? By volume of

catch or by price per pound? Dutch Harbor or New Bedford? The National Marine Fisheries chose New Bedford as the top US port, siding with the fourteenth-century Islamic scholar and jihadist Ibn Taymiyyah, first to describe the law of supply and demand: *If your desire for something goes up while your chance of getting it goes down, you'll be willing to spend . . . but if there's a lot of it, who cares?*

Dutch Harbor would have to wait. When its catch plummeted, it, too, could achieve greatness. A plethora of labor and a sea full of fish was only halfway there.

Livy knew she wasn't the only one looking for work on a crab boat. After all, goldfish are as cheap as pennies and bad jobs get measured in parts per million. But money could be made as long as there was something to catch. Like all hustlers, cabbies, and strippers, she believed in her own luck. That faith had not been destroyed by recent months, only shaken. There had to be a job for someone who could work without sleep. She'd failed so far, but her future was her own.

Livy was on the deck of the *Dinah* when she first saw the Makushin Volcano, a presage of arrival in Dutch Harbor. A man in an Elizabethan ruff flickered into view next to her. It was the same man she'd seen when she was on the highway with her sister. This time he introduced himself as explorer and venture capitalist Sir Walter Raleigh. Doffing his feathered cap, he looked over the rail of the *Dinah.*

"You look different than you do on cigarette packs," she said.

"I feel different," he said.

Raleigh squinted at the island shore then dismissed it with a sniff. "I would advise you not to plant," he said. "This is a terrible place to grow tobacco. Hold off until we get to El Dorado."

"How do you measure wealth? Fish or money?" asked Livy.

Raleigh pointed to a sounding whale. "Perfume! It's in their heads and bellies. A fortune!"

But the whale he pointed to was not a sperm whale and its head was not full of perfume.

"I lost my investment," said Livy. "I owe people money that I cannot pay."

Raleigh shrugged. "I lost an entire colony." Reaching into his doublet he retrieved a cigarette rolling paper on which was drawn a pencil sketch of a three-year-old. "Have you seen this girl?"

Livy shook her head. He folded the paper then clapped her on the back.

"Speculation! It's how money dreams of itself. You owe nothing!" he said.

Livy was not sure she agreed.

Raleigh flickered again.

"Be bold!" he boomed. "Be a citizen of the world!"

Then fading more than flickering, he held the fragile slip of paper above his head and let the wind take it; turning, about to say something else, he disappeared.

Looking at the shore, Livy saw glaciers and green shoulders folded and cut by fjords. She felt a rise in her sense of the possible. Maybe Raleigh was right. Maybe she owed nothing. She was not the first person in the world to lose money on a gamble. She would make it back. Three or four times over. She was here and Dutch Harbor was the home of the crab fleet. A billion dollars moved through this port every year. Surely she could catch some of it.

Coming into the port, though, her confidence fled. She took in the beaten little town of Unalaska. Whatever wealth had moved through there had kept on swimming.

Livy and Michael holed up for a week at an inn that looked like an abandoned grain shed. Every day they dock-stomped for work. Rumor had it that a boat called *Eliana* might need crew, but she wouldn't be there until mid-September. In the interim, they squeaked by on day labor and Bisquick.

Livy sent Kirsten her address at the inn but the only letter she got back was disappointingly short. A horoscope that Kirsten had annotated and a few updates. Cheyenne was living at Neighborsbane; Essex was doing okay at boot camp. A week later she got a letter from Essex. It was also short but came with a picture of him. With his new crew cut he looked like a bouncer.

Dear Livy,

I have found perfect working socialism and it is called the Armed Forces. You get food and a place to live, health care, education. I'm getting that root canal I've needed for years. Boot camp is beyond words. They actually make you do all those stupid things you see in movies. Sometimes I don't feel the way I'm supposed to about it. They make you care about things by holding other people hostage, though. It turns out you do all sorts of things for other people you would never do if it was just you.

Don't lose a finger or an eye (I don't know how to end letters).

Love, Essex—also, I have a bank account and get regular deposits. They give you ten days between boot camp and training. I'm going to go home and buy something for Kirsten. I'm not sure what. What do you want?

I want money, I want a job, I want to come home with something . . . Livy folded the letter and put it in her back pocket. Thinking of Essex made her think of Cheyenne. She felt a twinge of guilt.

The next afternoon she found a necklace in the lining of her jacket that must have slipped down through a hole in her pocket. The necklace was one of Cheyenne's favorites. Livy had taken it to sell in an emergency. She held it up, a Chinese jade pendant on a 24-karat-gold chain with two fixed gold beads to accentuate the collarbone. Livy went to see if she could find a pawnshop of any kind but still couldn't make herself sell it. She pushed the necklace back down through the hole into the lining and sewed it up. After all the money her sister had cost her, they were even.

Weeks passed. Ferries stopped running. The season changed. Finally, the crab fleet amassed. The *Eliana* came but the captain offered them a single job that they could split for a flat fee at greenhorn pay. Take it or leave it. Having no alternatives, they signed on.

On the day before departure, the docks changed. Livy could see the electricity running between people. Their eyes sharp and shark-like, they moved faster. It was contagious. Whatever this crab season would be, it was about to happen. She and Michael climbed the hills of subarctic grassland above the old Russian Orthodox church. They found wild ponies standing in a few inches of snow, already fallen. The water and sky were every gradation of blue, passing through shades but arriving nowhere. Michael told her about a forest of drunken trees. Drunk? Drunk. Leaning. He wanted to go into the church on the way back. It reminded him of his mom and being a kid. Livy agreed but didn't really want to go. In the seat next to him, she waited out the service, ignoring what she could. This is where they send them out, fishermen, like they did before electricity, like they did before radio, out through these white painted timbers, out into the ocean. Out like Essex. To wherever.

32 The Crocodile and the Clock

KIRSTEN SAT before the oncologist, shifting back and forth in time.

The closest she'd ever come to death was her pregnancy. Her labor had not gone well. At thirty-nine weeks she woke up in a wet bed at dawn and called Margaret. While she was on the phone, Ann drank castor oil and started walking loops around the block. By the time Margaret arrived, Ann was in labor as well. Ann delivered quickly, but Kirsten was not progressing. Margaret raised the possibility of transferring her to a hospital but Kirsten begged her to wait. At thirty hours, Margaret gave her a tiny injection of morphine to allow her to rest. She woke up disoriented, in hard labor.

It was not so different—loss of appetite, cramps, nausea. You think something is wrong but then you think, no, it's always like this, pains, moods, things come and go. They run tests and say . . . *You're pregnant. You have swallowed a watch. Now the crocodile will always be able to find you.* Then later, you don't eat like you used to and get nauseous. There are ghost pains—but isn't it always something? The stress of scrappy living, hormonal changes. You're fifty-two. What do you expect? They run tests and come back and say . . . *We have found a clock inside you. But it's the windup kind.*

———

"You shouldn't feel like you did something wrong," said the oncologist. "Stomach cancer is often undetected until stage three or four. It's like ovarian. What we have to do now is begin treatment."

"I don't want to rush into surgery."

"You're not a candidate. Have you spoken with your children?"

Kirsten heard the light clicking of her own teeth as her jaw trembled and wondered if it was audible outside her head or only visible.

"You're free to do what you want," said the oncologist, "but in your case I think aggressive treatment is the only real option."

"This from the people who brought you floating wombs, Lysol douches, cigarettes for pregnancy weight, and episiotomies," said Kirsten.

"It's your choice."

"Not really it isn't."

A fat tear ran down her cheekbone.

As a teenager Kirsten had pranced into Margaret's office and announced she was not terminating her pregnancy. Margaret did not crown her with praise or throw her a party.

"Women died so you could have a choice," she said.

Puffed up like an affronted pheasant, Kirsten said, "I made a choice."

"The hell you did. A real choice has three questions: What the fuck am I going to do, and who are these bastards I'm talking to, and is this bullshit even real? Which of these have you asked?"

As an adult she knew how to ask those questions, but no matter how she asked them, the choices looked no better.

SHITTY FUCKING OPTION #1: Do rounds of chemo and
    radiation and hope it works for a while.
SHITTY FUCKING OPTION #2: Go to Mexico for experimental
    treatment. Consort with rich people afraid of death. Start a
    blog.
SHITTY FUCKING OPTION #3: Do nothing.

———

Kirsten had seen stars in total blackness once. She'd been twenty-one. She was driving across the desert her first night away from the girls and there it was, the galaxy, uncountable specks of dust moving in circles lighting the dark. She drove under the canopy, vacillating between an awareness of brilliance and sorrow—because she hadn't known magic was real until she saw this, because she'd never really been anywhere and now probably never would.

Two years. Two years. Two years of Cheyenne awake while Livy slept. One sick then both sick. One bleeding because the other knocked her down. She'd learned to parent with stomach flu, with fevers and food poisoning. Two years. Two years of never going to the bathroom alone, showering with the curtain open so she could hear what was going on. She'd learned not to scream at them in the grocery store when she couldn't keep them from running through the aisles. And she'd learned not to cry when all the other mothers looked at her like she was trash and made comments about controlling her children. At night after she put them to bed she'd walk into the living room stunned by the day. She'd sit in a chair and sob. She'd made the wrong decision. On everything. Everything— her deep independence and love of autonomy, her night-owl ways and desire for solitude, her dreams of travel—it was all gone. She couldn't stand a single thing about her life anymore. She hated being a mother. But she loved her girls.

She was in a metaphysical bookstore—because it didn't take a genius to know she was more than materially fucked and symbolically fucked but archetypally fucked on a grand scale—trying to speed-read a book on tarot when Cheyenne pulled a whole row of books off the bottom shelf and Livy ran out the door.

A young woman in the Feminine Mysteries aisle ran out, snatched Livy up, and brought the furious eighteen-month-old back to Kirsten, who already had Cheyenne by the arm. After passing the flushed and kicking Livy back to Kirsten, the woman cleaned up the aisle, putting the books back. Then a miracle happened. She offered to watch the girls so Kirsten could finish reading the chapter on tarot. An act of kindness so powerful it broke her life in two. Kirsten before that, Kirsten after.

A month later she and the young woman dedicated themselves to the Goddess, and for Kirsten's twenty-first birthday the women of her newly minted coven took her kids for the weekend, filled her tank with gas, and sent her to a hot spring in the desert.

Driving across a desert free of light pollution, liberated for two nights from motherhood, Kirsten searched for her planets but couldn't tell them from planes. The constellations had also been easier to see on paper. The only things she recognized were the Big Dipper and the North Star. Propelling herself toward a nameless star at the top of her windshield, counting up the miles behind her, she tried to outrun motherhood. Hitting 110 miles per hour on the freeway, the car rattled, breaking apart in the atmosphere. Holding the wheel her arms shook; burning up in the waves of gravity, battered by planetary tides, shards of a life, violence of light, she was never going to get there.

Option #3 it was.

33 Hathor

CHEYENNE WALKED UP to the ticket kiosk in the basement parking garage and tapped on the bulletproof glass. Kirsten slid the window open.

"I got a message you have something for me," said Cheyenne.

"Wait in the locker room. I have to clock out."

Kirsten pointed to a door in the corner of the garage.

Cheyenne found the lockers but didn't sit. She was still angry. She'd come ready to let Kirsten have it. Seeing her in the kiosk, though, in such an anonymous position, was unsettling. She also had no idea what was coming or what her mother wanted to give her.

The locker room had gray tile walls and a hamper. There were three OSHA posters and a sink without a hot-water handle. It reminded Cheyenne of the women's changing area at the public pool where Kirsten made them take swim lessons in grade school so they wouldn't drown if they fell off the ferry deck. Coming home reeking of chlorine, deaf from screaming kids and lifeguard whistles, with hunger headaches, their hair stiff from chemicals, eyes burning, they'd burst into the apartment where, instead of beans and rice or mac and cheese, Kirsten would have vegetarian lasagna or shepherd's pie with mushrooms waiting. They would devour it, skip homework, and go to sleep. She could see Kirsten as she was then. Long hair, horselike muscles, wildly alert—she wanted that Kirsten.

The door opened and Kirsten came in. She sat on the bench and unbuttoned her fake–cop uniform shirt. Underneath was a cheap white bra with light brown stains at the armpits. Her belly was a series of gentle rolls. She seemed to have lost weight, which gave Cheyenne a prick of concern because Kirsten didn't diet. Diets were a form of violence used to keep women self-obsessed and small. But then Kirsten also didn't work as a wage slave.

"You gave her my address," said Cheyenne. "Which means you had hers all along."

"Whose?"

"Oh don't be cute about it."

"Do you remember what you said when you first brought Essex home?" Kirsten asked. "You said, I don't want him but he needs to go somewhere. I cried like crazy. You were seventeen. Do you know why I cried? It was the first time I knew that I was a good mother. First, because you couldn't leave an eleven-year-old on the street with no one. And—don't look at me like that—second, because you brought him to me."

Kirsten dialed the combination on her locker.

"How much have you talked to Ann?" Kirsten asked.

Cheyenne looked at an OSHA poster. She had written a letter but nothing came back.

"She had a choice in what happened," said Kirsten.

"Are you saying someone can't regret a decision they made? 'Cause I sure as fuck do."

Kirsten reached in her locker and took out a packet of letters. She set them on the bench.

"This is every letter I have from Ann. Not one missing. Look and you'll get answers."

Cheyenne felt anger come through her skin. "Why don't you just tell me?"

"They're not my questions," said Kirsten. She pulled out her keys and worked the Toyota key off the ring. She put the key on top of the letters and slid them toward Cheyenne. "Do what you want. Go." Kirsten's eyes teared up.

"Don't do that," said Cheyenne, "don't you dare. None of this ever had to be secret. You made your own bed. I don't feel sorry for you. What's happening now between Livy and me is your fault. Essex joining the marines is your fault."

"How the hell is Essex joining the marines my fault?" said Kirsten.

"You want him to be what he's not. He's never living up to his potential. None of us are. I'm sick of being told I have something exceptional in me or that Livy does or Essex. It's such bullshit. I can't just work in an office. Essex can't just drive a cab. Livy can't just paint a fucking boat. It all has to be part of some stupid story line about our path and manifesting some agenda. You know, I met a lot of people who believed that shit back East and they're different from us. You know how? They're rich."

Cheyenne remembered that whenever she intervened on a conversation with something astute, Jackson's friends acted like she was a fish that suddenly began to speak. They marveled. They listened. Then they congratulated themselves on discovering a talking fish. Kirsten didn't witness it. Jackson missed it because he was it. And it's not like there was a manual for all the rules either. You can't say "black." You can't call someone a Mexican. Don't ask how much something costs or what someone makes at their job. If you find a bargain, keep it to yourself unless it comes from a thrift store, then brag. The part she never mastered was how to talk about her life. She wasn't an up-and-coming lawyer or filmmaker or founder of an NGO. She wasn't an academic. Tell me about yourself. She hated the question because it was not a question. It was a command: Present an entertaining (short) monkey dance about your life, a sentence or two to relieve the listener of having to think about you—*Dana is a brilliant surgeon who fell in love with a woman who works with rescue horses and now writes children's books and lives with her in Texas . . . Robbie is a genius mechanic who can fix or build anything (you really*

should get his number), who's rehabbing this spooky, haunted house into
a bed-and-breakfast a few miles from our summer cabin—a vocation,
connected to an aspiration, connected to a place. She couldn't do it.

Cheyenne shook her head and folded her arms. "You know I'm
not sure what you thought you were teaching us but it's not helping."

Kirsten stood up fast and yelled in a sharp voice, "I am not
going to apologize for thinking the three of you have possibilities.
For thinking what you have inside you may be of some use in the
world and suggesting you get off your ass and figure out what that
is. And I'm not going to buy into the Man's rules about who can
be someone and who can't." She lowered her voice. "This is just a
transition time."

"See?" Cheyenne shouted. "That's how you undermine every
moment. It's never enough to just be somewhere doing something
lame without any fucking reason. No, we're all supposed to be dragging some rock of karma up a mountain at the same time." Her
voice cut out because her larynx clenched and she couldn't get air
and a sob burned up through her throat. "I don't think I've ever felt
free in my life. That's why Essex isn't here. Because he thinks it isn't
good enough to just be alive. You're going to kill him and I will never
ever forgive you."

Kirsten turned the color of ash. Tears left claw marks on her
cheeks. Splotches of red appeared on her pale chest and arms.
"That is not true. That's not true. Don't say that."

Cheyenne snatched the letters and the key and left.

Halfway across the parking garage, it occurred to her that the
sound of their fight would have rung loudly in the building, ampli-
fied by the tile and tin of the locker room, and further by the concrete hallway and the shape of the parking garage. Everyone within
two hundred yards would have heard them yell. Security guards.
Clerks in the office. Patients. Doctors walking to their cars. So why
had no one come to see what was going on? Or was it just that the
sound of two women screaming didn't scare anyone?

———

Cheyenne had $326 dollars of her rent and bill money. She could sleep in the car. If she drove south then across, most nights would be warm. At the co-op she bought a nine-pound vat of peanut butter and in a proud moment of thrift, passed on the tampons. She would roll her own. Without a word to her landlord, the next morning she put her keys on the floor of her room and drove away from Neighborsbane. *Fuck me if I ever see it again. The girls' karma is their own. If they're meant to find me they will.* Anger at Kirsten choked her.

She drove east through Snoqualmie Pass. Blades of sunlight cut between ridges, blinding her on the curves. Radio stations dipped in and out. The Toyota sounded like a cheap hair dryer as it gained elevation. At lunch Cheyenne pulled into a Dairy Queen. Queen? For a moment she imagined the great lover Hathor, her cow's head looming, drunk, over the grill, dreaming of bloodbaths and rivers of beer. But the girl who made her milk shake was not Hathor. She was a teenager who wrote tickets in backward-slanting round script.

Cheyenne saw a picture of a toddler taped to the register.

"She yours?"

"Three next Monday," said the girl.

The girl tucked a piece of frosted hair into a bobby pin. She was just the type Jackson's friends liked. They would have said she was great. Great like a kitschy oil painting. Great like a sixty-foot statue of Paul Bunyan. Cheyenne spooned peanut butter into her chocolate shake when it came. She had more in common with this girl than she had with the people she'd spent the last six years around.

In the parking lot she went over the letters again, but all she saw was someone devastatingly young. Justine described the other novices scathingly . . . They barely laugh and I have to admit, there's a lot more bowing and counting than I expected. I'm starting to wonder if this is about liberation at all. It seems more like watering yourself down and pretending to be Japanese. Yesterday in Zazen I wanted to yell, "You know the Japanese are famous for vibrators too." They could use a clit tickler here. I love how you aren't threatened by me. And in another letter . . . I was thinking about what you said about the importance of holding your head up. I do. Forgive me but rolling over isn't something to celebrate . . .

and . . . I'm tired of what people think. If freedom was an animal, the first fucking thing they would do is stun it, throw it in a cage, and take pictures with a caption reading "Wild." The letters came from Vermont, India, California . . . I like the idea that you can drop whoever you were and be something new. But I have to ask myself, if I am not who I was, was I ever really that? Right. And if every social circle Cheyenne had ever drifted through ended up at the same party, they would have all left.

After the Great Prairie Monastery in Montana, Justine had gone to a monastery in California. Then she was in Los Angeles, which was burning . . . In the street everything was shattering and everyone was shouting. The cops beat a man right on the corner I was standing on. A window got smashed behind me. People poured through like a dam that broke. They flooded into the store and grabbed everything. They took some high-ticket things, but mostly took whatever—cheap toaster ovens when they probably had better ones at home, black-and-white TVs that you could find left on the street, pencils, staple guns—that's when I saw. It wasn't contraband. They were totems. A semitruck was stopped at a light and they moved there. Later I heard they took the man out of the truck and that, too, made sense. She related what she saw to things she'd read in the Upanishad and to her own destiny . . . You talked about greatness and I do sense a greatness in myself but I don't know what kind. I feel like there's something I'm about to find or figure out, like I'm on the edge of some kind of understanding. One thing I can say, I've learned more in my first week here than in my entire time at the monastery. Like about the Jains, states of enlightenment. WTF?? Nobody ever talked about them (!!), not at Tassajara or Great Prairie. That's what I want. I want to see through all of this and be free for real.

Yes. Free for real.

34 The Well

THE *ELIANA*'S CAPTAIN was a physically unimpressive man with a forgettable face and a voice that faded into background noise. Livy had to turn her ear toward his mouth to catch his words. They were finding crab steadily. But whatever came over the rail, pots empty or crawling with king crab, his face remained illegible. She wondered at first if he'd had a stroke or some palsy but saw no evidence of paralysis, only something unfinished, an expression akin to memory loss, not so much grasping after the past as releasing the idea that it mattered. As she watched more closely how he interacted, with her, with Michael, with the four other deckhands, she began to read his quiet expressions. It was like a code that she earned her way into, and as she got better, his respect grew. She saw it in the barest shift of his mouth, his esteem for her uncomplaining nature.

From the outset the experience was different. Livy had never worked in such seas. Soon they would be plunged into shamanic darkness. Morning would come later and later as the light left. The lengthening night was already affecting her more than she'd expected.

Although the brutality of the job was legend, she preferred living at sea out of sight of land. She spent every waking hour grinding cod and pushing pots. She loved how it required everything. How her mind didn't wander. How her body preached. She cut bait when she couldn't feel her hands or arms and sorted crab when she could barely open her eyes in the freezing spray. She knocked ice off the rail with a sledgehammer and almost went over twice in her first week. The darker the days got, the deeper the troughs, the blacker the rolling waves, the more the *Eliana* was sheeted with ice—and what do you do when there's more work than can be done? They almost never slept.

Once, when they were following the crab out into the abyss, Livy saw an island lit up on the horizon. It looked like a spaceship landing on the water but turned out to be a drilling platform.

"They're all over," said the captain, who had come up behind her.

"I've never heard anything about them."

"What happens out here is invisible," he said.

The idea of something so massive going totally unseen made Livy light-headed. A whale to the side of the boat slapped the water with its tail and dived. Sir Walter Raleigh took shape beside her. He raised his hands in the air in a gesture of delight. *Their heads are full of money and land!* Then his face fell and he dropped his hands. *Not a whale, only history.* He clicked his tongue, disappeared. Waves rippled out from where the whale had not sounded. On the surface, a rainbow slick of oil undulating on the water.

The early test wells in the 1970s had come up with little and the amount of oil they found wasn't worth the cost to get it out. But that was a different time. Rarity. The last drop worth more than all the drops before. Looking at the drilling platform, Livy became nervous in a way she couldn't explain. She felt the sweep of a world more powerful than she would ever be. No matter what anyone said, if there was money to be made, people like her would always go—down into the ocean, out into space, into the middle of the Bering Sea.

The size of the rig was beyond anything she'd seen before. She had a sense of vertigo, or maybe it was more like looking out the window on a fast train when you know you're going forward but it feels like slipping slowly backward. As they approached, she could see the name. PRAJNA Deepwater. PRAJNA. Deep wisdom. Fed by the breath of the universe. Vital life force. What asshole names their drilling company PRAJNA?

An alarm bell rang, marking a shift change. White floodlights bombed the decks all at once with a new and sterile day. The blaring, buzzing sounds louder than any Livy had ever heard. She covered her ears. The searing whiteness of the industrial lights made her shade her eyes, but still she saw workers filing in lines up onto the rig's deck. It was an eternal factory without night. Heat from the center of the earth vented through the rig and billowed to the sky.

"I still can't believe they built it," she said.

"You can do anything you want here and nobody will care," said the captain.

Then he walked away. Someone yelled at her to get the ice off the rails. She picked up the sledgehammer.

Alone in a bunk for a rare nap, Livy closed her eyes and the world went black. She slept more heavily than she ever had in her life. Even her dreams had no shape, only moving shadows blending into other shadows.

She woke up with someone on top of her. She thought it was Michael crawling in to sleep, but it was the captain. He put his hand over her mouth and leaned his weight on his forearm. His elbow dug into her shoulder just below the rotator cuff and cut her circulation off. With his other hand, he reached down and grabbed hold of her base layer and yanked them down. Michael came down the ladder and stopped. She couldn't call out because the captain's hand was over her mouth but he saw what was happening. Their eyes met. Terror flickered on his face and he turned and ran back up the ladder. The captain started pushing up inside her, jamming her neck against the back of the bunk. A minute later he came, whimpering. A bell rang and he rolled off.

"We better get up there," he said. He zipped his pants and went above decks.

She was in two positions in time. Three minutes before was one time. Now was another. The whole thing was gross, marginally painful, and quicker than a sneezing fit. How could it be anything at all? She found a kitchen rag to wipe herself off and threw it in the trash. Snapping herself into her foul-weather gear, she went up and two crew guys were waiting to come down. Passing them, she couldn't look them in the eye.

On deck she was sent to the rail. *Get that ice off!* She felt like she'd stepped into a painting of a boat and was not on the boat herself. She went to work on the ice, then hooking bait to the pots. All her life she'd been told what to do in this situation, but none of it applied here. Why couldn't she just get raped in a parking lot like everyone else? Lowering a string of crab pots into the sea, she had a clarity beyond any she'd known. She could see the crystal structure of snow. She saw the size of herself and the size of the sea.

That night in the galley the captain treated her as he had the day before. She looked straight at him. Michael brought her a bowl of chili. But Michael she could not look at.

Something important happened.

Nothing important happened?

She crushed a couple of saltines over the chili.

This changes lives?

This is no more than a bad day.

The captain was concerned about the temperature. The temperature was dropping and the captain worried the crab might freeze.

She hadn't bitten his hand when it was over her mouth.

"Eat if you're eating," he said.

The danger is falling off the boat.

The danger is staying on the boat.

She went to the head and shut the door. She made herself cry the way someone who's swallowed a bunch of pills makes themselves throw up, because it's the responsible thing to do. A few shallow tears was all she got. The rape had lasted longer. She gave up. His opinion of her, her reflection in the captain's face. All that tantalizing withholding, the way he held the ring over her head, for his respect for her fortitude, his appreciation for her skills. She felt sick.

Now that made a tear roll! She laughed, brash and ugly. Never trust a woman who cries when she's angry.

She was near the rail when she saw the captain heading in her direction. He was thirty feet away but froze. At the last moment, she stepped back to let him pass as a heavy wave broke and she lost her footing. He grabbed her upper arm but she couldn't tell whether he was pushing or pulling. She reached for the rail. He jerked her upright.

"You'll go right in if you fall here," he said.

She searched his shapeless face. She had no idea what he was telling her.

She needed to get to land. But they were days from going in.

The temperature dropped and the seas grew bigger. They lowered a second string of pots. A deckhand near Livy tossed the shot and a length of rope snaked through the blackness. Livy watched transfixed until the last buoy bobbed past. Michael came over.

"Stay away from me."

"Let me help."

"I can deal with what he did. What you did was awful."

"I'm sorry. I don't know what happened. I froze. I don't know why."

His words were too close. He didn't get to have those same feelings. She pushed him aside.

"I have other problems."

But he didn't get it. It never entered his mind.

She had a hundred and twenty hours to find a morning-after pill. Seventy-two were gone.

Livy had to get off the boat and find a plan B. She'd slept what hours she was allotted only in the presence of two or more crew, and never when the captain was in the cabin, but she couldn't come down from the state of paranoia and was starting to see trails. An aura over the crab in the hold, a sparkle over the deck. Sometimes she saw Raleigh on the bridge but he had nothing to say to her.

Fifty-four hours.

She was at the rail when word went around. Crab was freezing in the hold. A few had exploded. They went full steam for the processing plant on the island of Akutan to transfer what crab they could before they lost it all.

Forty-eight hours.

35 Akutan

LIVY SAW THE ISLAND'S LIGHTS emerge from the dark.
She had to get off the boat. It was animal, not logical. The second
the captain stepped off to do paperwork, she had to be gone. They
docked. He walked toward the bright lights. She bolted. Leaving
behind her hard-weather gear, her seabag, and all her work hours,
the only money she had in the world, her only chance at coming
home with something. She left the *Eliana* with nothing but what she
was wearing.

Akutan. With its sharp slopes of mineral-rich vegetation, its
hyperactive stratovolcano, its wide caldera and lava flows pouring
forth new shorelines on the Bering Sea. With its deep and natural
harbor, it is where the Unangan people settled and, later, where venture capitalists saw a whaling station. Despite new sources of fuel,
the whale processing plant processed bowheads and humpbacks,
though mostly for dog food, before being abandoned. Oral histories
collected in the great anthropological boom of the 1930s capture
the memory of locals who were children at the time, brought to
the station on field trips. They spoke of the smell and trying not to
slip in the whale grease and blood on the docks. One girl described
seeing the giant head of a sperm whale with a hole cut in the top
where buckets lowered in and came back up again and again filled
with milky oil. Years later, a new processing plant was built on the
edge of the Unangan village. This time the company made its own
harbor, blasting into the volcanic rock and ice, dynamiting, taking

a half-circle bite out of the mountain. Now, at water's edge, the processing plant: a cannery for a thousand workers with everything needed to work in the perpetual dusk of summer and the perpetual night of winter.

Once ashore she had no idea how to get off the island. She was halfway out on the Aleutian chain. There were no ferries or planes and the fishing boats weren't going anywhere except back out to fish. Walking toward the village she asked a cannery worker how people left when they had to. Hovercraft, helicopter, he said, but not in this weather. She counted back the days. Her chance of getting pregnant was high.

There was a clinic at the plant but there was no way in hell she was going there so she went to the one in the village where a very nice Unangan woman told her they were out of morning-after pills but could order them. The woman called the clinic at the plant. Same story. She tried Unalaska. No luck.

"A few days," the woman said.

"I don't a have a few days," said Livy.

"You'll have to go to Anchorage when the weather clears."

Outside the clinic, Livy was at a loss. She walked through the mud streets between the few scattered buildings that made up the place. Shadows seemed to eat whatever electric light there was. She saw someone coming toward her but didn't realize it was Michael until he was three feet away.

"This is all I have," he said, holding out two crumpled twenty-dollar bills.

She snatched it and kept walking.

"I might be able to get more. A guy at the bar last time said he'd pay me for a blowjob. I've never done that but I'll do it for you."

"It's not the same thing, you know. You can't make it right."

He looked away. "What are you going to do?"

"I'm going to get out of here."

"How?"

"I don't know!" she yelled. She turned and walked back to the clinic. "Don't you dare follow me."

The woman at the counter was surprised to see her again.

"This situation," Livy drew a vague circle around her body, "is not my fault. I did not choose it. I am a very careful and thoughtful person. I am a responsible person. I have great self-control. I would not forget to use birth control." Her throat tensed. "I am also a private person." She paused. "Do you understand? I cannot," she pointed toward the harbor, "get back on my boat. Help me."

The woman rubbed her temple. "The nearest real police station is in Unalaska."

"I just want a morning-after pill. I have a hundred and twenty-seven dollars. And thirty-six hours to take it. Help me get out of here."

The woman nodded and picked up the phone. "I have a cousin who works for the airline. They get discounts."

The woman dialed. Livy stepped back as the woman spoke to her cousin. She heard the words *jump seat* and *favor*. She heard *unofficial* and *family* and *thank you* and *beer*. The woman covered the receiver with her hand and motioned Livy closer.

"If you can get to the airport in Unalaska, she can get you to Anchorage."

Livy took a deep breath. Another idea surfaced.

"Wait. Don't hang up. Can she get me to Juneau? My last skipper is there and he owes me money."

The woman asked. More *thank you*. More *beer*.

"She says she can get you to Juneau, but you have to get to Unalaska by tomorrow afternoon. Some of the guys run skiffs between the islands. Ask at the bar."

"Thank you."

Livy turned to leave.

"Do you have a place to stay?" asked the woman.

Livy shook her head. The woman drew a map of the village with an X by a house. "You can come to me later."

"Thank you. Really, thank you."

Outside Michael was waiting.

"You want to help me?" Livy said. "Find me a skiff."

When the woman from the clinic came home, Livy was sitting on her steps. The woman let her in and showed her where things were. It was a two-bedroom T1-11 ranch house with brown carpet and couch and a kitchen table with orange place mats. The walls were filled with pictures of children and grandchildren who had left for the mainland.

"I know they say don't shower," the woman said, "but it's in there if you want."

When Livy came out of the shower there was a grilled cheese sandwich and a bowl of cream of tomato soup on the table for her.

"The shower help?"

"Yeah, but I probably shouldn't have," said Livy.

"Those cops would shower if it happened to them. Do you want to sleep? I can set an alarm."

"I'm afraid I won't wake up."

"Pull the door shut when you leave then. It'll lock on its own."

The skiff left Akutan at what should have been the light of dawn but wasn't. It took her to the next island, Akun, where she would have to wait. A small plane went from there to Unalaska. She would have to pay for that trip, but the woman assured her it would be less than what she had. The guys who took her across the water warned her that there was nothing on Akun. No services, nothing. It was a rock in the middle of the ocean with a landing strip but there was a place she could wait, a shipping container converted into a holding area next to the tarmac.

The plane ride was scary as hell and she'd never felt so close to dying. She admired the pilot's calm. She could see it was a front but that didn't mean it wasn't true.

BOOK 3—METAL SLOVAKIA

My name it means nothing
My fortune is less.

—Lyric by Geezer Butler,
  wrongly attributed to John Michael Osbourne
  by an argumentative teen coming down off acid

Lone Pine

US ROUTE 395 passes between Sacajawea State Park and the Hanford nuclear plant. Over the lands of the Umatilla and the family graveyards of Kennewick Man, over the water-carved Channeled Scablands that dug the Columbia River Gorge and freed the great river, which, now dammed, floods the west with light. Cheyenne drove through the old mining settlements where Chinese workers had lived in "Tiger Towns." What had Justine said? I want who I am to have nothing to do with anyone else.

Cheyenne rolled the window all the way down to let in the crystal-clean air. She did eighty miles per hour as the highway slipped south between the mountains through towns founded by speculators who came without permission long ago. Drawn by the promise of the Comstock Lode they drilled and blasted the Virginia Range and the local natives could do little but watch as they went after the silver.

A generation later, in 1890, a Paiute man with messianic visions manifested a dance. Drawing on elements from other nations, the dance united the spirits of the indigenous dead with those of the living. It infused the People with the powerful magic necessary to halt colonial expansion. Whites who saw it performed, unnerved by the spectral aura around the dancers, called it the Ghost Dance. It spread across the country. In a rage of eerie faith, it scorched the battlefield at Wounded Knee with ghostly fire.

I want to see through all of this and be free for real.

Cheyenne spent the first night in a rest area in central Oregon but the cold kept her up. Livy would have had sweatshirts, a fisherman's cap, and a sleeping bag. Livy would have had money and a plan. Cheyenne had a bucket of peanut butter. At dawn she drove through low hills scorched by the summer fire season. The blackened spears of trees—even with the windows up, the car smelled like smoke. There were patches of green pine where the fire jumped and the sky filled with golden eagles. She spent another terrible night in a rest area. Coming into the Inyo valley she watched for black ice as the sun burned the mist away, exposing the forest floor, a tinder of pine cones, also a ghostly dance.

The landscape flattened into the foothill canyons and scrubbrush creeks. The Alabama Hills came into view. Named during the Civil War for the Confederate raider CSS *Alabama,* the hills are where *Gunga Din* and *The Lone Ranger* were shot. They are where the Arapaho attacked in *How the West Was Won,* back when it was greener. They are a dusty gladiatorial arena in ancient Rome. They're Afghanistan. The Owens River, stolen and forced three hundred miles west by the Los Angeles Department of Water and Power, no longer feeds the land. It is also a ghost. Haunting aqueducts, disappearing within sight of the sea.

Cheyenne felt the spook of familiarity everywhere. Justine rode in the car beside her.

I sense a greatness in myself but I don't know what kind . . .

She pulled into a gas station and parked by the bathrooms. She'd had little sleep for two days. Joshua Tree was only half an hour west and would probably have safer places to park her car and nap. Jackson had mentioned that a former student of his, Ben, was living there now. She might be able to find him, though she wasn't entirely sure how that would go. She and Ben had been close once, and not under the best circumstances. The idea of seeing him made her slightly nauseous. She'd had genuine affection for him at one point. But then again there were a lot of ways to tell the story of those years and most were not a portrait of victory. She doubted she liked his version. Still, in an emergency she wouldn't feel weird about calling him, maybe, like if she got stabbed. Because that's the great thing about emergencies: Everyone has to drop everything they think about each other and act like a human. Sadly, her being a fuckup wasn't an emergency.

Outside, the Mojave Desert stretched before her. She made a sandwich on the hood of the Toyota. She was lonely. It wasn't a new feeling.

A few feet from where she stood the poured concrete of the gas-station parking lot ended and the desert began. She hadn't expected it to have a sound but it did, a baseline noise of rattlesnakes and sidewinders, camel spiders and drone flies. The wind blew at the back of her legs and through the scrub brush.

She pulled out the Kennedy half-dollar she'd put in the ashtray. You'll never go to jail if you're riding with a Kennedy. She rubbed it between her hands. Heads, straight east to El Paso. Tails, Joshua Tree and a safer place to park for the night. She tossed the coin and caught it and slapped it onto the back of her hand. Heads. Which is why flipping a coin never works.

37 Blood Tree

ON THE MAIN ROUTE through Joshua Tree, Cheyenne found a café and ordered a tuna melt. She had been there an hour and the midafternoon sun was streaming through a window when two men came in the back door. They were dressed casually in faded T-shirts, but even from where she sat she could see the expensive watches, the well-made shoes. She had to look twice before she realized that one was Ben. She laughed before she thought of why. Kirsten whispered in her ear . . . *Meant to be.*

"Shut up," said Cheyenne.

Ben's face was leaner than the last time she'd seen him, but he'd been barely out of his teens then. He saw her.

"Cheyenne?" He came over and wrapped her in a hug. "Man, you look exactly the same. How is that possible?"

"People's faces don't change once they're adults," she said. Out of her mouth. The very first thing.

Ben waved his friend over.

"Carter. This is Cheyenne," and the way he said it, she wondered if he had told the man about her; her heart began to race.

They sat and ordered beer.

"Have you been to Joshua Tree before?" Carter asked.

"No. I'm just passing through. My mom's in a monastery on the East Coast. I'm going to visit."

"What kind of monastery?" asked Carter.

"She was Zen but now I think it's nothing."

"Man, I can't believe you're here." Ben turned. "Cheyenne and I met when I was in college."

"I wasn't a student," said Cheyenne.

Carter looked confused.

"She was married to my American studies professor," said Ben. "I was in the student union with friends talking shit about this one professor who insisted on calling all six of us on campus who weren't white African Americans. One dude is English. Two from Jamaica. One from Brazil. So only two of us are actually American. We were drunk and obnoxious and torturing the pale kids so we started polling the other students: *Hey! What am I?* We get the usual, black, African American, tan—yes seriously, fucking tan—one poor frosh mewls, 'A person of color?' and the other American yells, '*No, man. This is the USA. I'm a person of interest.*'" Ben laughed. "The guy just scurries away. Then the Brit sees Cheyenne. '*Oi, what do you call this?*' He holds my arm up. 'Carob,' she says. '*Carob? What the fuck is carob?*' he says. I told him people raised by hippies never learn their colors." Ben smiled at her. "And that's how we met."

Carter laughed. Cheyenne did too. But why that story?

"Remember Elan Marquez?" said Ben. "He's out here too."

She felt a prick of nerves.

"I'll check on the beer," said Carter and went to the counter.

A line had formed. He was going to be a minute. Ben turned back to her.

"That was a rough time back then," he said.

"Yeah, it was."

"I don't want it to be weird."

"You know it's not like I was a million years older," she said. "You were an adult."

"But there is a difference. Between twenty-seven and nineteen."

Cheyenne looked at the door. "I felt out of place. I think I thought you did too," she said.

"It's not like it was just me."

"What I did was tacky but it wasn't criminal," said Cheyenne in a low voice.

"You were part of the institution, though. A professor's wife? That's power."

"Don't act like I was the first married person there to fuck up by sleeping around or having sex with a student."

"Students."

She started to get up and he put out his hand.

"I'm not trying to be a jerk," he said. "You're right. It was a bad time for everyone. I just didn't want it to go unsaid."

"No, of course not."

He gave her shoulder a gentle squeeze.

Cheyenne looked out the window. She had many hours of driving ahead.

Carter arrived with beer. "You should stay the night," he said. "We're having a massive party. Half the town will be sleeping over. I'm sure you can crash there."

"You should," said Ben, "for real. We can all meet up later."

She felt a sense of relief. She would sleep and lay a bad situation to rest. Maybe some things are meant to be.

The directions were easy; she found the place and parked where she was told. The party was being held jointly by two households, neighbors. Carter said they were putting meat on the grill about five. There was a fire pit set up on the property line of the land between them and both houses had food and drink. By the time Cheyenne got there at least forty people were already milling around. It was past seven, but the grill wasn't hot yet and guests were raiding the houses for chips, eating what garnishes could be found, and filling up on beer.

Someone offered her a beer and a shot. She took it and explored the property. She ran into Carter and a little while later she saw Ben by the fire pit and went over.

He looked at her as if she were a stranger. She thought he was playing and laughed. He turned and walked away. It took her a second to realize he meant it. She ran to catch up, rifling through a catalog of their interaction for whatever she might have accidentally said.

"Did I do something?" she asked.

He refused to look at her and kept walking toward one of the houses. She stopped. Her skin got hot with panic and she didn't want to cry in front of strangers. She headed up the road to go but when she got to where she'd parked, the Toyota was blocked in on all sides by rows and rows of cars. The party had turned into a bash. She was there until morning.

Trudging back to the party she made a plan: avoid the houses, blend into crowds, sleep in the car. She was starving, though, and the smell of meat and smoke was driving her crazy. People were lining up by the grill but she was afraid to go over in case Ben and Carter were there, so she joined the group at the fire pit. The woman next to her passed her a bottle of tequila that was going around. A little while later the same woman said she was going to get food and Cheyenne asked her to get a sausage for her. Eating something made her feel a little less insecure, and when it was fully dark she hazarded a trip to one of the houses for a glass of water.

In the kitchen doorway she saw Carter and his girlfriend by the sink talking to Ben, and she stepped back. They were talking about her.

"That's fucked up," said Carter. "I'm surprised you were so nice to her. It says a lot about who you are, man."

"I thought I could let it go but then I thought, why? And get this," said Ben, "not one white guy. Not one."

"That's serious slave and master's wife shit," said Carter.

Cheyenne wanted to scream. Half of those guys were princes! Princes with actual servants. She hadn't even known people like that were real. Or went to college. She thought they were just in books. The loneliness of being on that campus hit her like it was happening again. She couldn't take it. She stalked into the kitchen, went over to the sink, and found a glass. She filled it with water, drank it, filled it again, and turned to Ben.

"You know you shouldn't be so proud of yourself. I kissed my little brother four years before I ever met you. Talk about an uneven power dynamic," she said and realized what a horrible mistake she'd made.

An hour later, she was still trying to tell the story right to a man she'd cornered on the porch.

"He was only, what, seventeen? Hadn't been to school for almost two years. My mom, well she might be my mom—but I really truly hope not because she tortures you with mystical archetypes, it borders on abusive—said Essex was going to end up as muscle for some second-rate dealer so I said I'd kiss him in front of his friends if he got his GED. My point is that there are reasons. Even feeling out of place somewhere. That's a reason. But then sometimes you make a mistake and end up having sex with bratty little scions and princelings, which is problematic—*problematize,* by the way, is not a real word and neither is *othering.* It's just a bunch of bullshit people say to lock the gate behind them. Anyway Essex always wanted to kiss me and he had his GED in under a week. Know what he used that for? 'This only takes a signature.'" She waved her hands. "'This only takes a signature.'"

On the periphery she heard a name, Dhamma Dena. It rang her mind but in her current state she couldn't attach it to anything. Dhamma Dena.

The fire was raging and she was shivering so she went back to it. Staring into the blaze, she reminded herself over and over that none of these people mattered. The second she left, they'd be gone too. I want nothing I am to have to do with anyone else. I want nothing I am to have to do with anyone else. I want nothing I am to have to do with anyone else.

The guy next to her was talking about DMT and freight train this and freight train that and can you believe there hasn't been a band called Machine Elf? Oh there is? Are they any good? She couldn't figure out what they were talking about. 2C-T2, 2 . . . who fucking knows. *I'm totally game to try it,* the man was saying, *I just can't prom-ise what it's going to be but it's designed by the same guy—*

"Try what?" she interrupted. "What are you talking about?"

"A psychedelic a friend gave me. It's supposed to be in the 2C family, similar to T2T7 but doesn't last as long, maybe a little more like DMT."

"Do you have some here?" she asked.

"It might be pretty visual and it's definitely going to have some kind of a body rush. Have you done stuff like this before?"

"Probably. I do a lot of things, apparently."

He looked a little hesitant.

"And I'm a fucking adult."

Cheyenne swallowed the capsules he handed her.

Within half an hour the drug hit Cheyenne like a building collapse.

She came to on the edge of the party in the dark. Pinned to the sandy ground, she toggled between two types of hallucination: the kind you have with your eyes closed and the kind you have with your eyes open.

Closed, she saw three people and a fiery barge they were pushing into the current of a wide river. There was also a cave with a chatter-ing golden skull surrounded by human leg bones.

Open, she saw cubes and Cartesian planes and some strange tri-angles covered in flames. Most of the triangles were walking around but there was one big one in the center, which turned out to be a bonfire. The others turned out to be people.

It took her a while to remember that she was also a person. But even in the moments when she did remember she was a person, a person with relationships to other people, she was afraid to move because there was something wrong with them. There were rules. Because you treat some of them one way and some another. If they're strangers you're not supposed to touch each other, but then you're also not supposed to touch some of the ones you do know. She didn't think she could keep it straight. She knew there was a Ben and a Carter but wasn't certain she'd recognize them by their faces. To be careful, she stayed where she was. Eyes closed, golden skull. Eyes open, triangles. She sat back down and watched the stars move. The world like a bowl around her.

Her stomach twisted. She stood up, freaked. She couldn't tell what was happening in her body. She started toward the fire where there were still people standing. Halfway there she realized it was just that she had to go to the bathroom.

Looking up at the bright lights of the two houses on either side she saw that they were not homes but operating tables. No way was she was going into one. She walked into the desert looking for the compost toilet she thought she'd seen. There was one, which gave her some confidence. She tried to piece everything together. She was a person on a drug. Now she was in an outhouse.

Moonlight came through the slit in the door and she could see a little. What was wrong? Why was there blood? Oh right. She was a person on a drug who had a deal with the moon. She wasn't the only one. The moon. She felt around for toilet paper and found it. When she made it back to the fire, a small crowd still stood. They had their hands out over the embers. She put her hands out.

"Jesus," said a woman, "your hands and shirt are totally covered in blood."

Cheyenne nodded solemnly. "I may have killed something."

The woman turned white.

Cheyenne tried to think back.

"No. Wait." She held up a bloody hand. "Don't worry. It was only me."

There was the name again. A few feet behind her. She turned. Dhamma Dena. It clicked. It was in Justine's letters . . . The stores are empty sockets and the streets are covered in trash. I keep hearing people on the news say: How could they do that to themselves? Why burn your own neighborhood? Maybe I would see it that way, if I wasn't here, but all I see is will. The will to destroy everything around you and prove again you can live with nothing. It's something beautiful in a way. The people I'm staying with are freaked out. They want to get out of town. They know about a meditation master at a place called Dhamma Dena.

If people were talking about it, it couldn't be that far away.

She saw a man walking down the road looking for his car.

"Do you know where Dhamma Dena is?"

"Take this road back to the crossroads and follow the road left up the hill. You'll come to another road but just keep going the way you are. It'll be on the right about a mile on."

She walked back to the Toyota, which was unblocked. Starting the car, she was released.

On the crest of a hill where she'd been told to look, she saw a series of low shacks and a single-story building made of corrugated tin and wood. She parked where other cars were parked and when she got out, she heard chimes in the wind. She followed a sign that pointed to a room where the morning meditation was taking place. Standing there she decided she didn't want to go in.

There is no mirror like the desert. That's what Justine had written.

Now it was morning, though early. She felt her mind almost fully back. The cold was helping, the light too. Two coyotes appeared on the horizon, behind the closest house. They trotted side by side in a perfect tandem gait. One seemed slightly bigger than the other, but it might have been the angle of approach. They came in her direction and crossed within six feet of where she was. Then, without a pause or look between them, the two coyotes split at the very same second. Not a beat apart. They tapped a new vector into the sand and dirt. She realized that despite the misery of the night, no matter how hard she tried, she couldn't quite give up the idea that the world was a wild place where anything could happen.

38 Neptune

THE DRUGSTORES WERE CLOSED when Livy got to Juneau. She didn't want to go to a hospital for emergency contraception if she could help it. She couldn't take the blare of entrance-way lights, the cacophony of nurses, pens, and clipboards.

You are not you, but you say: Several times a day the cycle hum that is you downshifts. I reach for the cord on the diving bell and find only ocean . . .

She only had a few hours left, but at least she had a few hours. In the phone book she found a rape crisis center. It was downtown in a basement on a side street. Unofficial, unfunded, and run by volunteers, it was just the kind of place where Kirsten would have worked, which made Livy feel closer to her mom.

The woman who did the intake had a rash of carrot hair lighter than gravity. It sprayed around her ghost-skin face. Large freckles. Dressed in a tan army surplus shirt unbuttoned to her sternum, she said her name was Sarah. She apologized when she introduced herself but Livy had no idea what for.

"I'm going to have to ask some questions."

"You're the most Irish person I've ever seen," said Livy.

"I'm not Irish. I hate St. Patrick's Day. You should see this place the day after."

"So you're Scottish?"

"Icelandic," she said.

Livy tilted her head, raised one eyebrow, and gave her a half smile. "I didn't know you all looked so Irish," she said.

"It's a reaction," said the woman.

"What is?"

"Flirting."

Livy shifted her weight. "I've always been a flirt. Am I supposed to stop because of some asshole? Let the terrorists win?" She winked but there was no charm in it and her cheeks flamed.

The woman, Sarah, smiled. "The lack of control is part of the violation," she said. "Was the incident more than ninety-six hours ago?"

"Five days. I was fishing."

"Have you showered since then?"

"I've showered."

"Was the assailant known to you?"

"I know his name."

"Do you have the clothes you were wearing?"

"I'm not filing a report. I want contraception."

"I have to ask, sorry," said Sarah. "Are you in danger now?"

"Only of pregnancy."

"Can I get an emergency contact, just in case?"

Sarah handed Livy a form. Unlocking a cabinet, she pulled out a shoe box filled with morning-after pills.

"What's going to happen when I take the pill?" Livy asked.

"You might get a headache. Sometimes there's spotting. Do you have support where you're staying?"

Until getting here everything had been about getting here. Now she was here.

"An old skipper of mine lives in town," said Livy.

"Is that where you're staying?"

"He owes me money," said Livy.

"Do you have a safe place for tonight?"

Livy looked at the clock.

"Or enough money for a hotel?" Sarah asked. "You shouldn't be on the street. If you have cramps or bleeding you're going to want to be in shelter."

Livy popped the morning-after pill in her mouth and swallowed. "I have everything I need from you," she said.

Livy stood. Sarah stared at her desk.

"Okay," said Sarah, as if Livy had asked her. "You can stay with me." Sarah gathered her things. "I'm a volunteer. They can't fire me."

Sarah's apartment was across from a totem pole near the top of a hill. They huffed up a set of grille-metal stairs to get to it.

"My roommate just moved out."

On the yellow walls was a faded poster of a Tlingit dancer in a Chilkat blanket. An upright piano was in the corner, covered in dust.

Crossing the threshold, Sarah relaxed. She began to talk incessantly. About music. About the roommate who left. About the benefits of rice over quinoa (which she thought was a marketing hoax). A form of mental motion sickness overtook Livy from trying to follow the conversation. The woman was hot in a weird way, but too birdy.

"I was a page at the Capitol when I was a teenager. I worked for NGOs but they're all fucked. We never did anything but write grants to continue writing grants so—you're gay, aren't you? Heartbreaking, the oil companies. I was no longer a true believer—but admitting that is like coming out. I shouldn't compare it to being gay because that's its own thing. Coming out is, and I felt like my soul was being sapped for nothing and all the oil companies just—you know I really shouldn't compare it to coming out. Also coming out was way easier for me than for my native friends. I shouldn't lump it in with food politics either. Like what I said about quinoa being a marketing hoax." She stopped. "What do you think?"

"About quinoa or politics?"

"Either."

"I like quinoa Moroccan-style with fruit. I think people do what they do and call it politics later."

Sarah opened the door to her own bedroom and paused in the doorway.

"I don't mind you being here. I wouldn't do it if I did. Do you need anything before I go to bed? An extra blanket?"

You are not you, but you say: I was raped while my friend watched and did nothing. I say: Bring me his mother and sisters. You say: They are specters on the sea. The ocean is different now.

"I don't need anything," said Livy.

39 Every Rifleman

ESSEX LIKED BEING a marine more than he thought he would, though he didn't like the part of himself that did. Whatever. Steamroll my opinions. Give me a job I'm good at. He was relieved to finally stop wondering what to do.

When he'd first arrived at boot camp, everyone was yelling for him to throw his personal items into the red plastic tubs, but he had nothing to throw in. Now, days from graduation, he had things, but they all were invisible—digital money, health care, the ability to actually help someone.

He and Jared and two others weren't going to Camp Pendleton with the rest, but east to Camp Geiger, then on to Camp Lejeune. Essex felt a tingle in his neck and saw the marine's marine with anchors and globes and eagles.

Jared was thrilled to be moving along. School of Infantry. He liked the sound of it.

"Every marine is a rifleman," said Jared.

"Not you," said Essex, "you can't hit shit."

They were back at the barracks the night before graduation. There was a thrill going through the men, a crack of energy; families would be arriving. It reminded Essex of grade-school plays. Kids flushed and excited, peeking through the curtains to get a glimpse of their parents. It was the same. They would all perform. The moment would happen. And then everyone would rush off to find their loved ones. *You were such a good goose. You were such a good prince. You look like a real soldier.* Essex considered offering to fly Kirsten out but spending all that money for a two-day trip made no sense, especially for something she didn't necessarily approve of anyway.

All the recruits had ten days' leave. Jared had booked his ticket but Essex still hadn't. He wasn't so sure going home was such a good idea. He was in between. Changing but not changed. Too long at home and he might end up back where he was.

"I might start SOI training early," said Essex.

"Are you crazy? Think how easy it'll be to get laid on leave," said Jared. "People love to have sex with people who aren't going to hang around."

"Getting laid is not really my problem." Essex took off his socks so he could feel his skin on the floor. "It's kind of like how they say don't look back or you'll never get to leave the underworld." He stopped to brush a tiny spider off his ankle. "Or like how if you do it anyway it turns you into stone or salt?"

"Girls, boys, I don't care. Do me!" said Jared.

Which was pretty much how Essex felt about the marines. It's all okay. Do me.

"Are you really going to go straight to SOI?" Jared asked.

"I'll probably go home for a few days and see everyone. I just don't want to get stuck."

Jared laughed. "You don't have to worry about that. They'd find you and throw you in jail."

Sadly, jail also sounded okay to Essex.

Flying into Seattle, Essex peered over the wing of the plane at the islands in the sound as they made the turnaround for their approach at Sea-Tac. After deplaning, he walked through the airport. People stepped aside and smiled at him.

Someone thanked him for his service. He wanted to tell them he hadn't done anything yet and that he might never do anything worthwhile, but it would have taken too long to explain and everyone would have felt worse afterward. People's expressions were remarkably similar. They all said the same thing: *Thank you. I'm sorry. Boy, you're not too bright, are you?* He would never have believed that such a conflicting set of messages could be conveyed in a glance. He wondered how Cheyenne would look at him if she didn't know him.

He had planned to pay up several months of rent for her as a peace offering, but it turned out she was gone again. Kirsten had given her the Toyota and she was off to meet Justine. He was relieved in a way, something he didn't expect.

Cheyenne's disappearance with the Toyota also gave Essex something real he could do for Kirsten. The second day he was there he took her out car shopping and bought her a used 1988 Corolla with a decent clutch that sailed through DEQ. Being able to just go out and do something like that was so unreal that he took a picture of the car, angled to show off the current tabs, and sent it to Jared.

The day before he left he went to the expensive grocery store and filled a cart with enough organic food to stock Kirsten's refrigerator and freezer for a month. She seemed a little thin for her and her skin was a little wan. He had seen her this way before, usually when she was living on cereal and toast and peanut butter. She made him dinner from the fancy food he bought, and he slept on the couch. He started to tell her about Camp Lejeune, how he felt good about it. Like it called to him. He had expected they would stay up talking, but Kirsten said she didn't feel well and went to bed early.

In passing at breakfast, she mentioned that Cheyenne was also going to North Carolina. Justine lived in some place called Bolivia. Which was the second unreal thing, the idea that he and Cheyenne would be so far away and so close at the same time. He was pretty certain that she didn't want to see him. Strangely, he didn't really want to see her. He liked getting to make up who he was all over again.

Kirsten gave him the address anyway.

Getting back on the plane he felt a wave of relief. He wouldn't have to make decisions about any of it for at least another month. And even then, he might decide not to go find her.

Because there were two ways to be a marine. Squared away or a shit bag. If you're squared away, all your superiors are all over you making a big deal out of every mistake you make, which means they're going to trust you not to get them killed. If you're a shit bag, no one says a word. Jared, he knew, was a shit bag. Essex liked not being a shit bag. But he wasn't sure that if he saw Cheyenne, he could still be squared away.

40 Riding with a Kennedy

CHEYENNE HAD GOTTEN OFF the interstate and taken a southern route through the heart of the desert and the tiny Toyota fan couldn't take it. She had to stop every forty miles to let the engine cool.

She had never been anywhere so hot you couldn't touch metal. Trying to open the hood to check the water she burned her palm. Even that thick skin blistered. She put a sock over her hand to drive so she could shift. She saw Livy cackling like Medusa in the wavering fumes. Her sister would never be so stupid.

Half an hour later, the engine hit 120 degrees and she had to pull over. The left side of her face and arm were turning scarlet and there was a new burn on the side of her elbow where she had accidentally touched the door trying to adjust the mirror. She rolled the window all the way down to wait and reclined in her seat.

When it was safe to check the radiator she carefully popped the hood. Wrapping her backup jeans around her good hand she twisted off the engine cap. The well was dry and she'd gone through all the water. A truck went by and the driver laid on the horn—*Look everybody I'm here! Notice me. I'm afraid of myself.* She poured her gas station coffee into the radiator to get her a little farther down the road. She slammed the hood shut.

Driving, she saw an empty boxcar out in the desert and wondered when the last train had come through. A billboard with date palms went by. She saw what looked like cotton gins far out on the flat land next to what looked like bunkers from another time. The engine was hot again. Plumes of white-blue steam billowed from under the hood. She saw a spark, panicked, and turned off the ignition. The Toyota coasted to a stop.

Across the road was a compound of single-story structures that had been built in one shape and worn down into another. Cheyenne left the steaming car. When she got closer she saw the place was made of old railroad ties and corrugated tin. She saw a door with a brass bell, knocked, and stepped in. A cat was draped over the counter and another sunned itself on the desk next to a woman with leathery peach skin and bottle-blond honey curls.

"My car overheated. I need water. There may be something else wrong."

The woman went outside through a door behind her and Cheyenne followed. She entered a world entirely made of cats. They sauntered and batted at each other, rolled off things and attacked one another around stacks of tires. Cats circled her legs and leapt at her shadow and a litter of kittens mewled under an abandoned Chevy hood. She saw a kid's rusty metal slide from the '70s. Two kittens were trying to climb the ladder to the slide that ended in a large sandpit, which was being used as a giant litter box.

"Jesus. How many do you have?"

"I say between eighty and ninety. Pedro says we're well over a hundred. They're harder to count than you'd think."

"Is that even legal?"

"It's the desert." The woman cupped her hands and yelled for Pedro.

Cheyenne heard a sound that turned her lungs to ice. A growl hit her ears and vibrated through her body and she didn't need to look to see what it was; it was genetic. She froze. There was a second growl and adrenaline surged. She bolted forward into the desert in a full run until she heard the woman laughing.

"He's just saying hi."

Cheyenne turned. She hadn't seen the cage. Inside, two full-grown tigers paced. One brushed against the bars, scratching its face; it chuffed and made a whirring sound, which was a kind of purr that died with each breath.

"What is this place?"

"Originally it was a whorehouse. There was an air base nearby. Then carnies bought it, which is where the tigers came from. The cats were an experiment of ours that got out of hand. We're sort of a stop-off for illegals. Hey, you're not FBI, are you?"

"God no, I—"

"Just joshing," said the woman.

A man came out of one of the rooms. "Whose car is out there?"

"It overheated."

"Better get it off the road before some teenage cholo hits it."

"This is Pedro," said the woman.

Pedro helped her roll the Toyota into the compound and filled the radiator with a hose. Cheyenne turned it over but nothing happened. Pedro lifted the hood and had her try it again.

He phoned a friend, speaking in Spanish.

"Beer?" said the woman. "It looks like you had a rough night."

Cheyenne glanced down. In addition to coffee stains and engine grease there was still blood on her shirt at the hem. She went to wash up. When she emerged a few minutes later, three men had gathered around the Toyota. They were drinking vodka and talking about the car in Spanish. No one touched the engine, just passed the bottle. Cheyenne recognized a few words—*water, crazy, heat, asshole.* An old man held up his hand and everyone shut up. He started to whistle and circle the car then reached into the engine, unscrewed a part, and tossed it into the yard where a startled cat hissed at it.

He looked at Cheyenne. "It's fine now."

The others clapped him on the back but the old man brushed them away.

Cheyenne looked dubious.

"Really," said Pedro. "He's always right."

She got in and the car started.

———

The sun went down behind her and cool night air whipped through the windows. Coming into El Paso she took an exit for a filling station close to the freeway off-ramp on a frontage road with few working streetlamps. She pulled up to a pump before realizing the station was closed. She pulled out but the car stalled. When she turned the key in the ignition, it clicked. She was going nowhere. Reclining her seat, the emotional damage of the past twenty-four hours that had made her mind race finally overloaded and tripped a shut-off valve. She was a blank.

An hour later she was thrown sideways as the Toyota was hit by a car doing a fast three-point turnaround in the lot. The driver hadn't seen her until he backed into the front of her car. The impact knocked her both over and sideways so that the stick shift nearly cracked the back of her ribcage. A second later there was a tire screech as the car squealed off and everything was quiet again.

Cheyenne got out and looked at the tire marks. Her heart gave a little. There was a large dent between the midline and the driver's side headlight of Kirsten's car. The rubber part of the fender had been torn away and was hanging detached. She got back in and laid down again.

Someone knocked on the roof of the car and she jumped up. A young Latino man in eyeliner with an ankh around his neck leaned into her window and motioned for her to roll it down.

"Lady, you can't be here. It's four in the morning. We're closed."

She rolled the window down. "My car doesn't work."

"Your problems are yours, not mine."

"The starter clicks. I had someone look at it today but I think it was more of a healing than a repair."

The man drummed his fingers on his collarbone; he had black fingernail polish with little flower decals. She pointed at them to say something nice but he shook his head.

"Call someone to come get you," he said. "Call your insurance company."

"I don't have insurance. Can't I just sleep here?"

"Absolutely not. I'm meeting someone. It's business. I can't have you around."

A car came down the frontage road. The young man's eyes tracked it as it passed.

"Okay, come on, you're going to have to wait in the store," he said. The man opened the car door and waited.

"I need to go to the bathroom," she said.

"Let's just get inside."

"I also would love a glass of water."

"There's water inside."

She grabbed her backpack and followed him to the convenience store, which was adjacent to a garage festooned with razor wire and lit solely by glowing beer fridges.

"I'm going to lock you in for a little bit and then we can figure this all out."

Cheyenne was about to remind him that she had to go to the bathroom when the car came back. The man shooed her into the corner by the milk cooler and pointed to a chair.

"Don't go anywhere until I come get you," he said, and left without locking her in.

She saw the car roll by and a white guy get out with a duffel bag. She heard them talking outside about border crossings and shift changes. Cheyenne was cold and wanted to get a sweatshirt from her car. She slipped out but as she came around the side of the building, a spear sailed by within inches of her head and sank two feet into the door of the men's bathroom.

"Holy shit!" said the white guy who threw it.

"Was that meant for me?" said the guy with the eyeliner. "Are you trying to kill me with a fucking spear?"

"I'm just trying to prove it's real Aztec!"

Cheyenne turned and walked back into the convenience store. She was finally sick of caring about shit that didn't matter.

She watched the sun rise through the store windows. There had to be meaning in this. Why else would it be so stupid?

The young man came back in and made her coffee. "We have hazelnut cream."

"I need a starter," she said.

Half an hour later one was in her car.

"What do I owe you?"

"Nothing. We almost killed you with a spear."

She started to back the Toyota out.

"Wait." He leaned in through the window. "Don't forget, you're in Texas. Don't stop or get out if you don't have to. They'll fine you hard for driving without insurance. That dent looks like a hit-and-run and with the out-of-state plates, you're cop bait."

"Don't worry." She smiled. "I can't go to jail." She pulled out the ashtray so he could see the half-dollar. "I'm riding with a Kennedy."

He started to laugh.

"What?" she said.

"You might want to rethink that."

"I don't understand."

"Lady. You're in Texas."

THE NAVIDAD RIVER cuts through the black prairie lands before emptying into a lake damned and full of catfish. On both sides of the river, stands of live oak twist and shelter, and small painted churches dedicate themselves to the patron saints of Slavs.

In the 1840s, Czech immigrants, driven by failed European revolutions and poverty, trickled then poured in. They arrived at the port at Galveston, a scourge of liars, putting false names and false homelands on their documents, a contagion of temporary workers, no longer Slavs but Germans, no longer peasants but blacksmiths and butchers, they pooled in south Texas, the unassimilated papists, Moravians pretending to be Bohemians, liars.

On the edge of the Civil War in the freefall of Bleeding Kansas, a group of Moravians wandered north. They hadn't gone far when it started to rain. They took cover under an ancient oak just as the water crashed down. Looking out through the branches, they saw no reason to leave. Settling there, they built the town of Dubina, Texas. Dubina, "oak grove" in the mother tongue, the oak, sacred to the Slavic god of thunder. Today Dubina is a specter, having been razed by fire. Its history, however, has been preserved in the University of Texas archives and uploaded into the decentralized databases of modern ancestry websites. You can see their names in census taker's neat cursive. A woman of either twenty-two or twenty-seven, born in Bohemia or Moravia or Austria, claiming ten or twelve children, half of whom are dead. *For the record,* the census taker says, *tell me where you lost them? Did you eat them? Olga, Elisabeth, Frank, Anna, Catherine, Joseph, Walter—where are they?* No, she says, I did not lose them. I did not eat them. They are under the black prairie. They are in the mud of the Brazos tangled in cottonmouths.

Crossing Texas, Cheyenne slipped into a dream state where her body drove but her mind, her mind . . . Over the last four years every idea she'd had about who she might turn out to be spiraled to the ground. Justine, it seemed, might have gone through something similar.

I meditated on charnel grounds and got sick of my own daydreams. I want to be a blank. I want who I am to have nothing to do with anyone else.

She had stayed in the desert for several months . . . I look around in every place I go and see the same people—Ponytail Guy and Dr. Massage and That Chick Who Can't Stop Blubbering. They say there are two kinds of truth—relative and absolute. The world being full of stupid people is absolute . . . and eventually went into silent retreat.

Cheyenne had never seen anything as wide and flat as West Texas. Once she reached the plains, the sky touched the ground everywhere. She passed decommissioned oil rigs, machinery rusted into place. Coming into Odessa there were functioning wells, hundreds. Rigs pounded the earth methodically, a horrifying sight. They looked like dying black cattle yanked by their heads to the ground. She started, held her breath as she passed as if it were a graveyard.

In Abilene, she heard about the storm with hurricane-force winds sitting on top of Fort Worth. According to the cashier at a Mexican restaurant that let her use the bathroom, roads were flooding. It would go on for the next twenty-four hours. She thought about waiting it out but also considered what the man at the gas station had said about not stopping any longer than necessary and turned south toward San Antonio and east again.

Outside of San Antonio she saw a state trooper. She decided to turn off and see if she could find a parallel route. The land began to roll in hillocks, green again. She could feel the pressure dropping. Cumulus clouds formed in gray, pink, bronze—the colors of sunset.

There were only ranches and farms around now. She looked for a place to pull over. She saw a stand of oaks off the road by a tractor turnaround. Water from a drainage ditch fed the underbrush, which buzzed with insects and whistled with birds darting in the tall grass. It was going to rain; the air was an electrical field; she was not separate from it. Rain. Rain hard. Make me eight years old again. Lightning shock my heart; make me cry for real. She saw drops fall on the road and smelled wet concrete. She thought she might choke from relief. What was it? This feeling.

She parked and got out. She wanted to feel the air and electricity on her skin. Then the rain really came. She grabbed the peanut butter and bread and ran for the oak trees. Under one, she found a spot to watch the clouds move. Branches touched the ground around her. She felt something sharp. It was a metal plaque embedded at the root: Heritage Tree. A thousand years old. Not ceremonial, a surveyor's mark. Do not cut. Do not sever. But the tree had grown around the plaque; it has folded it into its roots and buried it in soil.

The rain bounced off the road. Glorious. Don't stop. May singing atoms crown us all. The sky turned to jade and the clouds merged into a giant wall coming toward her. There was a roar of hail. The Toyota was getting pummeled. She saw the wall of clouds descend in fangs biting the earth. Lightning struck and flashed in a cloud. She began to count. At three, thunder boomed. A second later a barrage of hail drowned all sounds.

She could try to outrun the storm but she didn't think she could see enough to drive. Another sideways strike lit the road white. The cloud lifted leaving only filaments. The winds died. The storm slowed coming across the fields. The hail turned into a hard rain. She stepped out from the protection of the grove but something else was happening. The cloud began to turn.

There was a gap between what she saw and what it meant. Then it clicked: tornado. The word changed shape as she watched the cloud, not a box but a cage, not a cage but a net, not a net, something ephemeral and utterly incapable of containing the experience.

The wide trunk of the ancient oak strained—this tree has been here for a thousand years, this tree was here when Vikings came, this tree lived at the time of the Toltec, this tree, this tree—and there was a new sound. In the field across the road a twister touched down and spun earth into clouds; it tore a trench through the adjacent field; it hit a herd of cattle and one fell, broken, to the ground a few feet away from where she hid. She saw another come down not far from the first and threw up into the dirt. The ancient tree seemed to lift. She could feel the great roots loosening. The tornado jumped across the road and came toward the oak grove. Everything got dark then light and flickered like a silent film. She saw the tornado pass in front of her. It picked up the Toyota and spun it into the air. The debris cloud was everywhere then. In the jet-engine sound, her mind went blank. She let go of the roots and closed her eyes and covered her head with her arms. There was a massive crack as a bolt of lightning struck the field behind the trees. She was now under the storm. A boom of thunder, then hard rain. It came in sheets through the oak branches, beating her back as she crouched with her knees tucked, hands over her head. Then there was only the sound of the rain, deafening.

She raised her head but she couldn't see. At the bottom of her ribcage she felt a sharp pain and realized it was the vat of peanut butter. The tree was unharmed but for one large branch twisted off at the joint. As the rain stopped, she could see the debris scattered across the two-lane highway. Water flowed over the road, which was now a river shaped by branches and dead cows, torn siding and tin. The Toyota was nowhere.

She couldn't feel her legs. She needed to find the car. The wind blew in one direction now. It was still loud but different, like a chopper landing; it beat slowly on her eardrums. She walked along the center line of the road where it was highest. She kept her head tucked but felt the wind on her chest. She thought she'd seen the car go this way but really it had just gone up. She found it in the middle of a large field. Wading in, mud kept sucking off her shoes so she gave up and took them off. Sharp reeds cut her feet.

The bumper of the Toyota was peeled off and all the glass was gone. The front of the car had been crushed to half its size. The front doors had popped off. She didn't see the driver's side door anywhere.

She saw her backpack under the front seat on the passenger side. She climbed through a window socket but couldn't reach the strap. She had to get on her belly and lie flat across the backseat to get to the strap but it still wasn't coming loose. She squirmed down so that her face was against the carpet pressed into the glittering chips of safety glass. Working from there, she freed the backpack. Putting the strap in her teeth, she lifted herself back out of the car window until she could swing her one leg down and climb out.

Going back to town made the most sense. But then she noticed a dot on the horizon half a mile away, miles closer than town.

Cutting through fields she came to a long unpaved driveway that led to a farm and followed it, though it was mostly a creek now.

The farm came into full view. But it wasn't a farm. It was a tiny castle.

42 Metal Slovakia

THE CASTLE WAS BORDERED by an honest-to-god moat. On the other side of it was a wall blocking her view of the lower half of the castle, clearly unfinished. There was Tyvek on the main tower and plywood had been used as a bridge over the moat, a trench filled with storm water and displaced snakes, and she saw one on the mud bank—a copperhead or a cottonmouth; she'd never seen anything but a garter snake.

On the other side of the plywood bridge was a wooden gate. She tried to open it but she had the vat of peanut butter in one arm and the other gripped a bag of water-logged bread.

"Hello," she called, "is anybody here?"

She thought she'd seen a car around back so she followed the wall, made of gray stone, carefully mortared, with built-in arrow slits at head height every ten feet. The moat ended and she saw the shell of an ancient blue Volvo in the grass; its hood leaned against the perimeter wall near a gap in the stone, through which she saw a trailer.

"Hello," she called, stepping into the castle yard. "Hello," coming to the trailer.

A light went on inside. A man near sixty opened the door. He seemed to have been sleeping. His hair was long and in a ponytail at the top of his head, salt and pepper cascading from his crown in all directions.

"Wow, man. You are really out in this. That's crazy." He looked up at the sky and pushed the trailer door open. "Come in. She might come back. If she does we go to the castle."

He stepped aside so Cheyenne could enter.

There was a love seat with a crocheted throw. A stained-glass bird dangled from fishing line by the window. A blue Formica table was bolted into the floor surrounded by an orange half-circle couch. The thin bang of the tin door closing behind her as he let it go woke her up. She couldn't remember how she got there.

He invited her to sit.

"What shit is this? Fifteen years I am here. One tornado. Not this crazy end-of-the-world shit. Hold on. I look outside the wall and see where she is."

He opened the door again, shook his head once, and stepped back inside.

The little sink was full of cups and glasses. A pitted peach lay in two halves on a cutting board. On the side of a cabinet, hanging from a triangle of picture wire, was a Pegasus stenciled on a mirror. She looked at her feet and wondered where her shoes were.

The man sat across from her.

"Where is your car?" he asked.

"In a field."

"I help you with it later."

"It's crunched into a square," she said.

He considered her. A small gust of wind rattled the trailer.

"It's okay," he said. "We deal with all later." His voice was the ocean gently rocking.

He pulled the crocheted blanket off the love seat and put it over her shoulders. "My friend, I think you may have shock."

"My car's just stuck."

"You said it was crunched into a square."

"Yes." She paused.

"Give me your hand."

He examined her fingers, took her wrist and turned it over.

"Were you in the car when the tornado hit?"

"I was looking for a place to make a peanut butter sandwich." She stood up, alarmed, and looked around.

He pointed to the vat of peanut butter. She sat. He took her pulse. His nails were clipped to the quick, dirt on the pads of his fingertips, the nail beds dotted with white splotches and white streaks. There was a black beauty mark on his cheekbone. He wasn't as old as she'd thought. It was only the deep lines by his mouth, his eyes, between his brows and across his forehead. Like the apple heads she'd carved as a kid that became old ladies, once dried.

He felt her forehead then patted her shoulder.

"You're going to be okay. I have some slivovitz. Plum brandy. I make it myself. Give me your clothes, I put them in the dryer."

He pulled a bottle from a cabinet and got a robe, scarlet. A mangy crushed velour. She took it into the bathroom, which was a closet made of vinyl paneling with a small frosted window and a shower door that didn't seal. Naked, with bruises all over her body, she looked in the mirror. Her pupils were dilated. Her hair had twigs in it. Her overgrown bangs were plastered to the sides of her cheeks. Her face was covered in scratches.

The man tapped on the door. "Are you fine, lady?"

"I'm staring at my face."

"It would be good if you come out."

"Give me a minute."

She bundled up her wet clothes and put on the robe. Stepping into the hallway, she handed the bundle to the man. She saw there was now a bottle of brandy and a glass on the table and next to it a pack of Marlboros. The pack was newly opened and one cigarette was pushed forward. A box of matches lay on top.

Sitting, she tried to feel anything about her situation. The car was gone. She was in a stranger's robe in a trailer behind a castle.

"Try it." The man filled her glass. "In the shed, the dryer," he said, and left.

She drank it like water. He came back and sat on the other side of the table.

"Do you have family here?" he asked.

"Why is it clear if it's brandy?"

"Maybe you call." He took out a cell and clicked his tongue. "No signal. We try in while."

Taking up the pack of cigarettes he pushed one toward her with his thumb.

"I don't smoke," she said, and he lit one for himself.

"Why are you building a castle?"

"I want to be King!"

He laughed but she had no reaction.

"Just fucking kidding you, man. I hate kings."

He poured more brandy into her glass.

"Are you Russian?" she asked.

"Fuck no, if I was Russian I'd have to kill myself for being such an asshole. I'm from Czechoslovakia."

"That's not a country," she said.

"What do I care about what some fucking politician says?"

She froze, confused. "I think I was trying to be polite," she said.

"It's okay. I know this. It's not you. It's these fucking people. They don't know potatoes grow in dirt."

She drank and he poured her another glass.

"So lady, where are you from?"

"Seattle."

"Do you have friends in Texas?"

She giggled but the giggling turned into an unfamiliar kind of laughter that became coughing, only not coughing but laughing.

"Why do you laugh this way?"

"I don't have friends."

From his face she could tell it wasn't one of those jokes you can explain and still have it be funny.

He put out his cigarette and reached for the pack, pushing another toward her.

"I don't smoke."

He took another one for himself and lit it.

"Maybe we try the phone now?"

He handed it to her. There was a signal. She dialed Kirsten.

"Hi, just checking in." She switched the phone to her other ear. "I'm in Texas." She looked at her bare feet. "Everything's fine." She hung up.

"Your mother?"

Cheyenne didn't say anything.

"We try again later. No stress. Maybe we make your car drive."

"It's her car."

"Your mother?"

"She doesn't have insurance." She started to giggle again.

The man took a plate out of the cupboard and got a banana and a peach from a wire basket. He sliced the banana into little ovals, cut the peach in half and set the plate beside the brandy bottle.

"So lady, here."

"She doesn't have any money."

"Your mom?"

"Basically."

"It's okay. We take everything slow." He pushed the fruit closer. "My name is Jirshi. What is yours?"

"Cheyenne."

He smiled. "You are Indian?"

"No, I'm not Indian." She could see he was disappointed and she wished she'd lied. "I'm sorry," she said.

He shrugged. "That's all right. I also not."

She ate a piece of peach to make him feel better.

"She likes Indians, your mom?"

"I was named Cheyenne because my mom thought she'd found an ancestor that wasn't a colonizing fuckhead."

"Maybe you are part Indian."

"We're not anything good at all."

She felt a shudder. Her hands were starting to shake.

Jirshi thumbed another cigarette forward.

"No thanks," she said.

He lit it for himself.

———

She slept in his bed while he crashed on couch pillows in the kitchen. The wind picked up but the storm didn't come back. In the morning there wasn't a cloud in the sky, only the castle.

Her clothes were dry and folded by the bed and Jirshi had left her a pair of canvas tennis shoes. They fit enough to put on but not enough to wear without blistering. She heard a saw outside. When she found Jirshi, he was behind the castle, shearing stone under running water, gray from mineral dust.

"Good morning, lady."

His hair was wrapped in a paint-stained T-shirt and twisted into a Sikh's turban. His forearms were gray from where the water had splashed as he worked. At his hip was a homemade knife. A steel chain dropped in a loop from his belt to a large leather wallet sticking out of his back pocket. She looked at the growing stack of stone blocks, buckets of sand, and powder.

"You're a mason." She looked at the castle. "Can I go inside?"

"I show you later. I've been thinking we need to get your license plates. They tow it maybe and charge your mother."

"God, that never even occurred to me."

"It's okay. I help you."

He undid his T-shirt turban and dipped it into a bucket of water, then wiped down the table and threw the shirt back in the bucket.

"Maybe your car is not so bad and runs if I work on it."

The giggle came again. "Yeah, let's check out the car," she said.

Jirshi filled a bucket with tools and grabbed a couple of quarts of oil out of a shed.

Cheyenne scanned the castle grounds. "Where's your car?"

"I have a truck but I lend her to a friend who goes on vacation to Oaxaca for two weeks. I think—I take a break from building these fucking patios and ugly kitchens, work on the castle, finish the wall—if I have my truck, a job comes? I have to say yes because you don't know if it comes again. But if I have no truck what can I do?" He shrugged. "I say no and it's not my fault."

Once outside the fortifications Cheyenne shaded her eyes but couldn't see Kirsten's car.

They waded into the high grass.

"I go with her once to Oaxaca. They have good fruit. You can walk on the beach without getting tar on your feet. Not like Galveston."

She shook her head. "I don't really know this part of the world."

"I like it except for the people."

They reached a field where the grass was beaten flat from cattle.

"How did you end up here?" she asked.

"I have a great-great-uncle. When I was young he told me stories of a Czech man here that gives any Czech coming a job."

"So you came for work?"

"No, that was a hundred years ago. That's how my uncle came. The land I build on was his."

They came to a dead steer tossed by the tornado. Its body was contorted and buzzing with horseflies. Cheyenne got light-headed. Jirshi bent to look for the brand.

"I think I know whose she is. This poor stupid cow. I don't eat them. I eat only fruit so it's okay for me but this," he gave a quick nod to the steer, "is no good for anybody. Not only cows but people. A couple of stupid cows gone and," he made a gesture of washing his hands, "like that, you're done."

He took the pack of cigarettes out of his pocket. There were two left and he offered her one. She shook her head. They started walking.

"I was raised in a communist country. We always talk of freedom. Like rock and roll and saying whatever you want without being afraid. I live for this then. There at least you could drink and play music in the woods all night, have a fire and sing, maybe talk—no one bothers you. You get it out, whatever it is. Here cops come at ten. Quiet, quiet, quiet, everyone shh, always this shhh. But I am no fucking mouse. I want to go home but I think it is gone forever, that place. Do you like heavy metal?"

"More the idea of it."

"Everything is a copy from now on, I think. Not like Ozzy. I wanted to be a drummer. I see Black Sabbath on their first show in Prague. They start 'War Pigs' and everyone loses their mind."

He played a drum-fill in the air across a rack of toms and belted out, *"Gen'rals gathered in their masses . . ."* but his voice, loud and nasal, didn't carry in the humid air.

"After the show I have sex with my girlfriend for the first time, and I think, maybe it stays like this from here on. The wall is down, we're teenagers and we go." He clapped and sliding one palm off another made the sound of a jet and a knife-edge cut to the sky with his hand. "Gone."

"Who deals with the dead cattle?"

"They get their bodies. Like your car. Someone has to come."

He smoked, tapping the ashes into the front pocket of his black jeans.

The smell hit her of the hot wet soil mixed with the scent of dew evaporating on the blades of green shoots and bramble leaves. "I think I'm done hearing about the end of the world," she said.

She stopped to reassess their position. "I'm not sure we are going the right way."

There were oak trees on the other side of the highway but she couldn't quite tell if they were the same oak trees.

They started to walk.

"Are you traveling or on vacation?" he asked.

"I'm not sure I've ever had what people think of as a vacation."

"We do that all the time when I grow up. I love travel. Always. I go anywhere. Before I start the castle, I take lots of holidays. I go to Turkey—I become a fruitarian so I go for this—and to Laos and Burma. Terrible government but the people. These are fucking great. Real people. They have a fruit I like, rambutan. Do you know it? It looks like a sea urchin. Crazy. But I like it so much so I go there for that. They have it here sometimes but by the time they ship, it has no taste."

"Can you really live on fruit?"

"Yes, why not?"

She saw two trees bending over a depression on the other side of the road. "What kind of trees are those?"

"Pecan," he said.

"I saw trees with no bark."

"Tornados can do this."

The sun was high and the dew gone. Every part of her was damp from sweat. It was good to have slept and be clean in clean clothes, even if the blood didn't wash all the way out. She didn't mind the sun burning her cheeks or the flies.

"So lady, where is it you need to get to in this car?"

"North Carolina. I'm going to meet a woman who might be my real mom."

"You are adopted?"

"One of us was. I have a sister. It might be her."

"Your mother doesn't tell you?"

"She does not, in fact."

"Maybe she has a reason."

They hit a fence she didn't remember with a gate over a cattle guard and went through it into another field.

"I don't think she is my mother, the one who raised me."

"She tells you really nothing?" He stopped. "Is that your car?"

In the dip of the field was the Toyota. It was half its original size with a corona of safety glass around it. The rear axle rod had snapped in two and one shaft was driven several feet into the ground.

"You are a lucky lady. I think no one lives in this car."

When they reached it, he circled the driver's side, then took off his belt, squatted down, and whipped it beneath the car to clear the grass of snakes before crawling under to look at the chassis. He came out shaking his head.

"Can we get money for the metal?" asked Cheyenne.

"Toyotas of this time have not much metal. The tow truck cost more for sure. Best we can make sure there is no way for these pigs to find a name. No name, no fees. The storm is maybe good here. With this crazy tornado if they can't find who owns it? They forget it."

They pulled the license plates and filed off the VIN numbers where they could. Kirsten didn't have insurance and did her own maintenance so there was zero paperwork to worry about. Cheyenne carried a wheel, Jirshi carried the bucket of plates and handles, the jack, and the spare, and they trudged back across the green pastures toward the castle.

In the trailer, Jirshi made coffee. He got some star fruit out of the fridge for lunch. Cheyenne felt like she'd done something wrong by showing him the car but couldn't explain what it was.

"This woman," he said once they were sitting, "the one who might be your mother, can she help you get to where you need?"

"She doesn't have any money."

He dug his thumbnail into the grooves of the exposed plywood on the table.

"My last paycheck I spend on stone. All of it. I think, if I do this, I must finish my wall."

She took some star fruit.

"My truck is in Mexico. I owe everyone money. Maybe in a month I have a job but I have no way to help you now. Even when my truck comes there is no money for gas to take you to North Carolina."

"I have gas money. One way anyway."

He smiled briefly. "I am not a pretty lady like you. Nobody helps me and I get stranded."

She finished the star fruit. He washed some cherries and put them in a cup. She ate them because he'd done it, not because she was hungry. He washed the cutting board and wiped the knife.

"You said I could see the castle," she said.

Against the backside of the castle, directly across from the trailer, piles of wood and brick were stacked next to a low scaffold that, now partially deconstructed, reached nowhere. A bale of hay had come unbound. Opening from the center out, blown by the storm, it covered the scaffold base in straw. Twelve feet up the wall, under the lip of a wooden corbel that ran around the castle, Cheyenne saw several hornet nests.

"We start here." Jirshi pointed. "This is the orchard."

Cut into patchy grass on the south side of the perimeter wall was a rectangle of broken-up ground but nothing was growing in it. A small tarp sheltered saplings in pots, little green sprigs now dead and splayed on parched soil. Jirshi ignored them as he passed, as if they were no longer speaking.

"I plant fig trees here. Apricots and pears, there. Peaches I maybe must put outside the wall for better sun. They do better that way, I think. I also try this way of splitting the tree so that it grows sideways, but it dies. I am still learning. What is it they say? Master, master, where's the dreams that I've been after? So funny, these words but I make my orchard for sure. Master, master—do you know this?"

She shook her head.

"I like it very much."

They stood at the edge of the empty orchard. Cheyenne wasn't sure what else she was supposed to see. She bent her head and platted her hair into a short braid, but having no rubber band, it unraveled as soon as she moved. Jirshi walked to the wall, dumped rainwater out of a compost bucket, flipped it, and set it beneath an arrow slit so she could look out. She got up on it and leaned into the embrasure. The field behind the castle was a strip of green and tan and sky. Two cows moved across the arrow slit.

"When I start, I think, maybe a hilltop fort. This is really no hilltop, though, so, okay, I make a wall. I make a real castle. A real castle is a fortress so I measure the angles."

"Do you really think you're going to get attacked?"

"No." He laughed.

Soft cheeks, pink under his black-and-gray stubble. He took a fresh pack of cigarettes out of the breast pocket of his sleeveless jean jacket. Opening it, he arched an eyebrow at her. She didn't respond.

"Anyway." He lit a cigarette for himself. "Attacks do not come like this now, yes? For these you need a mental wall."

He took a few drags. She turned back to the field. Black birds filled the upper half of the arrow slit then vanished.

"Everything to be great is here," he said, "but they don't make it, I think. When I was a kid, I read books about Indians and it makes me so sad, I think when I come here, I want to meet some but when I came I find only Mexicans. I think, okay yes, I understand this. But then I see how they are to their own Indians and I say, what—is this whole world crazy? Okay. Then I'm crazy too. I build my castle."

She stepped off the bucket.

"Why doesn't the moat come back here?"

"I run out of money to rent the backhoe. Spring maybe. There will be no water for a long time, though. I make my castle eco. I use the leftover stone pieces from the roof and the wall to make the bottom of the moat. Otherwise it just goes away, the water. I think like this for everything."

"So it will be stone."

"Yes, sure. For now, no. Only the wall."

"Are you going to make a drawbridge?"

"I think about it but a drawbridge is too far."

She looked at him with a wide smile and started to laugh in a bell-like way. It was a sound she'd never heard come from herself before.

"Okay, yes. I know it's like this." He stubbed his cigarette out. "But still. It is too much, a drawbridge. Like haha. 'A castle.' Maybe, though, I make a portcullis—is this the same word? My English gets so bad when I am alone. Growing up, I must learn Russian then Italian when I work in tourism. Then I must learn German when I leave. Now, I don't care. I say good enough."

She looked at the masonry, at the beveled embrasures around the arrow slits, the variegated hand-cut stone tiles on the castle roof, the corbel framework.

"But why? Why do this?"

"Why? Because everything is ugly. I want to show how something beautiful is made."

"So you'll let people come see it when you're done?"

"No. I think not. Maybe I change my mind."

She examined the back wall of the castle. The exterior wall was no more than fifteen feet with the tower rising another fifteen and the spire another five beyond that. Even with these, the whole thing was not so much bigger than a large house.

Square in front of them was the keep. Just above the main tower in height, without corbels or buttresses, it was a tall solid block, Soviet in its simplicity. Attached was a small circular tower with a steep spire. It was the highest point on the building and what she'd first seen from the field. It was how she'd known it was a castle. He pointed to the roof of the turret.

"I fell off that. I was sure I broke my back. I can't move for hours. So much pain. I crawl to the trailer. I know I must have broken my back. I spend two days on the floor. I shit myself. I don't care. Awful."

"Why didn't you call someone?"

"Who wants to live with a broken back? Shoot me like a horse. So I wait and it was fine. I finished it a week later."

He walked over to a barn door in the back of the keep. Grabbing a large handle with both hands and putting his body into it, he slid the door sideways a couple of feet and the sun coming through the crack hit the interior wall, painting on it a second bright doorway. They stepped in and he rolled the door shut. They were in darkness again.

"Our eyes adjust faster this way."

She blinked. Brown shapes appeared in the corners. A square of dull light from a window high above fell on the ground.

"This is for a siege, the murdering hole." He raised a finger toward the window, which had no glass. "For pouring hot oil down on bad guys." He laughed. "But I think I make it for no reason."

The keep was colder than she expected. She crossed her arms and rubbed her shoulders. The walls were framed but not sheeted. Building materials were stacked on pallets in the corners, and in buckets and on shelves were strips of wood.

"Go up and take a look," he said, raising his chin toward the stairs at the other side of the room.

She climbed the stairs, pausing to test the boards. Looking out of the first window, she saw a pecan tree growing on the other side of the wall and what appeared to be a juvenile oak behind it.

She crossed 2x8 planks laid down as a platform to the other window.

Close to the trees she could see a small ravine with a creek that disappeared into a bush.

"What will happen to the forest when you build the moat?"

"I work around her."

"And the creek?" It was barely a trickle but the idea that it wouldn't be there made her sad.

"I don't know," he said, "we see." He hovered over a thought. "What do you think?"

"Of what?"

"Of my castle," he said quietly.

She shifted nervously. He'd grown tender. She looked from the vantage of the scaffolding up at the spire beams then out at the wall.

"I don't understand it," she said.

"Ah," he said, "don't worry, lady. You are not alone. Most people not." He offered her his hand as she came down the stairs but when she got to the bottom she noticed the hurt. He couldn't look directly at her so she turned slightly so he wouldn't have to.

He took her back to the hallway, pitch-black again because she'd looked out the windows. But soon she saw brown bands across the floor where the hallway opened into other rooms with other small high windows. In a workroom she saw more shelves, neatly organized tile, a workbench, and, in the amber light, pieces of glass and wood cut into geometric shapes, glued or soldered together, parts of greater designs.

He took her into the great hall, which—like the kitchen that served it, the royal bedchamber, and the orchard—was empty. There were no windows in the hall and had there not been one in the kitchen behind her, she wouldn't have been able to see the thick curtain that hung between the hall and the tower.

"I don't want a god but a church is maybe good."

He pulled aside the curtain and sun poured across the floor.

Cheyenne walked to the center of the tower room. It was an octagon and each side was not a wall but a window, tall and Gothic, filled with daytime. The floor was a parquet of handmade starburst tiles like she'd seen in the workroom.

"It is not finished of course," he said, but she could feel his pride like a wounded animal breathing behind her.

Vaulted arches rose thirty feet above the ground to meet in an eight-way cross at the top. From there blue-and-white tile formed a star whose points almost touched the peak of the empty window frames.

Light was everywhere and came in from all sides. On the wall in front of her was a kaleidoscope of gold and pomegranate red, amethyst and dragonfly-green light. She turned to see where it came from. On the south-facing side of the tower, high above the roof of the great hall, was a stained-glass window. The bottom was made up of thin panels that used elements of Alhambra geometry inside a carnival barrage of color, nothing uniform, no two hues alike. Above was a circle with a rose in it. The petals had been constructed of busted pool-table lampshades and opaque, ballet-slipper-pink transoms and sidelights salvaged off tacky suburban doors. The rose reminded her more of a heavy metal tattoo than something from Eden. Yet it was exquisite in its diligence. As if it had been a real rose dipped in nitrogen and shattered into shards, each a piece of all that was worth it about the world, collected by the mason to make it whole again.

"The national flower of Czechoslovakia," he said. "Now Czech Republic and Slovakia. We cut it in half like a baby. I hate these stupid ideas. We are done with our tour. We have a snack."

He took a mandarin and a Granny Smith apple out of his jacket.

"Like I said, she is not finished."

He handed her the mandarin and, taking out his knife, cut the skin off the apple in a single waxy spiral.

"It's just a hippie myth that you can live on fruit," said Cheyenne.

"I know soon enough, anyway, so I don't care. If I get sick, maybe I know the hippies are lying."

She passed on the apple he offered her on the end of his knife and leaned against the wall.

"Maybe you could make weird stained-glass windows for people," said Cheyenne.

"It doesn't work. Everyone wants the kind of beauty only they can own. In Prague we have a clock from plague years. Still telling time. As a kid I am crazy about this clock. The man who makes it? They blind him so that he makes no other. Like the Caesars. Tourists come and say, haha, funny story, but when I am a boy and hear it, I don't know whether to love this beautiful clock or hate it."

"Will you keep making things?"

"I don't think I put out my own eyes."

She ate a mandarin wedge and tried to put it into words.

"When did you get okay with being nothing?" she asked.

He scraped the apple peels into a pile on the floor with the back of his knife.

"I'm sorry," she said.

"It's all right. I'm not mad."

"Do you know what I mean?"

"Yes, sure, I know what you mean."

Just this. The not having to explain, something fell from her shoulders.

"Building the castle helps. It's good to have something to do that is very hard but has no point." He tapped the starburst inlay with the butt of his knife. "A month of evenings after work, this takes me. Each square. And before I must figure out how to do it and what I like, every day. I do it over so many times till I find the right way. But what is she for? To walk on, so what?"

"Like a Zen garden?"

"Fuck no. I hate these guys."

"I think my mom is one."

He put the apple scraps into his jacket pocket. "Well maybe she's okay."

"She might be more of a guru. I'm not really sure."

"Gurus are better. They live off rich white people, not poor stupid villagers."

She picked up the mandarin peels.

"Leave them. I love this smell. Like my orchard." He stood up. "Tonight we grill peaches with cinnamon and I make mangoes with cayenne. This is how the Mexicans do it."

Leaving the castle, Cheyenne wanted to be alone but didn't know how to do it without being rude.

After dinner Jirshi got a chunk of hash out of a mint tin on the counter. He stuck a couple of rolling papers together, then broke the filter off a cigarette and sprinkled its tobacco over the papers.

"So lady, do you know what it is you do yet?"

"I'm going to go in the morning. I can hitchhike. I'd rather do that and have money for a night in a motel if I need it."

"Okay sure."

He crumbled hash on the tobacco and rolled the cigarette up with the filter inside. He lit it and offered it to her. Afraid the drug effect from the other night might return, she declined. Everything was weird enough. He took a drag and exhaled. Silence charged the room. It was that moment, the one that always comes when maybe you're going to have sex and maybe you're not, and it only takes the slightest movement to tip it one way or another, just that whisper: Be human, be human, in this very place. She let the moment pass. Because everything was weird enough.

43 Luck

LIVY POUNDED ON THE DOOR. Jeremy had not been that hard to find. Returning without a boat, fish, or money, he had crawled back into the apartment by the wharf that he'd lived in for years.

"Let me in, you bastard. The guy in the hall says you're here."

Jeremy unlatched the door.

"Pay me what you owe me."

"You got your share of nothing just like I did," he said.

He opened the door and walked off. He was wearing only a short green terry cloth robe and made a point of stretching to expose his butt cheeks before halting in the center of the one-room efficiency. He looked around like the room was a surprise to him too, barely any furniture, a plaid armchair folded out into a cot, a blue beanbag that had sprung a leak. He sat on a stool by the island counter of the kitchenette. His robe split open to show his fuzzy chest. A toilet flushed in the apartment above.

"What?" he said.

"You left us stranded."

"I couldn't look at that fucking boat another day," he said.

"You think I wasn't sick of that duct-taped fiberglass floatie piece of junk? You owe me. You don't even know how much. You had fish tickets from our last haul. I saw them. What did you do with them?"

"Cashed them for the plane ride out."

"Sell your permits," she said.

"Sold weeks ago."

"What about permanent fund money? I know checks went out. Where's yours?"

"In my ass!" he barked. "Come get it." He opened his arms baring his chest. "Help yourself," he said, "it's right here."

"I hate you," she said.

"So what, me too."

"I have no pity for you. Find something."

Slope-shouldered, he retied his robe, then began to growl. He jumped up, startling Livy, and rounded the breakfast island and went to the fridge.

"You know what?" he said. "I got something." He opened the freezer and started throwing things on the counter. "Macaroni and cheese. Salisbury steak dinner. Another Salisbury steak. Mini tamales. A bag of Cajun tater tots." He held up a box and shook it at her. "This is a chicken pot pie. I've been saving it because it's my favorite but you can fucking have it."

"You know," said Livy, coming around the counter, "I will have it. And whatever else you have too." She pushed him aside and looked into the freezer. "Pound cake. That's actually one of my favorites." She threw it on the counter with the rest of the food.

Jeremy looked like he was about to cry. She couldn't watch. She started jamming frozen food into her backpack. She picked up the chicken pot pie and paused then threw it back into the freezer.

"Thank you," he said.

"Don't talk to me."

She'd known he was broke. But she'd expected to pry $50 out of him at least or a stereo or a watch. Her head was aching and she felt cramps coming on. It could be the morning-after pill or the situation. A cloud bank hid the mountains. Trash was strewn over the sidewalk by bears. Ravens pecked at burger wrappers in the street, then flew to the power lines when cars came.

She tried for on-dock work. Even if boats had been going out, she could not have made herself get on one. Offering to pull garbage or do maintenance, she asked around but no one took her up. All the male faces. They reminded her of the men she'd fished with and the men she'd played pool with, friends and brothers of friends, cousins of girlfriends. Men who had also made her who she was. Young beautiful men. She should have fucked one of them. Then there'd be less to take.

By midafternoon the abdominal cramping was more intense. She passed a shelter with a window full of men milling around with coffee and couldn't help but feel like she was on the wrong side of a glory hole. All that light, all that bareness, better to keep walking. She found a cold beach, a creek that glinted gold. She saw the black slippery heads of harbor seals and the silver flash of escaping salmon. It was getting dark. She was going nowhere. She had to turn around. Asking Sarah if she could stay another night ran against every instinct.

Returning to the apartment she made her pathetic speech. Sarah said she was welcome. Livy handed her the partially thawed boxes of Salisbury steak she had been carting around all day. The apartment was warm, the radiator hissed, local radio was on in the kitchen.

"I got you a phone from the domestic violence people," Sarah said. "They get them donated. There's minutes on it but I don't know how much."

Livy felt her own anger burning. Sarah knew she'd be back. But it wasn't her fault and it felt good just to be inside. Then the chatter started.

"You'd think they'd give phones to runaways but they're afraid of turning them into drug dealers and hookers. I mean they give the homeless people phones and I always think, so it's okay for them to be dealers and hookers?"

She was fluttery. Circling the same idea, asking variations of the same question.

"Beer?"

"Sure."

"Some people are stone-cold addicts and behavioral mod doesn't do anything but for the rest of us it's great. What do you think?"

"I don't know what we're talking about."

"Whether social services should give phones to everyone in at-risk populations or just domestic violence groups," said Sarah.

"I don't know. I hate phones. If you have one you're supposed to answer it."

Sarah threw two Salisbury steaks in the microwave, stacked crossways, and set the timer for eight minutes.

Livy watched the dinners rotate.

"I don't think that's going to work," she said.

"Why not? Four minutes for one. Eight for two. Why do you think it won't work? The microwave."

"I just don't think microwaves work that way. They're also half thawed."

Sarah shrugged. "I was at a laundromat where a guy threw a frozen pizza in the dryer to cook it. You should call your family either way because being stoic is a setup. I see it a lot. Hang on. Why wouldn't it work if you double the time?"

"Wait, what happened to the pizza in the dryer?"

"He checked it after six minutes and it wasn't done so he threw it away. But there was no reason it couldn't have worked, and by family I don't mean literal blood, chosen family, whatever. Anyone who really loves you."

"My family would make too big a deal out of this. It would only make it harder."

Sarah opened the microwave, restacking the paper trays before starting it again. Five minutes later they sat down to eat.

"You can stay here," said Sarah, stabbing the Salisbury steak with her fork, "I'm moving out in a few weeks. The rent's paid. I don't mind."

"Why are you leaving?"

"I'm going to Panama."

Livy knew she was supposed to ask more, show a little curiosity, buoy her side of the dinner conversation, but she couldn't.

After dinner she wandered down the hill to a bar, but as soon as she entered she felt like an extra in a movie. This film takes place in Alaska. The hippie rednecks and the natives are drinking beer. Something is about to happen, but you're not involved. She went to the bathroom to wash her hands. Her skin was dry and her lips were chapped. She looked at herself. The few freckles she had were nearly invisible, nothing like Sarah. Two girls came in, talking, spraying their hair to death, reapplying lipstick. Their eyes and hers meeting occasionally in the mirror. But all of Livy's desire to flirt was gone. Because if I can't touch myself, I'm certainly not going to touch you.

THE FOLLOWING MORNING, Jirshi walked down the driveway with Cheyenne.

"I wait until you get a ride," he said.

"Okay, but stay in the bushes or no one will stop."

He handed her a bag. "Apples for your peanut butter."

It was such a thoughtful act that she had to swallow a couple of times so she wouldn't cry.

"Thanks. I like apples with peanut butter."

A car passed. She didn't try to flag it.

Jirshi hiding in the bushes didn't work. There wasn't enough cover and all the cars that passed just saw a guy crouching by a ditch. Once he left the next car stopped but only took her two miles down the road. She might as well have walked. For a while after that cars didn't stop so she did walk, along the narrow dirt shoulder, making up new words to the ABC's song, "My Country, 'Tis of Thee," and "Row, Row, Row Your Boat." Then the melodies got stuck in her head and made her crazy. The castle tower occasionally appeared in her mind as she'd seen it looking up, the intricate interlocking wood and stone, the star patterns in the floor, and the idea of being okay with being nothing.

A guy in a Lexus pulled over. He was on a business trip to Fort Worth, which wasn't the way she was going but he said she could pick up I-20 and it would be the same, so she got in. She made it to a Dallas truck stop by midday. By then another song was stuck in her head.

> *It was in the month of June*
> *All things were bloomin'*
> *Sweet William on his deathbed lay*
> *For the love of Barbara Allen . . .*

She got a ride with a trucker to Birmingham, which is where she said she was going. He didn't believe her but didn't care. She said she'd called a friend from a pay phone and her friend was waiting in Alabama. Just outside Birmingham. "We're supposed to meet in this motel where she works. Just off the interstate."

> *They rode to the east*
> *And they rode to the west*
> *Until she came nigh him*
> *And all she said when she got there*
> *Young man I think you're dyin' . . .*

Hours later, past dark, she saw a billboard for a motel. Here, she told the trucker, here. She got out in front of a glowing sign advertising rooms cheap enough even for her. The woman at the desk said they were full. A bus of college kids had checked in for a game. She hadn't had time to change the vacancy sign. Cheyenne could see she felt bad, and that she wasn't lying but that didn't help because it was getting dark and she was stuck.

"You really don't have anywhere to go?" the woman asked.

"I'm going to North Carolina to see my mom."

The woman rolled a pencil back and forth over the glass counter.

"My car was destroyed in a tornado in Texas two days ago," said Cheyenne.

"Well you don't look very dangerous," said the woman. "Pretty sure I could take you in a fight. I also have a gun in my purse. You can stay on my couch. I'm off at eleven."

The woman answered calls and handed out towels and micro-wave popcorn. At eleven sharp she locked up the laundry room and they drove a few blocks to a small house.

Cheyenne heard an explosion.

"Fireworks. My neighbors are having a party," the woman said as she showed Cheyenne the couch.

In the morning the woman drove her to a truck stop after giving her a peach-colored T-shirt with a large air-brushed bunny on it. The woman had said, "You can't see your mother in that dirty shirt." Cheyenne found a ride all the way to Georgia. Halfway through the morning she realized she'd left the peanut butter in the woman's fridge, but the trucker bought her lunch. She rolled tampons out of toilet paper in the bathroom. How many days had she been bleeding? Who had she been when it started and how different was she now? She bought crackers and bean dip and gummy worms in the store.

When they hit the weigh station she hid in the back of the trucker's cab. Atlanta went on forever. From Augusta she got a ride to South Carolina. She saw a honey locust growing in a strip between a gas station and an undeveloped lot. It had huge thorns and was surrounded by cigarette butts and used condoms.

The rest of the way it was a series of shorter rides, mostly in cars. Then it was: a right turn before the Cape Fear River, stay between the Green Swamp and the Boiling Spring Lakes, look for a temple in Bolivia.

She got to Bolivia, or almost, and asked a man outside a convenience store how far she was from the temple. He said she'd never find it.

"It's not walking distance," he said.

"How far isn't walking distance?"

"My friend might run you there if you wait."

Ten minutes later she got into a taupe Prius.

"Are you here for the festival?" his friend asked.

"Yes."

"It's mostly over," he said.

The road to the monastery was clogged with cars. The man dropped her off.

The temple was built on pilings with columns. Asian people flooded in and out of it. Through a set of doors she saw a shamrock-green Buddha on a golden dais, spear-point hat nearly touching the ceiling. Men in ocher robes moved through the crowd—*I'm looking for my mother*—but they turned out to be visitors too. She followed the crowd toward a little creek where people were placing paper blossoms into a stream. Laden with candles, with cash. Some more like crowns than flowers. They floated away on black water shining from candlelight, and made their way through the forest. Not in Bolivia. Not Chiang Mai. Dixie.

She felt a hand on her shoulder. "Are you Cheyenne?"

She nodded.

"Justine said you might come. She's through the forest. I can take you."

"Doesn't she live here?"

"We take her mail but she's not really part of the monastery."

The forest floor was sodden in places and fully underwater in others. She followed the man down a narrow wooden boardwalk through the trees. Palmetto fronds fanned on either side of her. The farther they got from the temple, the less dry land there was. The palms disappeared. Oak and shagbark hickory too.

"It's always wet but not normally like this. It hasn't drained off from the hurricanes this year."

The boardwalk branched. He stayed to the left. Rooted in an island in the swamp under a hole in the canopy that let in sun, a young and deluded swamp chestnut oak sprinkled crimson leaves over the water.

"She's a great woman."

The creek widened until there was no ground left. The boardwalk ended in a dock in a glassy pond. He pointed into the forest. Across the water she saw a large yurt in the woods.

"We need to wade," he said.

"Aren't there snakes?"

"We need to wade carefully."

He didn't have shoes on. She hadn't noticed.

"It's not far." He rolled his cotton pants up to his thighs. "There's a makeshift footbridge that connects to the shore between the Cypress and the Tupelo. You'll see it when we're closer."

It was near dark. Everything was cast in blue shadow. He stepped into the swamp water and sank to his knees. She took off Jirshi's shoes and rolled up her jeans. She was taller than the man was so the water only came to the middle of her calves. The fear of snakes was so intense she could barely breathe. Her mouth was dry and her tongue tasted like metal. She sank deep into the silt mud at one point but found a root under the water to stand on. The yurt was directly ahead.

They reached the footbridge, a stray piece of the original board-walk over a few buckets of packed dirt. The man offered her an arm but she handed him her shoes and stepped up by herself. They dipped their feet in the water several times to get the mud off.

"How long since you've seen her?" he asked.

"I've never seen her."

Someone in the yurt turned on a lamp. The brightness shot out of every window, a lighthouse beam.

"That's her," he said.

Justine looked out over the swamp. She couldn't see them, though they could see her. She was searching. Lamplight cut angles on the water. Even at this distance Cheyenne would know her face anywhere.

She looked exactly like Livy.

BOOK 4—UPRIVER

And the wheel's kick and the wind's song and the
white sail's shaking,

And a grey mist on the sea's face, and a grey dawn breaking.

—Penned by John Masefield,
sung loudly by the starboard watch of the rebuilt *Neva*
as they shivered on deck waiting for morning

45 Waves and Light

STANDING AT THE BEACHHEAD—not all that far from the Roanoke River, or even from Hatteras Island, a place of ghosts— looking east, the ghost of Sir Walter Raleigh is caught in a loop of time. Every night, he flees his lost colony and sails for El Dorado. Because on the inhale the Virgin Queen blessed the East Indies Company, and on the exhale she handed Raleigh a use-it-or-lose-it charter for the New World. *Go east young man, go west. Go wherever the hell you want.*

Behind him, and inland down the North Carolina roads toward Jacksonville, is the Marine Corps Base Camp Lejeune where thousands of troops skirmish daily. The base is home to the 2nd Marine Division, which was formed on the cusp of the twentieth century when a fledgling empire felt the need for a bodyguard. Conceived in the White House, born in the Philippines, schooled in Panama, Cuba, and Guadalcanal, the division provides ground forces to North Africa and the Middle East.

Lately Raleigh's taken to wearing a wreath of tobacco around his neck and carrying a lock of a blond child's hair. In the distance, off the North Carolina coast, ship-like factories of whalers head for the Horn. Going deeper and farther out as they approach peak oil, they sail for the Great Offshore Grounds. Barefoot, Raleigh digs his toes in the oily sand. Ankle-deep in surf, he whispers his mantra: *I am not liable. I am not liable.*

On the beach around him, marines practice for night landings on foreign shores. The tidal estuary that partially surrounds Camp Lejeune is considered ideal for training amphibious assault units. Sadly, taking the beachhead over and over for forty years did have unintended costs. The camp's drinking water became poisoned with benzene and engine degreaser, which resulted in birth defects, cancer, and lawsuits. Because while gold cures impotency, alcoholism, and poverty, and whales cure machinery and darkness, there is no antidote for benzene poisoning.

John A. Lejeune emerges from the sea with the Tuscarora people behind him, first as the crest of a wave then as foam on the sand. Raleigh turns into lightning bugs. Lejeune averts his solarium eyes. One, the explorer and brand-creator, the other, logistics and deliverables.

Having fled north at the founding of the colonies, the local Tuscarora people were gone as a force but not gone forever. A hundred years after the Carolina colony subdivided into north and south, they remerged in the white imagination as the Union sloop of war the USS *Tuscarora.* This projection marked a subtle shift in the moral center of the country, repositioning itself outside the role of proud aggressor into the victimized center of the haunted colonial unconscious: *I am not the cowboy but the Indian. I did not take the hill. That city is not mine. I am not covered in salt.*

On the eve of the Civil War, the USS *Tuscarora* was sent to intercept that soon-to-be notorious Confederate raider the CSS *Alabama,* for which the Alabama Hills would be named, hills now overrun with gladiators and lonely rangers. The order given to the USS *Tuscarora* was simple. Sink the CSS *Alabama* before it crosses the Atlantic—because who better than the Tuscarora understood the need for this? Who better than they understood the cost of failure? How if allowed to land, invasive seeds might take hold and colonize an entire garden and become very hard to eradicate later. The USS *Tuscarora* did fail, though. It did not stop the CSS *Alabama.* And the ship too, then, was forced to flee north. Ever-returning and reemerging, though, the sloop later sailed around the Horn to Valparaíso where it encountered ghosts, mostly the giant Galápagos turtles set on fire by the sailors of the whaleship *Essex*.

The failure of the USS *Tuscarora* to intercept the CSS *Alabama* was very likely cheered by John A. Lejeune's father, a devoted Confederate captain, though such things are impossible to know. Perhaps the elder Lejeune's heart was never in the Confederacy so much as devoted to those whose hearts were—because who will not do things for a person whom they love that they would never do for themselves? Either way, the elder Lejeune's allegiance to the Confederacy did not pass to the next generation. John A. Lejeune, a marine's marine, though a plantation-born Southern son of a Confederate captain, lived and died a defender of the Union.

Lejeune served in the Spanish-American War covering troops in the aftermath of the Battle of San Juan Hill. He fought in the battle for Guantánamo Bay, establishing Cuba briefly as a US colony. He commanded the USS *Dixie* in Panama when the United States took over construction of the canal. An opener of doors. The soft speaker. The carried stick. John A. Lejeune.

In the summer of 1905, Lejeune remembered, the USS *Dixie* was rerouted to assist in the French colony of Algeria. They were tasked with helping to set up a scientific station from which to view the total solar eclipse. Lejeune arrived in August. He toured the city of Bône, which had been the site of a paradigmatic shift of force and brilliance. Grateful that he was there to absorb and not slaughter, he wandered alone. These were the streets of Hippo where Saint Augustine had walked. Augustine, who looked at the expansion and excesses of Rome and saw that its destiny was not divine but a glitch in the narrative of becoming. From the physical realities of the aqueduct and the arches, Augustine constructed a new and holy city set upon a hill, carved in salt and light, but invisible.

In the moment before the 1905 eclipse, scientists checked their equipment. They had Algerian servants lay down bedsheets to catch the shadow bands. Then the eclipse began. The temperature dropped. Stuttering light danced on the linen and the corona of the sun was captured with spectroscopes that owed much to Augustin-Jean Fresnel's theories on waves and light. Such an elegant instrument, the spectroscope, only a prism. A couple of mirrors, a slit in a box, yet able to reveal the elements in complex radiation. For this reason, it is often used in the classroom to demonstrate spectrometry. The experiment is simple. Take a candle that's been used before. Put sodium chloride in the well by the burnt wick. Then look at it burn through the spectroscope. In the dark a single bright yellow line will appear, also made of salt and light.

Essex and Jared had each joined up on an open contract, so unlike other recruits, they had no idea what their military occupational specialty would be. The idea had been to cast the die for real. See what fate held. After taking the assessment test they awaited the results. Maybe a collection of skills and aptitudes captured on the assessment test would describe a new self. Brides in an arranged marriage, they hoped for the best.

The Armed Services Vocational Aptitude Battery didn't hold very many surprises, though. Essex and Jared both scored high on Assembling Objects and Electronics Information and tanked General Science. Essex aced the Word Knowledge section then totally blew it on Verbal Expression. Which only made sense when he thought about it. His record of saying what he meant in terms that anyone else but him understood did seem criminally low. But whether this or any of these attributes made a difference to the marine charged with giving them their MOS is unclear. They were both assigned to infantry. Jared as a basic marine. Essex as a rifleman.

The Lejeune complex was a hundred square miles, larger than Seattle. Essex was struck by how different the land in North Carolina was. Much wilder than the hills around San Diego. The humidity of the South was like nothing he'd ever known. It was October but didn't feel like fall at all. The air was wet but the plants were dry. Unlike the Pacific Northwest, they had no deep greens or blues. The only gray was pavement. The trees were not triangles or spears but bushes and hands. Pickle-colored cotton balls on parched grass, either in a thicket or planted in rows along the tank-wide avenues of the base.

The satellite facility that would be his first home on the complex, Camp Geiger, was ten miles south of the main base, which meant it was also seventy-three miles north of Cheyenne.

Once Essex settled in and his infantry training began, he forgot about her most days. He practiced patrolling and getting ambushed and sleeping under the stars. He preferred to be in the field than in the barracks.

During the day he worked hard at excelling in anonymity. When he had a few hours of liberty, he wandered. Sometimes when he was alone, exploring what drainage ditches and creeks he could find nearby, the ghost of John A. Lejeune walked beside him, bending where Essex bent to look for crawdads in the dark pools under the rocks. So accompanied, Essex found he was more himself. On the base the standards were high and hard to meet, but the why was no longer his. Do you miss it? he asked the ghost. Do you miss not having to go where you're told? But the ghost of John A. Lejeune only shuddered, whispering, *The president's own, the president's own . . .*

46 Justine

CHEYENNE HAD BARELY KNOCKED when Justine opened the door. "Cheyenne," she said after a beat. Justine thanked the man who'd led Cheyenne through the swamp and dismissed him.

Cheyenne walked into the room like she'd forgotten what she was looking for. Justine came closer. She smiled but didn't try to touch Cheyenne, for which Cheyenne was grateful.

"Do you want some tea?" asked Justine.

Cheyenne said no but Justine put the kettle on anyway. Watching her move around the yurt, Cheyenne was riveted. Justine's face was square more than round, with a solid jaw and wide cheekbones and a dusting of freckles—like Livy. As a young woman, her hair might have had the same subtle mahogany undertones as Livy's, though it was mostly gray now; she wore it in two efficient braids, also, strangely, like Livy.

"The swamp," said Justine. "It's not always this bad."

She stopped and took in Cheyenne.

"I would know you anywhere," she said, and laughed.

Cheyenne's throat got hot. She tried to speak her sister's name but her mind was full of noise. Justine squeezed Cheyenne's hands and she flinched.

"I have a burn."

Justine turned her palm over and held it to the light.

"I opened the hood of my car when it was overheating."

"I have aloe."

Justine got a bamboo box from the bottom of a dresser.

"It's gone," said Cheyenne.

"What?"

"The car."

Justine handed her a small plastic bottle of aloe. Cheyenne squeezed some onto her palm and gently spread it over the blistered skin. The lime-green gel, the cinnamon aura of Justine's hair, the white-noise breeze buzzing against the window screens. Cheyenne was sweating from the swamp and humid air, which she had never before experienced but knew almost from instinctual memory, it was in her body like the terror of tigers had been.

Justine unraveled a strip of gauze from a roll. "We should wrap your hand too."

Cheyenne heard Livy's voice. When Justine wound the bandage around her hand she saw Livy's movements. In the sparse interior of the yurt she saw Livy's personality.

Justine put the bamboo box back.

"I wondered how it would feel to see you," Justine said.

Cheyenne had looked at the Polaroid so many times. How had she missed it? Their faces were not at all alike. The woman in the photo had a soft moonlike face, not square like Livy's, and her coloring was paler. But then Cheyenne's own face hadn't sharpened into what it would become until her early twenties, and what was Justine in the photo? Nineteen? A teenager who had just given birth, captured in an overexposed shot, head shaved, her face plump from pregnancy weight.

Justine sat on the bed. "I was worried that I'd feel nothing when we met."

Cheyenne wasn't sure what she was supposed to say.

Justine smiled. "I can't hide my feelings," she said.

"Neither can I."

"It's a way we're alike then."

Cheyenne felt the pit in her stomach get heavier. Justine patted the bed. Cheyenne sat at arm's length.

"Tell me about your trip." said Justine. "Was it good?"

"It was horrific."

Justine looked at the sunburnt part in Cheyenne's hair, her wet feet. "You must really have wanted to get here," she said. "I like that. I don't like half-assed people." Justine tucked one leg up beneath her. "You don't seem like the half-assed type." Her expression changed. "I want you to tell me about your life while you're here. What it was like until now—I know that's hard to boil down."

"Actually it's pretty easy. My teenage years were a mess. I married a professor and slept with a bunch of his students. I hate clerical work but nobody hires me for anything else."

Justine laughed. "I can imagine that. Well better to fuck up for real than rack up a bunch of misdemeanors. It makes you interesting."

In that moment, Cheyenne wanted to be interesting more than anything.

Justine looked at her. "Can I ask you a question?"

"Of course."

"Is that bunny shirt you're wearing yours?"

"No, a lady gave it to me because mine was covered in blood."

Justine cocked her head like a fox. Cheyenne felt the other woman's eyes run over her body. Then Justine laughed and shook her head.

"It really must have been one hell of a trip," she said.

She began unbraiding her hair, unweaving fast with all fingers, a ritual Cheyenne had seen Livy do many times.

Cheyenne had been so sure. If she got all the way here, if she showed no hesitation, if her commitment was absolute, that there would be a justice at its end to wash away all the years of poor judgment and make right all false starts. There should be a fucking prize for desire. But there wasn't.

"I'm glad you came," said Justine. "I hope you stay a little while." She pointed to the windows. "Every morning when the light comes in it's like waking up in a tree house. You'll see."

Justine showed Cheyenne how to get to the outhouse and handed her a flashlight. When Cheyenne returned there was a cot made up for her against the cold woodstove. Cheyenne, unsure how much to undress, got under the top sheet fully clothed. Her jeans twisted as she turned onto her side but she didn't want to make noise straightening the sheets or herself. She wanted to be inaudible, invisible, visible. She wanted to be someone else. The lights went out and she watched the moonlight dance on the vines and leaves. She closed her eyes.

I'm not going to tell Justine that she looks like Livy. I'm not going to tell Livy. I'm not going to tell anyone.

47 Miss Thailand

SUN COMING THROUGH THE TREES filled the yurt. Justine started a small fire in the woodstove, threw in some palo santo sticks, latched the door, and watched the flames catch through the window.

Cheyenne rubbed her eyes and sat up.

"You're lucky," said Justine. "Normally I teach an early meditation class but it's the weekend."

Cheyenne looked around the yurt. With light coming in so many windows it looked bigger than it had the night before. The bed was queen-size, the kitchenette more like a kitchen, the closet where the cot had been folded like a clamshell, large enough for several cots. In the center of the room a circle of sunshine from the hole in the canvas roof played on the floor.

"There's a propane shower next to the outhouse if you like. I left a clean towel on the bench."

Justine went to the closet and pulled down a box of clothes. She found a pair of jeans and a faded denim shirt with pearly buttons.

"It may not be your style. But it doesn't have bunnies or blood on it."

The back of Cheyenne's hands burned. She couldn't tell if Justine was stating a fact or making fun of her. She took the clothes and went to find the shower.

Outside the leaves were just starting to turn. The swamp was a perfect mirror. An insect skimmed the surface, which rippled briefly before reflecting sky and branches again. When she came out of the shower, she dried off on the wood steps and dressed. The smell of Justine was in the shirt, familiar in a primal way. The scent unearthed a bedrock longing older than words.

Walking back to the yurt she could smell the coffee. The sweet wood was now burning in the stove and the sounds of Justine moving around, the clank of mugs in the sink, brought tears to her eyes. It was strange how raw hospitality made her now.

"I thought we could spend the morning talking," said Justine, sitting on the floor by the stove. "I'm sure you have questions."

Cheyenne got a cup of coffee and sat down across from her.

Justine pulled her unbraided hair to one side where it cascaded over her collarbone and down her breast. She looked east toward the sun. The corneas of her brown eyes flashed with amber. Cheyenne saw faded discolorations on her cheeks, old freckles, terrain. Livy was everywhere. In her gestures, her coloring, her voice. Justine turned back to Cheyenne.

"How is Kirsten?"

"She's okay. She got a job as a security guard."

Justine nodded imperceptibly, her mouth open slightly, the bottom of her teeth white and even beneath her upper lip. "She could always do so many things I could never do," she said.

Cheyenne tensed and Justine laughed.

"Relax. I'm not saying what you think I'm saying. She's just never been a restless person. Whereas I've always been looking to solve something that can't be solved, she's able to be satisfied with things that are more attainable. Our imaginations are just shaped differently. It's not a slam. I just need more." Justine blew on her coffee. "And I bet that's how you are too."

Cheyenne's skin got hot. She felt something cut loose inside her. It wasn't completely untrue. Kirsten's life, though untraditional, had an iron framework.

Justine crossed her legs.

"I went west because I was bored of college. It was full of little boys taking philosophy. Have you ever noticed that girls take psych and boys take philosophy? You see it everywhere you look, this idea that women should be so interested in what someone else thinks. I'm not. And that, it turns out, is a problem for people. Cyril was the first straight man I knew who wore eyeliner. We met because I made him share his table at a coffee shop." She grinned. "He likes to be pushed around."

"Kirsten doesn't."

"You're right. That's why I liked her. You should have seen her back then. Mall jeans and a pentacle choker. She'd say borrow when she meant lend and called soda, pop, which I'd never heard before, and she still had that wall of bangs from back in the eighties—I don't think she'd ever eaten out anywhere that wasn't a chain restaurant. But she was a refreshing and natural person in a world of posing little scenesters." Justine paused. "I envied her quite a bit. Did you go to college?"

"Sort of. Some."

Justine nodded. "It's not all that worth it. One good year is probably all you need. A semester of philosophy, a decent literature course, something about media and art, and you basically have it."

Justine got up to get more coffee. She talked about Seattle, how it was then, how it was different now. Cheyenne watched Justine's face, which was beautiful and raw and moved through emotions so subtly that they were only discernible in the moment of transition. A long time ago someone, she didn't remember who, had told Cheyenne that white wasn't white but all colors at once. Justine's face was like that, capable of showing all feelings simultaneously. What do you do with that kind of charisma?

Throughout the morning Justine talked and asked questions. She didn't press, which Cheyenne was grateful for because she wanted Justine to like her and talking too much felt like a risk. At various points, Cheyenne brought up Livy but Justine didn't seem that interested so she dropped it.

After breakfast they sat at the table, finishing slowly. Cheyenne was about to get up and do the dishes when Justine motioned for her to wait.

"You can ask," she said. "Did I love him?"

Cheyenne looked at her blankly. "Who?"

"Cyril," said Justine. "Don't you want to know?"

Cheyenne's mouth opened then closed. It wasn't a question she'd ever asked herself. "I don't know," she said. "Did you?"

"To be honest, I didn't," said Justine. "I just wanted to see what he looked like in love."

Cheyenne felt a faint revulsion.

"Did you love him?" asked Justine.

"You have to know someone to love them," said Cheyenne.

"That is obviously not true."

Cheyenne flushed with shame. Justine was right. It was not true. Because, after all, here she was.

They spent the rest of the first day walking through trails in the woods. Justine had a limited relationship with the temple. She'd taught there for a while but something hadn't worked out and a new arrangement had been found.

"Most people aren't ready for what I have to offer," she said.

"Most people aren't ready for what I have to offer either," said Cheyenne.

Justine laughed. Cheyenne felt a glow around them.

"Are your parents alive?" Cheyenne asked.

"Yes."

"Do they know about us?"

"No. Why should they?"

The flatness startled Cheyenne but it was also a relief. A plain statement of fact, something nearly impossible to get out of Kirsten. As they walked, a new hope emerged, a trickle, a brook; maybe Justine really was her mother.

They continued to travel deeper into the woods. The trees were different from those Cheyenne knew. They weren't like the cedar, spruce, or fir at home or the maple, birch, and elm near Jackson's college. These were overgrown with brush and tangles and often she couldn't see through the canopy. They walked the edges of a place called Half Hell Swamp then went east to Boiling Spring Lakes where they turned down an old railroad grade.

Cheyenne stopped and sniffed the air.

"How close is the sea?" she asked.

"Maybe fifteen miles?"

Justine pulled a leaf from a nearby bush and toyed with it, twisting it around its spine.

"Do you ever regret leaving?" Cheyenne asked.

"It barely entered my mind until you came," said Justine.

Cheyenne felt the wind get knocked out of her. Maybe she had misheard. She asked again. "Do you mean that you never thought about it? Or that you never let yourself think about it?"

Justine tossed the wrecked leaf aside. "I didn't think about it," she said. Her voice was as clean as a sword stroke.

They continued walking until they reached the beach.

"Say a mother leaves her children because she thinks she isn't going to be a good mother. According to most people, that's somewhat horrifying but understandable. Maybe even noble. Or say a mother leaves because she doesn't care that much, but she's torn with regret later and it ruins her life: also, in its way, forgivable. Now, say a woman thinks she'd be a fine mom but leaves her children anyway and never feels any guilt at all. People are terrified of that kind of freedom."

Cheyenne watched her mouth, the skin around her eyes.

Justine pointed toward the ocean. "There is a lighthouse, an old one, not far from here on the coast. Apparently the waters around the Cape Fear River are treacherous. You should see it before you go."

Cheyenne felt like a stone statue of herself.

"For more than two hundred years that lighthouse has sent out a signal to fishing boats, slave ships, colonists, tourists—no distinction, no moral judgment; it lights everything. All around it sea turtles are hatched. We rush to protect them because we're afraid to watch, or afraid of the part of us that can watch. But the real truth is that only some turtles make it to the sea. Many people never get to freedom. They're just incapable. You're not. I can see that. So I'm going to say it again: I left you and I wasn't torn with guilt. I knew what I wanted to do and acted on it. I never thought about it much until you came. Now, how free do you want to be?"

Cheyenne felt a terrible awe. Justine was fearless. She had no remorse or doubt about anything she'd ever done. She had the will to move ever forward, a quality prized in great men. Maybe this was just what it looked like in a woman.

"We should go back," said Justine.

On their return to the yurt Justine talked about her upcoming trip to India. She went occasionally, she said, on retreats, sometimes for years. Her relationship with the temple needed to change, she said; she'd done what she could with it and now it was time for a change.

As she talked, Cheyenne saw it again, the unmistakable face of her sister.

"You should come with me," said Justine. "Get a little unfixed in who you are."

At seven the next morning Justine's students began to arrive, appearing out of the mist, sloshing through the swamp water. They took off their shoes and stepped into the yurt.

Cheyenne sat up on the cot. Glad she'd slept in her clothes.

"This is Cheyenne," said Justine, once everyone was in.

The way she said it, the tone, made Cheyenne think she was going to say more but Justine left it there.

"Let's start," she said.

Sitting down, she struck the meditation bell. Nothing happened.

People fidgeted or filled water glasses, they stretched. One rifled through a bag, another untangled a necklace clasp from her hair. It was as if they hadn't heard the bell at all. Cheyenne looked at Justine, offended for her, but Justine showed no sign of interest. Cheyenne leaned back against the wall of the yurt to wait it out. She watched them, forming a line to the coffeepot, staring vacantly out the window—who were these people anyway? Youngish, nowhere to be on a Monday morning. Ten minutes passed. The milling continued. Irritation crawled up her spine. Whatever agreement these people had, she wasn't in on it. No one had warned her. No one told her how to act. Do you know what this looks like from the outside? A student production of a French experimental play. A boring movie with the sound off. She had to go to the bathroom. She was still having her period and everything about the bottom of her felt heavy and everything about the top of her had been blown up into the sky. Irritation began moving up her spine as she realized she didn't know how long the meditation would go on. These people knew how long it was going to last so it was their privilege to set that thought aside. And is nothing so much a part of being a child as having no control over time, the land where everything is eternal until you are told different—why hadn't Justine woken her up earlier? Five more minutes passed and her rage got so bright and fast it burned the circuit. What was left of her was still and without current. The sounds had settled. Under her nails she felt the tender pink skin, and on her arms, the tiny hairs. Like a cut waiting to be sewn, open to everything. The meditation bell was struck once more. She could feel the waves of sound moving through her.

Justine shifted into a more comfortable position. "Death or fear?"

She waited.

"Who here has been terrified? I don't mean scared. I mean shit-your-pants terrified. Real terror. Like ice in your lungs, skin on fire, you can't breathe or speak, your guts turn to water—anybody?" Justine flashed a quick smile at Cheyenne. "Y'all should live a little more."

Cheyenne laughed but she was the only one.

"You've never been truly scared," said Justine. "Your fear is just a story. Your compassion is a story too. It's not-caring you feel. It's pity."

The idea that terrible things could just be a story had always enraged Cheyenne, but coming from Justine it sounded different.

"I met a woman in a truck stop when I first arrived, a waitress," said Justine. "She asked where I came from and I told her I was from the Midwest but spent time in Seattle and California. I named a few other places—I was very sophisticated. She had never heard of Washington State. I drew a map. She only recognized half of the country. Her whole world was the seventy square miles around where we stood. Anything that happened in those seventy miles would have been the End of the World. You know what she was doing? She was saving every penny to enter her five-year-old in a beauty contest in Huntsville to win a black-and-white TV. *My daughter is the most beautiful girl in the world.* She told me, 'If I take her there, everyone in the world will see it.'"

Justine looked at Cheyenne, then went on.

"I was in a Thai temple once and saw the body of a young woman rotting in a glass case. She'd been a great beauty, a former Miss Thailand. She died of a heart complication and donated her body to the monastery as training on impermanence. Death is always in the room. Here we lie about it. Teenagers have to make their own dead bodies just to show it to us. Collapsing bridges, ice sheets snapping in half—it's not important. Death is death." Justine's eyes fell on Cheyenne. "Why things happen doesn't matter."

Justine's gaze stayed for a few seconds and then she turned and went on, answering questions, asking some, all the time glancing back at Cheyenne, looping her into the secret conversation. The sense of connection grew until it was a physical thing in the room. It elevated her in a way she'd never felt. Not all daughters resemble their mothers. Not all people who look alike are related. When people got up to go, Cheyenne felt a rush of pride. That's right. You have to leave and I get to stay. She's mine, not yours.

As the door closed behind the last person, Cheyenne heard the solid swat of a hand slapping a counter.

"So many bugs," said Justine.

A man knocked. He was there to fix a leak under the sink.

"Oh, hi Jake. This is Cheyenne." Justine slapped the counter, killing the fly. "Cheyenne is a student of mine."

48 The Brochure

KIRSTEN LOOKED at the brochure the insurance broker had given her: SAY I LOVE YOU AFTER YOU'RE GONE.

There was no useful information in the brochure, like cost or exclusions. It was about selling their estate-management side, or so it seemed from the silver-haired men in the sunshine on a tennis court. Years ago, Margaret had taught her to look for the message beneath the message in advertising. Hint: It's usually paterfamilias. The broker went to ask the underwriter a question and Kirsten took out a pen.

~~SAY I LOVE YOU AFTER YOU'RE GONE~~

SAY GOODBYE WITH CASH

APOLOGIZE WITH MONEY?

~~SAY GOODBYE WITH MONEY~~

FREE YOUR SLAVES UPON DEATH

That was a message for sure, but not this message.

~~FREE YOUR SLAVES UPON DEATH~~

REST IN THE ILLUSION OF CONTROL

The broker returned. "Sorry about the wait. I'm new."

"Trust fund. Have you ever thought about those words? I mean trust is exactly what they're not about. That's what makes it funny," said Kirsten.

The broker gave her a vague smile. He'd never met anyone with a trust fund.

"I have a few more questions to get you a final quote. Are you the major breadwinner?"

"My kids are grown."

"But you want them to be secure after you're gone."

She laughed. "They aren't secure now."

"What about funeral expenses? Would you like a more comprehensive plan for when the time comes?"

"What's comprehensive?"

"We have plans for under fifty dollars a month that pay out at three hundred thousand."

Her mouth fell open. "I'm surprised you don't have more suicides."

"Well, we have precautions," he said but couldn't meet her eyes.

"You know, for someone paid to talk about death you're not very good at it." She sighed. "So how does it work?"

"You choose a policy. We do a health screening and start you on a plan."

"What if there's a problem with the health screening?"

"The policy might cost a little more, but we have pricing tiers to address most conditions. Unless it's something like cancer."

"No pricing tier for that?" she said.

"No, but it's not the end of the world either."

"Could be. You never know."

She faced the oncologist again with her insides displayed on the wall-mounted light box behind her.

"I'll do chemotherapy."

The oncologist fidgeted. "I'm not going to be able to keep seeing you," she said.

"I don't want to go over all of this with someone new."

"I know it's a very vulnerable time."

"You don't know the fucking half of it."

"You need a different type of care than I can provide."

"I have cancer. You're in oncology."

The oncologist cleared her throat. "Yes, but I'm on a different side of it."

She waited for Kirsten to understand but Kirsten didn't. The oncologist stood.

"I work with people who have a chance of getting better," she said. "Someone from palliative care will contact you."

The appointment was over, but Kirsten hadn't realized it until the oncologist stood.

Outside the sky was feathered with clouds. She was going to miss clouds. She was also going to miss the oncologist, which was ridiculous because she barely knew her, but all of a sudden the woman had seemed very beautiful. Kirsten stopped for a coffee and realized she was going to miss the barista who made her soy latte. She got on the bus and realized she was going to miss the bus driver even though she'd never met him. She looked around at the people on the bus. She was going to miss everybody.

She stopped by the grocery store where a woman from her coven worked and almost told her as practice, but then veered away from the subject. Once home, she cleaned her stove. She made a vegan Frito pie and cleared the cookies off her laptop.

It was her fault and she knew it. She had put off seeing the doctor and been dragging her feet on choosing treatment. It would be easier with money, but she wasn't the type to make a cancer Kickstarter campaign and blog; she had no desire to waste energy performing positivity for assholes. Photos of sunrises, her smiling in a bandanna—who was that supposed to comfort? But she wasn't a martyr. One of the kids was going to have to step up. She could write Justine and ask her to have Cheyenne call. But she was afraid it would sound like begging—and there's no way in hell that was happening. She wrote Livy at her last known address in Dutch Harbor.

Dear Livy, I have cancer of the stomach. I am going to die but
they tell me I will die less quickly if I try to kill my body first and fail.
I know it's not funny. I need you to come home. Love, Mom

She dropped the envelope into the glorious mystery of the US
postal system where it crisscrossed the mountains in flight, arcing
over the sphere until it landed on the harbormaster's desk. From
there it was shuffled into a box full of credit card offers and catalogs
to be burned as trash.

49 Sarah

JUNEAU WAS NOT AS DARK in November as it was farther north, but it was still darker than anything Livy had ever experienced. She'd gotten work doing minor repairs on a trawler owned by a snowbird living in Florida. That work led to other small jobs. She had no plans other than to get out of town, but that was turning out to be far harder than she expected. It's not like she could hitchhike on the roads that ended in the Tongass National Forest in both directions. Ferries and planes were expensive. Even if Sarah had that much money to spare, the idea of being in debt to a stranger made Livy's blood run cold. She had gotten herself here; she would get herself out. But every day she only made enough for food and a little bit to give Sarah for bills.

Cash in hand one afternoon, she stopped at the hippie grocery store on her way back to the apartment. All she needed was quinoa pasta but she got stuck in line behind a mother and daughter who evidently knew the cashier. The chatting was taking forever but Livy wasn't paying much attention until she heard the name of her old crabbing boat. *Eliana. Eliana.* She heard it again. Then the name of the captain came out of the woman's mouth. She spoke of the fishing season, best in years, according to her husband. This, Livy began to realize, was the captain's wife. Livy's skin started to vibrate. She looked at the girl, who was no more than fifteen. Slightly pudgy, dressed in a flannel shirt and jeans, hunched to hide her breasts: This was the captain's daughter.

The mother and daughter paid and left. Livy told the cashier she'd forgotten her wallet and followed them out. They got into a car and turned left out of the parking lot. Livy walked into the street. They drove just three blocks up the hill and parked. A porch light came on and they carried their groceries inside.

Livy walked slowly back to Sarah's, dropped the day's cash on the kitchen table like a dead rat, and went to bed. The next morning, she sat perched in the dark on the cold rung of a jungle gym in an old schoolyard. She watched the captain's house. Up and down the street everyone was getting ready for work or school. The porch light came on and the captain's daughter came out. She zipped up her coat and took out her phone, scrolled, and selected. The girl put in her earbuds and her face relaxed. She moved in small pulses, all motions circular, all angles rounded, trotting down her front steps. Livy followed her.

A few blocks later, the girl crossed a small footbridge and took stairs down the backside of the hill into a part of town Livy hadn't seen. A neighborhood of small, weathered, Easter egg–colored houses. The girl cut through the streets until they ended in an arterial that ran along the harbor in front of the high school. Livy followed her into the halls pressed with kids and teachers but lost her. A bell rang and the crowd thinned and she saw her again. The girl was alone. As alone as anyone Livy had ever seen. Students passed in pairs and groups and she never once looked around for a familiar face. A second bell rang and she took out her earbuds. As she wound the cord around her phone, Livy saw hatch-mark scars all over the girl's arms. Some healed, some new. Livy turned and walked away.

When she returned to Sarah's apartment, she heard a rustling sound in the kitchen, a scratching sound like an animal, and found Sarah with her nose in a family-sized box of cereal, shaking it, then going in with a fork to sift for raisins. When she found one, she carefully put it in a pile on the table. Then she shook the box again and looked inside, then drew back, fox-like, her red hair springing in all directions, and dumped the cereal on the table. When she had sorted out the number of raisins she wanted, she brushed the rest of the cereal off the table and back into the box.

"They always go to the bottom," she said.

"That's good, though. It makes the last few bowls taste like dessert."

"Yeah, but they're last. Tell me you're not the type who eats everything they hate first."

Sarah offered her the cereal box. Livy declined.

"The captain of the *Eliana* lives here. The *Eliana* was my boat, *Eliana*. He has a daughter and a wife. I was behind them in line at the grocery store and heard them talking. They are polite and buy organic and live just down the street. I followed them home then followed the girl to school this morning. I don't know why."

"What do you want to do?" asked Sarah.

"I honestly don't know."

She went out for another aimless walk.

Returning later that day she heard Sarah vacuuming her room. She'd only seen Sarah's room through a crack in the door. There was a mattress on the floor, a quilt for a sheet, a sleeping bag curled like a pill bug on top. Livy knocked and went in. The walls were covered with butcher paper with notes in different colors and arrows leading to bubbles of names that were underlined here and there with triple exclamation marks. Sarah shut off the vacuum cleaner.

She saw Livy looking at the walls.

"It's how I think," she said.

The word PRAJNA appeared several times on the butcher paper.

"Is this what you do?" Livy asked.

"Did," said Sarah. "I was a strategic planner for environmental campaigns targeting corporations, going after their client base to shame them into better behavior. It doesn't work. They're ashamed of nothing."

Sarah unplugged the vacuum cleaner and balled up the cord.

"People are assholes," said Livy. "They want to make money. You're never going to stop that."

Sarah pushed the vacuum cleaner into the corner and threw the cord over the top.

"What about talking to your family?" she said. "Have you thought about calling?"

"They wouldn't be able to help and then they would feel bad, and then I would feel bad about how they felt bad. Everyone would be worse. Did you know PRAJNA means deep universal enlightened wisdom? It's from the Upanishad."

"I know what it's from," said Sarah. Her tone was biting and Livy flinched. "Did you see any of the wells where you were fishing?" Sarah asked. "We tried to run a ballot initiative against the new drilling but got outspent."

"I think I saw a woman with a clipboard talking about that in a bar in Homer," Livy winked, "but I managed to duck her."

"Tell me you vote," said Sarah.

"Well I haven't but—"

Her perfect non-voting record had always been a source of pride. Now she had come down in Sarah's eyes and it bothered her more than it should.

"You're a gay woman," said Sarah. "What the hell is wrong with you?"

"It's not like whatever you think. I believe in democracy. I just think my whole life is a vote. Everyone's is." Livy pointed to photos taped to the wall, oil-covered sea otters and shorelines on fire. "Everyone voted for that."

Sarah sighed. "It's too bad you aren't a drunk," she said. "I was thinking about ways for you to get home if a job doesn't turn up. Or at least a place you can go. You're welcome here but I'm leaving in a few weeks. But if you were a drunk, you'd have more options. We could get you into a treatment center or a halfway house. Could you say you are? Who's to know? They'd have to take you at detox. I think they'd have to check your blood alcohol level but I suppose we

could get you really, really drunk—like alcohol-poisoning drunk—
and take you into the emergency room. They'd send you to detox
and we could advocate for a bed in a halfway house from there,
which is a stronger position and you'd only have a shitty headache
and the shakes."

"You said you were leaving. Where again?"

"Panama. PRAJNA is getting ready to drill down there too."

"I thought you quit."

"I did. Why do you think your family can't help? You should call
even if you don't say anything about what happened."

"Who?" asked Livy.

"Your mom."

"I—"

"I knew someone in a halfway house who replaced his windshield wiper fluid with vodka and ran a small hose into the car so
anytime he wanted a shot he just toggled the wiper arm. He'd sit in
the driveway and get plastered. They kept searching his room and
his car but could never find out how he did it. Ingenious. You might
like those folks. The control-freak part of you would be in agony but
they're charming in their way. What do you think would happen if
you called her?"

"My mom?" asked Livy.

"We could role-play the conversation if that would make the call
easier."

Livy looked horrified. Sarah laughed.

"Got it. Not your kind of role-play."

Sarah crossed her arms and looked at Livy. She walked toward
the kitchen then turned and came right back.

"You know it's not just you. I grew up here and that asshole lives
in my town."

"Sarah, you should see his daughter. That girl doesn't need one
more thing to make her life harder."

"You don't get to decide alone." Sarah's jaw tightened and she
burned holes in the carpet with laser eyes. "This is how they do it.

They force you to choose." She jabbed her finger in Livy's direction. "They force you to be the better person and act magnanimously. They rely on it."

"I do not have a magnanimous bone in my body," said Livy, "trust me."

Sarah tapped her thumb against Livy's collarbone in agitation.

"You should see her," said Livy. "It's written all over her. I don't think she has anyone. I'll be fine but she's a mess. Please."

"Fuck! Okay. Fuck. I will not out him publicly but I will warn everyone I know."

"That's fair."

"And tell them to warn everyone they know."

"Also fair."

Sarah paced in a tight circle then let out a long breath. Livy thought it was over so she started to make a grocery list on the palm of her hand with a pen but then Sarah screamed, "I fucking hate this!" at the top of her lungs and Livy dropped the pen. She stared wide-eyed, on alert for more yelling, but none came.

"I'll respect it," said Sarah after a minute, "but I think you're wrong."

"Thank you."

"By the way. We're going to have guests. We'll need to set up the room you're staying in."

"Of course. Just let me know when they're coming."

"I don't know when they're coming. They're tall-ship sailors."

"Tall-ships sailors? How are they getting here?"

Sarah rolled her eyes.

Livy was on her way to work a week later when she saw the high square sail of a fully rigged 1800s tall ship sailing up the Gastineau Channel. She heard commands shouted by a single voice and repeated in chorus. *Fenders up! Fenders up.* White eggs in the morning dark, the floats were raised from the water. When they reached the dock, a woman by the bowsprit threw a coil of yellow line. More lines and they made fast to the bollards. *Starboard watch coil and hang! Coil and hang. Portside watch lay aloft! Portside watch laying aloft.*

A crowd formed, watching the sailors climbing the shrouds. A hundred feet up in the dark, leaning out over the yard, tipping forward and back like seesaws. Livy heard the command to harbor furl followed by cursing. A gangway went down between the ship and dock. A burly woman with brown hair, a flat face, and wide-set puffy eyes carried a sandwich board across.

Discover the days of sail! Tour the authentic Russian ship the *Neva.*

Livy noticed that the ship on the sandwich board wasn't the same as the one docked before her. This *Neva* had three masts where the one in the picture had two.

That night Livy heard the sailors on Sarah's porch before she got halfway up the hill. She counted five voices in the dark in at least four conversations.

So we're making for Death's Door to avoid Hell's Asshole . . .

And they throw us a party, roast a pig in our honor, set off fireworks, open bar, trays of chocolate, and we're starting to sea stow and go . . .

Yeah, well I heard you went all the way to Liverpool with your sea cock hanging out.

Laughter.

Oh fuck you. There was some pretty valiant shit done on that boat you know nothing about.

The gun captain's gone full Crazy Larry.

Not speaking ill of the dead. I just think someone should have taken them to court years ago.

No, Cinderella, we changed our minds. Not until you harbor furl.

Hotter than a welder's ass.

Say again?

Hotter than a half-fucked fox in a forest fire.

I heard he was third mate when it went down.

Some things are unnecessary.

Blacker than a cow's insides.

Sarah opened the porch door and told them to shut up and get inside. Livy entered on their heels. In the kitchen, she was introduced to the sailors of the starboard watch, mostly all women. The one who'd set up the sandwich board was Marne. She was also the one giving the other sailor hell about the sea hen, or sea cock, whatever.

Three sailors bunked in Livy's room that night.

So they walk us right through the sandwich line and out the back door with only a plate each. All these re-creationists coming up. Hi! I'm Jim Smith the tinder. Elijah Owen the blacksmith, if you need a horse well-shod, I'm your man. And we're crawling with chiggers in our tarries and James is wearing that tie-dyed Phish shirt and Shaney just dyed her hair blue.

I remember that day. I got hit on twice by the Mayor of Imaginarytown.

Did he want to see what you looked like dressed as a handsome cabin boy?

I slept on the deck and got woken up by fucking musket fire.

Livy asked them to be quiet. They apologized. Two minutes later they were whispering to each other like drunks.

Yeah, totally, on my last boat you weren't supposed to clip in. Someone was washed over, gone.

A bunch of fucking yachties is what they got . . .

Yeah, well you can go over just walking around on deck.

I love these bastards who say it's not traditional to clip in. Sailors used to lash themselves to shit all the time in big weather.

A hand for you, a hand for the ship.

Say again?

One hand for you. One hand for the ship.

At 2:00 a.m. Livy gave up and made for the living-room chair. Sarah heard her and invited her to sleep in her room. A lit candle flickered in a jar by the mattress. She looked at the butcher paper on the walls and it seemed different. It wasn't gibberish but something more delicate; Sarah's mind captured on paper, how she thought of the world. Looking in the candlelight now, words and names, Sarah was tracking gossamer belief systems, childhood relationships. Her creativity reseeded itself on each wall, tendrils, vines.

Livy lay down nearby. She was nervous. She wasn't sure how close to Sarah she should be. Her meters were failing.

"What do you think of them?" Sarah asked.

"They seem to mean well. How did you meet them?"

"Marne and a couple of the others were part of that coalition against PRAJNA last year."

Livy could feel the heat from Sarah's body so she scooted back. Her hands were shaking. Her own body was untrustworthy.

"They're my free ride to Panama," said Sarah.

"That's a slow ride."

Sarah took out her gold drop earrings and put them by the base of the candle jar.

"What's your deal with Panama?" asked Livy.

"I like the sun."

"They don't make sunblock for skin like yours."

"It's called clothing."

Livy smiled. "And buildings."

Sarah got into her sleeping bag.

"But really, why there?"

"Oil companies. Capital. It's one of those places assholes meet and hide their money."

"I thought that was everywhere," said Livy. She ran her hand across the carpet. "Sarah, I don't know how to say this." She paused. "Don't waste your life on politics."

Sarah didn't say anything. Livy felt like she was staring so she looked away.

"Have you thought about what you're going to do?" Sarah asked. "My landlord might let you take over this place. It's not bad with a roommate."

But Livy didn't really hear any of this. Behind Sarah's flame halo of hair, words flickered and blinked in the candlelight. Circles and circles, arrows and arrows. Sarah shifted and those went away, now lost behind her shoulder, exposing a list of names. Some were underlined, others had stars by them. One was her father's name. Livy turned her head slightly as if seeing it in the periphery would make it make sense, but when she turned her head back it was the same.

Livy gestured toward the wall. "Who are those people?"

Sarah twisted around to look. "Board members. Investors." She resettled herself.

Cyril's name was now slightly higher over Sarah's head, as if it had risen in the night sky. The importance of his name, a shell containing a vapor, nothing at all. The strangeness of it next to the rightness of it, because everything in this moment was right. Livy wanted it no other way. If he was part of it, so be it. Whatever it was, let it all come.

Just before Sarah blew the candle out, Livy traced again the line of her shoulders with her eyes. Sarah's body was unlike other bodies. Her narrow ankles and bony elbows, her long neck and thin limbs, they were not brittle like Livy originally thought but made of unbreakable silver metal. Her arteries painted fine blue lines on her arms and wrists and temples. She was almost translucent and reminded Livy of the plastic doll she'd had as a kid that was clear so you could see its organs. Livy wondered if the blue veins leading to and from Sarah's heart would be visible on her breastbone.

You can't fall in love in two weeks. Anybody who says so is lying.

You can't fall in love in three weeks. If you do, you're in love with a projection.

Livy could deal with the idea that her feelings might be lies. But the idea that Sarah was just a creature of her mind, that was unbearable. Even if today was the last day she ever saw her, it meant a great deal to Livy that Sarah was in the world.

50 The Proposal

IT WAS EARLY NOVEMBER when Essex was granted a full day of liberty. He decided to rent a car and drive south to see if he could find Cheyenne. Kirsten had given him Justine's address, but that was more than a month ago. Given his sister's ability to burn through entire social scenes in under a week, it was just as likely that she was a thousand miles away as it was that she was in North Carolina. But having nothing better to do he drove, taking the scenic route, not rushing, but heading generally toward where Cheyenne might be.

Parking at the monastery, he wandered into the temple where he found a man dusting an enormous green Buddha. The man had a coastal Southern accent, the kind Essex had come to love and associate with an open welcome. When Essex asked about Justine, the man's expression changed and a reserve set in, but he was polite and told Essex where he needed to go.

The deciduous trees were bare, the swamp as much mud as water. Once on the small dock he saw Cheyenne through the windows of the yurt. He watched her for a minute, stunned that she could not feel him, then knocked.

She looked up but did not move because he could not be there.

"Aren't you going to let me in?"

She jumped to open the door. "Is everyone okay?"

"They're fine," he said, pushing on the screen door, which was swollen in the humidity, until it popped open and he walked into the yurt.

"What's your problem?" he asked.

"I thought you might have bad news."

She hadn't seen him in almost five months. He had become oddly muscular and his hair was shorn. His blue nuclear-reactor-pool eyes followed her. He shifted in his cheap Mexican shirt with roses embroidered at the collar. It didn't quite fit in the shoulders, so he rounded them to compensate. She noticed his caving posture but attributed it to something else. There was still a shadow of late-summer tan fading on the back of his neck and on his forehead. Damp from crossing the swamp at dusk, irritated, his ears reddened and the skin around his hairline turned pink while she took him in.

"You look like you should have a serial number tattooed on your neck," she said.

"You should see us in uniform. We're a bucket of matching marbles."

"What are you doing here?"

Justine called from the dock, "Get the door. My hands are full."

Essex saw panic on Cheyenne's face.

"What is with you?" he said.

He opened the door for the woman because he was closer.

As Justine came in, he stepped back to give her room and was standing behind the screen as she passed. He saw immediately what Cheyenne had seen when she first arrived: Livy.

Justine set the groceries down.

"This is my brother, Essex," said Cheyenne.

Justine introduced herself then went back out for another bag of groceries. As soon as she was gone Essex turned on Cheyenne.

"Does Livy know?" he said.

"Know what?"

Annoyance crossed his face.

"Livy doesn't care about any of this," said Cheyenne.

"What about her?" He pointed to Justine. "Does she know?"

Cheyenne said nothing.

"You know what, I don't care," he said. "What you do is your business. But if Livy ever asks me I'm going to tell her the truth."

"She won't ask."

"Just letting you know I'm not a part of this."

Justine returned.

"So you're Kirsten's boy," she said.

"Not biologically," said Cheyenne.

"Yes," said Essex, "I am her son."

"Aren't you supposed to be in the Midwest?" said Cheyenne. "Or on some kind of island?"

"They sent me to Lejeune for infantry training. It wasn't my choice."

Cheyenne laughed. "I'm sure it wasn't."

"Do you know where you'll end up?" asked Justine.

"Wherever they want him too," said Cheyenne.

"The Middle East most likely," said Essex, looking at Cheyenne. "Not yet, though."

Cheyenne started to put groceries away. An animal scurried across the steps. The sound was followed by a small splash into the water. Essex straightened like he'd woken up.

"What time is it?" he asked.

Justine glanced at the west-facing windows. "About six."

"It feels later," he said.

"It's the swamp," said Cheyenne. "The sun sets earlier here because of the trees."

"The sun sets at the same time with or without the trees," said Essex.

"No, it doesn't, because we turn around the sun and what we see or don't see is relative. And since we invented the whole sunset thing, if it appears to be dark earlier, the sun sets earlier."

Essex brushed the wrinkles out of his shirtsleeves. He was sure she was wrong.

"I have to be back in a few hours. I want to take you to dinner," he said.

"You should go," said Justine. "There's a spaghetti place about twenty minutes north of town. You'll have just enough time if you leave now."

Cheyenne grabbed her jacket and a flashlight. Justine waved them off.

At the dock's edge Cheyenne shone a light on the black swamp water. Essex stepped where she directed but his leg disappeared up to midcalf and he wondered if she was doing it on purpose.

"You should have taken your shoes and socks off," she said.

"They were already wet."

She stepped into the swamp with her shoes on and went around him.

"I can't believe you haven't told her," said Essex.

"Save it for the restaurant, please."

He stopped, cupped his hands around his mouth, and shouted into the trees. "Justine looks exactly like Livy! Livy, Livy, Livy, Livy . . ." adding the echo the heavy swamp air couldn't offer.

Cheyenne turned to slosh back to the yurt but Essex grabbed her arm. "Come on. It's a joke."

"It's not a joke. I'm sure she heard you."

"What's going on with you? You're not a liar. You've never even been able to keep a secret. What are you doing?"

"Justine and I could be related. We're alike in ways that aren't physical."

He looked at her in shadow light.

"You don't need to be ashamed about being wrong. No one is going to hold it against you. You've been wrong lots of times and you've certainly fucked up plenty."

She stopped. "Apologize for that."

"I'm not apologizing. It's true." He threw back his head and sang, "Livy, Livy, Livy . . ."

The spaghetti place was not a spaghetti place but a diner that advertised Chinese and American food with two pasta dishes, spaghetti with meatballs and lasagna. After five, the paper place mats went away and were replaced by red-and-white-checked vinyl tablecloths. Oil candles in scalloped glass holders shaped like eggplants were lit at the end of the day.

"Get fried rice or orange chicken and I'll split it with you," said Cheyenne.

"Order a full meal."

"I am. I'm having lasagna too."

"I'm having sweet-and-sour chicken. You can have some of that."

"Chicken candy doughnut," she said.

Essex smiled. "That's about right."

Cheyenne glanced sheepishly at the napkin dispenser. "I didn't make it up. A friend did."

"See what I mean? You aren't a liar. You don't take credit that isn't yours. What the hell are you doing?"

The server came. They ordered. Essex was quiet for a minute; he put his finger on the center of his knife and spun it like a dial.

"Kirsten said you had her car," he said.

"I got caught in a tornado in Texas and had to pull the plates and leave it. The whole thing was," her mouth twitched, "wild. Mostly in a bad way but also in a now-you-know-your-universal-address way."

She looked out the window. Her eyes were shining but on closer examination Essex realized it wasn't tears, only a reflection of passing taillights from a car in the parking lot.

"You don't have to worry about it. I bought Kirsten a car when I went back."

She couldn't imagine him buying someone a car.

"She gave me the title in case you needed to sell the Toyota," he said. "Obviously not applicable."

"How was she? When you saw her."

Essex shrugged. "Seemed fine. She thought she was getting the flu but she wasn't super down about anything. She said she's only gotten a postcard from you."

The server brought egg drop soup and lukewarm jasmine tea.

Cheyenne watched a new car pull into the parking lot, dump trash in the restaurant dumpster, and leave.

"What's it like being a marine?" she asked.

"I'll tell you when I feel like one." Essex poured tea into the plastic cups.

Cheyenne jittered her legs under the table.

"What do you think of Justine?" she asked. "You should read her letters. She's awake in a way most people aren't. She really doesn't give a fuck what other people think."

"Is that a good thing?"

"Of course it's a good thing."

Essex was no longer sure that was true.

"I wanted to talk in case we don't get to talk later," he said. "We should both be realistic about what might happen. I know you would feel like shit if I died and our last conversation was you being an asshole to me so I decided to come here and save you from yourself."

"I go into silent retreat in a few days. Justine says silent retreats were the place she really learned not to care about everyone's opinions."

Essex rolled his eyes.

"What?" she said.

"It's just hard to imagine you in a silent retreat."

"Well I am. For a month. There's a smaller yurt not far from Justine's. I go there, they bring me food, and I come for dhamma talks."

"I kind of like to think of you in a shed out back not talking." He smiled and she made a grossed-out face.

"Marry me," said Essex.

She laughed.

"I'm not joking. Put everything I've ever said about us aside. This isn't that. This is about money and security. Someone should have the benefits I have now. There's health care, there's everything. If you marry me, you get it. They'll take care of you."

"You have to be kidding."

Essex shook his head.

"You should ask Livy."

"I did," said Essex. "Apparently even a fake heterosexual marriage is unbearable."

"Well, finally we know what wins the war between cheap and gay," said Cheyenne.

"She said she'd rather peel her own eyeballs. Look, for real. They have all sorts of things you can get." He opened his mouth and pointed to a molar. "I got a crown and they didn't charge me a thing."

"My teeth are fine."

"How do you know?"

"Jackson had dental insurance."

"That was, what, five years ago?" he said.

"Teeth don't go bad after you're a kid."

"Did you make that up? Please. This is a chance for at least two of us to have something. If you get sick, you'll be taken care of, and if I get killed—"

"Spare me the drama."

"If I get killed at least it's something. There'd be money for you."

"Livy really said no?"

Their food came and the subject of marriage was dropped. Several times he caught her staring at him. When he didn't think she saw him, he glanced at his watch and the clock on the wall. The simple thought of Essex having to be somewhere on someone else's schedule was eerie. She was seeing someone else in her brother's body. The alarm went off. Wake up! Like Kirsten with a job, like Livy refusing to talk to her, like Justine having no real relation to Cheyenne at all—something is wrong, something's wrong, something is terribly wrong.

The waiter cleared the plates and brought fortune cookies with the bill.

Essex slid a couple of twenty-dollar bills to the edge of the table.

"All they need is a driver's license and something with your social security number on it. Tax returns, W-2s, anything," he said.

"I lost my social security card years ago. I'd never get a replacement in time."

Essex laid his hand on her wrist. "Life is about choices, Cheyenne," he said in his best psyche-nurse voice. "You can actually choose to shut up any time you want. You don't have to wait on anybody else."

She pushed his hand away. "I'd have to talk it over with Justine," she said.

"If you have to, but I may not be here in a month."

"What's it like taking orders?"

"Honestly I don't mind letting someone decide things for me for a while."

"That's pathetic."

"You're the one who thinks you have to ask permission to marry."

"Advice isn't the same as permission."

"I'm just saying. I'm tired. You must be too. Marry me. Take the benefits. Use everything you can. They're just going to sit there if you don't."

Cheyenne considered. "How long would it take—if I did have proof of my social?"

"Instant. We go to the Jacksonville courthouse, one day. I file all the papers with the corps the next. Done."

She nodded. "Hand me your phone."

Cheyenne dialed Kirsten's number. She hadn't spoken to her since she'd driven away six weeks earlier.

Kirsten answered. "Essex?"

"No, it's me," said Cheyenne.

Kirsten cleared the gravel from her throat. "Are you with Essex?"

"Yes, but we're in a restaurant so I can't talk long. I need you to look for something. You know those collection notices I get? The ones for my student loans? They're usually yellow or bright pink. I need you to send me one of those notices. You'll have to overnight it."

"Is everything okay?"

"Yeah, it's just paperwork."

Kirsten started to say something but Cheyenne cut her off.

"I'm in a restaurant. I'll call again soon."

51 Everything You Do

KIRSTEN OVERNIGHTED the paperwork to Essex. After, she changed her sheets and cleaned out the fridge, which had several things rotting in it because she didn't eat like she used to. A call came in but it was from an unknown number so she let it go to voice mail. It was many hours before she remembered to check the message.

She set the phone on the kitchen counter and played the message on speaker while she sorted the bills. Sarah's voice filled the room. It was soft, shaking, and relentless. Kirsten put the bills down and watched the phone while Sarah spoke. When it was done, she picked it up slowly and hit Play again. She held it to her ear like a conch shell but there was no ocean, only the quiet static of a bad connection cut through by Sarah's voice. Halfway through the message she called the number back but it went to voice mail. She hung up and called again. On the third time she left a message. She had no idea what she said. When she was done she set the phone facedown on the counter. She never wanted to touch it or turn it over again. She stepped back and looked around the room.

Every fucking thing you do. Every fucking thing you teach. Every candle lit for the safe passage of girlhood through this world—and what's the fucking point? If none of it was ever going to matter, what's the fucking point? Kirsten kicked over the coffee table and trashed the living room like a rock star. She smashed one plate after another in the kitchen. She called a friend in the coven to practice saying it. She howled until she could say it then said it until she could whisper it, *Some asshole raped my daughter, some asshole raped my daughter, my beautiful little girl.*

52 The *Neva*

THE SECOND NIGHT the *Neva* was in port sailors from the other watch filled the apartment. They were just as chatty as the starboard watch had been but drunker. This time Sarah got drunk with them and Livy drank too. She watched Sarah move around the room, aware that every time Sarah looked at her, she was already looking at Sarah. By 1:00 a.m. Livy was solidly drunk like everyone else. Sarah invited her to stay in her bedroom again.

"You can sleep on the mattress and I can sleep on the floor if you want," she said.

"That's ridiculous, it's your bed. Are you leaving? With them when they go? You said they were your ride."

Sarah shook her head. "We're going to meet up somewhere down south. I have things to tie up here first."

Livy nodded. "I know him."

"You know who?"

Livy crossed to a wall where a list of names appeared on butcher paper.

"I know him." She tapped the fourth name down. "He's an asshole. He's married to a teenager—well she's probably not technically a teenager—he's rich and prefers Tibetans."

Sarah gaped. "How? Do you have his address?"

Livy laughed. Sarah's cheeks flushed. A patch of red blossomed across her collarbone and her lips turned faintly purple. Livy dropped her hand from the paper.

"What?" said Sarah.

"What you look like when you're really excited. It's how I thought you would look."

"Are you making fun of me?"

"I'm drunk, never mind," said Livy. "This name—" She rubbed it a little hard putting a tear in the paper. "This name, Cyril. I know him. You don't need to know him. He won't help you do anything. He's just the classic Allfather with too much power and— Hold on. Make fun of you? You're beautiful and smart and—why would I ever make fun of you? I wouldn't. Not for anything."

The room spun slightly. Livy turned back to the wall.

"A jerk of sky-god proportions who lives in Singapore and has no daughters." She slapped the name Cyril.

Sarah looked confused.

"Don't worry. Never mind. I'm just talking trash," said Livy.

Sarah came close, so close that Livy knew if she closed her eyes she would still know exactly where every part of Sarah's body was.

Livy leaned back against the wall pulling Sarah with her and kissed her, but right when it was getting good Livy started crying.

"Fuck. I'm drunk. It's not you. Sorry. Kiss me again," said Livy.

"I have to tell you something," said Sarah.

"I don't want to know anything."

She put her hands lightly on Sarah's shoulders.

"It's important. I did something bad. I thought it was good but it was bad."

"Nope," said Livy, shaking her head. "I still don't want to know."

"I called your mother."

Livy became still. All the small movements of her body, the swaying and shifting stopped. There was only her breath.

"I should have told you," said Sarah.

Livy lifted her hands from Sarah's shoulders and lowered her arms.

"I pulled her number from the emergency contact sheet at the center and called."

"Why would you do that?"

"You weren't going to do anything about the captain. I'm leaving and I don't want to be the only one who knows what's going on with you."

Livy moved off the wall and sat down where she'd slept the night before.

She couldn't think of Kirsten. She hadn't been able to for weeks. Because when she did think of her, Livy was little again, afraid of trees at night, afraid of being reincarnated as a mouse and not seeing the owl, all those strange untranslatable fears from the dawn of memory.

"I need to sleep," she said.

Livy crawled under a blanket. Sarah lay down on the mattress and blew out the candle. The room was dark and silent but for breath and rain.

The next morning Livy found Marne on the docks. They had spoken several times on the night Marne had stayed at Sarah's and Livy was pretty sure if any of the sailors were in charge of anything, it was her.

"I need to leave Juneau," Livy told her. "I have experience at sea. Do you have a job?"

Marne said nothing.

"I'm good at knots," said Livy.

"Round turn and two half hitches is all I'd let you do—and anyone can do that," said Marne.

"I don't really care what you make me do."

Marne shrugged and took her below to meet the captain. An hour later Livy had signed papers waiving all liability and was assigned a canvas seabag with a number on it and a hammock inside.

"You're going to need a rig." Marne tapped the knife and marlinspike on her belt.

"I lost my marlinspike."

"I've got an extra. I'll make you a knife when we're under way. Just find a belt."

"What kind of gloves do I need?"

Marne smiled. "We don't use gloves."

Livy spent her last afternoon in Juneau walking around downtown looking at jewelry in windows. Even the smallest pendants were more money than she had. After a while, she found herself in the makeup aisle of a drugstore staring at gaudy necklaces.

On a plastic arm between necklaces with saucer-sized peace signs or dollar bills or bells, she saw a charm bracelet with three charms, one of which was a captain's wheel. She slipped the bracelet off the rack and dropped it into her inside pocket.

At a coffee shop she took the bracelet apart, then used a pen to work open the stitches in her pocket and fish out the necklace she'd stashed there. She slipped the jade pendant off Cheyenne's necklace and replaced it with the captain's wheel. Whatever she left Sarah, she wanted it to come from her alone. Or at least as much as possible. She put Cheyenne's jade pendant in her coat lining. Taking a flier from the wall that advertised a show long over, she wrote Sarah a letter on the back in case she didn't see her before she left. She thanked her and apologized. Then she folded it around the necklace with the captain's wheel and borrowed tape from the barista to seal it shut. Sarah was home when she got there, though, so when she wasn't looking, Livy left the envelope in the key drawer.

Sarah wasn't surprised when Livy told her she was leaving.

"I have a belt. It's leather. You can have it," she said. "I got it for free. It has a buckle with a Big Dipper stamped into it but I guess that doesn't matter."

Livy put the belt on but pulled her shirt down over it.

They stood on the porch.

"My mom would like you," said Livy.

"She left me a message saying I should be banned from ever working in a domestic violence shelter."

"You should."

"And that she was going to call and get me blacklisted."

"She will," said Livy.

"She did. Yesterday."

Livy smiled. "How did she sound?"

"Angry. It was just a message. I didn't call back."

Sarah crossed her arms and shivered. She'd stepped out onto the porch without her jacket.

"She thanked me too," she said.

"That also sounds like her."

Sarah fixed her eyes on the rain glinting under the streetlamp. She forced a smile. "I'd like to stay in touch."

Livy stepped into the field of Sarah's radiant body heat, kissed her, and stepped back.

"I'd rather you didn't," she said and left.

The *Neva* got under way the following morning. They took up the shore power and water. The dock lines were singled and taken, fenders pulled and stowed; they motored out into the current.

53 Jacksonville

THE STUDENT LOAN collection notice that Kirsten had overnighted to Cheyenne was hot pink and written in ALL CAPS using whatever font they use on drunk-driving billboards.

"That is your paperwork with your social security number on it?" said Essex when he picked her up.

Cheyenne laughed out loud. The idea that this might be the piece of paper that would finally serve as her ticket into the lower-middle-class lifestyle was too much. Or it was perfect. She couldn't tell.

"I got rings," he said and dug two plain bands from his pocket. "I got silver so they wouldn't look like wedding rings unless we were together. They're real sterling." He handed her one. "See if it fits. I got a third one, too, that's a little bigger if it doesn't."

She put it on and held out her hand.

He smiled. "You like it."

"Yeah, they're pretty. If I was going to have a wedding ring, I'd like one like this."

But of course she'd had a wedding ring and it wasn't like this, so that was a dead end.

She took it off and handed it back.

"I need to get something to wear," she said.

In a thrift store they found a denim halter dress and rope-colored wedge sandals. At a pharmacy she bought lipstick and a floral scarf for her hair. Essex was in uniform.

Jared waited outside the courthouse. As soon as he saw her, he started laughing. Another marine was there too, from the South by his accent, a second witness.

Cheyenne began to feel it. In every administrative action, in the stamping of papers, the signing of documents, and transfer of fees, there was a quality of tenderness. Even the justice of the peace seemed to perform his duty with more gentleness than the state required. When it was time to kiss, the Southern marine had tears in his eyes.

"Make it look real," Essex whispered in her ear.

Outside the magistrate's office everyone congratulated Cheyenne so sweetly that she nearly died of guilt. A car waited on the street, a loaner with "Just Married" soaped on the back and a few cans tied to the bumper. Everyone was trying. Everyone wanted them to have something to hang on to. It was too much. Cheyenne ended up crying too.

The marine held the car door for them before sliding into the driver's seat next to Jared.

"Where are we going?" she asked Essex.

"They got us a motel."

She pinched him. He refused to look at her.

"Well they better not want proof of anything," she said.

The motel was not far from Camp Lejeune. When they unlocked their room there was a vase of flowers on the particleboard dresser next to a bottle of champagne and fifty bucks. Essex picked up the note. It was from his commanding officer.

"He likes me. I don't know why." He put the note down. "He's a dad who didn't have a dad. I think he has a soft spot that way. I thought they'd all be assholes but they're not."

Essex hung the jacket of his dress uniform carefully in the closet.

"You make it sound like a quilting circle," said Cheyenne.

"It's definitely not that."

"The Marines. One Big Quilting Circle. The Few, the Crafty—the Marines."

He laughed.

She looked around. "How long do we have to stay here?" she asked.

"You have to sign some things in the morning. I need to report back by lunch tomorrow."

They got a bucket of ice. They reconned the blue kidney-shaped swimming pool and decided it wasn't worth buying bathing suits. They peeked into the exercise room and saw a pink man drenched in sweat running on a moving belt. They drank champagne then made a beer run and played hands of casino and rummy.

"Are you as bored as I am?" Cheyenne asked.

"Not really."

"Let's rearrange the furniture."

"I'm pretty sure it's bolted down."

The motel carpet was oppressive. The TV kept staring back. Occasionally there was action in the parking lot but it never amounted to anything.

The idea slipped into her head that there was one thing they could do. It's not like she hadn't considered it before. She had. But it didn't seem fair. Still, Essex had charm. A rare kind of confidence that came from nowhere and was based on nothing. None of the guys or ex-students she'd slept with in the past two years had that. The little colonials, the little Livingstons, what seemed to be confidence with them turned out to be only entitlement. Essex wasn't like that. Other things weighted it down. And he was an adult. She didn't need to make his decisions for him.

"Your bet," he said.

She tossed her cards on the table. "I fold." Getting up she went and hovered over him. "Exactly how bored are you?" she asked.

"I'm not bored at all."

Cheyenne knocked his arm off the chair with her knee. He put his arm back on the armrest keeping his eyes on her the whole time. She knocked it off again.

"You're a bully," he said.

"If we do this, can you promise me you won't make it a thing?"

It wasn't a fair thing to ask and she knew it.

"I promise," he said. "Not a word about it."

Thirty seconds later, pressed up against the wall, feeling him hard against her hips, she wondered why she had ever made such a big deal about having sex with him. But then again she knew, because he was in love with her and she was not in love with him and she was usually a decent person.

"Back up," she said, "I don't have any room."

He stepped back and she got down on her knees and started to unzip his pants but he stopped her.

"I'll come too fast. I've got another idea."

He grabbed a pillow off the bed and had her lie down on the floor with it under her hips. Pushing up the denim dress with two fingers, he pulled aside the crotch of her panties. She took a few breaths and closed her eyes then she sat up.

"Not here."

"Okay." He helped her up.

He took off his shirt and undid the halter tie of her dress, which fell to the ground. They stood close, her skin on his. He didn't want it to stop but she was already moving.

"Maybe the dresser?" she asked.

"The height is wrong."

"Yeah, probably. The handles would dig into my thighs too. Okay, the bed."

They went to the edge and she turned around and he bent her over the bed and she shimmied out of her panties while he undid his pants. He put his hand on her ass and she felt a rush of heat and wetness, then realized that he wasn't hard anymore.

He paused then shifted to the left, reached for the pillow and put it on the floor by the bed, then got on his knees to go down on her, but she slipped aside twisting herself up onto the mattress. They were suspended. He sat back.

"You don't want me to?" he asked.

"It feels a little personal."

He laughed. She glared.

"Okay then, what isn't too personal?"

"What we were doing," she said.

"Let's do that then."

But she didn't move. She chewed the edge of her lip.

He lay back. She crawled on top but didn't do anything.

Someone pulled into the motel parking lot blasting the Steve Miller Band. A jangle of guitar, a lazy abuse of the hammer-on, the reverb, a hallowing of the midrange. Cheyenne looked down at him.

"'Take the Money and Run.' *Texas. Facts Is. Taxes.* They're geniuses," he said.

She began moving back and forth across his body, brushing over him, leaning close enough to feel the hairs on his skin but not touching his skin. She could hear his breath in her ear and the places it caught. When she finally did touch his skin and slid onto him everything was fine. The song ended but no DJ came on.

"I thought it was the radio," she said.

"He's a true fan."

"If it's *Greatest Hits,* 'Rock'n Me' is next and he's a poser."

"No," said Essex, "because 'Take the Money and Run' and 'Rock'n Me' appear back to back on both *Fly Like an Eagle* and *Greatest Hits.*"

She sat up, drawing her knees in to press against his ribs.

"Damn. I had no idea you were such a fan."

It was a little too cool, a little cutting. Essex cocked his head and looked at her in a way she wasn't entirely comfortable with.

"I've had a lot of experiences, thoughts, ideas you don't know a thing about," he said. "Try asking."

He said it plain. She didn't think it was a jab but wasn't sure. There had been several points over the past few days where what he said made her wonder how much he might have changed. He gave her a half smile and she relaxed, but that smile, too, was an unfamiliar expression. It occurred to her that what he said was true. She didn't know him as well as she thought she did.

He began to sing: *"I ain't superstitious and I don't get suspicious 'cause my woman is a friend of mine . . ."*

"If you keep singing I'm going to stop fucking you."

When "Rock'n Me" ended, she was getting really close to coming and not thinking about the music at all. Her body was shivering in waves but then Essex stopped.

"Okay. You're right," he said. "It is *Greatest Hits*. He's a total poser fan."

She sat bolt upright and slapped him. "You're such an asshole! Oh fuck, I'm so sorry," she put her hands over her mouth, "I hit you. I'm really sorry."

Red spread across the inflamed left side of his face.

"It's all right. Just don't do it again."

"I won't. I'm so sorry."

She could feel him soften a little inside her.

"Do you want to keep going?" she asked.

"Hell yeah."

"People don't say hell yeah."

"Don't tell me what people say."

They were moving again and he was getting harder. He started to sing again: *"Don't get suspicious, now baby don't be suspicious, 'cause you know you are a friend of mine."*

"Stop!" she said. "If I start laughing you are definitely not hanging out inside of me."

It was a side of her he didn't know. She leaned down and kissed him. It was the first long kiss they'd had since he was a teenager and his whole body came alive. Hers too.

"You get on top," she said.

"Okay, but I want you to touch yourself."

"No problem."

A few minutes later he came and then she came, laughing so hard that everything around them shattered into little pieces. The rest of the evening was a world inside a world. Their tenuousness was replaced by a new language with stretches of silence almost like labor, stretches of intensity. Going all the way there, not going all the way there, singing because he couldn't seem to help himself, and a softer less rage-filled slap, because she couldn't either.

What a fucking show is chemistry.

After dozing for a few minutes, Essex rolled over in the bed. Cheyenne stood up and turned on the overhead light. His eyes followed her around the room.

"Stop looking at me," she said.

"Can't I look at my wife?"

She froze.

"It's a joke. I know it's not a real marriage."

"But it's not really a joke, is it?"

The anger passed and she just looked tired.

"I don't expect anything from you."

She laughed.

"I don't. I'm not a kid. I know we have a complex relationship."

"Yeah, we got married and spent the whole afternoon having sex. I can't imagine how you got confused."

Essex's phone rang and he answered it while she got dressed.

It was Kirsten. As she talked he felt like his organs were turning to lead.

"Put Cheyenne on," Kirsten said and he handed the phone over.

While Cheyenne listened, he made sure to stay a few feet away. He wanted to be close enough for her to know he was there for her, but he was no longer clear what he was to her so he didn't know how close or where to stand. Unable to locate who he was to her now—brother, friend, lover—he hovered between all points, hulking, awkward, in the way. When she crossed the room to the bed, he moved quickly aside to give her space. When she sat down by the end table, he sat on the corner of the bed. Cheyenne hung up and threw the phone with full force at the dresser beneath the TV, where it exploded into parts on the carpet.

"I fucking hate men. I fucking hate them!" She looked at Essex. "I'm sorry but I do," she said.

"It's okay, it's understandable. Tell me what you need."

"I need this not to have fucking happened!" she yelled.

She snatched up her denim wedding dress and put it on.

Cheyenne picked phone parts off the carpet by the TV and handed him the pieces. The part of her that could cry about this felt dead. She wanted to kill something she couldn't reach.

They drove to the monastery to tell Justine she was leaving. Essex waited in the car while she walked through the swamp so out of her body it seemed like she was playing a part in a movie; the brush and the trees, the patches of streaming sunlight, a cinematographer gone mad, and she, a small thing moving through. She saw Justine on the dock and the sense of distance broke. Her similarity to Livy overwhelmed Cheyenne and she lost it. Crying and breathless she heaved out the words. Justine put her arm around her. She tucked Cheyenne's hair behind her ear.

"It's not a crisis," she said, "it happens."

"I have to go."

"You'll do more for your sister by staying and doing your silent retreat."

Cheyenne drew back.

"Ask yourself," Justine said, "who does it really comfort to show up unasked?"

Cheyenne's mind went blank for a second. She looked at the older woman then she shook her head and went to get her things. There was no way she was going to sit in a swamp until she knew what was happening with her sister.

When she got back to the car Essex had finished taping his phone back together and Cheyenne called the airlines about tickets to Alaska while he drove. In Jacksonville they stopped at the bank and Essex put her name on his account. They got her a phone, added her to his plan. More documents for the military. Signatures. Outside official conversations, he made sure not to say the words *marriage* or *wife*.

At the airport he gave her sixty dollars. "Sorry it isn't more. They'll deposit my paycheck Friday. Once that goes through, you'll have enough for the return ticket."

Cheyenne looked past Essex. "I should have told her Livy was her daughter."

Kirsten had given Cheyenne Sarah's name and phone number. Outside of showing up, there was no plan. Justine was right. Livy would see this as an invasion. She shouldn't have come.

At the Juneau airport, she called Sarah and that's when she found out Livy was gone.

"She left this morning. I'm sorry. I didn't expect anyone to show up in person."

"How did she leave?"

"She got a job on a tall ship."

"Like one of those Disney pirate rides?"

"They're not really like that," said Sarah.

"I don't care what they're like. Where was it going?"

"Seattle by the end of the month then farther south. I assume Livy's getting off there but I don't really know."

"Does she have a phone?" Cheyenne asked.

"She left the one I got her on the counter."

Cheyenne looked at the grim channel and its fogbanks.

"You're going to have to put me up for a couple of days," she said.

Cheyenne was standing on the curb when a radically freckled woman with a feral spray of orange hair arrived at the Juneau air-port in a white mid-'90s Subaru. On the ride, Cheyenne tried to find out more but couldn't.

"Some women aren't forthcoming," said Sarah.

"How did she look?"

"She didn't have any bruises. She was mostly worried about getting pregnant. That's why she came. If she'd been able to get the pill herself, I don't think she would have come."

Sarah pointed at a road that turned off into the woods.

"Have you ever seen a glacier? We have one."

Cheyenne noticed the chain around Sarah's neck with the beads at the collarbone.

"Where did you get that?"

"Your sister gave it to me."

Sarah fingered the captain's wheel pendant.

"Livy doesn't give women jewelry."

"I think she may have stolen it."

"She doesn't steal."

Sarah made tuna fish sandwiches for dinner and talked about Livy. Everything she said seemed to circle back to that point of reference, Livy. She was infatuated. Through the course of conversation, Cheyenne saw something else. Livy told Sarah things she didn't tell people. Little things, things no one else would have considered private. Each story, a shiny object tucked into a nest. The more she heard from Sarah, the more certain she was. It was also clear to her that Sarah had no idea.

Speaking to Kirsten that night Cheyenne told her, Livy's in love.

"In love?"

"She's stealing jewelry to give it to her."

"That can't be true," said Kirsten.

Cheyenne paused. "What should I do? Should I come home and wait for her?"

Kirsten looked at the cans of Ensure on her counter and the stack of printed-out Internet research on heavy metal toxins.

"No. Don't. Take care of yourself. It's probably best you do what you're doing. I'll let you know if you need to come back."

———

It took two days for the money to appear in Essex's account—the account that they now shared. Once Cheyenne bought her ticket back to North Carolina, Sarah became agitated. She kept shuffling things around the apartment.

"I was going to San Francisco. To meet up with the ship."

Cheyenne felt like she was missing something.

"The ship that Livy is on," said Sarah, "I was supposed to meet them in San Francisco."

Sarah picked up a cheap lamp off a bookshelf and wiped away the dust that had gathered around its base so that there was no longer a circle but a swipe where her palm had been.

"Now they're not stopping in San Francisco, so I have to meet them in Seattle."

Sarah put the lamp back down.

"Does Livy know you're going to be in Seattle?"

Sarah shook her head. "I told the friend I texted on the ship not to tell her."

"Are you going to try to see her?"

"She wouldn't give me her address."

Coward, thought Cheyenne, you know you love this woman.

Sarah traced a wall switch to the living room overhead. "Do you think your mom would give me her address?"

"Not a chance in hell. Why can't you just wait for her to get off the ship?"

"Ships like that don't exactly have a docking time. I could easily miss her." Sarah paused. "Would you give me her address?"

"I can't do that either."

Sarah nodded and went into the kitchen to make coffee. Cheyenne followed and conversation turned to how to back-time leaving for the airport when Sarah blurted out, "That bastard lives here. That captain. Just up the street."

Cheyenne felt the hairs on the back of her neck ruff like a dog. "I want his name. Tell me where he lives."

"I can't," said Sarah. "I guess his daughter's kind of a mess."

"I'll trade you."

"She would kill me."

Cheyenne wrote the address of Kirsten's apartment on a piece of paper and handed it to Sarah. "Livy doesn't need to know a thing."

Cheyenne sat across from the captain's house. The lights were on but the blinds were drawn. A teenage girl came out and Cheyenne followed her to a coffee shop. The girl was waiting for someone, drawing on her jeans with a Sharpie, her hair cut into uneven chunks, maybe hacked off that morning. A man in his late twenties joined her. He had eyes in the back of his head like all the petty dealers Cheyenne had known, and from the way he ruffled the girl's hair like she was a Yorkie she could tell they were having sex. Cheyenne wanted to unfold her harpy wings and scour him with fire.

He asked the girl to buy him a hazelnut latte with extra hazelnut and an extra shot. Cheyenne studied the girl as she went to get the coffee. Her desire to be invisible was obvious. Then she saw what Livy must have seen, that every half inch up to the elbow of the girl's arm was scarred with deep cuts in various stages of healing.

Cheyenne dialed the base at Lejeune that night. She told them it was a family emergency and she needed to speak to her husband. Two hours later he called.

"That asshole is running around. It kills me. His daughter is the saddest kid I ever saw. Way worse than either of us at that age."

"Livy might be right to leave it alone," said Essex.

"Oh yeah? Tell me what all the real cutters you know had in common. Ten to one that kid hates her dad more than we do."

"There's a lot in the world that can't be fixed."

"Livy didn't file a report. There's nothing official."

Essex paused and the weirdness of what happened buzzed on the line.

"We're going into work up soon they say," he said. "I'll be overseas probably."

"This is not about you, what's happening. I don't mean the deployment—that's all about you and your stupid decisions—but this is about Livy."

Cheyenne felt like a jerk. Her frustration collapsed.

"It was sweet of you to marry me," she said. "Very thoughtful."

"My pleasure."

She laughed.

"You'll go to the doctor for a checkup?" he said.

"Yes."

"And the dentist?"

"And the dentist."

The line went quiet.

"Cheyenne, you'll do the right thing about the captain."

"I'm not famous for doing the right thing."

"You are to me."

"I wish I could talk to Livy."

"I don't know if it helps," he said, "but I've always thought of you as the scarier sister."

It wasn't hard to find out a few things about the captain. He had a pleasure boat and a truck. He used the gym at the Alaskan Club and hung out downtown when he wanted to drink.

Cheyenne hit the hardware store for traffic paint and grease markers. At 10:00 p.m. she went out. She spray-painted the dock by his pleasure boat, the dock by the harbormaster's office, the parking lot in front of Fish and Game, and the sidewalk in front of his house. On the capitol steps in highway-yellow she wrote: CAPTAIN MARLIN JENKINS RAPED MY SISTER. Just as she had everywhere else. She hit the bathrooms, men's and women's, in the bars with a grease marker. She paid for a movie ticket to get into those bathrooms, then she dialed 911 and said she'd witnessed a rape and gave them the captain's address.

Hiking up the hill at the end of the night she saw a shape crossing the street fifteen feet ahead. It saw her and stopped. Cheyenne had never been so close to a bear. She'd also never seen one this big. The bear turned in her direction and sniffed. In Cheyenne's backpack was an open package of smoked salmon. She'd forgotten all about it. The bear raised herself up on her hind legs. Her head was so big it blocked the moon. She gave another sniff then fell heavily onto her forepaws and trundled over to the unlocked garbage cans behind the hippie grocery store.

It was a sign. The great mother bear had given her a pass. They were sandblasting traffic paint off the sidewalk for days after she left the state. It was the least she could do for Livy.

54 Aurora

LIVY'S FIRST DAYS after getting off the dock in Juneau were hellish. Working without gloves, her hands were soon rope-burnt, and her blisters all torn. She didn't know where to be or what to do. She'd never felt so useless. None of the commands made sense and everyone was moving too fast to explain. When they heaved, she heaved. When they stopped, she stopped.

Handsomely on the bow. Dig in and hold. Come up!

"That means drop it!" someone yelled at her.

She let go like the line was a viper.

Marne took her on boat checks where they crawled around belowdecks on their hands and knees, lifting up boards to look for water.

"How many places do we check under this floor?"

"This is the sole. We don't have a floor. This isn't a fucking house."

In the mates' quarters Marne lifted another panel.

"Hole in the sole!" she yelled.

"Hole in the sole," muttered a half-asleep sailor.

"Say hole in the sole," said Marne.

"Why?"

"So I know you heard it."

"You're a foot away from me."

Marne waited.

"Hole in the sole," said Livy.

Marne clicked her headlamp back on and ducked under the raised board.

When they came above Marne took her over to the pinrail and tugged on a line Livy had secured earlier.

"Too tight."

"It was fine an hour ago," said Livy.

"It's not nylon. This is what rain does to real rope. I know you think it's bullshit to not wear gloves. But we have two hundred lines belayed to deck and every single one changes tension with the weather. We have a wood hull. It's going to swell and bend with the torque of the lines, the masts, how the yards are braced, the wind. This ship is a living thing that contracts and twists and breathes. Living things need to be touched by living hands. So no gloves. Nothing we do is for show. There's always a reason."

Marne eased out and coiled the line. Looking around she sighed.

"You have to understand. Once we're off dock the dog and pony show ends. Out here we've got nineteenth-century problems. The tractor motor in this thing gets you through still water but it won't get you out of a storm and a GPS is best at marking where you sank. If you're going down and the radio goes, every now and then you can get out an e-mail to the Coast Guard. Life rafts fail to deploy and there's no way to know if the CO_2 canisters that inflate yours works until you're in the water. So the best thing you can do, for all of us, is to forget what you think you know about being at sea."

"First mate's got the con," said a voice behind them.

"First mate's got the con," said Marne without taking her eyes off Livy.

Soon the next watch mustered and they went below. Hammocks were strung up tight between hooks in the overhead. Inside them sailors, wrapped like fruit bats, hung touching shoulder to ankle. Marne strung Livy's hammock, then took it down and had her do it. Livy got in. Her nose was less than eight inches from the overhead. She had two hours to sleep before she'd be up for her dog-watch. Two hours on deck then below for another four then up at midnight for her full watch, mustering in the dark.

Livy's pride was built on her competence. Here she had none. There were at least four different commands for how to let go of a rope and she didn't know one. She'd learned the names of things in books and did not recognize them contracted and strung together in commands—much less know what she was supposed to do to enact them. As the navigation got trickier, the commands came faster until they were an urgent, ambient barrage. Emphasis thrown from one syllable to another without apparent logic, she almost wondered if it was done on purpose to humiliate her. But of course this wasn't true. Not because sailors wouldn't do such things but because nothing on the ship was about her at all.

Once she heard the commands in rougher weather, she understood. The bending of the words was not laziness; each dropped vowel was intentional, designed to cut through wind and be heard. Marne was right. There was always a reason. This was a language preserved, not degraded, and premised solely on the need to act as one. It had been handed from sailor to sailor, literate and illiterate, English speakers and non-English speakers, shouted, repeated, call-and-response from Raleigh to her, down through time.

In her half-sleep on her forty-eighth hour out, cocooned in her canvas hammock, she saw Raleigh above in his velvet shoes and fur, stepping around the anchor rode. Beneath his soles, history. Gold and slaves, conquistadores and colonists, explorers, prisoners. Ships had carried all that. Crewed by poor people without better options, directed by those with only a little more, captained by second sons, driven by stockholders, seed-funded by merchants and queens—she was in the belly of all of it.

They were three days out when Marne came over and told Livy they were going aloft.

"Grab a harness. Check it for tears, empty your pockets, and come with me."

Livy followed Marne over to the portside rail. Stepping up and around to the outside of the shroud they began to climb. The first twenty feet were easy, Livy had been up a million ladders, but the higher they went, the narrower the ratlines she had to step on and the more slippery the shroud. She glanced down to find a better toe-hold and felt a wave of dizziness. Her boot slipped. She swung out but both hands were gripped to the shroud so she righted herself quickly, but a wave of fear rolled through her. She didn't breathe until she made it to the fighting top.

"I need to sit down."

"Just clip in," said Marne.

Livy wrapped one arm around the outer line of the shroud, her shaking hands fumbling with the clip. Marne casually dangled her legs over the edge. Livy kept her eyes on the yard.

"How high up are we?"

"About fifty feet. We can go higher."

"I can't. Not yet."

Marne nodded. "That's right. Never let yourself get bullied into something you don't think is safe. I had a friend who worked deep-draft container ships. He said there are these wells that fill with gas. They used to send sailors down to check them out. Guy goes down and keels over. They send another down. He keels over. Then they grab another sailor. Hey jackass! Go down and see what killed that other guy. No one wants to go but it's do it or you're fired. Mean-while bodies are piling up. It's kind of always like that. Nobody cares about sailors. We have to care for ourselves."

"That's how it should be," said Livy.

"Well maybe you'll make a sailor after all."

Aloft on the main! Aloft on the main.

Lay to deck. Laying to deck.

Going down was worse and Livy was visibly shaking by the time they got to the bottom of the shroud.

"You shouldn't feel weird," said Marne once they got back down. "Scares the hell out of most people the first time."

Livy gave her a grateful look.

"But it is the job," said Marne and walked off.

No one on the *Neva* pretended it was a good idea to sail down the Inside Passage in November in a knock-off 1800s sloop of war. They came apart with every nautical mile: the crew, the rigging, unspooling into dross. Livy got yelled at for things she couldn't have known and there was no time to show her anything. As she slept, the language of the boat ran through her dreams, tarries and ballantines, halyards and sheet bends— *Say again?*

The Russian oligarch who owned the *Neva* had grown bored with the idea of having his own tall ship, leaving it to float the oceans poorly maintained and under-crewed, ignored like a fallen satellite. Livy soon learned that people had been jumping ship since Yakutat. Unbeknownst to her, an ordinary seaman had jumped in Juneau. When they docked in Ketchikan, two of the better able seamen slipped off. *Fuck this sprung-beam rotting future fish castle!* Once back under way, the first mate just rebalanced the watches to compensate for their absence and not a word else was spoken.

By Petersburg they were short an able seaman, a bosun, and a mate, and of the three remaining mates, two had recently been promoted. The captain yanked a marginally qualified able seaman from the portside watch and promoted him to bosun. Livy came across the man botching a long splice and tried to help. Different ship, different long splice, he muttered, go away. In this manner, ill-maintained, abandoned by its backer, the ship, once a perfect technology of its time, transformed slowly into driftwood. For some of the crew that wouldn't matter. They'd be on the next tall ship that passed. For others, the *Neva* was less a ship than a raft. An international no-man's-land, a floating seedy youth hostel, a place where people used to being yelled at bartered their labor at a disadvantage. But to survive, the *Neva* needed money; to get money, it needed investors; and to get investors, it needed to look profitable, which is why in every port they called, they put on the funny clothes and did tours and day sails. An authentic maritime experience! Sail with the *Neva*, a piece of living history. But the *Neva* they sailed on had little in common with the original. It was a hack job cobbled together from several ship designs and muscled toward authenticity by Russian money and a lack of interest in historical detail. The rumor was that a real re-creation of the *Neva* was being built. Once a true replica was working the ports, they'd be done.

"Whatever," said Marne, "we're the most authentic ship around. We're miserable, they're screwing us on pay, we're doing stupid things for investors—that's authentic."

"If people keep jumping, we won't be able to sail."

"We just need to get her to Panama," Marne said. "After that I don't care."

In talking about Panama, Sarah's name came up a few times, mostly in relation to PRAJNA and the work she and Marne had done last year. But every time Sarah's name came up, Livy found other things to do. The doors Marne opened in the conversation, she closed, at first because she didn't want her mind on Sarah, and then because she did but it was private. Marne realized it was a dead subject and stopped mentioning her, and Livy filled that silence with her own thoughts.

Hard weather descended: There was nothing but dark and fog, and all conversations stopped. Sir Walter Raleigh appeared, pacing the quarterdeck, at home. His sea legs planted on the Douglas fir deck, his fists on his hips, he took a sharp intake of air then blew a cloud of hot breath back at the stars only he could see. He began to sing a song about a sun that had set and cedars, and a troubled ocean that beat its banks. Then in the middle of the verse he stopped.

For days, the only words Livy heard from anyone living or dead were commands. The wind kept switching directions. Dying off then coming out of nowhere. They set sails only to strike them moments later. The waters got choppy and enough of the sailors got seasick to keep the remaining ones working almost around the clock with half the crew needed. Buckets of vomit, if not emptied fast enough, tipped over, and the watch slipped on the deck while sweating the lines in icy rain. In the red light belowdecks, in the hammocks between work shifts, they swung against each other with the rock of the ship. Every time the sailor on Livy's left bumped her, she woke in terror, the *Eliana* fresh in her mind.

A week out, Livy got her first regular period. She hadn't known she'd been waiting for it. But it didn't fix what was happening. Other things were growing in her, too, as a result of the rape. The world hit her—and didn't notice. She noticed it now, but it blew by without a look back, a relationship that was no longer mutual. Once such a power differential, such a loss of reciprocal impact would have spurred in her a fierce drive for parity at all costs. Now the feeling bred no ambition; the part of her that touched the world spun without friction.

The weather began to clear. She was on a dogwatch when Marne found her on lookout.

"I told you never to do anything you didn't think was safe but I need you to get over your fear and help me up on the t'gallant. I need to see why it's not setting right."

Livy had gone aloft only once since her first trip. She had stayed close to the mast and clipped in and was in a fearful sweat the whole time, able only to look as far as the sail in her hands. She had never been up above the crosstrees.

"We're going to have to go pretty far out on the tops'l yard too," said Marne. "I can wake someone up if you can't do it, but you have to tell me now."

Everyone was getting less than three hours of sleep a day. The idea of waking someone up because she was too scared to do what they did was something Livy could not manage.

Marne held out a harness.

"It's not a bad night for it," she said. "The moon is out so we'll be able to see."

Livy followed her through the shadows cast on deck by the main and topsail to the starboard edge of the ship. They began to move out. Livy paid attention to her hands and her grip. She tested the ratlines with each foot before putting her full weight on them. The wind was gentle and steady. She made it to the fighting top and paused.

"You good?" asked Marne.

"I'm good."

Livy looked up to where the shroud met the mast on both sides. Above that was the crosstrees, a small arc of metal to stand on, no more. It was only thirty-five feet above where she was but she would have to climb the futtock shrouds.

They started again. The wind changed above the topsails. There was more of it to catch and less cover. It buffeted her jacket and stray hairs tickled her face. As the shroud narrowed to attach, the footholds were so small she could barely get a toe in. She was now at the base of the futtock shroud. The web moved up and out from the mast before wrapping around the crosstrees.

"It works best if you just do it fast," said Marne. "And when you're climbing, think of pushing the ratlines away with your feet, not down. You don't want to end up dangling. Momentum is what will keep you on the shroud when you're upside down. Once you start don't stop."

Marne scrambled up the shrouds, out and over the side of the crosstrees until she was standing again on the strip of metal.

"Like that," she said. "Go."

Livy went. With strong quick movements crawling backward, eyes glued on nothing but where she was grabbing hold. Shaking, she was upright on the outer shroud again and could swing to the inside where she found footing.

"I'm not sure I can do this," she said.

"You can."

Livy did what Marne asked, keeping her eyes on her hands. The whole time, fear like a chatter. When they were done on the t'gallant Marne climbed down to the topmast.

"When you step out," Marne pointed to the line of rope dipping in scallops beneath the yard, "you have to warn anyone out there because they're standing on the same line so you say 'laying on' and wait till they answer. Same when you're coming back to the crosstrees, you say 'laying off.' Gives them a chance to get hold of something if they're not clipped in. This," she slid four fingers under a thick line across the top of the yard, "is the jackstay. That's what you hold on to until we get to where we'll clip in. I need to work closer in so you're going to have to go out first. Just keep hold of the jackstay and I'll tell you everything else as you go."

"Laying on," said Livy.

Marne waited for Livy to get used to standing on the line.

"Laying on," she said.

Livy didn't answer.

"Say 'laying on.'"

"Laying on," said Livy.

Marne moved out onto the yard. As soon as she stepped on, Livy felt the line pull taut, lifting her slightly, shaking her from underfoot. A small gust came and she fought the urge to hug the yard. Marne told her to just hold on to the jackstay and push her legs out like a drawn arrow in a bow.

Once halfway out, they clipped in and went to work. Marne told Livy to reach into the sail and grab any loose lines and gasket coil them to keep them out of the way. A reef point on the tops'l had been sucked into the t'gallant sheet block. Marne got out her marlinspike. She worked deep into the sheet, prying on a tangle of lines to try to get things free. At times it seemed her feet were higher than her head and when she came up her face was red from the blood flow. They moved farther out until they were only a few feet from the end of the yard, which was now below Livy's center of gravity and at her upper thighs.

"We're almost done."

"There's nowhere to step," said Livy.

"There is. Just doesn't seem like it."

Livy couldn't get the terror in her body to stop her from shivering. She waited for a moment of steadiness between tremors then found the loop with her boot and stepped.

She was seventy-five feet up and thirty-five feet out on the yard, no longer over the boat but over water. Looking down she saw that Raleigh had returned. Strolling in the fall of white light, turning on his corked heels, she felt the centuries slip.

"I'm going to send you another line," said Marne. "Don't drop it or we have to do all this again."

At one point, trying to catch a line, Livy dove into the sail, kicking her feet out until she almost went headfirst over the yardarm. Righting herself, she passed it through where Marne told her. They were done and she turned to move back across the yard but Marne didn't move.

"Stop. Stop, look around," she said. "That's what someone told me the first time I came up here. Don't forget to look around."

Livy forced herself to do it. It was stunning.

Moonlight lit the glaciers, the current in the water, the sails, their hands; there was frost on the bowsprit and the yards ticked and cracked against the masts—*Bring me before the docket. Ask. Do you believe things happen for a reason? No. I don't. And I never will.* But inside Livy shame blazed. Because she was better now than she had been before. Whatever life the morning-after pill could not kill had taken hold, and she felt joy kick inside her, something new in the world.

An undulation of color caught her eye. Livy had seen the northern lights many times because, even in summer, a green curtain could ripple across the Alaskan sky if it was cold and clear enough. She had never seen them like this, though. A whip tail of pale yellow appeared from behind the mountain forest, and within minutes, flags of turquoise and fuchsia, of lime and violet fanned out across the stars. It was so remarkable that the starboard watch actually woke the portside watch. They came above, one by one, wrapped in sleeping bags and whatever layers they could find and stood in clouds of frozen breath, staring. It went on for hours, all night. Color like a shower of stars flung down on the rocky shore. Astral shards among the kelp. Like in summer, she remembered walking past stranded jellyfish, in red and yellow and purple, pulsing while they drowned in sand. She wanted to show this world to Sarah. Maybe the hardest thing to see straight is love. It's not the view through the window but the frame around it, and the glass is gone.

55 Salamander

ONCE OVER WATER, and again over Kansas, Cheyenne wondered if going back to North Carolina was the right thing to do. But what were her options? Move onto Kirsten's couch and wait weeks just so her sister had a bigger audience for her misery? And then they would both be there taking turns on the couch waiting for it all to blow up, which it would. Better to speak first then come home if Livy wanted her. In the meantime, she'd spend those weeks in silence. A boon to everyone, no doubt.

The small one-person yurt Justine had set up for Cheyenne's silent retreat was made for desert not swampland. The yurt's skin was like an old army tent, not breathable; it was cold and damp in the evenings and there was no electricity, but through the crown circle at night, Cheyenne could watch stars pass between the branches of the trees.

She got up at dawn, started the fire at Justine's, and sat in meditation. As she listened to Justine and the people who came to see her, they began to seem less like trust-fund refugees and more like masters. They decided what got to affect them, framing and reframing their advantage, and maybe that wasn't wrong. Perhaps who she thought she was or what she thought she owed people was only indoctrination. Maybe it was never her at all but a limit set by

Kirsten out of her own limits. Cheyenne had taken it on like it was real. An aerial view began to take shape.

After the dhamma talks, she returned to her yurt. Sometimes she waded through or walked around the swamp. Sometimes there was work fixing, building, or carrying things, which was a gift because her mind attacked her day and night. Repetitious horror shows of failure. Even her memory changed because time is made of memory and lifetimes are made of time and her memory was a glacier that, broken up, left behind a pristine lake with icebergs in a slow current, and it was this current that brought things to mind. Child thoughts bashed against each other in the faster waters. A broken bunk-bed ladder. The smell of a sink filled with soap high above her head. Disappointment because Livy had scarlet fever and still was not scarlet. Kirsten braiding her hair in the hospital because it turned into meningitis. Falling asleep her first time on Ecstasy and feeling cheated. An abandoned lot where she used to watch skaters that was now a high-rise for millionaires. Then blood rushed to her face and to her heart. She couldn't breathe and she couldn't get the feeling of freedom from people back. She thought of Livy and lost her mind sobbing.

Justine didn't ask about Livy when she got back but Cheyenne told her anyway. No one knows where she is, she said. On a boat somewhere between Alaska and Seattle. Cheyenne did not say, she's your daughter, even though every day the likeness became more and more unavoidable—but anyway, how exactly do you forgive yourself for your first thirty-three years and where do you start? Someone gives you snow and a woodstove and the title "wife." Your name on the blackboard, your name on the waiting list at the abortion clinic, your name in the prayers of people you don't like. Even if she had been able to speak she would have made no sense to anybody.

She remembered a line from Justine's letters.

Everyone has scars. People make too big a deal about them.

How could she have done the things she did to Livy over the years, to Kirsten, to Essex and Jackson? Stirring beneath the debris, she saw the real monster. Maybe she had never cared. Maybe whatever sticky thread wrapped people into the web didn't quite stick to her.

Burn down the structures around you, burn away the agreements . . . you talked about greatness. I sense a greatness in myself . . .

It had been three weeks.

Cheyenne knew every puddle and every snake. She knew the tree limbs individually by the sounds they made when they rustled. She watched the world as she never had. There was a mud salamander that lived in a burrow a foot from the step up to the yurt. She'd seen it once in the daytime. Its jelly-seed eyes under the cover of a leaf when a beetle passed. It must have eggs in the burrow. Under a full moon one evening, she watched it eat a smaller salamander, a salamander that probably also had eggs in a burrow somewhere. She didn't feel anything but curiosity. Even when she thought of Livy getting raped, her feelings were dampened. There's no way this kind of clarity can be wrong.

Sitting on the step of the yurt at dawn with an edge of light through the trees to the east, she watched a beetle trundle haplessly over a patch of rotted leaves and started crying. It had a two-tone shell, black with a scarab-blue sheen. Legs included, it was no bigger than the nail on her pinkie finger. How many species of beetles did they say there were? Three hundred and fifty thousand? Why couldn't she stop crying? The beetle stopped an inch from the edge of the salamander burrow. She saw the salamander blink in the burrow or thought she did. She had the urge to save the beetle. But you can't. That's the point. And the mother salamander needs to eat too. Three hundred and fifty thousand species of beetles, hundreds of eggs, all potential. Was that why she was crying? Let the salamander eat the beetle. How we feel about our lives doesn't matter. Because everything can't stop creating even when you wish it would. Grief can't catch a breath in this world.

That afternoon Cheyenne spilled coffee on her jeans and tried to wipe it off with swamp water but needed soap. She went to Justine's yurt, stripped off her pants, and scrubbed them in the sink. Justine came over and touched a thick scar on the side of Cheyenne's leg.

"Bike accident?"

Cheyenne started to respond but Justine put her finger to her lips.

"Don't say anything." She laughed. "Torturing people in silent retreat is a guilty pleasure."

Cheyenne started to cry.

"It'll get better," said Justine. "This is how we grow, isn't it? In stages."

She handed Cheyenne a towel to dry the wet spot on her jeans.

"I'll be buying my ticket to India in a week or two. We can take up a collection for your ticket if you want to come. We've done new-student scholarships before. I think it would be good for you, like I said. Think about it. I don't leave for another month."

Justine touched her leg again and guilt flooded Cheyenne.

"No bicycles for you, though," she said.

In the bright un-patterned mind of a child Cheyenne remembered the feeling of tumbling down concrete stairs on her tricycle. Like now. Without context.

At dusk she waited for the little salamander. She wanted to apologize to it. She scanned the twilight leaves for wayward beetles it might be after and saw none. She'd blown it. Her birthday was coming, which meant Livy's birthday was coming, and she didn't know where her sister was. She started crying again. *Everyone has scars . . .* but it didn't feel like a stage. *What you said about the importance of holding your head up? I do, always . . . Rolling over I won't celebrate . . . I can stop crawling and walk out of here teeth and all . . . This is my first birthday. I came out all new again . . .* She ran her fingers over the scar on her leg. She and Livy had gotten a tricycle for their third birthday and failed to take turns. After a fight, Cheyenne drove it off the edge of the second-floor apartment stairs. That was the scar.

Something in her mind clicked. She got out the letters. She needed to see if there was one from December of the year she got the scar. There was.

Everyone has scars. People make too big a deal about them.

She put the letters in order, writing out the dates on a separate piece of paper. As she did, her life and Livy's life began to take shape. All Justine's talk—of holding your head up, rolling over, crawling, teeth, walking, feeling like today is your first birthday—she was never making some deep statement on consciousness. Each letter from Justine was written a week or two after all the major events of the girls' lives. Cheyenne put the letters down. In her raw state a cascade of information hit her in a dark wave of enlightenment.

Kirsten had told Justine everything. Every milestone. Every accident. When something happened to either of them, Justine got a letter. Their first day of kindergarten. Livy's meningitis. Every crisis of their high-school years. Cheyenne's marriage. Kirsten made sure Justine didn't miss a single major event. What had Kirsten said when she gave her the letters? All the letters are there. In thirty-three years Justine had never asked about either of them.

The girls' karma is their own. If they're meant to find me they will.

Cheyenne found Justine reading a book by the woodstove.

"There's something wrong," said Cheyenne.

Her own voice after weeks of silence was a stranger to her. She cleared her throat.

"You never asked me about Livy's rape."

"You told me about it," said Justine.

"Only because you didn't ask. You never asked about Alaska. You could have asked me how it went in Alaska."

"How did it go in Alaska?"

"My sister is the toughest person I know. I don't know where she is. I can't stop thinking about what it would mean for her, specifically her, to get forced into something."

"We all face demons."

Cheyenne's mouth started to tremble. "She looks exactly like you. Exactly alike and anyone could see it. I saw it. Essex saw it. It's obvious."

Justine set her book aside and shrugged. "She's my daughter."

Cheyenne felt like she had in Joshua Tree when the drugs had hit.

Justine laughed. "Did you think I didn't know?"

Cheyenne couldn't put anything together.

"I'm going to make some coffee if you want it."

She passed by Cheyenne, almost touching her.

Cheyenne's head twitched. Her voice began to change in her throat.

"If she's your daughter and you knew it, that just makes it worse."

Justine smiled. "You're both my daughters. Ask that nurse, Margaret. I'll bet she and Kirsten are still in touch. She'll tell you."

Justine wiped the counter with a sponge.

Cheyenne's body went numb.

"I don't believe you."

"People forget that it happens, but babies die all the time. Kirsten's did. I had twins." She rinsed the sponge in the sink. "She almost died too. She barely remembered anything about her labor. I'm not sure she ever knew what happened. I never said anything but Margaret must have told her at some point."

Cheyenne didn't believe it but couldn't think of a single reason Justine would lie about it. She started to cry. Justine came over and took her face in her hands. Cheyenne could feel Justine's breath on her wet cheeks.

"I'm offering you a kind of freedom," said Justine softly. "Take it."

She let go of Cheyenne's face. Cheyenne stared, trying to understand what she was seeing and what it meant. Justine's expression shifted from one complex emotion to another, landing nowhere. Was this the compassion she'd talked about?

"None of us have to carry on a story we don't want," said Justine.

Cheyenne saw something different in the movement of Justine's face. Sun breached the swamp, throwing vertical light against the windows, which cast rose-gold rectangles on the bed. Justine stepped away and turned the tap. She filled a glass and drank the water down. Everything in her manner was casual.

"India is wild. I think we should ask people to buy you a ticket," she said. "You don't have much holding you. Come with me." She turned. "Become a citizen of the world."

There were citrine flecks in her irises. The empire set in her eyes. She had a flirtatious love of destruction. The worst part was she couldn't help it. She thrived in acquaintance. She was the perfect teacher. She had nothing to offer.

A man came up the path and knocked on the door. Cheyenne wanted to yell and warn him, but how do you spell it out? What no one wants clearly said, this shameful desire—make me a student. Reinstate all this terrible potential like I never spent it.

Justine smiled affably at the man and left with him to look at the maintenance work. Cheyenne found the phone and charger Essex had given her, stuffed all she had in her backpack, and left, wading through the muddy water back to the road.

56 Postcard

KIRSTEN MADE A TRIP to the store for dish soap and a can of Ensure. What used to be a quick errand two or three weeks ago was becoming a major outing. She had turned an invisible corner. Now she couldn't walk all the way to the store and couldn't drive safely because her reaction time was too slow. She had to take the bus up and down the hill. Even getting around the store took twice as long as it had a month earlier. By the time she got back the mail had come. In it was a postcard with a photo of a spruce forest and an eagle flying over. It said, I know you know. I'm okay. I'll be there first week of December, love Livy. It was clear that Livy had never gotten the letter Kirsten sent to Dutch Harbor. Which meant her daughter was about to walk into another new and awful reality when she got to Seattle—and there was absolutely nothing Kirsten could do about it. She had been scheduled to start treatment ten days earlier but had postponed it, waiting to hear from Livy. Now she was waiting to see her.

Kirsten called the nurse navigator and left a message to say she needed to reschedule. She called Margaret to tell her she'd heard from Livy. Margaret lit into her about being a martyr and told her to get off the phone and call Cheyenne.

"Tell her what's happening and get her home now," said Margaret.

"I can't. She thinks I'm a control freak and that I try to choreograph everyone's life. Besides, she'll think my being sick is her fault."

"You talk incessantly about what the universe wants, but I bet it isn't telling you to die to protect your pride."

"You're a materialist atheist. What do you care what it says?" said Kirsten and hung up.

Suffused with anger, she decided to go to the convenience store on the corner for the toilet paper she forgot. It was more expensive but closer and she didn't have the energy for another bus ride. Even with extra adrenaline, though, that, too, took twice as long.

When she got back to her apartment, she saw a woman sitting cross-legged on the concrete landing in front of her door. She was camped out with an open box of cereal on her lap, which she was eating dry by the handful. The hood of her blue sweatshirt was pulled over her head so Kirsten couldn't see her face, only damp corkscrews of red hair springing out as if from a wild untended houseplant.

As Kirsten approached, the woman jumped up and brushed the crumbs off her clothes. She stuck out her hand.

"I'm Sarah," she said.

Kirsten didn't shake Sarah's hand so Sarah dropped it.

"Sarah who?"

"You called me in Juneau. I'm the woman your daughter was staying with."

Kirsten stepped back.

"Cheyenne gave me your address. Here, see?"

Sarah held out a piece of paper. Kirsten took it. Seeing it was Cheyenne's handwriting, she handed it back.

"Why are you here?"

"I was hoping to see Livy. Have you heard from her?"

"No," she said and unlocked her front door.

"May I come in? I need to use the bathroom. I came straight here from the airport."

Kirsten nodded. "Down the hall to the left."

While Sarah was in the bathroom, Kirsten got out the postcard.

When she came out, she showed it to Sarah. Watching Sarah's face as she recognized Livy's handwriting made Kirsten feel guilty for being so cold.

"You can stay for dinner if you want," she said.

Sarah shook her head. "I'm meeting friends. I should go. The *Neva* should be in port in the next day or two. Will you let me know when Livy comes?"

"Is she expecting you?" asked Kirsten.

Sarah shook her head. "Will you call me still?"

Kirsten looked at the young woman's face. So hungry, so tentative.

"I don't know," she said.

The Nurse Navigator

COMING INTO PUGET SOUND, Livy saw Seattle through a kaleidoscope of sun breaks and rain showers, the ship canal and the locks; she knew she was home, which meant she would have to face Kirsten. And what was she to say? It was nothing. It was everything. But different. People make too big a deal out of it, people don't make enough out of it. Thinking about the conversation she would have to have, she couldn't yank herself back from the gravitational pull of the Archean black universe that was her mother. Birther of planets, abuser of the phrase "personal journey," heroic myth generator— why Cheyenne felt like she needed two mothers was inexplicable; Livy couldn't bear the weight of merely Kirsten's feelings.

On the dock when they came alongside, she saw Kirsten shading her eyes and scanning for her. Something was wrong. She was gaunt. Kirsten had always been a little heavy but healthy, solid. The extra weight that seemed so natural to her body was gone. Her hair didn't shine and she was bundled in a winter coat even though it was fifty degrees.

It took more than an hour to get the cutter out, run the lines, double them, and get the chaffing gear on. When the gangplank went down and Livy jumped off, Kirsten wrapped her in a hug that lasted too long.

"I'm fine," Livy said, extricating herself. "Can you please not look at me like that?"

Kirsten could feel Livy's warmth from movement, her broad

muscled shoulders, the rough skin of her hands. Her skin, its winter tone, her hair braided and slept in and shaped at the crown by sweat and her knit cap. She checked for every part of her as she had when she first counted her toes and fingers. Her daughter was intact but could not look her in the eye.

They went to a nearby café and Kirsten ordered soup but did not eat it, though she cupped the bowl for warmth. Livy noticed that her mother walked slowly and had not taken off her coat.

"What is going on with you?" she asked.

The lie came right out of Kirsten's mouth with no thought at all. "I got E. coli from a salad wrap. They kept me in the hospital for three weeks. I just got out. I'm fine. Just weak."

Kirsten pushed her soup away abruptly, spilling it over the sides into the saucer beneath.

"You get raped," she said. "Raped. And you don't even call. I find out from a stranger."

The word *raped* was too strong in the air for Livy's comfort.

"Lower your voice. It's not everybody's business," she said.

"The hell it isn't. They—" Kirsten's voice got louder. "They," she waved her arm at the lunchtime rush, "get off too easily. It's not your shame. It's theirs. They're the fucking rapists."

A couple of women at the next table paused with salad on their forks. Anger brought color to Kirsten's skin. This kind of moment, embarrassing and thrilling, was so familiar to Livy that she started to laugh. Because Kirsten, without money or property, acted like she owned the world and held it accountable. Kirsten daubed the spilled soup on the saucer with a napkin then set it aside.

"I met Sarah," she said.

Livy froze.

"What are you talking about?"

"Cheyenne gave her my address. Your sister went to Juneau to find you, you know."

"Why is Sarah here?"

"Ask her."

"What the fuck is Cheyenne doing handing out my address?"

"Well if you had actually called us, she wouldn't have had to go find you and wouldn't have met Sarah at all so you can thank yourself for it," said Kirsten.

Livy speared a tasteless slice of a salmon-colored tomato and put it in her mouth. Swallowing, she looked at her mother's untouched soup. "Is something wrong with it?"

"Too rich," said Kirsten.

Livy asked for a to-go cup. The waiter brought it with the check.

"I like Sarah a lot but there's a time and place and we had ours," said Livy.

Kirsten put a twenty on the table. "Tell her yourself. She's at the house."

When Livy came in, she saw Sarah on the couch, uncomfortably vivid, even more weirdly stunning than she was in Livy's imagination. The feeling that she couldn't control her life was back. It was the last thing she needed.

Livy dropped her backpack.

"Sarah, I know you mean well and I'm grateful for all you did but we can't both be here. If you need a place to stay, I'm happy to sleep on the ship."

Sarah scrambled to pick up her journal, a pen, a coffee cup, a phone, all scattered over the coffee table. "I'm sorry. I'll go. Cheyenne thought I should come," she said.

"I don't blame you at all. My sister thinks a lot of things."

"At least let her have some lunch before you kick her out," said Kirsten.

"Yes, of course," said Livy. "I'm sorry. I'll make you a sandwich."

Watching Livy and Sarah eat at the kitchen table, Kirsten was struck by their awkwardness with each other and how sensual it was. Kirsten had forgotten how beautiful people were when they were in love. Around Sarah, Livy shivered with life. Sarah was so different from what she'd imagined Livy would want, but that's better, isn't it? We shouldn't be able to know for sure what people desire. It should be a mystery.

Sarah ate her sandwich slowly, stalling, drinking water in between every few bites. When she was done she stared at the plate.

"I guess I should leave," she said.

"If you want some coffee to take with you I have a thermos," said Livy.

"I can get it back to you."

"No," said Livy. "You can have it. When does the *Neva* leave?"

"Marne said they'll be in port a week."

Their eyes locked and Kirsten saw it happen. All that electricity between them, Livy sent it to ground; she simply switched the channel. Kirsten felt the weight of it in her abdomen. Cheyenne was right. Livy was in love. And was going to do absolutely nothing about it. Worse, once Livy knew about the cancer, Kirsten would be her excuse.

They said goodbye in the doorway like casual acquaintances and did not touch.

Later, while Livy did the dishes, Kirsten tried to raise the subject of Sarah but Livy interrupted, asking about her health and what her doctors thought about her eating so little.

"It's normal," said Kirsten. "They said to drink some stupid poisonous fake milk protein if it gets bad."

She pointed to a can of Ensure on the counter. Livy nodded, wiped the counter, and said she was going out.

Kirsten knew she had to tell Livy about the cancer but couldn't find the words. She also had to get Livy on the ship to Panama, and she couldn't think of a way to do both.

After Livy left, Kirsten called palliative care to move her appointment.

"I need to reschedule," she told the nurse navigator.

"There's a point at which intervention makes no sense."

"I just need one more week."

"We're not holding your weeks," said the nurse navigator. "No matter how many times we reschedule you, we can't stop time."

58 Ishtar

ESSEX SPENT most of his training time out in the field. In camouflage, in ditches, under leaves and trees, and at night under the stars. It was easier to stay distracted that way. Back on the base, Essex thought about Livy all the time. He began to look at everyone differently. In every interaction he had with a man he wondered: Would you do it? Would you rape someone if you knew no one would know? He stared pointedly into the eyes of every woman he came across and wondered what had happened to her before that moment.

One night, Essex sat around with a bunch of the guys listening to a corporal who had just come back from "over there." Soon Essex would probably be going "over there," wherever the new "over there" was. After that, according to the corporal, he would have one job. Stay alive, don't get blown to bits at a checkpoint, don't get shot in a market square, make it back to the base at night and you're a model employee.

The corporal showed them a picture. In the foreground was a soldier. In the background an ancient city. Seven thousand years old, the marine said. Essex looked at the rich blues that were baked into the clay tiles. The wall around the city, weathered and breached, pockmarked with bullet holes, was still beautiful.

"Do you think they hate us?" Essex asked the corporal.

Jared came up behind him. "Does who hate us?" Jared said.

Essex didn't acknowledge him.

"The people there," he said to the corporal. "I mean I know they hate us, but do you think they all hate us?"

The man said nothing.

Jared put his hand on his breast. "You can hate all of the people some of the time and some of the people—"

"I'm pretty sure you can hate all of the people all of the time," said Essex.

"Well if they don't try to shoot me, I don't care if they hate us," said Jared.

Essex passed the photo back.

"They used to worship Ishtar in that whole area," Essex said.

"Who is Ishtar?" asked the corporal.

"She's the Sumerian fertility goddess of war, love, and sex."

Another grunt laughed. "That's a fucking weird thing to know."

"You'll never beat him at goddess trivia," said Jared.

Essex looked at the grunt. "My mom is a witch. My sister is a fisherman. I like Ishtar because when they tried to keep her out of the underworld she said, Fuck you. I'll break your doors and smash your locks. I'll raise zombies to eat the living. She walked into the underworld naked and nobody could have sex until she came back. She got to decide. It was her call. All the way her call."

Essex got up and left. He could feel the men staring at his back and he didn't care.

There were people on base he could have told about Livy, people he respected and trusted, but Livy would hate being the subject of conversation. Of course it wasn't really her that he was protecting. If he had ever had any wish it was to stop being useless and yet here he was, trained in combat, armed with health insurance and a debit card, and none of it prevented Livy from getting raped. Strange rages were hitting Essex. Rages like when he was a boy on the street and had no power. *Kick me out, push me around. Look through me like I'm hollow.* They came up when he remembered something intimate about her. *These things are private. These things are public.*

They came up over nothing. Like wet dreams, they surged through his sleep. It had been weeks since he found out and he had to tell someone.

Eating breakfast next to the marine he was closest to, a deep and kind man, one of the few his age, Essex almost asked him if he had time to talk. The man would have said yes. And if Essex was going to confide in anyone, it would be him. Scraping his plate Essex practiced the words. *My sister was raped and I couldn't stop it because I'm a fake.* But those words were never going to leave his mouth.

Essex took the soft way out and decided he would tell Jared because it was easier since he had no respect for him, and also Jared was a shit bag of a soldier so who cares about his opinion?

Essex found him in the barracks half asleep.

After months of brutal physical training, Jared's wiry long body had barely changed. Which was only fitting because certainly not a damn thing else had changed about him either.

He reminded Essex of a dirty penny. The drab of his clothing, his buzzed copper hair, two sides, loyal and bullying. Jared had never been the type to pull wings off bugs, but he wouldn't have stopped it either. He was perfectly happy to be around whatever was going on. In any setting, he sank to the lowest common denominator.

Essex pressed his knee into Jared's ribs.

"Wake up. I want to go on a walk."

Jared groaned. "Later."

"We have to go now. It's going to rain."

They walked for a bit under heavy clouds. Fine, vertical striations appeared on the horizon to the south. The humidity was so high that Essex felt like he was in a warm mist.

He told Jared.

"Do you think she maybe sent the wrong signals," said Jared.

"What the fuck is wrong with you?"

"I'm just saying a woman fishing with a whole bunch of guys isn't exactly a good idea."

"I can't talk to you," said Essex. He turned and walked off in a different direction.

It was soon evening but he had an hour left of his two-hour liberty: Liberty. Liberty to do what? Think?

Down the road Essex saw John A. Lejeune. The marine's marine had charged the North Carolina shore under a full moon at dusk. Emerging from the phosphorescent surf, his ankles tangled with glowing seaweed, he began the forward march, his eyes on the western shore of the nation, and beyond that, China. Ever fixed, ever focused. The Tuscarora flickered behind him, sometimes a People, sometimes a Union ship.

Coming upon Essex he stopped.

"Rage," said Essex. "What do you do with it?"

"I have seen so many beaches. I have earned so many stars," Lejeune said.

Essex saw that rage ran through Lejeune too. How else could it be? In this Southern son. Yet in Lejeune it had come out as drive and been transformed into coordinated movement and discipline, strategy and will. Whereas in Essex it was loose, electric, and sparking.

59 Static

HAVING RUN OUT OF JUSTINE'S and trudged through the swamp, Cheyenne now stood on the small highway in wet tennis shoes and swamp-soaked jeans without a plan. She started walking. One car passed, then another. What was she to do? Wave like she was drowning and flag them down? Help. *My life is an emergency of my own making. Save me.*

Images ran through her head in random order: the blown second chances, burnt relationships, twisted cars—all spent on a ticket to get to here, this moment.

The preposterousness of Justine's story rang in her head, echoing in a closed universe. Little interactions returned backlit with new meaning, the way Justine spoke of freedom, the way Kirsten handed her the letters, the hints of something over the years that may or may not have been something at all because she really didn't know what Kirsten knew or what was true at all.

Her mind, scrambled from weeks of silence, bounced. *I've seen this in a movie with the cave and a jungle or maybe it was a cave in a jungle. There were skulls but they were bone, not golden so there's no way any of this is real.* Insane thoughts. *If Livy was born first there's no way in hell I'm going to treat her like an older sister.* Quieter thoughts. *So this is what it's like to be thirty-four and have thrown it all away.*

She came to an intersection. A flashing yellow streetlight swayed in the wind next to a mini-mart with an empty parking lot. She walked in and was instantly baffled by visual noise—racks of Technicolor candy; neon cheese puffs; baby-blue and cotton-candy-pink marbled inflatable balls imprisoned in a black wire mesh rectangle.

The woman behind the counter had a face like a sandstone cliff and the manner of a bullfrog. She watched Cheyenne move around the store like a fly. Cheyenne grabbed a packet of powdered white doughnuts and went to the register. She tried to speak a sentence but the words didn't come out like she heard them in her head.

"I want to please plug in my phone."

"Where's your car?" said the woman, looking out the window.

"Texas."

Cheyenne tried to smile but wasn't quite sure what was happening on her face. She pulled out her wallet and opened it and took out the debit card Essex had given her.

"Please may I charge my phone?"

Recognizing the logo on the card as one used solely by service members, the woman's chin softened.

"I'll plug it in behind the counter."

Cheyenne handed her the phone and charger.

"I have a grandbaby in the service," said the woman.

Cheyenne, missing the invitation to talk, tore into the packet of doughnuts and began to eat, getting white powder all over her fingers and clothes.

She wandered down the aisles looking at soup cans and Kotex. She read the tags over empty racks by the travel packets of Benadryl and Midol. Rounding the endcap she passed cases of energy drinks and chocolate milk. Pausing by a row of microwavable popcorn she turned and looked at the woman.

"What's the wrongest you've ever been?" she asked. "'Cause I can't decide. It might be now. It probably is. But it could also be a couple of months ago. That was pretty bad—or a few months before that." Cheyenne's eyes wandered toward the Slim Jims and peanuts. "There's a really good argument for now but it could also be my first marriage. I really messed that up."

"Everybody gets a test pancake," said the woman.

There was something in her tone that made Cheyenne tear up. It was only kindness. She'd forgotten. There was kindness everywhere.

When the phone was charged Cheyenne took it into the bathroom and called Kirsten, who sounded strange. Didn't want to talk. Normally Cheyenne would have demanded whatever needed to be said, be said now and not danced around. But she, too, needed to have a longer conversation.

Leaving the bathroom, Cheyenne called a taxi company and told them she needed to get to Camp Lejeune. Whatever Essex had on the debit card would either cover the fare or it wouldn't. Either way she'd be closer to someone she knew.

She stepped outside. The bushes scraped and the trees rustled. Some creaked and scratched at other branches twisting through each other toward the sun. She watched the streetlight on the slack cable flash yellow. There was no contest. This was definitely the wrongest she'd ever been. Hands down.

Her phone began to buzz as a string of missed calls came through, downloaded from whatever satellite passed over like an angel, thinking nothing of her, not knowing she existed at all, orbiting. Because this is the way of it, the great exclusion.

The missed calls were all from numbers she didn't know. There were two voice mails. The first was from the office of Essex's commanding officer, but it was immersed in static. What words were audible, *incident, shooting,* chilled her lungs. She played it back and heard *investigation* and *field.* She played it again and got that the message was from the CO's office and that Essex had been involved in what seemed to be a friendly-fire incident with another marine but it was still under investigation. The number to call for information was garbled. The second voice mail was clearer. It was from Essex. He sounded shakier than she'd ever heard him. *I fucked up. I love you. I really fucked up.*

60 The Universe Returns

KIRSTEN WAS READING when Livy came in just before 3:00 a.m., made a grilled cheese sandwich, and joined her on the couch.

"What are those tall ships like to work on?" Kirsten asked.

"Hard."

"Harder than fishing boats?"

"Different hard."

Livy ate half her sandwich. "They're going to Panama," said Livy.

"I know. Sarah told me."

Kirsten watched her daughter.

"I should tell her I love her," said Livy, "but I don't really see the point."

Livy put the plate on the coffee table and leaned back. Kirsten waited to see if she would say more but she didn't. Three twenty-five a.m. filled the room. Livy laid her head on Kirsten's shoulder, something she hadn't done since she was twelve or thirteen. Kirsten sat still as if a hummingbird had landed on her.

That night the Universe sent Kirsten a dream.

There were two bags of gold coins. One with five coins and one with eight. She was only allowed to pick one bag. There were only three prizes she could buy. One costs less than five but more than three, one costs five, and one costs nine . . .

She could pick the bag with eight and try to haggle with the Man behind the counter, but she knows he will refuse. She could grab all the coins and run, but the Man said there weren't any prizes outside of the room. She could bribe the Man with sex, but she could tell he couldn't see her anymore.

Livy found Kirsten humming in the kitchen that morning.

"I think you should go," said Kirsten. "Get on that boat and see where it takes you."

"You're still sick and I'm broke. Maybe another time."

In the evening when Livy got back from looking for work, Kirsten was humming the same song. Livy recognized it this time. It was a track off some '70s record Kirsten always played when they had to do chores. At fourteen, Cheyenne gave it a name, Coke Damage Radio Hour.

Cheyenne would be on that boat. Cheyenne would go after what she wanted.

Livy went to bed. Kirsten's humming entered her sleep. It wasn't a song but a strategy.

At breakfast, Livy was patching the elbow of her foul-weather jacket when Kirsten stopped humming and started singing.

"Would you go if she promised you heaven . . ."

"Just say it," said Livy, putting her work down.

"What?"

Livy returned to the patch.

"Would you go if she promised you heaven . . ."

"It's 'Would you stay if she promised you heaven,'" said Livy.

"I can sing it however I want."

Livy packed up her needles and duct tape and got into the shower. As the water came down, she relaxed. At least her mother was better. She had eaten a real breakfast and done some laundry. She was singing, if only to torture Livy. She had even opened the curtains to let the day in.

When Livy got out of the shower, Kirsten was gone. She'd left a note on the counter. She was out of soy milk. Livy looked at the note and poured the last of the coffee into a cup. Her eyes flicked to where her foul-weather gear hung, patched, in the hallway, along with her marlinspike and knife. Livy looked out the window. At that same moment, in the harbor, the *Neva*'s crew was preparing to get under way. Stowing and lashing trunks of dishes, doing boat checks. Soon they'd go to stations and take up the lines. Between them was the kind of fog that wouldn't burn off. It would stay with them all the way through the sound. Floating on the lowlands and deltas, pooling in inlets, passing spectral through suspension bridges.

Kirsten would be back soon. Maybe they could order pizza and try to find a movie where the earth almost gets blown up and saved at the last minute.

Livy looked again at her foul-weather gear.

The gangway was already stowed when Livy got to the boat and she had to jump from shore to ship while teenagers heckled her, chanting, "Fall! Fall!" Once on, she scrambled down the ladder into the poorly lit captain's quarters. Three of the four mates' bunks were empty. The captain, with his thick gold rings and bad haircut, the epaulette with an N for Napoleon tattooed on his shoulder, stared at a chart table with no maps on it.

"Do you still need sailors for Panama?" she asked.

"I need a bosun."

"I can probably figure it out."

"Someone should," he said.

From Sarah's phone she texted Kirsten: *I'm aboard. Use this number to reach me. I love you. I'll see you in a month.*

Kirsten was on the bus when she got the text. She had just finished a box of strawberry-banana-flavored edibles when it came in and read it twice. It was a strange feeling. All the joy she could imagine, a rush of euphoria, then nothing.

BOOK 5—THE SEA

"What hills are those, my love,

That are so bright and free?"

"Those are the hills of heaven, my love,

They're not for you and me."

—Author lost to time

Ghost Ring

THE M4 CARBINE is a lighter and shorter rifle than the M16. Less cumbersome with superior targeting at close range, it replaces the M16 as the preferred rifle for infantry. Since armies no longer line up on opposite hillsides and charge each other, controlling certain distances matters less because if satellites and drones cover stratosphere to ground, and the M4 covers house-to-house, who cares about the middle ground? The enemy is either very far away or far too close. There is no longer an in between. Gone like the phalanx, one soldier crammed against another, rotating positions like antarctic emperor penguins, gone like the line, a meaningless shape in the geometry of warfare replaced by the vector, sweeping the sand at night, flashlight-like, checking underbrush for snakes or for the reflective eyes of a large cat.

Unable to fully abandon its past, though, the M4 carbine is equipped with a traditional iron sight. Just as a sailor makes an aperture with his hands to scan the horizon for objects, so a sight or ghost ring narrows the field of attention. With a trick of the eye, it can turn the body of the enemy into a dime-size circle, making it easier to hit. The M4 can also be fitted with a scope that provides a telescopic view of the target through an objective lens, though this doesn't necessarily solve the problem of parallax because what gets seen is never simple.

Telescopic sights evolved quickly during the Civil War. Unlike the iron sights before them, they didn't just exclude the distraction of an entire body and its context but magnified the enemy. A triumph of lens light, the scope prospered on the battlefields of Harpers Ferry and Antietam and throughout the war on both sides. Now, only what you want to hit is presented and all else is diminished. But the problem of parallax compensation remains. Because it turns out when you don't have another perspective, the depth of what you're looking at is impossible to gauge.

Jared had wanted to go shooting. Liberty came again. A real one when they could leave the base. Essex had taken to avoiding Jared after the conversation about Livy, but the downtime was killing him and Jared said he knew a place.

"What are we going to shoot with?" asked Essex.

"I got loaners."

Essex had assumed they were going to a firing range, but they ended up at an abandoned shack. When Jared got out the guns, Essex realized they were from the base.

"What the hell are you thinking? Do you know how much trouble we'll be in if we get caught?"

"I bought bullets. They won't know."

"I'm not getting kicked out because of you."

"Stop being a drama queen," said Jared. He held out one of the guns but Essex didn't take it. "Come on, man. We're in the middle of nowhere."

Essex gave in, and Jared handed him the bullets and he loaded the gun.

They set up targets in a beaten field. Essex took a couple of shots and hit the target both times. Jared shot and missed.

"Every marine is a rifleman," said Essex.

"Don't be a dick to me just 'cause Livy got raped."

Jared walked toward the target. Essex felt the rage like a tornado in his chest.

"They shouldn't let you go anywhere as a soldier," said Essex. "I'd never trust you in a dicey situation."

"I'll probably end up saving your life," said Jared.

"Spare me."

Jared missed again.

"I think it's the gun. Let me try yours."

"They're all the same. You're just bad at it."

"Give it to me."

Essex reloaded the gun and handed it over. As he did, he saw the safety wasn't on. Fuck him. Let him shoot himself. Essex went to find a bush. A second later the gun went off.

Essex drove Jared to the hospital on empty roads. The shot had gone through Jared's leg so he was upside down in the front seat to keep the blood inside him, with a belt tightened around his thigh. At the hospital, Jared was given blood and stabilized while Essex talked to the cops.

The MPs came and ushered him into a small room. They asked him nothing, but he tried to tell them anyway, that it was his fault, he was to blame.

"I left the safety off."

"Tell someone else," they said.

"He's an asshole but I know his mom. Should I call her?"

"We took your phone."

The MPs took up a position outside the door. Essex's pulse was still racing but his skin was cold. He felt like he did as a little kid locked in the apartment while his mom was out for the night. But Essex was not alone for long. The ghost of John A. Lejeune appeared beside him.

"My father was a Confederate captain." Lejeune looked through the window. "I've seen continents severed. I saw the Great Canal. I saw the solar eclipse in Algeria. You've seen nothing," he said, then walked through the wall, scrubbed for surgery.

Essex yelled for the MPs to call his wife, but there was only silence.

62 Realm of the Sky God

ALL THE WAY DOWN the California coast, Livy and Sarah were on opposite watches. One slept when the other was awake; one ate while the other washed plates. They saw each other in passing or when all hands were called to deck. Livy could feel when Sarah was near. The sunlamp of electric tension, her unmistakable presence. They couldn't touch or talk without being overheard, still everything between them deepened. Meaningless subjects carried the weight of all that was unsaid. Soon, Livy's awareness of Sarah expanded from ten feet to twenty-five to the whole ship, catching the movement of their bodies up in the ecstatic moment of where and who they were—Sarah in the hammock near the engine room when Livy came to wake the next watch. Livy with sailor's palm and needle repairing chaffing gear between fore and mainmast. With no relief possible, Livy began to work in a Tantric state of sexuality: the cheap manila rope running through her cold wet hands burned, that turned her on; the radiant heat of her own body in an afternoon's freezing rain, same.

Livy was used to working above the crosstrees now, and out on the yard. She could move across the crane lines without a thought. Her old autonomy back, if flowing from a colder source; she had sharkish clarity now.

Crossing into California waters, she texted Kirsten from Sarah's phone. Kirsten texted back a picture of Livy's horoscope. Livy texted Kirsten a picture of the Moss Landing Power Plant at night when they sailed past. The twin concrete towers like spires, the gasworks cube with a chassis of blinding industrial light all floating in the dark water. The photo didn't capture it, though. The power plant was a small yellow blur in a field of flat black. She tried again, but the power plant was an even smaller yellow blur and the blackness more complete.

Sarah came up behind her. "It reminds me of those PRAJNA rigs," she said.

Livy didn't take the bait.

"They have meetings in Panama they don't want anyone to know about," said Sarah.

"Everyone has meetings somewhere."

Livy turned away from the rail. But in her mind, she saw Cyril. Standing at an Olympian meeting of the gods in a skylit corporation penthouse spaceship of transnational capital throwing out envelopes like golden apples, setting things in motion. She remembered her father's face in the lighthouse. Scared at his own wedding.

"If you ask me a question I'll answer it," said Sarah.

"I don't have any questions," said Livy.

She could feel Sarah tense up.

"It's probably for the best," said Sarah.

Livy's watch was called to muster and Sarah went below.

Farther down the coast, Livy snapped a photo of a sandy beach and sage-green hills and sent it to Kirsten. *I'll call when we get to Panama.*

I love you, baby, Kirsten wrote, *don't rush back.*

South of Baja, in the lamplight just before her dogwatch, Livy opened the chest of lines to be spliced or repaired. She couldn't sleep so she'd come up early. It was quieter than it had been. The watch on deck was silent too, the Milky Way a spray overhead. She opened the tempered-glass panel of a small oil lantern and lit it. Outside of the red headlamps, it was the only light allowed at night because it didn't blind sailors who need to be able to work in darkness. Reaching down through a nest of lines that needed new whippings, she felt for a small ball of waxed twine. Taking it out, she closed the lid of the chest and set the lamp back on top. She measured a length of twine from the base of her middle finger to her elbow and cut it with her rig knife.

Moving the lantern closer, she leaned over the waxed twine, made a wall and crown, then pulled the strands apart to begin the sennit. She tested the length around her own neck a few times. When she reached the midpoint, she got out the pendant of Cheyenne's and set it carefully on the chest. It was a circular dragon carved from a light celadon jade. Livy was sure it was old. Maybe a hundred years or more. At some point, this piece of jade, too, had crossed the ocean. Turning the pendant slightly to catch the lantern light, it occurred to her that it might have been made under a lamp not so different from hers. Lit with whale oil instead of petroleum.

She wove the thin waxy strands in and out of the dragon until it was fully bound into a sailor's twine and continued the sennit to the end. She would send it from Puerto de Balboa. She would call Kirsten. She missed her mother's voice.

All the way to Panama, Livy tried not to think about her coming separation from Sarah. Sarah's devotion to the cause, whatever that cause was, was complete. Just like Livy's devotion to autonomy. Sarah would not stop. And Livy would not follow. Especially not for some kind of stunt, which would change nothing. In an effort to repair the fissure created by her lack of political interest, she asked Sarah what was going to happen in Panama, but Sarah was vague.

"I know you don't care about these things," said Sarah.

63 Hotel Titanium

ON THE TAXI RIDE from Bolivia to Camp Lejeune, Cheyenne tried to call Essex but he didn't answer and hadn't set up his voice-mail box. She felt a wave of fear. She'd been a bad friend. She'd done it all wrong. Now something had happened and it was her fault because she was lost in a fantasy jungle with a madwoman when she should have been answering her damn phone.

"Fuck!" she said aloud.

She met the cabbie's eyes in the rearview and looked away, embarrassed. She didn't need to come off as more aggressive than she was, especially if Essex's debit card didn't work and she had to play demure.

Then she remembered that Essex had given her a piece of paper with a list of resources on it for spouses. She tore through her backpack, then emptied her wallet into her lap. Dimes, pennies, her wedding ring—all rolled onto the seat or the floor or into the crevice between her thighs. Jammed in a pocket with a receipt from Alaska, she found the list. At the top, in Essex's best block letters, was the number for the family readiness officer. She called but no one answered. She hit Redial. She didn't care. She could hit Redial for the whole seventy-mile taxi ride. Or until her phone died again, whichever came first. Because she had fucked everything up. She hated being wrong just as much as Livy, but she'd always been able to avoid it by retroactively changing her intentions to match the outcome. It worked. Or had. What was she supposed to say now? At some point, you just see yourself coming. She wasn't all that different from Justine. Ambition. Crocodile tears.

Giving up on the family readiness officer, she began to work down the list of numbers and finally got someone who directed her to the judge advocate's office, which connected her to the JA assigned to Essex's case.

"I'm calling because my," she started to say brother, "my husband might have shot someone."

The cabbie's eyes met hers in the mirror again.

"He was involved in an incident of negligent discharge," said the JA.

"Who got shot?"

"Another soldier."

"Essex shot another soldier?" She couldn't believe it.

"No, the other soldier shot himself."

"So why is Essex in trouble?"

"Negligent discharge is a serious offense. Firearms were also taken off the base. Civilian and military courts are investigating."

"Is the other soldier dead?"

"He's alive but in the ICU. Theft of arms, that's the biggest danger to your husband. Or would be."

"Why would be?"

"He keeps talking about how he left the safety off and wondering aloud if he meant to shoot the guy."

"Can't you just tell him to shut up?"

"That doesn't seem to be working, ma'am," said the JA.

This, Cheyenne could easily imagine.

The debit card did work. She paid the taxi driver and checked into the Inns of the Corps late that afternoon. The lobby was full of marine families between housing. A soldier missing his legs carried a large duffel to the elevator, followed by a teenage boy. Looking around the lobby, the dining area filling with families coming down to dinner, she saw a new truth about herself. She had avoided contact. She had never known anyone in the service. She hadn't even known anyone who seemed to know anyone in the service. Now that she did, they all looked unique. Less like symbols. More like the people you would see in line at a movie, each different from the other.

She saw the marine who'd lost his legs emerge from the elevator. Had he really signed on for what he got? She thought of Essex. They either had all the choice in the world or none. She couldn't tell.

Unlocking her room with the plastic key card, she looked at the white bulbous lamps, the hospital corners on the sheets, and the mini fridge.

She called Kirsten to tell her about the conversation with the judge advocate but didn't get into anything else. They hadn't talked since she got back to North Carolina. Everything that happened in the swamp, the horrifying reflections of self, Justine's cavalier words, their revelations and what it all might mean—she couldn't say what she needed to say into a piece of plastic.

"I keep trying to text Livy," said Cheyenne.

"I don't think she has a phone."

"She really left you no way to reach her?"

"None at all. She wouldn't have good reception at sea even if she did," said Kirsten.

"She doesn't have good reception in general."

Kirsten laughed, then the line was silent.

"Did you find out what you wanted to know from Justine?" Kirsten said after a moment.

"I don't want to talk about it on the phone. What was it you wanted to tell me?"

"It can wait."

"They say I can talk to Essex tomorrow."

"It's good you got married."

Shame burned Cheyenne's throat. "There should be a better way to get dental work," she said.

"Why did you say yes?"

Cheyenne was no longer sure she knew.

"I don't know," she said after a few seconds. "He was so proud to have something to give us. Livy wouldn't take him up on it."

"He never asked Livy," said Kirsten.

"He did. She told him it would ruin her gay card."

"No, they hadn't talked in months. I asked. You know your sister. She would marry him for a better interest rate on a toaster."

Cheyenne's throat tightened. It was just another thing she'd been wrong about.

"Well that's a goddamned shame," she said, clearing her throat.

Taking off her clothes in the middle of the room, Cheyenne examined her body. She hadn't had a shower for days, which didn't matter alone in a yurt but did here. Her feet were filthy. She walked into the bathroom. There was a layer of dirt on her neck that she must have routinely missed with her washcloth. Rough, salty streaks ran over her cheeks. Her face had changed. She saw her sister. She saw Justine. She saw her own sharp green, brown, gold eyes—not far from the desert camouflage soldiers wore. She went to the mini fridge and got out a can of beer and some mixed nuts. She turned on the TV and scrolled through the pay-per-view options. They were not in the desert. She was not in the jungle of Bolivia. Everyone in this hotel was stranded on white sheets in the sterile florescence unable to hide from anything. She drank the can of beer. She ate the nuts. She chose a movie.

Her job was to wait.

In the morning she was told she would be allowed to see Essex. She wore the denim halter dress from their wedding, a private joke to remind him of their friendship. Putting it on, she felt closer to him.

She met the judge advocate and he took her to a room with an MP in the corner. Essex sat at a table inside. Seeing her, he jumped up. She thought he was going to salute.

He turned to the MP. "Can I touch her?"

The strangeness of permission cast a spell over everything.

The JA left and the MP stepped into the hallway. Cheyenne sat down. She waited for him to say something. Airless and dense inside a vacuum, she scratched her head and it seemed the sound filled the room; a small creak from a shift in his weight on the chair, a limb cracking from a tree, she started to say something but he reached over the table and grabbed her hand, pressed it between his and let it go. His face was changed. He looked at her like an astronaut returned to earth. Only half back.

She looked at the MP through the wire-mesh window.

"How bad is it?" she said.

Essex shifted and looked away, pale.

She closed her eyes. "I wish you never enlisted."

"I don't. I like being a marine. In the regular world, there's a veil between choices and consequences. A chain of events shaped like people, and you tell yourself it's okay because you meant well. Come on. Tell me you haven't said that about me a million times."

"You do mean well."

"I want to be someone people can count on, not like my mom or dad." He grabbed her hand again. "You can count on me, can't you? Say you can count on me."

"In your way."

She thought of him lashing Jackson's bed to the Supervan and burning his cab-driving job so she could go to the monastery.

"I might go to jail. They might kick me out."

"Why? I don't understand. You didn't shoot him. He did it to himself. So you took guns off the base. So what?"

The JA entered. Their time was up.

Returning to her hotel room, she slipped off her shoes and sat on the bed with her back against the headboard and knees pulled up to her chest. She began digging her heels into the mattress and pushing her back against the plywood headboard. Tensing every muscle, she strained like she was trying to move a cart out of the mud. But the headboard was flush to the wall so it didn't matter how hard she pressed because it wasn't going anywhere and neither was she. Giving up, she let the tension flow out of her body.

She was finally a blank. She was sure she would never sleep with Essex. She was sure she would never speak to him again if he became a marine. She'd known for sure she would be with Jackson forever and that Justine would be a great teacher. She thought Kirsten always knew exactly which girl came out of her body and lied about it out of a desire for control.

That one, at least, was a mystery she could solve.

She knew the name of Margaret's practice and called. She told the receptionist it was an emergency and had her forward the call to Margaret's cell.

Margaret was on a walk with a friend when she picked up the call.

"Hello?"

"Is it true Justine had twins? Are Livy and I real sisters? Just tell me the truth because everything is a mess."

Margaret excused herself from her friend, stepping back for privacy.

"Kirsten wanted—"

"Does Kirsten know? Just tell me," said Cheyenne.

"Not at first."

Cheyenne felt light-headed. She didn't realize until that moment how much she wanted Justine to be a liar.

"When did she know? When we were kids? How could she not have known?"

"Honey," said Margaret. "Honey, I need you to listen to me. Kirsten has stomach cancer. It is moving very fast. Get on the first plane you can."

Cheyenne couldn't feel her arms. Her heart pulsed in her ears.

"Did you hear what I said? You need to come now."

"Yes, yes, I will. Yes."

Cheyenne hung up on the nurse and tried Livy's number again

even though she knew it didn't work. She called the JA. *Essex has to come home. The woman who raised him is dying.* But the JA said it wasn't going to happen.

"Who are you to say no?" she yelled. "If he was some senator's son I bet he'd be on a plane now."

She hung up on the JA, too, and grabbed every piece of paperwork anyone had handed her in the last two days. She threw the pages on the bed and started to hunt through them. Everything with a name or a phone number on it, she pulled. She called the family readiness officer, who had no idea what to say to her. She called the department responsible for sending out casualty assistance officers, who said it wasn't their issue. She spoke with a secretary to a liaison in an office a few links up the chain from wherever they were. She tried to explain that Essex was not going to run: *He's got this fucked-up sense of honor and I do mean fucked up, and he wants to be with you guys even though I have no idea why but he's like that, he shows up, whether you want him to or not.* The man on the phone told her he was sorry and had nothing to offer her. She called more phone numbers. One was in Europe and had no relationship to anything because Essex had not deployed. When she got down the list, she started over. She left messages, shouting more than talking, pleading, starting in the middle of the story. *Please, please, please. His biological mom never did anything for him. She's useless, worthless. She shouldn't even be allowed to have her name on his paperwork. She shouldn't get to say she has a son at all. It's my mom! My mom. It was my mom who raised him.*

64 The Bridge of the Americas

ENTERING PANAMA BAY, Livy could feel the clock ticking down. A port authority vessel came alongside to pilot the tall ship toward the mouth of the Great Canal. Though the canal was already wide, the time-based economy of international shipping required ever more access so new construction was under way. An episiotomy to maximize efficiency, broader means of entry to satisfy growing demand. Soon, no one would ever have to wait at the mouth of the canal. Whole fleets could pass unhindered. Cruise ships, uncountable.

The Bridge of the Americas was ahead. As they passed beneath it, Livy looked up. Who cuts continents apart? Yes, this was the Realm of the Sky God. The Great Father spanned the Canal Zone, that awesome and liberal specter, that friend to Tibetans (as Teddy Roosevelt was to bears), governor of the colonies—*Hey, Sky Dad, tell me again. Which Indians forgot to be grateful?* Cyril had been in her dreams.

Not as much a man as a symbol of so much else, and Livy hated symbols. She hated the way they pacified, not bears but teddy bears, not Tibetans but Tibet, not daughters but a man's wild youth. Cyril and the child bride, Singapore, Panama—the scope of the imagination that cuts continents in half? She was nothing, nothing in their eyes. Gutted veins of copper. Shrimp strained from the sandy floor. A bravura of birds, a gossip of flames. The ditchdiggers unlading ships by the wharves—only a story to tell your kids when they're born, the little Manchurians.

Past the Bridge of the Americas she saw docks and the cranes of the port. Ordered and geometric, right angles and triangles of steel like a hangman's scaffold over the rectangular containers stacked on the ships and on the shore. The *Neva* sailed past, through water the color of Spanish olives, between mountains, emerald and eroded, until they reached a less populated part of the port where they could dock.

The captain took everyone's passports to customs and got them stamped. Then he went off to get drunk with the first mate and left the crew stranded on the ship.

In the heat under the canvas tarp raised to shelter the crew from the sun, they ate lunch sitting on deck chests. Sarah's back against the life-jacket storage, Livy's against Sarah, skin to skin. Dixie cups of orange sugar water, the salty dirt taste on their hands and necks, balancing paper plates of potato salad made with iffy mayonnaise on their knees.

When it cooled, Livy shoved Sarah's phone in her bra band and laid aloft to the crosstrees. She took pictures of Puerta de Balboa, but they didn't look like much. A white building with arched windows and a Spanish red tile roof, giant silver cylindrical tanks. A few high-rises against craggy hills in one direction and in the other, a ridge built of freight containers that blocked the lights of the city behind the port like a cloud over stars. She sent the pictures to Kirsten. *Balboa!* she wrote. *Named for the conquistador. That Man who discovered the ocean.* Kirsten texted back *Balboa and the Man's ocean* with a laugh emoji. Livy tried to call but it went to voice mail.

Are you okay? typed Livy.

Fine, said the bubble. *Just not anywhere I can talk.*

That night the captain and first mate came back so plastered they could only stand as a team. The crew heard crying in the night, the captain wailing in Russian, the mate trying to calm him. The next morning neither was at muster.

"Does anybody know what's going on?" asked a deckhand.

"It's just the fears," said an Irish sailor who'd come on in Seattle.

"The fears?" asked Sarah.

"You know, that sense of terror, panic, and black despair you get the morning after a solid drunk when you think you're going to die that instant because the hand of God is on you like a spider—don't you get them in America?"

"Never heard it called that," she said.

Second mate rebalanced the watches to compensate for an ordinary seaman who had jumped the last time they'd docked. For the first time, Livy and Sarah were on the same watch.

They scrubbed the ship together. They coiled and hung all the lines. They brushed against each other when they worked but were speaking less and less. With only hours left together, or at most a few days, every subject of conversation felt loaded.

After dinner they sat on deck by the spanker. The tiller was lashed and they were alone.

"What's going to happen?" asked Livy. "Are you going to burst into a meeting and drop a banner and shout about tax evasion? What's your big plan down here? Why Panama?"

"You don't have to talk about it like that." Sarah sighed and closed her eyes. "There's an exploratory well. They want to drill down here. We're going to stop it from producing but we have to get there first."

"You'll end up in a Central American prison."

Sarah shot her an annoyed look. "As it happens, I'm not going to the well. We're just helping to bring the crew to the boat that will."

The relief was so strong that Livy laughed. "You'll be back then and I can wait for you here."

"It won't be like that. When things happen they look for everybody." Sarah touched Livy's hand. "But you could still wait. Or come with me."

"And spend the rest of my life paying lawyers?" She shook her head. "I'm not going to risk jail for anyone."

Sarah flared but Livy reached for her waist.

"Don't be like that. We only have a little time."

The next day everyone got their passports back and Livy spent the afternoon with Sarah exploring Puerta de Balboa. She mailed the jade necklace to Cheyenne and tried again to get Kirsten on the phone. Just hearing her mother's voice on the message calmed her. Livy sent a text. *Waiting on money. Will call when I have ticket. Make sure Cheyenne has this number.*

65 What Hills Are Those

CHEYENNE BOOKED the first flight to Seattle that she could, then called Kirsten. She wanted her mother to say it wasn't true, that Margaret had exaggerated, but her mother was quiet.

"Does Livy know?"

"We've been in touch."

"And that means what? You said she doesn't have a phone."

"I forgot, she put minutes on her old one," said Kirsten. "I've been forgetting things."

When Cheyenne got off she texted her sister again: *Mom has stomach cancer. Come home. Now. Fast. Please.*

The judge advocate had said her request for Essex to travel was denied and to override the denial he needed permission from an officer above the one who denied him, but when she called his office his secretary said he was at Disney World with his family. Call him, Cheyenne said, yank him out of Magic Mountain. But for that, the secretary needed permission from another officer and that officer's secretary said the officer would be gone all day.

Pacing the sterile hotel room, Cheyenne looked at the polished mirror behind the TV and the unstainable rug and bleached sheets. She took a bright white complimentary robe from a hanger in the closet and tore into a sealed hygienic plastic bag that contained a pair of disposable slippers. In the absence of another direction to go, she decided to do laundry. Stripping to the skin, she made a pile of her clothes, dumped out her backpack, which smelled of sweat and peanut butter sandwiches, emptied pens and paperwork from the pockets, and threw it into the pile too. Balling it all up into her arms, she walked the halls past wet children, fresh from the overheated pool, chlorine eyes, skin tightening as it dried, mothers carrying goggles, also in bright white robes.

The laundry room was empty. She fed dollars into the change machine, bought a box of detergent, and threw everything in. In the glass circle of the washer, she watched her denim halter dress, her two pairs of jeans and three shirts, her four pairs of underwear and white sports bra, light brown at the underarm, spin itself into a torrent of gray froth. She'd clearly put too much detergent in. She didn't care. It wasn't the kind of thing that washed out. She was thirty-four and all she had to show for it couldn't fill a coin-op dryer. She'd been wrong. There were no points for boldness. When she got back to her room, the red message light on the phone was blinking. It was a voice mail from the JA asking her to call.

The order had come from the office of the battalion commander. Essex had seventy-two hours for travel. The JA waited for tears of gratitude, but she'd lost her manners and with it her sense of obligation to strangers and gatekeepers. An etheric rage took her.

"I've never seen anything like it," said the JA.

"You mean you've never seen it for a nobody like Essex," she said and hung up.

They hadn't been able to get on the same flight so Cheyenne had spent the last three hours waiting for Essex in the Seattle airport, looking up alternative cancer treatments on her phone and reading testimonials. A Vitamix. A diet of organic raw vegetables. Ayurveda. Lots of turmeric root. Move away from power lines. No microwaves. Keep cell phones and computers powered down. Throw out all cleaning supplies and check for hidden toxins in furniture, the curtains, the carpet.

Essex walked off the plane carrying a camouflage pack but wearing civilian clothes. His eyes seemed to her like bluebirds darting, looking for a branch to land on. *Find your own way,* she thought. *I can't do this.*

They drove toward the city in a rented hybrid. Essex randomly pressed buttons until he found the wipers. It was winter rain, heavy enough to last for months, marathon rain, which would slow but not stop. Vectors of cars and trucks appeared and disappeared on the windshield. Cheyenne rolled her window down to feel the rain on her face and the scent of earth was everywhere. The concrete and steel couldn't even start to bury it.

"It's not a done deal," she said rolling the window back up. "People get misdiagnosed. There's a lot of anecdotal evidence that other ways work. Clinical trials too."

"I think we should be married for real," he said.

"We are."

"You know what I mean," he said.

"You promised you wouldn't."

He turned on his signal and slowly floated into the left lane like he was back driving a cab, owning the road in a Crown Victoria. He tried to see the city as he had nine months ago but could not.

They came to a dead stop in the traffic.

"I'm not jealous, you know. If you think marriage to me is some kind of permanent sexual obligation, it doesn't have to be," he said.

"You promised you wouldn't do this. You swore," she said.

"I don't know how much time we have."

Their lane started moving and the car behind them honked. Essex ignored it. He turned to her. Behind him, drivers gave them dirty looks, cartoonish faces and gestures.

"What do you want? Honestly truly want?" he said.

"Drive!"

"For real. Tell me."

She threw her head back and glared at the gray fabric ceiling of the car. "What do I want? Let's see," she said in a choked voice, "I want to live in a public utility building, fall in love over and over until I die, have a job that doesn't suck, and see things change in a good way not a bad way. I want to go to sleep at dawn and wake up in the afternoon. I want to spend the first half of my day naked, wrapped in a sheet and drinking coffee, and the second half hanging out with people who only want to talk about shit that matters. Then I want to walk home after midnight, confess to mystical ideas, have sex, and go to sleep at sunrise. Every day. That's what I want to do every single day and none of it is going to happen. Now drive."

"I want to be with you."

"That's a lousy ambition."

They drove another mile bumper to bumper.

"You know how in *Little Women* everyone knows Jo should have married Laurie?" Essex said.

"You've read *Little Women*?"

"Kirsten made me."

Cheyenne laughed. "Of course she did." She yanked off her shoes and pressed her feet against the glove box. "You're not Laurie. You're one of the sisters. You might even be Beth. I don't know why I find it so disturbing that you've read *Little Women*."

"For real. A solid yes or a solid no. I don't want to go back wondering," he said.

Cheyenne nodded. They turned off by the university.

"I want to stop at a store," she said. "We should bring food."

They parked in the underground lot of an expensive hippie grocery. Essex opened his door but Cheyenne didn't move. She could feel the heat from his body on her arm but always bending to her physical attraction had messed up her life. It had burned through everything. Her relationship with Essex was not one she wanted to risk. Still, she felt herself wavering.

"Okay, what's the grand offer? I go live on some army base?"

"Marine base," he said.

"They send you to jail and I get to wait to see if they ever let you out?"

"It's what I've got to offer."

"Well I don't have anything to offer."

66 The Great Canal

ALTHOUGH THEY HAD FREE REIN to wander Balboa, Livy and Sarah stayed on or near the *Neva*. That space was theirs, separate and apart, and neither wanted to breach it and let the rest of the world in. Realizing it was useless, Sarah had stopped trying to talk Livy into coming with her. There were some kinds of risks that were simply not in Livy's nature. Just as there were some kinds of caution that were not in Sarah's. A line was drawn upon which they built a fence between them and hooked their fingers through, coming as close as they could with it there, as if it were a real thing and not something that could be brought down.

Livy could feel Sarah pulling away slightly. She spent more time with Marne and became distant in infinitesimal ways Livy could not name. Marne and Sarah were waiting on a meeting to take place in Panama City. After that, things would move. But until Livy had her money, she couldn't get a ticket home, and she didn't have to think about leaving Sarah. On the *Neva* with no sails to set, no show to put on for tourists, time expanded. She was a ruler of herself in a way she'd never known. *There is the ship; there is the sea. A sail is a fine winding sheet. May I never live to see the day when people cease to call me Queen.*

As long as she didn't look ahead.

A few days after getting their passports back, two deckhands jumped. It meant nothing to Livy but upset Sarah and Marne because one was supposed to be in the PRAJNA action. Gone without a word, a coal-mine canary.

"Why does it matter?" Livy asked.

"We need enough crew to sail this thing," said Marne.

"How far?" Livy asked.

"Into the bay of one of the islands. That's where we meet the other boat."

Livy looked aloft. "Well you might have enough to sail. The weather's decent."

Marne laughed and shook her head. "Maybe."

Sarah glared at the dock.

The third mate called the portside watch to muster.

Portside watch! Roll out all the hammocks and repair any fraying lines!

Roll out the hammocks and repair the lines!

Not like watching you bastards hit the ground in your sleep isn't funny . . .

Say again?

The captain, still drunk from another night ashore, slept on. Just before 3:00 p.m. the third mate, weighing his desperation to find work against the likelihood of getting paid, grabbed his seabag and left too. Another sailor followed. The first mate shook the captain at 5:00 p.m. Once alert and apprised of the situation, the captain and first mate went off to drink.

Livy joined Sarah on watch. The sun went down and yellow light from the oil lamp pooled on their hands and on the sea chest full of twine and rope. Underlit, Sarah's sharp bone structure painted strange shadows on her face, turning her eyes into dark sockets deeper than black ponds. Livy felt for a second like she didn't know her at all. Then recognition flooded back. This was her Sarah. She touched her cheek, lamplight along her forearm, she kissed her, lamplight on her ear and neck.

Over the next twenty-four hours, with the dwindling crew and the captain and first mate hiding in bars, the ship grew bigger and sometimes seemed all theirs. Livy knew she was lying to herself, knew it for a faerie mound, but as long as Sarah was waiting for the meeting and the captain held Livy's money, no one had to wake up.

With so many abandoning ship and no structure to their days, the sailors who remained on the *Neva* clung to discipline, largely enforced by Marne's moods and personality. They were foreigners, indigent without their pay and bound to the ship. Those with money from other sources gone, they waited. Livy didn't mind. *Let this go on and on. Here, here, here.*

As the day of the meeting with the PRAJNA coalition got closer, Livy tried to wear away the dangers of the future. *At some point we can meet again. You can hide for a bit then come back. I don't mind waiting.* But Sarah would not join her in this.

"These might be our last real days together," she said.

"You don't know," said Livy.

Sarah looked toward the bay. "Things don't always go as planned."

The morning before the PRAJNA coalition meeting, the captain called Livy to his quarters and handed her a check. She'd never felt so miserable getting paid. Crossing the deck, she saw Sarah standing by the mains'l in a stained white cotton long-sleeved shirt and straw hat, coiling down a line that someone had tripped over and tangled, probably herself. Livy held up the check. Sarah saw it and kept on coiling.

Livy decided to go to Panama City the next day to cash the check and get a ticket. Mostly so she could ride with Sarah and Marne who were meeting with the coalition to coordinate the PRAJNA action. Livy knew the rough shape of the plan—get the activist crew to the boat that would take them to the exploratory well, monkey-wrench it, show that they can be shut down, document the job with proof of international violations, upload planned location sites, and dox the hell out of everyone involved—but saw no way that it would change a thing. Her chance to change Sarah's mind was down to nearly nothing, and she felt like they were speeding toward a wall that would break them all apart.

On the bus to Panama City, Livy sat by the window. Sarah hung her head, motion sick, beside her. As downtown came into view, she laughed.

Livy smiled. "What?"

"It's such a—the whole downtown is like, I don't even know what to call it," said Sarah.

Marne popped up over the seat back in front of them.

"Oh yes you do," she said, "Try . . . h-a-r-d-e-r."

Sarah looked at the skyline. "Mirror dick garden?"

Marne applauded.

"I didn't think it would be so obvious," said Sarah.

The laughing died off. Everything was threadbare. None of this was funny.

When they arrived at the station, Livy held Sarah for a long time. Even though they would meet up in a few hours, everything would be different, Sarah's attention elsewhere.

A few blocks from where they separated, the foreign city moved around Livy, populated with foreign humans. She turned to see which way Sarah and Marne had gone, but they were nowhere.

Livy found the bank and waited in line pressed between business suits, breathing in cologne. Her own dirtiness became more acute. She started to shrink, then her mother's voice echoed so loud in her skull it seemed everyone could hear. *They get off too easily. They destroy everything!* They, the dominant culture. They, the rich, the power brokers. It was Kirsten's view of the world.

Once out of the bank, Livy tried to call her mother but was sent to voice mail. She texted, *Turn your ringer on.* Kirsten texted back a picture of the apartment's courtyard, its lake-like puddles, its defunct fountain clotted with rotting leaves. *Cheyenne's coming tomorrow,* wrote Kirsten. *I'll be home soon,* Livy wrote. *Follow your heart,* wrote Kirsten. But Livy couldn't.

Wandering back to the appointed meeting place several hours

later, she tried to run the options in her head and found none. She felt Raleigh behind her and turned but it was only a day trader, or someone dressed like one—respectfully sketchy with a racing heartbeat—well maybe she was a day trader too.

When she got to the bar, Sarah and Marne were at a table in the corner, already drunk.

Sarah had her elbows on the table and was holding her head.

"Two years," she said. "I wasted two years of my life."

"What happened?"

"We shouldn't talk about it," said Marne.

"I don't care." Sarah threw her head back. "Arrest me. Maybe I'll meet some real activists in jail."

It took Livy a few minutes to get the full story. The exploratory well was not where it was supposed to be, and they could not get to where it was.

"Why can't you try again another time?" said Livy.

"The coalition blew up," said Sarah. "Half the crew that was going to do the work left."

"People got spooked because the information was bad," said Marne.

Sarah pushed the last of her scotch toward Livy, who drank it and tried to flag a waiter.

Sarah grabbed her wrist. "It was so fucking simple. Get the coalition crew to the *Neva*. Get the *Neva* to the boat. Get the boat to the well." Sarah let go of Livy's wrist and stared at the room, letting her eyes go to soft focus.

"Try not to look so happy," said Sarah. Her voice cracked with bitterness and despair.

"I told you," said Livy quietly, "I'm not political."

Sarah put her hand up. "Show some respect for those of us who are." She looked with bleary eyes at the room. "It should have been easy." Sarah groaned. "I just wanted to stop that well for one day. I used to think if something wasn't permanent, it wasn't worth it. Now I feel just the opposite. I'm getting old." Sarah got up. "I want cigarettes. Do they sell them here? They must."

Livy looked to Marne.

"Our information was wrong. The well is much farther out than we thought," she said.

"What time's the bus?" asked Livy.

"We already missed it. I got us a room at a place down the street," said Marne.

"Want to see where the fucking thing is? Give me my phone," said Sarah.

Taking it, she typed in a set of numbers she'd written on her arm, which turned out to be longitude and latitude, and handed the phone to Livy.

"All I see is blue," said Livy.

"Zoom in."

Livy zoomed in. "I just see blue."

"Right, because that's where it is. Now zoom out."

Livy backed out until land appeared. On one side, she saw the Marquesas and on the other the coast of South America. Somewhere in the 4,500 miles of open sea between these two points was the new PRAJNA well. Joy filled Livy's chest. Sarah wasn't going anywhere.

She relaxed like she hadn't in months. Sarah wandered off for cigarettes, swaying badly.

She returned and held up a pack of Gauloises.

"You don't smoke, do you?" said Livy.

"Neither of us do," Sarah said. She tore the cellophane off the pack. "Fuck this year," she said.

"Fuck this year," Marne said.

Yeah, fuck this year. But looking at Sarah, Livy couldn't say that. Sarah lit a cigarette from the oil lamp on the table. Marne did the same, took a few drags, then blew out smoke.

"It doesn't feel like it used to," she said.

"It will," said Sarah. "You just have to keep smoking."

"Are you going to stay on the *Neva*?" Livy asked Marne.

"I hate that ship. If I get on a tall ship it'll be the *Columbia* replica. I like barques. The real *Columbia* is fully rigged and lives in Disneyland. And guess what? I don't care. I'm sick of other people's fantasies about the past."

Sarah set her glass down on the table too hard.

"For fuck sake. We have the location of the well. Why can't we just find a bigger boat?"

"It would have to be a tanker to carry the fuel we'd need." Marne kicked back and began to count off on her hand all the things in the way. "After the fuel there's the time it would take to get out there. Keeping a secret for a few days is one thing. For a month? Someone would start talking. They'd find the boat long before it got there. Radar when they knew where to look. The navigational system. Trust me. They'd find it."

"Yeah," said Livy. "What you two need is some kind of magic ship that requires no fuel and a crew that can navigate without electronics."

Sarah sat bolt upright. "Wait! That's us."

"Pull the radar block and the reflectors—we're not big enough to register and the *Neva* has a wood hull. Out of sight, we're invisible," said Livy.

Marne laughed. "Nah, everyone would see us leave."

"How would you deal with the captain?" asked Livy.

"Wait until he and the first mate hit the bars then send someone to say Russian mob guys are on the *Neva* waiting for him. Tell him we'll find him when they're gone. He'll be hiding in a hotel for days."

"Is anyone really after that guy?" asked Livy.

"Only his own alcoholic imagination."

Livy smiled. She wanted the alcohol to take her. Because this was the kind of thing she loved. A theoretical problem in a world free of consequence, unclouded by emotion. Her love was with her and they were all together.

"Think about it," said Livy. "What makes the *Neva* the *Neva*?"

"Shape, class, deck length, how she sits in the water," said Marne.

"That's what we see," said Livy. "Most people see a tall ship with a stripe. From far away they just see sails. Change the sails. Rerig her. Make her a barque. Lower the yards on the mizzen, or cockbill them to look like gaffs from a distance. Cut the sails to string them fore and aft. Paint over the stripe."

"True," said Marne. "I guess the mizzen wouldn't have to draw. It's a downwind run in the southeasterly trades. But you'd need a week and decent sailmakers."

"Two days for a really shitty job. Tell the captain and first mate someone wants to charter the *Neva* for a couple of days and pay in cash. They'll be hiding out, thinking they really need the cash. Pick one of the islands with other little islands around. Come in flying as many sails as you can, drop anchor in the main harbor of the biggest island, run up flags, shoot off a few cannon blanks, let everyone know the *Neva* is there. Work the first day anchored in the harbor in plain sight then find a quieter cove with no one around to finish."

"And when we're not back in two days?" asked Sarah.

"Tell the captain the rich people want another day," said Livy. "Then it's just Captain Marne."

"No, you would be the captain because captain's a cunt and you're way more of a cunt than me," said Marne. "You are fishy to the spine."

"I speak shark," said Livy, louder than she meant.

"Can it work?" Sarah asked.

"Definitely not," said Livy. "We'd all die. It's thousands of miles of open sea."

"Shittier sailors than us have made it around the world in worse boats," said Marne.

"They had to."

"We could pretend we have to," said Sarah.

"It's a shit-talk, honey. I don't mean anything by it," said Livy.

Marne got up to go to the bathroom.

"I hate this day on so many fronts," said Sarah.

"It's not so bad." Livy took her hand. "I have a joke. What's the difference between fate and destiny? A six-pack of beer."

67 Above, the Fire

KIRSTEN'S APARTMENT was cleaner than Cheyenne had ever seen it. Members of the coven had been taking turns coming over. There was no dust, no dirty towels, dishes glinted in the rack, and the freezer was full of untouched food.

In a recliner in the living room, covered in blankets, was Kirsten. Her hair was still long.

Cheyenne had expected it to be gone. She expected to find her mother in a colorful bandanna, a charm around her neck signifying the eternal, looking worse than she did but in a temporary way, a stick image of survival.

Margaret greeted them, briefly obscuring Kirsten to give Cheyenne a second to adjust.

"I'm glad you're here," she said.

Cheyenne went to hug Kirsten but Kirsten flinched so Cheyenne paused. Every touch had the potential to injure; even this kind of love has violence in it now. Cheyenne leaned down to kiss her instead.

Margaret offered Essex her spot on the couch. Trying to slide in between the couch and the coffee table he knocked it and, spilling a cold cup of tea, tried to reverse direction to go get a rag, but Margaret motioned for him to sit. He settled, an arm's length from Kirsten, his knees jammed up against the coffee table, unsure of what to say.

Cheyenne, who was still standing by Kirsten's chair with her hand resting lightly on her mother's head, let it slide to her shoulder before taking it away. Cheyenne sat on the floor beside Kirsten with her feet tucked under her.

"You could have just told me Justine was a sociopath."

Kirsten smiled. "I try not to label people."

Margaret laughed abruptly.

"I could never figure out if Justine was born that way or if something happened to her to make her like that," said Kirsten. "You could only catch it in certain light."

Kirsten's gaze drifted to the door.

"She wasn't a good person. Isn't," said Cheyenne.

Kirsten shrugged. "Some people measure themselves by the distance they've traveled and others by how far they have to go. She was definitely a distance-traveled type."

There was a sound at the mail slot as envelopes were pushed through and landed on the carpet, fanned. Margaret gathered them and set them on a desk with others, also unsorted and unopened.

"I'm sorry you have cancer," said Essex. He cleared his throat. Cheyenne glared at him. He ignored her and scooted closer to Kirsten, knocking the table, spilling more tea.

"Me too," said Kirsten.

Tears in Kirsten's eyes, tears in Essex's and Margaret's eyes too.

"Can we not go there yet," said Cheyenne to the room, then turning on Kirsten, "Why the hell didn't you let us know? How long have you known? Since summer? That was why you were working at that stupid parking garage. How many months did you wait before going to a doctor? What the fuck were you thinking? What did you think you were doing?"

"Hey, hey," Essex said in quiet tones. "Let's dial back and deal with where we are."

"You're one to talk," said Kirsten, rallied in her anger. "All of you. None of you gets to say anything to me. None of you. Livy gets raped. She doesn't tell me. You get nearly killed in Texas. You don't tell me. Essex shoots his oldest friend—"

"He didn't shoot him!" yelled Cheyenne. "He just has a guilt complex."

"Stop immediately." Margaret's voice rang with thirty years of kicking people out of birthing rooms.

Outside, a pack of kids ran down the stairs chasing one another. Then someone bit it and there was crying and more running feet.

"It was a mistake," Kirsten said. "I thought I had time to decide. To see a doctor. I didn't want to end up talking to collection agencies the rest of my life." She paused. "I'm sorry."

Cheyenne had never seen honest guilt in her mother. Cheyenne felt her insides seize. Kirsten turned to her.

"I'm so sorry, baby," she said.

Kirsten sat forward, moving a pillow into place at the small of her back and got herself comfortable again. It was a labored gesture, but not undoable. Cheyenne's panic was premature. There was time. She began to breathe easier.

"Did Justine answer your question?"

"That woman is nobody's mother."

Cheyenne glanced at Margaret to see if she had told Kirsten she knew, but nowhere in Margaret's face could she find evidence of that. It wasn't hiding, it was the opposite. Margaret's expression held all possibilities equally; all truths existed in her face at all times.

Kirsten reached out without warning and brushed her hand across her daughter's forehead as if checking a child for a temperature. Cheyenne set her teeth because the tears when they came would not end.

"It's hot, isn't it," said Kirsten. "You're all overheated. I can turn the heater down."

"That's all right. It's a nice break from the rain," said Essex.

Kirsten straightened her blanket. "I don't even think I had real *I Ching* coins when Justine and I threw it. I probably used quarters or pennies. *Keeping still, the mountain. And above, the fire.* Pregnancy is a lot like a temporary prison in some ways." She laughed. "As opposed to parenting, which is more like work release."

"Oh thanks," said Cheyenne.

"You're welcome. You two were a nightmare," said Kirsten.

"You're the one who gambled your youth on a coin toss, so I don't feel sorry for you." Cheyenne's voice had an unintended edge because she did feel sorry for her, so, so sorry. It was one more thing she could do nothing about. "Livy should be here," she said.

"Leave her alone. She's in love."

"I don't care if she's in space," said Cheyenne.

"The *I Ching* is all about the Man," Kirsten said. "The Superior Man. The Great Man. What he does and doesn't do. I read it in my late teens and thought, Who the fuck keeps us alive? Not the Great Man." She sat up, repositioning pillows. "So you think it all came down to an unlucky throw. Is that how you see it? Ask me. Ask me what hexagram Justine threw that night. The night we decided I would take you both. Ask me what she threw."

"Okay, what did she throw?" said Cheyenne.

Kirsten slapped the arm of the recliner. "I had no idea." Kirsten glowed with victory, restored to her natural, unapologetic self.

Margaret's mouth opened. "You are fucking kidding me."

"Ha! There's the East Coast." Kirsten pointed. "It comes out when they're surprised."

"You tricked her?" said Cheyenne.

"Without a second thought," said Kirsten. "I let her throw the pennies then read her the entry for the Wanderer. *'The grass on the mountain takes fire. Bright light does not linger but travels on. All prisons are temporary . . .'*" Kirsten paused, letting victory slip. "It wasn't kind," she said.

Cheyenne took her mother's hand: As unfamiliar now as the wing of a fallen sparrow, it curled or splayed without resistance. "I'm glad you did," she said.

The room became pressured and airless. They were sea creatures going deep too fast. Kirsten extricated her hand from between Cheyenne's palms but hooked her daughter's fingers for a second, moving them back and forth like she had when Cheyenne was a baby.

"I was afraid that if I knew which of you was mine I might love one of you more. I didn't want to know." She pulled her hand back and kicked at her blanket, freeing her feet. "I was afraid of a lot of things. All the looks I used to get, at the DSHS offices and in the grocery stores. Because god forbid I buy you cupcakes with food stamps." She turned her eyes on Cheyenne. "I didn't want those looks to land on you two." She took a deep breath and let it out. "Do you know, if you go to an expensive school they will tell you from age five until twenty-two how great you are and how unique what you have inside you is. They'll make you write essays about your personal journey. You're always the hero. You always have a destiny to fulfill." She fell silent for a few seconds then grabbed Cheyenne's hand again. "I couldn't send you to expensive schools. I wanted you to have a myth of your own. So I gave you the North Star."

Essex looked down at the carpet. Kirsten blinked and let go of her daughter.

Cheyenne realized her legs were asleep, stood, and stretched.

Essex looked at Margaret but she was silent. He moved closer to Kirsten.

"How long do they say you have?" he asked.

"A month at this point. Maybe a little more." Kirsten's eyes filled with quick tears again.

"How could you let it get to this?" Cheyenne's voice cracked in anger and disbelief.

"I'm sorry," said Kirsten, "I'm so sorry. I made a mistake. I'm sorry."

"Don't torture yourself," said Margaret softly. "It might not have made a difference. This kind of cancer is fast."

"We need to make a plan for real," said Cheyenne, shaking off the moment. "Am I on her medical paperwork? I want to talk to her doctors directly. Has she had a second opinion?"

"It's not going to change what's happening," said Kirsten.

Cheyenne turned to Margaret.

"Cheyenne, I am more than happy to get you her doctor's number and help streamline any paperwork I can. I'll even call them now and find out if they have weekend hours," said Margaret.

"Do," said Cheyenne.

Margaret took her jacket off the back of the couch and stepped out onto the landing. Kirsten's eyes followed her.

"It's not her fault," Kirsten said, once Margaret was out of earshot. "When it comes to my body, it's my choice. She taught me that. Remember it. She only does what I ask. Even against her own opinions and wishes. Always has. Always will."

With no sound in the room, they could hear Margaret on the phone. The tone of her words as firm as concrete, the meaning, firing, wiring together, plastic.

Kirsten pointed to the shadow through the blinds. "I was fifteen when I met her. The eighties. A terrible time. Shoulder pads and nuclear war, wall of bangs—I was so alone. Margaret showed me how my mind had been shaped. She was the very first person to say the word *cunt* to my face. Not like a slam, like a calling. All liberation begins and ends with the body, she said. She could trace any political issue, no matter how abstract, right back to the body."

"I know she means well, I just think that we need better advice," said Cheyenne.

Kirsten ignored her. She brushed at something invisible on the arm of her chair. "There were all these other women she knew back East," she said, "living in funky houses and abandoned churches. She told me about this farm in the South that had the best midwives in the world. Totally radical. They didn't listen to what anyone said if it wasn't smart and those were the women who taught her. I didn't see it. I really didn't. How young she was then." She turned to Essex, who instinctively sat up straighter. "I didn't see it. I believed what she said about the world. I was like some little kid listening to her grandmother. I really thought that I was going to run off to all these places, meet all these women, and it was going to be some mystical experience. I didn't know." She turned to Cheyenne. "I didn't know it was already gone. All those collectives, all those little colonies, gone. Most anyway. It was awful, awful, when I realized it."

Kirsten turned back to Margaret's silhouette on the landing.

"It was like being told there's something great and important and beautiful but, hey, you missed it. Sorry. It was such a sucker punch. I stopped going to see her. We had it out one night about a year before you two were born. I told her she'd made my life worse. You know what she said? *Sorry you didn't get a torch, honey. You got a candle just like I did.* I thought she was telling me to suck it up and be grateful so I told her to fuck off and walked out."

Cheyenne laughed.

"I didn't get it for years," said Kirsten. "*You got a candle just like I did.* Her words, exactly."

Outside Margaret finished her call and came back in.

"Do you want some fresh tea?" Essex asked.

"No," said Kirsten.

"Are you warm?" he asked.

"Yes."

"Is there anything that you can eat?" he asked.

She shook her head.

Margaret studied Kirsten. "You need rest," she said. "Can you two give her a couple of hours?"

"Of course," said Cheyenne.

She bent over her mother's head and touched her dull hair. It was breaking off and thinning at the crown. Cheyenne kissed the line of gray skin where the hair parted, then went outside. Essex stayed only a moment then joined her, pulling the door shut carefully behind him.

Cheyenne started to say something but he took her hand, leading her off. They were near the stairwell when she pulled away and ran back to put her arms around her mother, encircling her, to hold her like a glass flower, hold her like a fragile painted Ukrainian egg—"I love you," she said. Releasing her, Cheyenne started to step back but Kirsten clutched her upper arms, digging into her muscles, pulling her back in. She reached for her daughter's head and brought it down to her lips. She kissed her daughter's temple. Holding her head in both hands, she turned her head and whispered into her ear, "I wanted to give you torches."

68 The Hostel

IN THE MORNING, Livy felt Sarah's body against her. They were on the bottom bunk of a hostel bed, their skin stuck together in the heat. Sarah's strong heartbeat, pulsing her body, lightly rocking Livy. When Livy moved, the world spun so she stayed still.

A few minutes later, Sarah woke up.

"I don't remember how we got here," Livy said.

"You were singing in the bar so we had to leave."

"I don't remember singing."

"It was some Cajun song about a guy who has three days to live and offers to trade two to spend one with the girl he loves. It was very romantic."

"I don't know any song like that."

"You were also yelling."

"What was I saying?"

"I know how to echolocate patriarchy."

Livy laughed. "I wasn't that drunk."

Although she did sort of remember shouting in the business district about Sir Walter Raleigh and an invisible fortress made of code and electronic fund transfers.

"Did the cops come?" Livy asked.

"Yes."

"I'm usually good when the cops come."

"You pushed one," said Sarah.

"I pushed a cop?"

Sarah gave a short laugh. "You told him you sprang in full battle gear from the brow of your mother."

"I've been missing my mom," said Livy. "I can't explain it."

"She's fine. If anything happens, Cheyenne will call. Kirsten has the number so Cheyenne has it too. She would let you know if something was wrong."

Livy raised herself onto one elbow and looked around. They were in a blue room with two other bunk beds, empty and stripped. Light came from a long window.

"All that stuff we talked about last night," said Sarah, "I can't stop thinking about it."

"I need to get up," said Livy.

Sarah moved aside. Livy sat on the edge of the bed. Her stomach turned over but she didn't throw up so she stood slowly, steadying herself on the upper bunk. Sarah got up behind her and came around.

"I want to try to do it, what we were talking about last night. Don't you want to change any of this?" Sarah gestured at the world in general.

Livy watched the sun find strands of gold in Sarah's red hair. She smelled coffee from the next room and heard children shouting in Spanish.

"No," she said, "I don't want to change any of it. I love this."

Sarah put her forehead on Livy's and her arms over her shoulders. Livy felt the room spinning slightly. She looked at Sarah's cracked hands, her cracked lips, the fine peach hair on her arms. She felt her warm breath on her skin.

"I won't do it for politics," said Livy. "I'll do it for you."

69 The Eighteenth Century

COMING BACK UP THE STEPS to Kirsten's apartment with a new blender under one arm, the other wrapped tightly around the waist of a paper grocery bag full of cruciferous greens, Cheyenne felt better about the future. No matter how bad it got, no matter how fast or slow it went, she was here. Essex followed, less assured.

An early-afternoon break in the clouds dappled the landing. They passed through streams of white sun, into the spotlight, out of it and offstage in the bright gray over and over until they reached the door. Stepping into the apartment, they were plunged into total darkness. Spheres of brown and amber appeared around candles, blue-lit faces, pale yellow tables, counters, mail, and a vase of flowers. They had walked into an eighteenth-century painting.

The woman coming toward her in the haze was Alice, a co-founder of the coven.

"Let your eyes adjust," she said.

Cheyenne blinked and saw several other coven members. The room wasn't dark. It was only the contrast. The women had pulled the shades for some sort of hippie ritual. She felt a flash of annoyance. They meant well. She lowered the blender to the floor just as Alice enfolded her in her arms.

"Look at you," she said. She kissed her forehead. "I'm sorry this is happening, baby."

"I need to put the groceries down," said Cheyenne. Crossing to the counter she gave the other women a nod. "Is she lying down?"

Two of the women exchanged glances.

Cheyenne took the kale and dandelion greens out of the bag and set them on the counter.

"Can someone please turn on the lights?" said Cheyenne.

No one moved.

Cheyenne, frustrated, came around the counter island and stalked down the hall to the bedroom door, but Essex got there first.

"Let's just go slow," he said.

She could see Kirsten behind him. The lights were out but a thick aromatherapy candle burned next to the bed. She was lying down. Margaret stood in the corner. The air smelled like oranges but also something sour and metallic Cheyenne couldn't place. Essex moved aside so she could see. She could feel others gathering behind her.

Kirsten still lay under an electric blanket she'd had for years. Her hair was braided into thin black twine, ending in the finest of paintbrush tips at her breast. Her eyes were closed. Cheyenne had never seen her mother's face that color. Not ashen like nausea, not flushed like when she had the flu, but an entirely new color made of other colors, unmixed, unnameable. Violet hues, tinted complex grays, a wash of indigo tempered with gunmetal and slate. A trace of white like the weathered, dingy fur of an old wolf, barely visible in the purpling skin, highlighting the brow bones, the crest of the cheek, the chin: This is what she saw.

Cheyenne stepped into the room.

Cheyenne reached over to a switch on the wall and flipped on the overheads. Sallow light from the compact fluorescent bulbs in the ceiling fixture spared nothing. The dresser was not an altar with tea lights and flowers, it was a particleboard box with two drawers and a scarf thrown over it. Her mother's skin was not all the rainbow colors of titanium but a flat purple-gray. Stains on the carpet from previous tenants covered the floor. Lampshades pilled with dust.

Essex turned off the lights.

"I think this may be how she wanted it," he said.

The candle, senseless, danced.

"But I'm back," said Cheyenne. "I said I'd be here and I am."

She heard one of the women behind her start to cry. A wave of fear then a quick shock of rage went through her. Cheyenne took a few steps into the room. She stopped. There was a noise. She listened. Soft crashing waves looped quietly nearby. She looked around for the source and saw a phone facedown on the floor by the dresser. Margaret motioned for her to come closer. Still in the corner, half in shadow, her face was unreadable. Cheyenne walked around to where Kirsten was. The bed had no frame. Even with a box spring it barely came up to the lower part of Cheyenne's thighs. She looked down at the body of her mother.

"But I'm here."

She sounded like a child even to herself.

Raising her gaze, she saw Essex on the other side of the bed with his eyes full of tears. Dreamlike. So unlike any dream. She got on her knees and examined her mother's face. All those features she had mistaken for Livy's, or for hers, they belonged to Kirsten alone. Sovereign all along.

Cheyenne ran her fingers lightly across the pads of her thumbs to feel herself and could not. She reached out to the body slowly, moving through space, a little girl waking her mother from a nap, she touched Kirsten's neck and recoiled.

"My god she's still warm. Call 911."

"It's the blanket," said Margaret.

Cheyenne got up quickly and Margaret put out her hand.

"Honey," she said, "it's the blanket. It's still on."

Essex found the cord and switched it off.

"Did you do this?" Cheyenne asked.

Margaret's hand was now on her forearm.

"Did you do this?"

"This is what she asked me to do," she said.

"She wouldn't do that." Cheyenne's voice was sharp and raised. "Did you do this?" she demanded.

Essex looked at Margaret. "Was she in a lot of pain?"

Margaret nodded.

"Get out," Cheyenne said.

Margaret gave a short sob and caught her breath.

"Get out!" Cheyenne screamed.

The candle by the bed flickered.

I came back. I came back. I said I would and I did. I'm here.

When Essex returned, the candle beside the bed was guttering. He asked one of the members of the coven to bring another from the living room and she came back with two. One, she put on the altar, the second she handed to Essex. Essex came around beside Cheyenne. She had entwined her fingers in her mother's hair and laid her face on the bed by her hip.

He set the candle down and went to blow the other out.

"Don't touch it," said Cheyenne. She raised her head. One cheek, pink from the draining heat of the blanket. "Don't you dare."

Kirsten had lit the candle with her own hands. It still burned. She was still here.

The Letter

I HAVE MADE A DECISION you probably won't understand.
I try and explain it but every way I think to say it only says something
else. In all honesty, I'm not sure the place I'm going even exists. If it
does, I have no idea what happens when I get there.

Know that I truly believe I will see you again.

These past few days I've felt like a stranger in my own body.
I want to control what I can't control. I wake up and recognize
nothing. Have you ever been so in love that everything you ever
said about yourself before sounded like a lie? The best part of me
decided to do this.

Livy sealed the letter to her mom belowdecks under the red light of
her head lamp. They were within hours of sailing for the PRAJNA
well. Livy thought of Raleigh and El Dorado, Cyril and Singapore.
Maybe the ocean is the bardo and everywhere you land is karma.
The one thing her mother and Cyril shared was a belief in the ultimate morality of cause and effect. Livy had no such conviction. She
addressed the envelope and went above.

Marne had dealt with the captain. Livy had called for a pilot
boat, and now they were escorted back under the Bridge of the
Americas and into the bay.

In the shade of an island they performed the queen of all shoddy
jobs. They brought down the cro'jack and rigged some blocks on one

of the mizzen yardarms, which took some serious lashing and carpentry. It was the beginning of a job in which every corner was cut.

As they finished over the next two days and looked around, they tried not to think too much about what they saw. It probably wouldn't hold in anything more than a five-foot chop, but it might get them out of the bay. As long as no one got too close. If they did, they would see the paint over the stripe dripping down the side of the ship like tears through mascara and the Frankenstein-stitched sails. But distance was not their only protection; if no one sued or filed an insurance claim, it mattered to no one what happened to them. *Drown. Break to pieces on the rocks. Wash ashore on whatever beach the tide sends you to.* Their greatest invisibility lay in their own insignificance.

71 Vigil

THE POLICE HAD BEEN CALLED. They spoke to Essex and Margaret in the living room. Cheyenne heard voices but no words. They wanted to see the body. They needed more light. Cheyenne stood. Margaret didn't have the right paperwork to prove she had acted on Kirsten's behalf. The coroner was coming. The police would wait. They turned out the lights. Everyone left the room but Margaret.

Cheyenne was on the floor with her back up against the bed. Her knees drawn in, arms folded on top, she rested her forehead so all she could see was the dark well of her own body. The blanket was cold. Kirsten was cold. Margaret sat down on the corner of the bed.

Margaret took a breath. "I'm going to say this to you now and you can hear it later. Your mother had all sorts of ideas I didn't agree with. She made a million decisions I'll never understand but I have never known anyone who knew herself so completely." Margaret cleared her throat.

Cheyenne raised her head. She craned her neck back and ran her fingers through her hair but kept her eyes closed.

"Your mother was her crazy sense of entitlement. She never let the world off the hook but she also understood that life owes us nothing. She was entirely without self-pity."

Margaret waited but Cheyenne had no reaction.

"What I'm trying to say is that she wasn't happy about the cancer but she didn't feel wronged by it. She was okay with how she was. She was okay with how her life went."

Swallowing, Margaret took a breath. "Which one of you has the big freckle on your foot?" asked Margaret.

Cheyenne opened her eyes and took in the room anew. "Livy." Her larynx was so tight it ached.

"You were born first. That makes you the older sister."

Cheyenne got off the floor and found a half-moon spot on the edge of the bed, the weight of her mother's body still anchoring the sheets. She placed her hand on her mother's abdomen.

Someone knocked on the front door. Voices in the living room got louder. Something hit the doorframe on its way in. She moved her hand to her mother's collarbone. In the periphery, Cheyenne saw Essex in the doorway. She wasn't sure how long he'd been there.

"She was okay with how she was," said Margaret.

"You said that already," said Cheyenne.

"It matters."

Margaret heard the noise of the gurney coming.

"I'm going to say something else and you can save it for after all this. I've seen a lot of death. That's not where people struggle. They struggle with how fast life comes back. Even when you don't want it to. Life doesn't have the decency to quit."

The gurney was in the hall.

"The coroner is here," said Essex.

Margaret stepped back to give room for the gurney. The lights came on and they rolled it into the room. When Cheyenne understood what was happening, she jumped off the bed.

"You can't. Not now. Not yet. You need to leave." She blocked the narrow passage between the corner of the bed and the dresser. She put her hands up and the young man who was wheeling the gurney around stopped.

"We have to take her. There are laws about how long we can wait."

"Don't touch her!"

Essex talked to the police and because the law is twenty-four hours they agreed to come back in the morning.

The coven brought more candles. Essex turned out the lights. They left Cheyenne alone with Kirsten, and Cheyenne returned to the body. Her mind cleared. It was as sharp and ventilated as it ever had been. She had the whole truth of it. How death was the most mundane thing of all. The cloying smell of the bergamot in the perfumed candles, the diminished pageant. Standing over the bed, she looked down at the body of her mother and wondered what she had fought for. What was she trying to save?

Wearing only her underwear, she climbed into the vacant side of the bed. Under the sheets, bare skin against Kirsten's nightgown, flickering breath, slow and skipping heart, her thoughts flowed back and forth, pouring into something totally normal then back out into the void. Kirsten was changing again. Her wrists and fingers were suppler, if only slightly. Margaret was right. It had no decency. She put her head next to her mother's and twisted their hair together. One by one, as the women left, the apartment filled with the refrigerator hum of ancestors. Or maybe it was just the idea of ancestors vibrating through her, the subsonic frequency of all the things we come from that we cannot see.

In the morning when they returned for the body, Cheyenne let the gurney pass. She was calm with the great absence all around her. Then when they slid the pillow out from beneath Kirsten's head, she dove, wrapping herself around her mother's legs. It's a trick! she shrieked. A trick! They just want the body. They think they can do whatever they want to it. They think it's theirs. They always have. They think they own it. They are insatiable.

72 The Southern Cross

AS THEY GOT UNDER WAY, leaving the islands behind, Livy watched the garish skyline of Panama City pass slowly in the distance. Had she been on shore, looking out at the sea, she would not have seen a ship at all; without running lights or lamps, the ship was only a small abyss on the horizon, a space without starlight.

Marne came up beside her. She pointed. "That's the Star of Magellan. It's part of the crux of the Southern Cross. Have you ever seen it?"

Livy shook her head. "I've never seen anything."

"It's how we'll be guiding soon. Between that star and the one there," Marne drew a short line with her forefinger, "you can trace down to the south celestial pole."

Livy turned instinctively toward the direction they had come from. Polaris was low in the sky behind her. Soon it would sink beneath the horizon entirely. The North Star, gone.

Everything you navigate by has to change.

Ahead, the Southern Cross, its blue giants, red giants, hot white stars seen and unseen.

Name those dear to you, count them as present, they are still here.

A whale breached nearby. The white of its fluke flashed against the dark sea.

"Humpback," said Marne. "They navigate by geomagnetism. They can find a direct path over five thousand miles of open ocean and arrive exactly where they mean to."

"We should be so lucky," said Livy. "Dead reckoning. That's what we'll have."

Marne smiled. "A sailor's last recourse."

The low hum of the engine was only noticeable now that it was gone. Every slap of water against the wooden hull, every snap of a sheet, the slight whir as a properly coiled halyard line ran free was audible, these were sounds that ancient sailors knew. They sailed past lighthouses that stood like giant chess pieces along the shore. Great rooks, they presided, each painted differently, daymarks, they said: *You are here! You are here!* At night they warned, they worried over the rocks they knew: *Look out! Look out!* These shoals, these shores. Each, a unique signal not to be confused with any other in the world. This specificity had seemed merely practical to Livy, but now it seemed quite beautiful; the differences between things, between people—she had misjudged it. She had scoffed. With eight billion people, how much do differences matter? She saw her sister and her brother in the light of the Fresnel lens at Cyril's wedding. Not to be confused with any others in the world. How could she have missed it? All the ways slight angles reveal an unseen facet, sending new light everywhere.

The *Neva* turned to catch the trade winds that would take them out to the Great Offshore Grounds. Before leaving, Livy had collected everyone's cell phones in a pillowcase. They couldn't chance someone making a call and getting traced. Once fully past Panama City, she grabbed a hammer and went below. Desperation, the kind they needed to survive, couldn't be faked. She sat on the sole with the pillowcase full of phones between her legs. Fishing out Sarah's phone, she set it aside. The rest she smashed to dust.

Picking up Sarah's phone, she felt a strong urge to turn it on one last time and see if there was a voice mail from Kirsten. She wanted to call Cheyenne even though she knew the number she had was old. She wanted to e-mail Essex. Her mind ran to Sarah's skin.

How it felt on hers when they were stuck together by sweat in the hostel bed. Raising the hammer, there was absolutely no debate in her mind. She brought it down full force sending plastic and metal skittering in all directions. You shouldn't have to choose. But if you have to, choose love.

73 The Grief Channel

CHEYENNE STUDIED the motel-room wall. She didn't remember checking in. Essex shifted next to her in the bed.

"How long have you been awake?" she asked.

"I didn't sleep."

"I was hysterical. I made it worse."

"You'd been up for thirty-six hours. Everyone understood."

She rolled over, putting her head on his chest. She pressed her palm against his heart but his muscles tightened and he slid his thumb under her palm and removed it. He didn't let it go, but with a forefinger, traced her lifeline down, while her hand closed around his.

"You're like one of those plants that curl up when you touch them," he said.

He put the butt of his palm against hers. She spread her fingers. Her fingers were shorter, but not by as much as she would have thought. She felt his calluses and didn't know how he got them. Outside, the rush-hour sound of trucks and cars.

She remembered his touch in the living room of the apartment after they took Kirsten's body. The cops and coroner gone, she'd yelled at him. *What am I supposed to do now? What am I supposed to do now?* She remembered her hips against the kitchen table and his stomach against the small of her back. Crazed and anonymous. Nothing but the body. She remembered feeling so insanely alive. She made him start again when they were done. Afterward, standing in the hallway, she yelled once more. *What am I supposed to do?* As if he knew. She kissed his legs and put her cheek against them. Where had all that sorrow been before this? Then they were in a car. He was talking. She kept trying to touch him and he wouldn't let her. He was driving. He kept pressing her back. In the motel room, he had not. When he was very close, the air was rain and sweat, not illness. She could smell it now. Her temple just under his clavicle. She went back to sleep.

An hour later Essex drew the curtain of brown flame-retardant shades from one side of the large window to the other, letting the day in. She sat up in bed. He stood shirtless by the window looking out. They were on the ground floor. Across a shallow parking lot was an arterial road.

Essex bent his head, his shoulders caving slightly. With a flick of a gaze at her, he went back to looking out the window. Two homeless men argued at the bus shelter. Essex's blue eyes followed them, the brightest thing in frame.

"How long did I sleep?" she asked.

"Maybe three hours."

"What happened?"

"Like you said. You were hysterical. Not in a bad way."

"Hysterical in a good way." She drew her knees tighter to her chest. "Was it okay what happened between us?" she said.

The splash of daylight behind him blinded her and she couldn't see his face.

"I'm not totally sure. You were begging me to have sex with you. And it was also the only way you were going to go to sleep," he said.

"But how do you feel about it?"

"I think it's probably okay."

He sat back down on the bed and put his hand over her ankle. He took a manila package off the nightstand.

"Move over." He scooted his back against the headboard, taking up most of the bed. "This was in the mail at Kirsten's."

Cheyenne took the small padded envelope. The postal stamp said Panama.

Cheyenne just looked at it. Her sister had stranded her on the East Coast. She had not called her in all the months she'd been in Alaska. She had not called her when she came through Seattle. That she could forgive, but the idea that she had seen Kirsten and not warned Cheyenne was a gulf between them.

"You shouldn't be mad at her," said Essex. "I found Kirsten's phone and it had about a million texts and voice mails from Livy. She doesn't know."

Cheyenne pulled the strip and bits of gray padding rained into her lap. A note fell out, taped on all sides so if you tried to open it with anything other than a knife or scissors, you'd tear it. "She did that on purpose," said Cheyenne. She shook the envelope and a necklace fell out. The cord was delicately worked twine with a jade pendant knotted into it. "My dragon charm." She touched the intricate knot work Livy had done. "I didn't know she could do this."

"Let me see," said Essex.

She handed it over, picked up the note, and chewed a hole in one corner. She tore into it carefully but there was nothing inside but another note, also taped shut. She finally peeled the tape back enough to open the note, which had been folded into a compact square. It was one line written in her sister's blocky hand: THANK YOU FOR JUNEAU.

She showed Essex, who laughed. She could feel the tears rolling down and could taste them in her mouth. How many times a day can you cry?

"Put it on me," she said.

Every time he touched the back of her neck trying to get it clasped, she flinched. She turned around, fingering the charm. She looked like a teenager. Nothing filtering out the world.

"I leave in twelve hours," he said. "And things are definitely going to get worse."

"Livy should be here."

"Are you coming with me? Now, next week, a month from now. I need to know."

She wanted to, or her body wanted to, but she couldn't make herself say it.

"I can't help but feel that you and I are a case of jelly holding up jam," she said, and touched the jade charm. "You should just go to Canada. Walk over the border and live off the grid."

He put his hand on her knee rocking it back and forth and gave her a half smile.

"Want to walk over the border with me?"

She didn't say anything.

He took his hand off her knee.

"There are a lot of ways I love you," he said. "This isn't one of them."

She got out of bed, put on her jeans, and gathered up the clothes she could find.

"Your bra is in the corner," he said.

She walked to where he pointed. It was on the floor near the electrical socket under the table with the laminated Wi-Fi instructions and unplugged coffeemaker on it. One earring was on the wooden arm of the chair, the other glinted in the carpet. She put them on. Her socks were in her hand. Her shoes were by the door.

He started to say something, then just shook his head.

"Whatever you want to say to me, say it," she said.

"Margaret was right. Kirsten was okay with herself. It's true and you know it. And no matter what you think—and you know I care way too much about what you think—I am also okay with myself. And I'm pretty damn sure Livy is okay with herself."

She felt heat on her face and neck.

"I don't even know what's happening," she said. "She just died and you're asking me to commit to some kind of amorphous future."

"Anybody can make a decision between good options. Throw a dart, win a prize."

"I can't be what you want. If I lied about it, I would make it worse."

He looked like the wind had been knocked out of him. But

maybe it was only fatigue because none of this was new. He opened the door and the smell of diesel wafted in.

"What happens now?" she said.

"We go to the apartment to sort out what we can. Then I go back to Jacksonville."

The apartment was clean and dark. On the kitchen counter were three paper bags that Cheyenne assumed contained leftover food. Looking again, she saw the bags were each labeled, one for Cheyenne, one for Livy, one for Essex. Next to them under a mug was a page, obviously torn quickly from a spiral notebook. It said: The will is going to be read tonight on *The Third Spiral Galaxy*. Show starts at 3:00 a.m. Go to the bottom of the dial and wait.

74 Valley of the Kings

THE COMMUNITY RADIO STATION had been started by well-meaning white progressives at a time of great unemployment when airtime was worthless. As the city's youth population swelled, a new generation of more diverse and vocal activists took over and the coven grabbed the Sunday through Thursday 3:00 to 4:00 a.m. slot.

The coven's show's first incarnation was known as *The Apology Hour.* Divided into three segments, it began with a topical group discussion that resulted in a list of charges against the patriarchy. The list was then debated and refined in the second segment. Once consensus was reached, the list was read aloud in its final form and male listeners were invited to call in and apologize, but complaints soon mounted from other collectives that, since the third segment of *The Apology Hour* was usually twenty minutes of dead air, the coven didn't have a right to it.

The Apology Hour eventually collapsed for other reasons. Unable to maintain a quorum for the opening, they could not generate a list of charges, and how can you apologize for something you don't understand? Citing manipulation as a resistance strategy, the coven kept the time slot by co-opting dissent, voting in blocks, and stepping back when factions polarized, returning as queenmakers.

As the only radio show with in-studio childcare, the host was often interrupted by her own howling, disoriented kids. Livy and

Cheyenne had been the terrors of the station. One always woke the other with a hard kick, which was followed by retaliation. Tantrum screams bled through the soundproof walls into the booth. Kirsten did her best to ignore them when she was on air, but if it reached a certain pique, she'd have them dragged in and reprimand them live. After which, the call lights lit up and the rest of the night ended in a referendum on her parenting. Having built her daughters into indestructible hellions, they could not be harmed by her words. Kirsten herself had no such defenses. On one very bad night, after being told she was every single argument for family planning rolled into one, she lost it, screaming into the ribbon mic, "I'm fucking twenty-three! I'm fucking twenty-three."

But she also saved the show once. Right about the time the language of branding colonized all conversations, a new program director called a meeting. There was talk of listener quotas. All the shows were on the chopping block and a particularly virulent fight had broken out between the old guard and the program director over whether democracy involved a responsibility to educate and inform or was just responding to the will of the people. The story went that Kirsten, who had arrived late, listened to the debate for about thirty seconds then looked at the program director and said, "I don't care about politics. I want a show that a midwife or a woman on a crisis hotline can listen to without being ashamed of who we are." Argument stopped. Everyone looked down at their free trade coffee and, as the coven liked to tell it, remembered they were a fucking community radio station.

Following that meeting, culture at the station continued to change but the radical feminist radio hour remained intact. It morphed several more times before settling into its current iteration as *The Third Spiral Galaxy*. The format was simple. They read news about women. They broke down legislative attacks on the female body. They played music by women and ended each broadcast with mail, a list of local domestic violence shelters, and the names of errant teen girls the police didn't consider endangered: Her name is this. She looks like that. She's dating a real asshole, watch out for her please.

Tonight's show would be different. Following the invocation would be the reading of Kirsten's will. The rest of the hour would be devoted to her favorite music, regardless of the artist's gender, and time would be reserved for guests to call in. Kirsten, as the show's longtime astrologer, was well-loved and would be missed.

"I'm not ready for a wake," said Cheyenne.

Cheyenne and Essex decided to go to Gas Works Park. Take a blanket and a few candles. Listen to the radio show and open the paper bags up there. There wouldn't be enough time to come back to the apartment before Essex had to leave for his flight, so they would have to take both cars. She grabbed Kirsten's electric blanket, some candles, and all three bags. Essex looked around before closing the door to make sure he hadn't forgotten anything.

It was well into the night. Essex handed Cheyenne Kirsten's keys, which was another strange thing, an action like always, an action as proof it will never be like always, everything ringing in two worlds.

They stopped in the University District at a twenty-four-hour doughnut shop and bought apple fritters. The people at the tables were young and high, white but yellow-skinned from the light bouncing off the lemon walls. Neither Essex nor Cheyenne had slept much for days and the sound of sudden laughter was like cannon-shot.

It was after 2:00 a.m. when they arrived. The rain had stopped earlier in the evening but everything was wet. Moonlight turned the fishing boats to carved bone in their docks, swaying and clicking together like vertebrae. The rust-colored structure of the gasworks, backlit and black to the eye, guardrails ringing silos, huge pipes joined boiler to empty bell and thin ladders scaled the sides of barrels and peeked up over the top, scratching the sky like a woodcut.

The clouds were breaking up overhead and the temperature dropped slightly. Windless now, the lake was still, reflecting the city in bright spectrometer lines. Metropolis, Cheyenne proclaimed, opening her arms wide in mock stagecraft, Kirsten's electric blanket around her neck and shoulders, the cord trailing behind, ticking on the concrete path. They walked along low concrete walls in the shadow. A day-old moon was caught between the graffiti-covered welded steel tanks.

"I saw an Egyptian temple in a museum in New York," said Cheyenne, pointing at the tag on one tower. "It had graffiti on it from Romans and Napoleon."

"What did it say?"

"Same thing it always says: 'We were here.'"

He laughed and she smiled.

"Otherwise you might not know," she added.

"I don't know," he said, "I see us everywhere. The great buildings, the pyramids, the bridges—we built them. They're ours more than anybody else's."

"Except for the money, the building materials, and the zoning permits."

"I will not concede the greatness of our people to you."

"Sometimes it feels like all the big decisions of the world get made without us," she said.

The lake water lapped once against the shore. A car pulled into the parking lot with its high beams shearing and techno beat and bass rattling its fenders. The driver rolled down his window. A vocoder descant in round tones elbowed angel-ward, so sure of its place in the world.

"We can look for a spot by the sundial," said Essex.

They abandoned the lower park for the hill. Climbing the spiral path, the sound faded. The vista changed as they wound around the hill: downtown and the lake, the ship canal and the bridge, the parking lot, the gasworks again.

"You know what kills me is that all those women, Margaret and the coven, had a chance to talk her out of it."

"I don't think she wanted to be talked out of it," said Essex.

"They had time to get right with her and say goodbye."

"We did say goodbye, sort of."

"I didn't. Not at all."

They stopped just before the summit, breathing harder from lack of sleep.

"We should be able to get decent reception here," he said. "Where do you want to sit?"

Cheyenne pointed to a flat patch a few yards from the bronze sundial. "I want to see the lake. I want to see light."

The grass was slick from the rain. She ran her shoe back and forth, checking for rocks, needles, and broken bottles. Essex tore open one of the ponchos they'd bought at a gas station along the way and, shaking it into a circle, laid it down. She spread the electric blanket on top and sat.

"Open the other poncho. We can put the bags on it."

He opened it and handed it to her. She doubled it up then set the three bags down, positioning them carefully on the thickest part of the plastic.

"Wouldn't want our inheritance to get wet," she said.

Clouds thinned over the hills and more stars came through.

"Did Livy say when she'd be back?"

"Her last text said she was sailing," he said.

"She's already sailing."

"Farther out. I tried the number. No one picked up. It went right to voice mail."

Cheyenne stretched her legs out and zipped up her hoodie. A boat powered through the water on the other side of the lake. Seconds later ripples reached the shore, lapping then going quiet.

"I don't understand," said Cheyenne. "How can there be no one to tell?"

Essex drummed his hands on his thigh for a minute then changed position to sit cross-legged, forcing her to move over.

"Did you ever meet Kirsten's parents?" he asked.

"We never met anybody. When we asked about them she told us we were immigrants. She said we'd left the cultural old world in search of a better life."

Essex snorted hard then covered his mouth. His eyes shone. Cheyenne laughed.

"I know! Livy and I totally believed it too. Until like third grade we told everyone that we were first-generation Americans—What's with you? Why do you have your hand over your mouth?" she said.

He breathed out sharply through his nose and took his hand away from his face. "Every time I start to laugh, I cry."

Cheyenne nodded and looked over the tended wet hill.

"Sometimes I feel like everything she ever taught us was wrong," she said.

The damp from the ground seeped up through the cheap poncho and blanket and she shifted. Essex opened her backpack and got out the candles and the bag of apple fritters. After several attempts with the matches, he got the candles to stay lit. Scratching little burrows in the grass, he placed them into the cold mud beneath.

"I forgot how much it rains here."

"You'll like climate change then," she said.

Cheyenne broke a fritter in half.

"We should have eaten these when they were warm," she said.

"Do you remember when we were here last?" he asked.

Cheyenne thought. "I was here with Livy months ago. Seems like ages. But I don't remember ever coming here with you."

"We did too. The year you were married. You, me, and Jackson came up here."

"I remember being here with Jackson but not you."

"I can't remember why I was here," said Essex.

"Because you're a hopeless tagalong."

She handed him a fritter. Chewing, she looked at his profile. Little lines in new places.

A light gust brushed the south slope of the hill, blowing out the candles on Cheyenne's side. Essex leaned over and relit them.

"You know what my favorite wedding was?" he said. "You and Jackson. You were spectacular."

"Yup, and I'm going to feel bad about it my whole life. What I remember best from the wedding, though, is seeing you drag that heavy old mattress across the field by yourself. The one for the honeymoon tent."

"I don't remember that," he said.

"It's so vivid in my mind." She stared over the hill. "Our wedding was great in its own way too," she said.

The air was getting colder and the sky clearer. Essex checked the time again. The program was about to start. When he got the live stream from the station going he set the phone between them and turned it up. The earlier show was signing off. They were going out on a dub song about sexual orientation written and recorded by local high schoolers. After it finished, a woman's voice came on.

"Tonight, for the first time in two decades, you will hear male singers on *The Third Spiral Galaxy*," she said.

"Self-identified male," corrected another voice.

"Yes, thank you. Self-identified male."

"Don't be alarmed!" said a third voice in the background, pitched in a comic falsetto.

"God, the whole coven is there," said Cheyenne.

The sound fell away and the voice of the host returned.

"Is that Alice?" asked Essex.

"I think so. I can't keep their voices straight. They sound like geese to me."

"We lost our dear friend Kirsten this week," said the host. "This show is dedicated to her. We'll be back in a moment. Please stay with us."

They cut to a station ID recorded during a previous pledge drive, a musician nobody knew reading out call letters that nobody cared about. Cheyenne put her head down. She crinkled up the white paper fritter bag and jammed it under her pack.

"I am definitely not ready for this," she said.

The host returned.

"We are asking listeners to please hold all calls until the end of the show tonight."

There was scuffling. Someone dropped something. Another person asked if it rolled under the chair. Someone inaudible, interrupted by a cough. The host said something off-mic then returned. Cheyenne could hear her unfold a piece of paper, and the edge of that paper brush the table as the host took a sip of water and cleared her throat.

"To my children I leave clarity in emergency. The skills to calm a parasympathetic nervous system. The determination to fill out pages and pages of DSHS paperwork as well as the imagination to entertain themselves in the offices of Social and Health Services for as long as necessary. Most importantly, how to petition without begging and . . . hold on. I can't quite make it out." The host conferred with another person. "Yes, okay. I see." She cleared her throat again. "And an understanding of myth and the power of stories, a narrative other than the one assigned. The manners to negotiate with landlords. The cunning to open new bank accounts so you always have starter checks and free checking. The wherewithal to rotate through introductory offers at yoga studios so that you never pay more than five dollars a class. The skills to do medical research on the Internet. The ability to make kefir and kombucha at home for nothing. Proficiency in multiple methods of divination. Enough American Sign Language to be polite to the deaf and a working knowledge of the women's movement from 1865 to the present." The host took another sip of water. "The willingness to leave everything behind in pursuit of something more important and walk out with nothing. The determination to withstand the opinions of others and all my love forever. My good Le Creuset saucepan goes to Essex. My yoga mat goes to Cheyenne. Whatever's left of my herbs and medicine goes to Livy except for the Vicodin from my car accident. It's past-date but I don't think it goes bad. Just divide it between yourselves on an as-needed basis. It's in the bathroom cabinet."

There was more rustling of paper as the host flipped the page to see if there was anything on the back. A second later they could hear her refolding the will and sliding it into its envelope.

"That's it?" said Cheyenne. "That's her life?" She stared at the phone.

The host's chair creaked as she bumped the mic. "Please join us in a moment of silence."

"That can't be it," said Cheyenne.

She turned to Essex. He put his finger to his lips.

She looked down. Essex put his hand on her leg. It was trembling so she started to shiver . . . *The grass is alive in me and I can't make it stop vibrating. The mad garden's gone wild with seed; it winds through everything—leaking batteries, strewn clothes, sofas missing cushions, the people you love—knitting itself into something new and you say: I will not move forward. I will not leave you alone in this moment and let you slip into the past, but yet you are dragged away.*

"Thank you." The host exhaled. "She walks with her ancestors."

"Oh she'd love that," snapped Cheyenne. "Because we all know what a big fan of our ancestors she was." Rage was like a blight on the heart.

The music started. A baritone voice singing songs about weeping and mercy and ships.

Cheyenne tucked into herself like a pill bug, her face on her knees. She cried for herself and her sister and felt Essex's hand between her shoulder blades.

"Turn it down," she said.

"You should listen," he said softly. He moved the phone closer. "Shh. It's the sound of the home we came from."

In a cross-fade the baritone was gone and a young woman sang in his place. About another side, about another light that shines, about belonging to no one else. Cheyenne sat up and blew the air out of her lungs, shaking her head like a dog.

She stretched and was silent. The moon was over the gasworks. The singers on the radio were changing. The reverb and tambourine had died out and an overdriven guitar arced up and dipped under a single note. A drum machine kicked in. Soon it was drowned in layers and loops.

"I still can't believe you might go to jail," she said quietly.

He drew a long breath, stuttering on the exhale. "There's a chance I won't. If I do, you can hold my ashes for me."

He gave her a sad wink.

She put her hand among the green blades and twisted a thin root around her finger.

"You know I feel fine and then I don't. It's transcendent then it's not. The laughter feels right and then all of sudden it's worse than anything," she said.

His eyes moved when the seagulls by the lake moved but his expression didn't change. He tracked gulls as they took flight.

"Do you think they'd let me see her body again?" she asked. "I can't make it real." She wiped her face. "I'm sick of the taste of my own tears. Let's open the bags."

She put his on his lap.

"Wake up," she said and grabbed her own and Livy's.

"Shouldn't Livy be the first to open hers?" he asked.

"No way. I want to see what she got."

She reached into her sister's bag and pulled out a paperback. It was Kirsten's copy of the *I Ching*. The coins were in a little bag tied around it with a ribbon. She set it aside and kept going.

"I got her tarot deck," said Essex, holding up the worn box. "What did you get?"

"I'm still on Livy's bag."

There was a pair of dice made out of bones, a shark-tooth necklace, a scarf with silver threads that Livy used to tease her about wearing, a miniature statue of Kali, a honey jar full of barrettes and hair ties, and a journal with an astrolabe embossed on it that had the first two pages torn out but was otherwise blank.

In her own bag was a Toyota manual; a rune pouch; Kirsten's pearl-handle pocketknife; a fake antique necklace, shiny because the patina was gone; a painted candleholder; a box of playing cards with famous mountains of the world; and a Kennedy half-dollar.

"Oh score. Look at what I got," said Essex.

He held a lavender T-shirt against his body with one hand drawing the other across the shirt's faded script. *"Ain't No Lovin' Like Something from the Coven,"* he said. Said it like it was a fact, said it like testimony.

"That's not fair," said Cheyenne.

"I was her favorite."

He placed the shirt on the blanket with everything else. Then it was all there, a T-shirt, a scarf, some divinatory tools, a car manual, and fifty cents. Cheyenne looked at the blanket.

"I can't tell if this is great or pathetic," she said. "I honestly can't tell."

She picked up the Kennedy half-dollar. "Behold! The riches of the tomb."

She dropped it onto a paper bag.

She picked up the candleholder. "Potsherds," she said. "This is what we'll leave behind."

She set the candleholder back where it had been. Pushing her hood back, she ran her fingers through her hair. Her eyes were glassy and she was missing an earring. There were dirt streaks by her ear from crying while lying down.

"Did they make you go on field trips to Mount St. Helens in school?" he asked.

"At least once a year. We used to call it the field trip to a bus ride."

"Remember how you had to stay on the path so you wouldn't step on anything?"

"Yeah. They'd freak out if you so much as put a toe off the path. God, I hated those trips. You'd drive forever. Walk for an hour while they tell you about all the stupid people who died because they wouldn't leave, then they'd make you stop and ogle some sad half-inch sprig: Look! The glory of life. All hail, it returns. Then you get to pile back into the bus and drive forever then spend all night writing a report."

"Was the mountain all rocks when you saw it?" he asked.

"Like a moonscape."

"It was green when I saw it."

A cold breeze pressed briefly against the short winter grass and he shivered.

"I wish we could bury her on a mountainside," said Cheyenne. "Or here. Dig up the sundial and put her under it, like a secret tomb." She threw a fritter crumb down the hill. "I mean she tried really hard." Cheyenne choked and her voice broke; breathing, she got it back. "She made up all these myths and stories just so we would think someone was watching us and it mattered if we failed or succeeded."

She picked up the shark-tooth necklace and tossed it back onto the poncho. "But it only takes a look around to know that we don't count. All the decisions we make don't matter because the story isn't about us." She hung her head and laughed then looked up and gave him a rare and undefended smile.

"You're wrong," he said. "We're Valley of the Kings. Everything that's made and beautiful in the world, it's ours. They just get to name the stuff. We get to sign it."

"We Were Here."

"Right. We are. You know how they said nothing could live in Chernobyl after the meltdown, then they went back and it was full of wolves. That's what we're like," he said. "We come back first. We can live anywhere."

"Even in jail?" she asked.

He became less certain. "Even in jail," he said.

"Because we're Chernobyl wolves."

"We eat radiation grass. We're special."

She crossed her arms for warmth. "I do love you and I will miss you," she said.

"I love you too."

"Wait," she said, "what song is that? I know that song."

He picked up the phone and listened. "I don't."

"Turn it up."

An electric piano played simple chords under high male voices overlapping. *Sometimes, sometimes,* they sang through the phone's small speaker. The song was only half a song, though, and never really got going.

The host returned.

"That was for our beloved friend Kirsten, who passed yesterday at her home. I see the phones are lighting up. We have a listener on the phone from— Really? From all the way down in Cougar, Washington. Hello, caller, you are on the air."

Cheyenne grabbed the phone and shut off the stream. "I don't want to hear what anyone else has to say about her."

"It might help."

"I just want this moment to be ours. Why does it have to be so public?"

Essex shrugged. "She wanted people to know how she saw the world."

"Anybody she ever talked to would have known that."

Her eyes were full of tears again. She looked up and they ran down into her ears. It tickled so she wiped them away and looked back at him.

"I don't even know who we are to each other without her," she said. "Are you even my brother without her?"

Cheyenne watched him settle back into a slouch. The curve of his shoulders was so familiar in so many ways through so many lenses.

"You would tell me," he said, "if there was something I could say to make you marry me. You would tell me. You wouldn't make me guess."

She threw her arms wide and shouted, "Say: 'I can't live without you!'"

A startled bird flew off a bench.

Essex whispered into her ear, "I can't live without you."

"God, I was joking. Nobody should ever say that. It's super creepy.'"

"Why?"

"Because it's not like anyone even knows how they're going to feel a year from now."

"That's why they should say it. They know how they feel now."
She put her hand up.

"No," he said, "hear me out. People want credit for being honest but they're lying about the one thing they truly feel in that moment. They're cowards. They're afraid of their own emotions. I'm not."

He spun her toward him and she started laughing.

"I can't live without you," he said.

Now she was laughing hard and couldn't stop.

"Try it. It'll be great. I won't hold you to it. Promise," he said.

"I can't live without— No!" She pushed him back. "It's too stupid to even say. I get hit by a bus or leave you for a student I met at a bar and you do live without me."

"Exactly. That's what I mean. You lose nothing."

"Because it's lying!"

"Okay," he said. "How about I can't live the same without you."

She weighed it. "But you can say that about anyone you love."

"Yeah exactly. And some people more than others."

Cheyenne was too close to his body, in the realm of its heat. She moved back and started crawling around the blanket, throwing things back in their bags. She picked up the little brass Kali statue and threw it into her own bag.

"That's supposed to go to Livy," said Essex.

"She can find me and ask for it back."

She also threw Livy's *I Ching* coins into her bag and reached for the Ain't No Lovin' T-shirt but Essex stopped her.

"That's mine. You're not taking it. I'm serious."

She sat back hard on her heels. "Fine, I don't care."

Her lips were pale and there were pale blue streaks under her eyes. There was sand in her eyelashes at the corners and the edges of her nostrils were red.

"What are you going to do after I leave?" he asked. "I won't be able to help much longer. Is there anyone you can go to?"

"I'm an heiress. I'll be fine."

He put his hand on her head, fingers pointed down. "Your invisible tiara."

"Thank you."

"At least you have a car now."

"Which I can live in if I need to." She kicked out her legs and pedaled them to warm up. "I'll probably squat in the apartment till they kick me out. Get a job. Try and figure out if there's something I can do that's of use to anyone that doesn't make me want to shoot myself."

She smiled and leaned her head on his shoulder.

"It might go badly for me," he said.

"They're not going to kill you. You don't mean enough to anyone and neither does Jared."

"I could be in jail for a long time."

"Let's see what happens," she said.

He got to his knees and waited for the blood to flow back into his legs. "We have to go."

"Let's wait for dawn," she said.

"It's the Pacific Northwest. Dawn never comes."

She laughed. "The gray lightens."

"Not for another hour."

She didn't move and wouldn't look at him.

"Cheyenne, I don't have another hour."

75

The Fears

THEY LOST A SAILOR three days before crossing the equator. The weather wasn't rough. Still he went over. Livy saw the whole thing. He slipped in the headrig as the ship lurched in a sudden wave, the Irish sailor, lost forever to the fears.

It was the sailor's death that convinced Livy that Marne was right. They did need a ritual for crossing the equatorial line. Initially she'd balked, and yet when the Irish sailor went over what had they done? They wore ship and made a show of looking. And if that ritual had meaning then why not all others? But there were no shellbacks among them, no one who had been where they were. They were, each of them, new, crossing the line together.

"Keep it short and don't kill anybody. We still need to sail," said Livy.

Someone laughed. It was nerves. They already felt the absence of the Irish sailor, when they'd had to brace the main yard after the search, when they had to dig and hold without him.

Just south of what Livy guessed was the equator, they gathered on deck between the fore and mainmast waiting for the show. The ritual was a hodgepodge of Naval Academy hearsay, nautical-themed sports hazing, and community theater gags. The Lord of Misrule strutting as Diva Mermaid, demanding service, stripping dignity. There was one part of the ceremony that worked on Livy. Toward the very end, after the mad laughter of personal shame, Marne reappeared as Queen Davy Jones standing on the jack lines above the deck; she warned of the sea, of its chest below, and of the deep fall bodies take to its floor, floating, she said, down, slow, like summer leaves to the ground. A chill ran through each of them, the lost sailor everywhere.

Livy makes an entry in the ship's log. Star date: somewhere in time. Location: orbiting planet earth on a large body of water.

The wind that pushed the swell that took the sailor turned out to be the last breeze felt for many days. They moved forward for a time, but it was only inertia and proof of a frictionless sea. Doldrums stretched in all directions. With enough diesel for the backup generator but not enough to drive the ship, they began to float, torn sails and missing parts, peeling paint bubbled and flaking in patches to reveal the bright yellow stripe beneath, a toy adrift in a giant tub.

Late at night when the ship was silent, Livy charted. But she could only review past positions in the log and guess. Looking out across the ocean, she saw vast galaxies reflected. The horizon seam of sea and sky vanished. A starlit lighting bowl, the ship no longer traveled on the outside surface of the sphere but upside down and backward on the inside. Even if she had run the engine, even if she had spent the last of the diesel to move, they would still be nothing but a tiny tractor inching across hundreds of miles of space.

Raleigh came up beside her. He shot the stars with his sextant, also lost.

On the eighth day of doldrums when the sun was highest the crew sheltered under the tarp, ankles swollen and red, itching, bored, and international, they taught each other to curse in different languages, each sailor now a nation, they held terror at bay. Off the portside bow, Livy thought she saw a ripple, a whale perhaps, deep under, but said nothing. In these waters, even the flutter-kick of a frog's leg would break the glass-like sea.

Ship's log: These doldrums have no end.

Livy looks up into the equatorial sky. She sees a Japanese Zero. Its small-plane engine stutters. She blinks as it crosses the path of the sun. Running out of gas, the Zero circles down painting ensōs in carbons and hydrocarbons until it crashes into the sea, a twist of black smoke on the water. Looking to the south she sees the Galápagos yet lit by the fire of turtles burning in their shells.

Ship's log: Nothing is meant to be.

After sunset, Livy climbed over the anchor, rode up onto the fife rail that ran around the foremast. Sarah came over and Livy stepped aside to make room for her on the post. We are lost, she wanted to say. We are charting by history and hearsay. I know how far we've come but not how close we are. Leaning against Sarah's body, *goldene medina,* also a new world.

The next day Sarah wandered the deck in a long-sleeved white gauze shirt. Running her hand along the pins that belayed lines slackening in the hot dry air. She stopped to kick a neatly ballantined halyard coil into a pile of spaghetti. Glancing up she saw a loose line shiver.

"Wind!" she yelled.

Everyone ran to see.

"We should set the royals," said Marne.

Set the royals!

Set the royals!

Marne and a Dutch sailor laid aloft, scrambling up the shrouds to the crosstrees, dots at a hundred and twenty-five feet above. Sailors on deck secured and sent the royal yard, hoisting it with difficulty, their feet sliding when they tried to dig and hold. Once set, the royals puffed with air. Soon the breeze moved down and filled the topsails. They began to move again.

Calculating wind speed and adjusting for current, tracing angles, Livy charted the best she could. Farther south, they caught the trade winds and the ship came to life, lines snapping, bowsprit harpooning waves. A whale was sighted two points off the starboard beam. It wasn't close but when it sounded the water it displaced sent a swell that raised the ship, letting it smack back down onto the surface of the sea as the sailors cheered.

But it was not a toothed whale but a lost baleen whale, swimming without location.

After a week they sighted the oil well three points off the portside bow, a small black poke on the horizon. There was shouting and howling as if they were saved, as if they'd forgotten what they came to do. All afternoon the oil rig appeared and disappeared as the *Neva* sank in the troughs and rose on the crests. Sailors debated the merits of persuasion or hostage-taking. *We have musket! We have cannon!* Everyone laughed. Because they were not assailants. They were refugees arriving unasked on an island, which was not land but a symbol of it, stuttering in and out of time.

76

Testament

IN THE PARKING LOT, they dumped the trash. They got rid of the paper bags, which were damp now and on the verge of breaking, and Cheyenne wrapped hers and Livy's things in the hippie scarf with the silver thread, knotted it, and put it in her backpack. They stood there between the cars, looking at each other. She could see him at eleven and at fourteen, all the things that change, all the things that don't; he was sixteen passing for older, lost like a teenager, then twenty-two at her wedding and twenty-seven, driving Jackson's brass bed across the country. He kicked her foot. She put the instep of her shoe against the instep of his.

"You said I wanted you to be different than you are. I don't."

"We're all right."

Essex got in the rental and Cheyenne got in the Toyota. Turning it over, it wouldn't start. She pumped the gas then tried again. Essex came over to her window. She tried to roll it down but it would only go partway.

"Hang on." She pressed against the pane and rolled simultaneously until she could get it down. "I need to grease the track."

"What's happening?"

"I think it's just the ignition switch not fully engaging," she said. "Kore was like that."

"Kore?"

"Mom's red Subaru," she said.

She jiggled the steering wheel and tried to turn the key again.

"What was the name of the one you lost in the tornado?"

"It might have been something benign like Luna. She told me but I forgot. When we were little, she used to let us name the cars but then Livy and I would get in fights so she made us take turns. Livy named a car Shackleton."

Cheyenne turned the key and the Toyota rattled to life.

On the side roads in the dark, she saw that one headlight shone straight, the other angled. The car pulled to the left and the brake pads were almost gone. Easy things to fix, especially with a manual. Her mother was a genius at knowing when a car was bound for the junkyard. She could tell five repairs away. They'd always take a bath on selling, though, because Kirsten felt compelled to tell every potential buyer all the things she thought might go wrong next.

It was too much for Livy, even at ten years old.

"Why do you have to say anything?" she said one night over dinner. "Just take the money and let them find out."

Kirsten's eyes went wide and she snatched Livy's dinner plate away and dumped her food in the trash. Livy started to cry.

"Who do you think buys cars as shitty as ours?" Kirsten yelled. "People who don't have a choice. Poor people like us."

Points for boldness and grace. Her mother, at least, knew when to cut her losses. Cheyenne either quit too early or too late. But Kirsten was like a samurai. One sword stroke with full confidence and she was out.

Cheyenne's mind began to wander. She drove by instinct, seeing the city that had once been there instead of the city that was. Beaten old diners and car washes with giant elephants. There had been a junkyard far out on the edge of town. She and Livy loved it because it was like a city made of cars. Broken-down or wrecked, stacked as high as tenement housing, dark alleys paved with shatterproof glass, it was where they went when a car was destined for scrap metal. Kirsten would pack sandwiches and they would limp the dying vehicle out there, stopping every few blocks. If the car didn't drive, she'd get a friend to let her tie it to their back bumper with a slipknot around the hitch and they'd go slow on flat roads trying not to turn, with Kirsten steering and the two of them in the backseat howling like it was a ride.

The glory would wear off on the long bus journey back. Livy looking over the driver's shoulder after being told not to several times, Cheyenne switching seats and pestering strangers. Kirsten staring out the window like she wanted to run as fast and as far away as she could. She would get so distant that Cheyenne would get scared and sneak over to scratch her hand. Sometimes it took a second, but always, Kirsten would turn, looking first at Cheyenne as if she were a stranger, and she would smile and there was no distance between them.

Cheyenne felt that way now. Like she wanted to drive and never stop.

She wondered what the real cost of getting the body back from the coroner was going to be. There might be storage fees at the county. There might also be fees around investigation if they thought the body was abandoned. Her gaze skated over the freeway. She blinked and saw iridescent pinpricks and halos. The cost-benefit analysis of body disposal? Weigh it against a feather.

The airport was coming up. A few minutes later she exited, following the signs to rental return, and pulled into the stall next to Essex.

He checked the backseat of the hybrid.

"Are you going to come in?" he asked.

"I'd rather just say goodbye here." She pointed at the air traffic control tower. "See? The sky is lighter gray. We made it to dawn."

He kissed her forehead at her hairline.

She squeezed his hand and he walked away. As he reached the edge of the parking lot, she saw him run his hand across the back of his neck and glance toward the control tower, then disappear. She leaned against the Toyota. Pulling her backpack off the floor of the car, she hunted for a leftover fritter inside, but there was none. She zipped up the pack and hugged it to her chest. She had a working car, a few weeks of dental, and, prior to eviction, a place for a month or two with dishes and clean clothes. More than she'd had of her own for a long time.

Five moves from here? She didn't know.

Think of all the times you've been naked. You have a dollar. You have a magic rock. You have something someone said to you that you hold precious, a vague idea, a plan, nothing, you have nothing. Now think of all the times you've been wrong. You end up with a broken heart or chlamydia, a wristband and disposable slippers, you're pregnant, you're not.

There's no shame in freedom.

Years of being embarrassed over nothing. Like everyone else could see. She shut the car door and began to walk before she even knew she'd made a decision. And her mother's body? The coroner would search for next of kin. They would knock on electronic doors and find no one. You never give the Man what he wants. Eventually her mother's body would be marked abandoned. They would burn her as an indigent, as a witch. But they would keep the receipt. And maybe it would find its way back to Cyril as a bill.

She began to run. Bolting, backpack looped around one arm, she tripped and hit the ground hard, wiping out on the concrete, bashing her knee and tearing a hole in her jeans. Getting to her feet, she danced in a circle. She could see the blood welling and winced. A man from the rental car company was coming to see if she was okay. Looking back at the Toyota she threw the keys at it as hard as she could. They sailed in an arc and landed on the pavement.

She caught up to Essex in the carpeted tunnel to the terminal.

She was right behind him and he didn't know she was there. How could he not know? She took a quick skip forward to match his gait and grabbed his upper arm.

"Don't stop," she said, "don't stop."

She felt her way down to his hand and locked her fingers in his. It wasn't as bad as she thought, walking like this, exposed as she was. Just a new kind of naked.

The blood running down her ankle into her shoe tickled. She stopped to scratch it through her sock. Standing again, her knee was stiff. It was already starting to scab. Essex put his mouth by her ear.

"You look like you spent all night in a park."

"Keep walking," she said.

Coming into the main part of the terminal, people cut across their path dodging carts, looking at signs to other terminals and shuttles. Essex opened his wallet, took something out of the change pocket, and pressed it into her palm. She felt what it was and laughed. She put the extra ring on her finger next to the first one he had given her.

"We get to make it whatever we want," he said in her ear.

"Don't look at me."

"No one's watching."

"They are watching."

"Who cares."

He pulled her toward a crowd gathering, forming a line, waiting for the ticket counter to open. A woman in her fifties with frosted hair, peach lipstick, and a robin's-egg blue neckerchief stepped behind a computer and began her day.

"Can you even buy a ticket at an airport counter anymore?" Cheyenne asked.

"Don't worry, I doubt my credit card even works."

"They're going to look at us like we shouldn't even be here."

There was blood on the carpet from her leg. She tried to smudge it out with her shoe but Essex stopped her. "They deserve it," he said. She shifted, only half there. He squeezed her hand to let her know to move up. The woman with the robin's-egg blue neckerchief was now close enough to hear. She spoke in the tonal language of transaction and permission.

They stepped forward in line.

"Don't forget," said Essex, "we're Chernobyl wolves. We eat radiation grass."

She leaned into his ear. "Valley of the Kings," she whispered.

Epilogue

OFF THE EAST COAST of North America whalers head for the Horn. Cutting through the waves of glowing seaweed in the bioluminescent surf off Hatteras Island, they head for the breeding grounds. Ghosts.

And so, what if someone told you, whispered in your ear, you, you are exceptional. Shh . . . the rules do not apply—but don't look down. Yet you look down. Or maybe you're on a hill and build a city but the hill was never empty, what then?

Hometown. City of your birth. Ghosts everywhere.

The first white Christian child born in North America entered the world at Roanoke but went missing at the age of three and her body was never found. Some say she was born un-locatable. Others say little Virginia Dare was only location. Contemporary investors split on the impact of her disappearance. Under the right circumstances, would her absent bones spur or deter investment? Was she warning or cause? Girl or brand? Coal-mine canary or kick start? Futures unpredictable, stockholders revolt, board meetings devolve—so perhaps her body is to blame? Or never mattered at all, a pin drop in a map of colonial imagination, Virginia Dare.

Flickering in and out of accountability, Raleigh closes his eyes. Half-filled ships wreck against rocks on foreign shores. He paces . . .

I am spirit . . . I am spirit . . . Trembling, Raleigh doffs his blame-taking body for the cutting-edge technology of economic imagination, the joint-stock entity. Co-creating a new world, incorporating over and over until he is no longer a blamable individual with a body, but a simulacraic choir of self-replicating cells, a new form of life. Raleigh, founder and corporation, strides forth. *Toward sunset!* Angels ring; sailors shout through a spray of seawater and sun.

Shaking off his losses, he sets sail for El Dorado and catches, in the periphery, the spectral child Virginia racing along the Outer Banks as his ship sails past. He squints but cannot make her out, seeing at once a milk carton with a child's face then a sad man surrendering on a horse. She stops and begins to turn in a circle, Santa-doubting-Shakespeare-sister Virgin Queen of tobacco fields rending her Quantico dress and laughing. Training his mind, Raleigh turns his intention toward El Dorado (which rumor has is many miles up that wet jungle-mouth delta of Orinoco to the south), only he doesn't know where it is. So many things have happened since he left that he can't tell how far he's come. And because he's never been to El Dorado and it's only an idea, he can't tell how close he is. He practices EMDR and taps . . . *I am spirit . . . I am spirit . . .*

The problem of location has never been simple. Do you fix a point and aim at wherever you want to go? Or do you locate yourself in relation to the shore, memory, and landmarks?

Baleen whales navigate this way. Toothed whales do not. Early sailors preferred celestial navigation—best to rely on something outside the grasp of this world—but celestial navigation doesn't solve the problem of unknown shores and cloud cover, which is why dead reckoning is the fallback of sailors.

A fixed beginning, speed, and trajectory.

Dead reckoning is how wolves cross snowy hillsides, how pumas slip between desert ridges in the night. Out of satellite range in open ocean without lighthouse beacon or buoy, dead reckoning is a sailor's final hope. But solve one problem and it has puppies. Give a man a fish and it's not his fault, but teach a man to fish and he eats everything in the ocean.

Starting point, mode of transport, goal.

Rome, St. Augustine, Hill City;
Gravesend, Roanoke, El Dorado;
Nantucket, *Essex,* the Great Offshore Grounds . . .

Raleigh takes the bridge and calls to his sailors. *Never forget the depths of this world!* He shouts, though they cannot hear him over the squall, *Strangers!* He shouts. Shh . . . strangers. We are strangers to these waters, only cartographers. Mark your head. Look sharkish! And tell me what you see. A sailor, peering across the lens of curved horizon, frames the sea. *L7 . . . I spy . . . I spy with my little eye a sun, a cloud, a mast . . . I spy . . . I spy with my little eye . . . a sister, a highway interstate system, a statue of Jefferson Davis.*

A song breaks out:

> *They grew to the top of the old church tower*
> *They couldn't grow any higher*
> *They locked and tied in true loves knot*
> *The rose around the briar.*

Raleigh never saw the tidal estuary at what would someday be Camp Lejeune or the river that fed it or its relationship to the ocean of moon jellies or the pods of right whales heading south to give birth. And who can say what happened to him when they cut off his head? Did he wander a Christian bardo? Did he explode into a Shinto grapeshot of small ticking souls haunting tobacco fields in the New World? Did he return as a barnacle bound to a whale swimming southward coming ever closer to but never making it up the hot humid delta river-mouth he was certain led to El Dorado?

It is known that Raleigh's physical head was embalmed by the Crown and handed to his widow in a velvet bag, but as embalmers tend to guard their secrets, the exact method of its preservation is unknown and traditional approaches vary by region. Some involve soaking a head in saltwater. Others prefer to bury it in hot sand.

Sun flashes on the sea.

Sometimes Lejeune and Raleigh sit at a fold-out table on deck of the *Neva* and play cards. *For Virginia!* shouts Raleigh when he lays down a winning hand. *For the canal,* says Lejeune. A Confederate captain circles the table, a long line, a through line, a red line.

Livy opens a letter from Cheyenne. It says: *What's the secret of empire? Location, location, location . . .*

Livy crumples the note and throws it into the ocean. A white paper flower, it blossoms on the water's surface unshaping itself in the waves.

Livy shades her eyes.

Inescapable, whispers Raleigh, inescapable, all this salt and light.

At night, the well was an illuminated pinprick on the edge of the world. Though the sea was quiet, and though the well was only a speck, Livy's ears filled with the buzzing and deafening alarms and sounds of metal slamming metal she'd heard when they'd passed the massive oil rig in Alaska. She had the sense that they were not moving forward at all but were caught in a whirlpool, circling around the exact point where it had all gone wrong.

Raleigh emerged from the cabin for the last time and went to the starboard rail. He extended his arm then lunged, reaching for something close but unattainable in the flush of dementia.

"It's in their heads!" he said. "Perfume and cigarettes and transmission fluid, cures for epilepsy and solar systems, whole solar systems!"

Livy tried to calm him but he didn't know her.

Just before dawn, he shook her awake.

I have terrible things to confess . . . terrible things . . .

She sat up to listen, but he was gone.

Livy went above. The sea was full of constellations. The North Star was beyond the curve of the globe. She relieved Marne on the bridge.

Captain's got the con.

Captain's got the con.

As they closed on the rig it looked less like a deep-sea well and more like a sinking ship. Covered by a low fog but just under the crown block, affixed to the tower, Livy saw the flag of her homeland. In the predawn light it appeared in grayscale: its stripes, bone bars over black; its stars, the whites of the eyes that seemed to Livy imprisoned in the darkness. It pillowed once in the wind then was pressed by a breeze flattened over the struts, sunken against its emaciated ribs. On the deck below was a child with tangled hair waving so frantically it seemed she might fly. Livy could barely make her out, dressed as she was in fog and shadowed in violet light.

And what if someone said to you: You were conceived in a cracked lighthouse that has no keeper. While there might be a faint glow up top, it is only a ship's lamp.

Ask me a secret. Whisper. I won't tell. Promise?

. . . I still love my country . . .

You have no country.

. . . I love the idea of my country . . .

Whose idea?

My idea, mine. That exceptional flame. A country not yet born.

Below the derrick, Virginia Dare covers her eyes with her hands as the sun torches her hair gold. She yells over the water with all the power of her three-year-old lungs words garbled in the din of whale song and ghosts. Her ankles are in the water. She looks in all directions to see how to swim. Baleen whales navigate by memory, but she has no memory. Toothed whales navigate by echolocation, but she cannot even hear herself. She slaps away the water, now over her knees.

On the horizon, a bright line shot in either direction as the corona of the sun touched the water behind them. Livy squinted in the advance of the coming glare and made an aperture with both hands, a ghost ring to target the oil rig unblended by reflection. Just before sunrise the fog rolled back to reveal the drilling platform. It was at the waterline and Livy saw that it was sinking, slow and inevitable. Then the sun like a scythe cut the sea from the sky. A beveled and perfect lens signaling through space: *We are here! We are here!* It swept over the waves and began to climb the well strut by strut until it reached the flag, which caught fire in the flash of dawn. Call-and-response, moving together, like swifts, like submarines, listening to the sound of shapes, toothed whales cross the ocean. Sonic and concentric waves radiate out from their great bodies filling the space between locations with an unceasing chant: *How close? How close? How close?*

ACKNOWLEDGMENTS

Novels are like doomed marriages. You start with great expectations—in love with all the characters—then things take a turn and you have to walk away. When you're not sure whether to stay or go, you need your friends, and sometimes outside professional help. This novel took a very long time to write and edit. Everybody mentioned here was needed.

At its inception, I was greatly helped by the Bingham family in the form of a PEN/Robert W. Bingham Prize, and by the MacDowell Colony in the form of a fellowship. In the middle years, I was sustained by readers who kept me company, my mother and father, Alex Ney, Nili Yosha, Angus Durocher. Kirsten Evenson, a poet and fisherwoman, read multiple times and offered her invaluable experience in the Bering Sea.

During the course of research, I was fortunate enough to work on the US Brig *Niagara,* a replica of an 1812 square-rigged, two-masted warship. I am grateful in particular to Joe Lengieza, who made it possible for me to come on as a sail trainee for nearly a month; to Jen Dexter, who took me to work aloft for the first time; and to Matt Kent, who clipped me in when we were up at the crosstrees and got hit on the beam by a freak wave train and swung side to side like a metronome for four minutes. In addition to assuring me we would live if we held on, he also kindly offered to let me throw up on him if that helped. Tom McCluskey, of HMS *Rose* and *Bounty,* brought his considerable experience as mate and bosun to these pages, making valuable correc-

ACKNOWLEDGMENTS

tions. Therefore, all mistakes regarding tall ships are mine alone, and something always gets past me.

In the end, I needed outside help. My agent, Sarah Bowlin, helped shape the novel and find it a home. Tim O'Connell, my editor at Knopf, and assistant editor Anna Kaufman were patient and unafraid of a good debate. Brilliant editors are a gift, and I can't imagine doing this book with anyone else. My friend and former publisher, Richard Nash, was and remains my greatest champion. These stellar humans were essential to this novel's existence.

The deepest support I received, though, was from my family. Throughout the writing—and it took years!—I did not do my share of dishes or drive my daughter to band practice. I did not pay my fair share of the bills or move my share of boxes from apartment to apartment. These necessities fell sometimes on Blake Wright, but most profoundly onto the shoulders of Stefan Jecusco. Stefan worked far more hours of manual labor than anyone in their mid-forties should. When there was a financial crisis, he burned his credit to cover the gaps. He often supported my artistic life and growth at the expense of his. From 2015 to 2019 I struggled with depression and despair. I became antisocial and morbidly self-involved. At a certain point, I decided only politics and organizing mattered and saw no point in writing novels. I told Stefan I wanted to quit and was sharply informed that the decision was no longer mine. They had all put their labor into this, my family, friends, and other believers in my career.

So here it is, and thank you all. I truly hope that I have not let you down.

A NOTE ABOUT THE AUTHOR

Vanessa Veselka is the author of the novel *Zazen,* which won the PEN/Robert W. Bingham Prize for Debut Fiction. Her short stories have appeared in *Tin House* and *Zyzzyva,* and her non-fiction in *GQ, The Atlantic, Smithsonian,* and *The Atavist Magazine,* and was included in *Best American Essays* and the anthology *Bitchfest: Ten Years of Cultural Criticism.* She has been, at various times, a teenage runaway, a sex worker, a union organizer, an independent record label owner, a train hopper, a waitress, and a mother. She lives in Portland, Oregon.

A NOTE ON THE TYPE

The text of this book was set in Plantin, a typeface first cut
in 1913 by the Monotype Corporation of London. Though the
face bears the name of the great Christopher Plantin (ca. 1520–
1589), who in the latter part of the sixteenth century owned, in
Antwerp, the largest printing and publishing firm in Europe,
it is a rather free adaptation of designs by Claude Garamond
made for that firm. With its strong, simple lines, Plantin is a no-
nonsense face of exceptional legibility.

Typeset by Scribe, Philadelphia, Pennsylvania
Printed and bound by LSC Communications, Harrisonburg, Virginia
Designed by Anna B. Knighton